T0060763

SOPHIE GRAVIA

What Happens in Dubai

x

Sophie Gravia grew up in a town just outside Glasgow and has always had a love for the English language. At a young age, she found herself writing funny stories or poems to friends and family for special occasions, and after high school she undertook a performing arts diploma, flourishing in her creative writing class. Sophie now works full time as a nurse in a busy city hospital.

In 2020, Sophie started writing again as a distraction from the ongoing pandemic, cheered on by fans of her hilarious blog, 'Sex in the Glasgow City'. *A Glasgow Kiss*, her debut novel, shot straight to number one in the erotic charts and has been a word-of-mouth sensation ever since.

SOPHIE GRAVIA

What Happens Happens in Dubai

x

ORION

An Orion paperback

First published in Great Britain in 2022 by Orion Fiction,
an imprint of The Orion Publishing Group Ltd.,
Carmelite House, 50 Victoria Embankment
London EC4Y 0DZ

An Hachette UK Company

9 10

A CIP catalogue record for this book is
available from the British Library.

ISBN (Mass Market Paperback) 978 1 3987 0670 5
ISBN (eBook) 978 1 3987 0671 2

Typeset by Born Group
Printed and bound in Great Britain by Clays Ltd, Elcograf S.p.A.

MIX
Paper from
responsible sources
FSC® C104740

www.orionbooks.co.uk

This book is written for any woman who aches for more. You are the star of your own novel – don't let anyone make you feel like an extra. If you are waiting on someone to walk in and change your life, simply look in the mirror and do it yourself.

I believe in you,

Sophie x

Chapter One

Remember when I thought I had my life in order? Well, it turns out that I definitely fucking didn't.

Within a few short weeks of my transformation into a happy single gal no longer obsessing over men or marriage, I realised I was, in fact, the same old Zara.

The thing is, on the outside, my life looked terrific. I am, after all, a successful aesthetics nurse in one of the most exclusive clinics in Glasgow. I work with my best friends, Raj and Ashley, and still occasionally take on a couple of shifts a month as a nurse when I need to feel more fulfilled in my profession. I am no longer scrimping to get by and this year I have purchased a bundle of leather shoes instead of my Primark plastics, which do not cope well with the stress of the Scottish rainy season, every fucking day. But even with my new-found comforts in place, it only really meant that as my life spiralled out of control this year, I appeared a smidge classier than usual.

The problem came at night, when I was alone with absolutely no distractions except Netflix and Pornhub. My once-unhealthy obsession with settling down with categorically anyone seemed to have evolved into an even worse habit of *shagging* literally anyone, with no real interest in them afterwards.

I seemed to develop the ick at an alarming rate – during or immediately after sex.

Anything could put me off, from an outfit they wore to the way the poor fucker sneezed, or merely the unmasculine way they drove their car. I was incredibly picky for someone who once fantasised for several months about a stranger who held a door open in a shopping centre for me, wondering if he felt the connection too. My attitude to men and sex had done a complete one-eighty. I couldn't find a man who kept me interested in them for longer than a couple of dates, and even my Penguin-loving Mark got ghosted when someone more interesting came along. After slating the shagging type on Tinder last year, I recently grasped that I am now the Glasgow gigolo and my list of accomplishments that I had fucked and chucked my way through this year was expanding rapidly.

I hadn't seen much of my ex, Tom, since I was working less at the hospital and practically full time at the clinic, but I'd heard rumours of his aesthetic business folding. Not that I cared or even gave him a second thought – I was thriving. But I couldn't help thinking the way he treated me had left me psychologically scarred and unable to form a real attachment or even a tiny bit of interest in any male after they'd penetrated my increasingly large vagina. The only person I could trust was myself and I wasn't prepared to take any shit from any man ever again.

Ping.

It was a frosty Tuesday morning in January, and I rolled over in bed to retrieve my phone after hitting the snooze button for the third time – six new matches and a message from William.

Morning beauty, looking forward to tonight. Enjoy work x

I planked my phone back down on my pillow and stretched widely, letting out a large groan.

Another day of work at the clinic. I rolled to the edge of the bed and sat up, looking around my chaotic bedroom.

This place is a fucking disgrace.

I stood up, kicking aside mounds of clothes to create a pathway for my feet and opened the wardrobe to find suitable attire for today's shift. Raj had been stricter with our dress code as a flurry of new aesthetics clinics had swept the city recently, and he was keen for us to stand out and insistent we all looked our best. A black midi dress, gold waist belt and small black pumps would have to do. Everything else seemed to be getting tighter as I took my December hibernation Dorito diet to the extreme. I opened my underwear drawer, rummaging for a clean pair of knickers, disturbing my growing stacks of dildos as I did so, but none could be found.

Shit.

My eyes scanned over Bin Laden's cave till I spotted a black thong still tangled up in an old pair of work tights. I picked them up cautiously, and gave them a little whiff, feeling utterly disgusted with myself. Commando it is then. I ran my brush through the tugs

3

in my messy hair and managed to slip it into a neat ponytail, then glanced at my watch: 8.48 a.m. *Shit*. My first client was due at nine. I only had time for tinted moisturiser, so I began rubbing it frantically into my cheeks while brushing my teeth at the same time. *Shit, shit, shit! Why did I insist on snoozing my alarm so many times today?*

Grabbing my leather jacket, I ran to the front door and headed down the cold stone steps onto the bustling streets of Glasgow. The wind was blowing fiercely, so with my head down I battled through the wintry weather on my usual ten-minute walk to the clinic. I saw the '*Individualise*' sign light up a gloomy George Square and breathed a sigh of relief. *Finally*.

As I walked in the door feeling dishevelled, I checked the clock above the reception desk and felt pleased I was only a few minutes late. Ashley was standing behind the desk awaiting my arrival, looking immaculate as always.

'Morning!' she said and beamed her brightest smile at me. I couldn't help but grin back at her infectious energy.

'Morning. You look pleased. Dave putting out this morning?' I replied, taking off my jacket, suspicious of her contentment.

'Ew, as if. His morning glory disappeared along with Oasis. No, I just love product day! Such a skive.' She was pottering about the desk, humming cheerfully away to herself.

I had completely forgotten it was product day. On the first Tuesday of each month, our product branding rep

Andrew comes to the clinic to pitch us new products, filler and treatment ideas. We had all become good friends, and because of the overall success of the clinic, Andrew gave us tips and constantly kept us up to date about new concepts in the industry and what products the other clinics were buying in. He had been the brand rep of Individualise for years, but as I previously worked part time, I had never got to know him. I would occasionally pick up his name in conversations between Raj and Ashley, but it was only when I qualified and increased my hours that we were finally introduced.

If I had remembered it was product day, I would have got out of bed a little calmer this morning as it meant I only had a few clients before spending the afternoon ogling Andrew. He was incredibly charming, chatty and funny. Initially, I wouldn't say he was a complete ten but the more he spoke, the better-looking he got, and the hotter he became. Ashley would make jokes and slip in some uncomfortable questions to find out his status, but he always had a witty comeback prepared for her, which made us even more curious.

I walked through to the treatment room and slipped my dress down before shoving it into my desk drawer, keen to keep this room tidy. I peeled on a set of navy blue scrubs that were hanging on the door, *these things must be shrinking in the wash,* and neatly set up my sterile trolley: *OK, so – needles, product, wipes.* Then I sat on the stool and examined the room, which was now *my* room. My certificates hung proudly on the wall, and my desk sported two large silver frames, containing photos of my graduation day, one with my mum and sister and me, and the others with my friends. Some days I forgot how much I had accomplished and others, like today, I felt proud and warm inside thinking of the opportunities I'd had.

There was a gentle knock at my door, which snapped me from my daydream.

'Zara, Mr Patterson's here for his top-up.'

'Yip, I'm coming!'

I stood up quickly and headed to the reception area.

'Peter, how are you?'

'I'm great. How are things, darling?' he replied, standing there in a pristine suit. Peter was one of my favourite clients. He worked as a top banker in London and would commute back and forth to Glasgow for work. He was initially one of Raj's clients from years before, and when I started training, he offered his face to me as a guinea pig for injection techniques and since then had remained on my client list. We got on exceptionally well and often commiserated about the gruelling task of online dating.

Together we walked into the treatment room, and I shut the door.

'So, just a top-up today?'

'Freeze me please – as much Botox as I can handle!'

I giggled at his demands.

'Deal!' I had prepared the syringes already, anticipating the large amount of product he was going to request, and began marking his face with a tiny white pencil.

'Look up. OK, big frown. Perfect.' I headed over to the sink and washed my hands.

'So, how's the dating life? How's the restaurant guy from the last time?' Peter asked.

I sighed a little, slightly embarrassed that I had moved on so quickly.

'Ehhhh . . . aw, nothing exciting. It didn't work out, but I do have a date tonight!' I turned around to him smirking. 'What about you?'

'Oh, never mind me! I've not been in the same place for two nights running! I'm living off other people's dating stories. Spill.'

I put my gloves on and sat down on the stool beside him, feeling uncomfortable at my tummy bloat.

'Well, his name is William. He's older than me. Considerably older, actually. He's like fifty-five but very DILF-y.'

Peter let out a big laugh.

'Oh, Zara, you crack me up. Nothing wrong with a DILF but at that age he could be a grampa you'd like to fuck! Where are you guys meeting?'

I leaned over Peter, trying to concentrate without giggling as I began injecting his forehead.

'Meeting at The Ivy for drinks. Just a couple – I'm working tomorrow.'

Peter's eyes were blinking as I got closer to them with the needle. I carried on for a few minutes, holding his head.

'That's you done, I'm just putting pressure on the bleeding.'

7

'Oh, it feels better already. It's been too long between appointments. Can't wait to shave off a few decades now. Oh, maybe you could inject your new man? Have him looking in his thirties again.'

We both laughed as I handed Peter a mirror.

'How the hell did you meet him anyway?' he asked, smising in the mirror from the treatment bed.

'Tinder,' I shrugged.

'What fucking age range do you set, Zara?'

I blushed, remembering that I'd recently had to expand the limits at either end of the scale as I had exhausted all my swipes, having either shagged, messaged or ditched my original group of suitors. This resulted in Tinder itself messaging to say *No more potential matches are meeting your criteria.*

'Right, come here, you.' Peter leaned over and kissed me on the cheek. I felt his expensive, strong aftershave hit the back of my throat. He always smelled amazing.

'Stay safe, Zara. I'll square Ashley up. Enjoy your night, sweetheart!'

I smiled back at him as he walked over to the desk, shaking his head.

'Thanks, Peter. See you soon.'

I wiped down the bed and set up another sterile trolley before heading back to the reception desk just as Peter was leaving. I waved him out the door.

'Who's next then?' I asked.

Ashley stared at the computer screen. 'Jan Hark? I can't remember who that is again, can you?'

I paused for a second, trying to recall.

'I know the name but can't think.' Ashley began searching the client database with her extra-long and pointed acrylic nails until we found a picture of Jan.

'Oh yeah, I remember, she's nice. I'm sure she's lips and Botox.'

I sat down on the swivel chair at the reception desk beside my friend, but as soon as my legs expanded on the flat surface, my scrubs felt like they were about to burst open at the seams. I gasped uncomfortably as I observed my stomach drape over the struggling elastic waistband.

'I'll need to steal a pair of Raj's scrubs again, Ash. I swear the scrubs are shrinking. Look at this – I've got more rolls than Morton's.' I was squeezing my stomach jokingly.

Ashley shook her head, looking annoyed, so I instantly shut down my *White Chicks 'Tina the Talking Tummy'* impression that was coming next. She had heard my moans so often and could only reassure me so many times. Right now she seemed more concerned about changing her hair parting using the computer screen as a mirror. I watched on enviously. Her perfectly curled blonde hair suited any part and any style. The last time I tried a side shed like that I just looked like fucking Hitler. Ashley stood up eventually and walked around the desk to the filing cabinet, before handing me a pair of freshly ironed scrubs from the bottom drawer. I smiled gratefully at her for providing Raj's spares. There I was, fitting into men's clothing while she was rocking a tight pencil skirt with a short crop top tied at the front, managing to look trendy but still professional.

'So, is it tonight you have the date with the old guy?' she asked, finally satisfied with her hair.

I slapped her arm jokingly as I giggled.

'Don't call him that. He's not that old, is he? I'm in my thirties now.'

'Aye, just. No, I totally agree he is fit-looking but there's no denying he's ancient. Are you talking to anyone else?'

I sneered up at Ashley while I retrieved my phone from my scrubs' top and held up a picture of another Tinder match I had been chatting to.

'What do you think of this wee belter? I'm also messaging him.' I began flicking through pictures of Luke. A student architect, he was young, muscly, blond and incredibly flirty.

'He is also very, very good-looking, but . . .'

'But what?'

'Zara, he looks about twenty!'

I started to giggle, zooming into incredible abs and the large grey jogger bottom bulge he sported.

'He's twenty-four actually.'

'Oh my god, Zara! You're like fucking Goldilocks. Nah, this cock is too old, hmm . . . This one is too young. You need to sit on one that's just right.'

We started laughing loudly, the sound of it filling the shop around us.

'Stop judging! And by the way, they all feel the same after a while, to be honest.'

Ashley's eyes were shiny with tears from giggling.

'Absolutely no judgement here! At least you're getting some!' she exclaimed. 'Every night Dave has a fucking moan. "I'm too tired" or "Wait till I play FIFA, babe". You'll notice he's the one waiting after that. Oh, and the other night I was doing my fake tan and he waltzed into the bedroom absolutely livid because he finally wanted to have sex, but I had just done my tan so he couldn't! Mate, if it's him or the Fake Bake, I know who I'm choosing.'

I was still snorting with laughter when the door opened. It was my second client, looking puzzled at all the hilarity.

'Hi. Morning, Jan. Sorry.' I cleared my throat, trying to remain professional as Ashley sniggered beside me. 'Right, how are you? What are we doing today?' I asked.

'I think I walked in at the wrong time, girls. At least you lot can have fun at your work! I'm thinking half a mil in my lips and three areas of Botox please, Zara.'

'Sure. I'll set up for you and let Ash take some snaps. See you shortly.'

'Not a problem. Let me fix this hair first, Ashley, before you take any photographs – it's blowing a gale out there.'

I shuffled through to the treatment room, grasping the bigger pair of trousers tightly in my hand, still smiling from the banter with Ashley. I carried on with work that morning, injecting a couple more faces, chatting along the way, while discreetly performing a prolonged pelvic floor workout, feeling ever so paranoid about the size of my vagina.

Later that afternoon Ashley and I were gossiping in the staff room when Raj popped through the door.

'Ladies, how was your morning?'

I nodded happily while trying to swallow my Koka noodles.

'Yeah, good. Peter was in,' I smiled, knowing it was still a sore spot for Raj to lose a client.

'Oh, was he now? I still can't believe you poached him, Zara.' He squeezed my shoulders jokingly.

I started to giggle but remained engrossed in my noodles.

'All right, people.'

We looked out towards the clinic floor as we heard a deep voice. Andrew.

Raj immediately went to greet him while I slurped the rest of my noodles down and quickly followed a few seconds behind.

Andy smiled over to me as he removed his dripping wet jacket and placed it over the desk, shivering slightly, still feeling the cold from outside. I was gawking at him as if he was in a Coca-Cola advert until I noticed him watching me back. 'How's it going, Zara? How are you?'

'Yeah, not bad thanks, Andy. How are you?' I asked, fiddling with my ponytail while checking him out from a distance. He was wearing a tight Ralph Lauren shirt which was carefully tucked into his dark denim jeans. The strong, masculine scent of his aftershave filled the room, which made me immediately turn my head a little to the side, taking in a deep breath, inhaling his scent. I could feel my face turn warm as he continued the conversation.

'Yeah, can't complain. Did I interrupt your lunch?'

'No, no, not at all. I'd literally just finished. You're totally fine to start.' I walked over to the large white sofa in the centre of the room, glad of the slight breeze escaping from underneath the front door which was cooling my flaring face as nerves took over.

'Well, you'll probably be hungry later on,' Andy said. 'Half of it's down your uniform.'

My flirtatious smile dropped as I glanced down at my scrubs, which were encrusted with curried noodles. Raj shook his head in disgust.

'Aw, Zara. Are those my bloody scrubs you're wearing again?' Raj huffed.

Shit. Shit.

'What? No. Well, I don't think so. Oh, wait. Are they? Sorry, I must have lifted the wrong ones from the desk this morning.' I glanced over to Ashley who had her hand over her mouth discreetly hiding her smirk.

Well, thanks for that, Raj. Now the guy I fancy knows we could shop jointly in Burtons together, even share sizes. It took a few minutes for my heart to stop pounding so loudly into my ears, till I could sit back, relax and finally admire our sales rep.

Andrew must have been in his mid-thirties, with a shaved head, bright blue eyes and great body that peered through his designer shirts. He had broad shoulders, large forearms and was pretty muscly uptop, with a slight pot belly. Normally this would instantly put me off someone – even though I personally felt like Pavarotti's sister, I wasn't a fan of podgy men. Nevertheless, *his* slightly bloated abdomen always seemed adorable. Combining all of this with a glistening smile and laddish patter, Andy really did seem to be the full package.

'Right, troops, have you got the sales figures from last month?'

Ashley handed him the spreadsheet and he skimmed over it.

'Yeah, looks pretty OK. A bit of a dip mid-month, Raj, eh?'

'Yeah, and it's getting more of a dip each month, Andy. It's that bloody new place that's opened right across the square, Botox Boxx. I mean, the council must have approved their premises when we're right here. It's a joke. They are stealing half our clientele. I've seen more than a few of our regulars pop up on their Instagram feed having had treatments there – cheap treatments.' He rolled his eyes at me, sitting at the other end of the sofa.

'I know, ma man, but that's the business you're in. Aesthetics is building, and more and more people are training in the industry,' Andy replied.

'Yes, well, I wish they'd move further afield,' Raj muttered back.

'I think I can do something that could help. Anyone ever been to Dubai?'

Ashley gasped. 'Me!'

Raj and I looked at one another curiously.

'Right, basically Dubai is where it's all happening just now. Hundreds of influencers; big party girls – and boys – are flooding the streets of Dubai. The richest, most photogenic city in the world but there's no fucking decent aesthetics out there. None. The company is expanding their products and have managed to book a luxury penthouse in the Palm for one day only. We need practitioners to go out there to deliver our product and set up the aesthetics correctly for a shoot. That's it. The models will then take part in some fancy photoshoot and you guys can chill. You'd be on standby in case you need to show them how to hold the needles but basic work. They've hired top influencers, and of course you can take behind-the-scene content – fucking fantastic for your social media and followers as well. It's half a day's work at the most, and honestly, Raj, the publicity will be unbelievable, mate.'

My mouth dropped open and Ashley began screaming, clapping her hands and stamping her feet. Raj was totally calm.

'Wait, Ash, shh, calm down,' Raj said. 'Do you have dates in mind? I can't afford to cancel existing clients. I'm trying my hardest to keep them sweet in case they go elsewhere at the minute, Andy.'

'Well, that's the only thing: it needs to be next week. Next Friday to Monday, all flights and accommodation paid for. You would arrive on Friday and not need to work till Saturday, another day shopping or whatever you like on Sunday then home the following day.'

I was hanging on every word Andrew said with my herb-stained grin beaming over my face. I looked at Raj hopefully, who was deep in thought, contemplating the idea.

'God, it's tempting. It really is. It's just the clients, Andy.'

'Well, I thought I'd give you first dibs on it anyway. I know it's short notice, mate, but if Individualise decline, I need to ask Botox Boxx next. Only because of their recent sale figures, my boss insisted. And see, if I'm being one hundred per cent honest with you, Raj, I know they will snap this shit up.'

'Raj,' I interrupted, 'we don't have to cancel any clients. We can rearrange appointments and do a couple of late nights this week. I could even come in on my day off. This is a great opportunity.'

I looked at my friend as he bit his lip, wholly lost in thought.

'You think we could do it, Zara?'

'Fuck, yes, of course I do,' I yelled enthusiastically.

Raj didn't say anything for a few seconds. I could see him working things out in his head, weighing up the pros and cons, of which I could think of exactly zero. The man would be stupid to say no. As his silence stretched on, I could feel my heartbeat racing and Ashley, standing like a ball of tension beside me, ready to burst.

Finally, Raj looked round at us and then turned to Andrew.

'Looks like we're going to Dubai, mate!' he blurted.

'YESSS!!' Ashley stood up and began screaming. 'Oh my god! I can't wait till you guys see this place. It's insane. I'm ready to cry. I'm so excited. Oh. My. God. I can hardly breathe.' She was flapping her huge nails in front of her face enthusiastically.

'Wait, Ash. Sorry, hen. There're only two tickets,' Andrew said. 'You cannae go.'

Ashley's face fell and her energy suddenly popped like a balloon. The room fell awkwardly silent.

'Aww what! I cannae keep that going. I'm only pulling your leg. I told my boss better make it for three. There's no show without Punch.' Andrew burst into hysterical laughter. Raj and I followed, Ashley ever so slightly smiling as she took in his cruel joke.

'Right, so, you're all up for this? I'll take a few details and finalise everything.'

I nodded my head frantically, still trying to take in the prospect, while Ashley stood clasping her hands tightly with excitement.

Raj smiled at us and shook his head. 'Individualise is taking over Dubai!'

Chapter Two

That evening as I scurried around my flat hiding the accumulation of dirty clothes anywhere that would fit, there was an excitable bubble in my chest that I hadn't felt for a long time. I was going on holiday next week! The cold, frosty Glasgow air would soon be traded for a rich, warm, sun-kissed breeze and it couldn't come quick enough. Tonight, however, I had my date with a mature older man, and I couldn't wait for a civilised meal, preferably three courses, with lots of boasting about my upcoming holiday.

I was meeting my date outside The Ivy, a popular high-end restaurant in the city, at 7 p.m., and it had passed six before I even contemplated beginning my date-night preparation. I was finding that the more dates I went on, the less I could give a fuck about the getting ready part. Dating, which was once a novelty, had become a far too familiar process for me, and the excitement of preparation and willingness to look my best had vanished.

I eventually swaggered into my bedroom after watching one too many episodes of *The Vampire Diaries* and started spraying my long black hair with a generous amount of dry shampoo. Earlier I'd had ambitious plans of washing it before the date, but unfortunately the original family of vampires had taken up permanent residence in Mystic Falls and my plans to conceal a week's worth of grease, long work hours and the likely remnants of other men's bodily fluids had become second choice. After swooshing my hair with a generous amount of product, I realised quickly it was a bad idea as my hair was sticking up like Jedward's. I attempted to pat it down, with no luck. Somehow, I managed to manoeuvre it into a beehive. *Great, no one's wore this style since the seventies. Still, this cunt will remember that decade well,* I thought. I proceeded to smear a mound of foundation across my face before finishing the look off with some black mascara and shiny lip gloss. *This will have to do.*

I headed to my bathroom and squeezed out a last-minute pee before having a little council wash in the sink. I ran the water for a few seconds, allowing it to warm up, then shunted my tights and underwear to my knees, splashing my vagina at the sink. I lathered up some Radox and began shaving my bristly bush, wincing at each thick, stubborn pube that didn't want to budge. By the time I was finished, my fanny appeared to have been sheared by Sweeney Todd. I gasped at how raw and severely wounded it looked, but at least it felt smooth. I wasn't planning on sleeping with William, but with the way my dating life was going, I wasn't ruling it out either. I hoped to make the decision quickly after meeting him as, with my hair growth, I had roughly three hours tops before the cactus returned.

William and I met on Tinder. He had Super Liked me, and I suppose, *as always*, I enjoyed the attention. We'd only been chatting for two or three days before he asked to meet up and when he suggested The Ivy, I had to oblige. He seemed really articulate, smart and occasionally cheeky in his text messages, and although he was older, he looked remarkably fit with an impressive set of broad shoulders that immediately caught my eye from his profile pictures. He ran a boxing class for kids, and after a decent amount of Facebook stalking, I found his club and watched sexy videos of him pounding the punch bag. I got turned on scrolling through to 2017 as he embarked on the 'push-up challenge', hoping one day I'd be lying under his sweaty pits getting pumped! If his profile didn't declare his age, I would never have guessed he was anywhere near his fifties. He did, however, have a few grey streaks glistening through his dark hair at the sides, which hinted at his years but in my opinion made him appear even more sophisticated and utterly fuckable in his photographs. Tonight was sure to be an interesting one.

I walked back to my bedroom and flicked through my wardrobe, conscious I only had fifteen minutes before I was supposed to be meeting him. In a rush, I pulled a black oversized woollen dress on, yanking it at the shoulders to attempt to make it more fashionable. My tights were still on from earlier and, unfussed about changing them, I bent over to give my feet a little sniff and shrugged. *Not absolutely awful but not the pleasantest either.* I took some deodorant and sprayed them, hoping I could mask the stench for a few more hours at least. *Let's hope he's not got a foot fetish, Zara.* In a rush to leave, I had one last look in the mirror, feeling unimpressed. I grabbed my phone and forced my feet into a pair of Doc Martens before heading for the door.

Outside, the wind was bitterly cold, and I felt glad I had opted for such a sensible outfit. I wondered what William would be like. I hadn't been nervous about seeing him the entire day and had only responded to a few of his messages, but walking down the street to meet him, I suddenly felt anxious. *What the fuck am I doing? He's old enough to be your dad, Zara!* I suddenly had an overwhelming fear, but I was committed and would never let someone down last minute. I was approaching Royal Exchange Square and the restaurant was only a few steps away. I could feel my heart pounding with nerves. I brought out my phone to text Ashley when a message from William popped up.

I'm here x

Great. No backing out now. I took a cool deep breath and carried on with my walk, pretending to be distracted by my phone, all the while my arse was making buttons and my heart was leaping out of my chest.

'Zara? Hiya.'

I looked up and smiled at the shadow of a tall man standing outside the large flowery entrance to the restaurant.

'William?' I replied, cheekily biting my lip, trying to see his face under the black night sky.

He was standing with his hands in his jacket pockets. I walked over to the silhouette in the doorway to greet him properly. He leaned over and kissed my cheek.

'It's lovely to meet you in person. Right, after you.' He opened the heavy restaurant door for me. 'C'mon, I'm bloody well freezing,' he joked.

I smiled up at him as I walked into the busy restaurant, intrigued at his upfront manner. The lights were bright, and it took my eyes a second to adjust. The smell of rich scrumptious food made my mouth water instantly.

'Mmm . . . I love this place, William. Have you been before?'

I turned to face my date and was surprised to see him rubbing his hands together, frantically trying to get a heat in them. *Probably bad circulation at his age,* I thought. But as my eyes gazed up to meet his, I suddenly choked in horror. William was sporting a full head of long, icy white hair. *What the fuck!* He most certainly didn't have that do in his profile pictures. I could feel my optimistic smile drain from my face as I began to wonder if people thought I was taking my gramps out for dinner.

Suddenly I was conscious that I was staring far too long at his head, hoping my eyes would make the colour magically reappear.

'You OK, wee yin?' he muttered, as I coughed slightly. He walked past me towards the server. I nodded back, snapping myself from my nightmare.

William was tall, his frame large and muscly, but he was wearing jeans that were frayed badly at the bottom.

I couldn't help thinking they were probably older than me, and over the years of wear and tear they had turned distressed all by themselves.

But even though I had been well and truly catfished, I was in The Ivy, and I was not willing to let an old man with bad dating etiquette ruin my dinner. When I wrapped my head around it, I strangely admired his boldness to turn up so dissimilar from his photographs and I also completely sympathised. He probably didn't expect me to be here without my spaniel lug filter or butterfly halo that I carefully choose to snap with as it seems to minimise my triple chin in photographs. He had after all, been a hunk back in the day; it was completely unfair that the ageing process had taken over and he now resembled a cross between Hulk Hogan and Karl Lagerfeld. I was sure I'd tricked many men over the years with my Instagram-filtered complexion looking as smooth as silk, when in reality I had more hair growth than the best of them.

The server was chatting to William and she smiled up at us.

'I'll take you both to your seat.'

I followed the pretty young hostess as William held back like a gentleman, allowing me to walk in front. As I went, I felt his hand scuff by my waist, and my back seized as stiff as a board. I felt like I was walking under a spotlight as I made my way past the tables neatly scattered round the lavish restaurant, hoping he didn't touch my back or make any suggestive signs we were on a date. The décor was magnificent: a 1920s vibe with relaxing music and a warm, friendly atmosphere. I felt as if I was in *Bugsy Malone*, only I was the only kid on this date.

We were shown to a small circular table in the corner which had pretty velvet bucket chairs at either side. William rushed round to pull mine out for me and I blushed, hoping no other diners were watching.

'Thank you,' I whispered, trying not to draw any more attention to us.

'You're welcome, Zara.' He walked round to his own seat, taking his coat off and hanging it over his chair. *Oh no*. He was wearing a plain white T-shirt with a grey checked waistcoat which jingled with an obscene number of buckles, belts and chains attached. I hadn't seen anything quite like it, and I could feel my face redden as I prayed he'd sit down quickly to avoid anyone else spotting the fashion statement.

As he sat, his chains rattled the side plate loudly. 'Oh, oops.' My eyes shut briefly hoping the moment would pass quickly. 'So, hiya, Zara. This is nice, eh. Good to finally meet you,' he said.

'Yes! It really is. This is one of my favourite restaurants. What do you fancy?' I was avoiding any eye contact, staring at the gin menu in front of me. I could feel myself get hotter with nerves. *Why the fuck did I wear wool?*

'I think I'll have the fillet of salmon; I checked the menu before I left,' he winked, hoping I'd be impressed by this, and I smiled back briefly, knowing I hadn't even factored time in to change my knicks never mind examine a menu.

'I think I fancy the fillet steak. Yes, I'll have that with a nice glass of Whitley Neill.'

'Jesus, Zara. A steak!!' his loud voice screeched. 'I hope we're splitting the bloody bill!'

I looked up at William's gobsmacked face. My heart was pounding, and my already sweaty body was perspiring even more.

'Haha, gotcha!' He pointed his large finger in my face so suddenly my chair moved back, and my legs swung out and kicked him under the table.

'Oh sorry!' I began to giggle awkwardly, as I watched my date discreetly rub his shin under the table.

'What the fuck have you got on anyway, Zara? A pair of rigger boots?'

I smiled politely at his shit joke.

'Eh . . . eh . . . what kind?' he pressed. 'I thought you women were supposed to dress up for a first date?'

I stared at him heatedly, unsure if this was yet another bad joke or not.

'They're Doc Martens; I believe that they are actually fashionable for people who were born in this century,' I snapped back.

'Waha! Yes, brilliant.' He began clapping his hands loudly at the table. 'I like how we can laugh together already, Zara. Absolutely brilliant patter.' He was laughing so hard at his own gag, while I still felt mildly offended by his dig at my outfit. I didn't put much into it but still, I looked better than his Jodie Marsh-inspired ensemble, I thought.

The waitress came over to take our order and I was pleased to finally have some alcohol en route to settle my nerves.

'So, tell me about you, Zara,' William asked.

'Well, I work in an aesthetics clinic just round the corner actually, and—'

'Right, be honest. Do you think I need some work done?' he interrupted.

'Oh, of course not,' I said politely. *But some Just For Men wouldn't go amiss, pal,* I thought. He winked across the table, liking my courteous reply.

'So, you're a boxing coach? That sounds like good fun, eh.'

'Well, I was – gave it up about five years ago now. Was getting too old!' he chuckled. 'I mainly work for the council now.'

What as? I thought. *A fucking lollipop man!* I felt completely deceived. Not only was my date using five-year-old pictures, but he was also tricking women into thinking he was still some big-shot boxer just to make him appear more eligible. I wasn't even sure if I felt angry or pitied him as he continued to reminisce about his boxing days and the numerous black eyes he'd encountered over the years.

While William chatted, I couldn't help examining his face. Yes, his hair dramatically aged him, but he was handsome. He had the brightest green eyes, tanned skin and a strong build. Did he really feel like he couldn't be his true self when creating that profile? I'm sure if he was honest and more realistic with his matches, he'd be a real catch for an older woman, who was more willing to listen to some dodgy patter and a few bad dad jokes.

Our food and drinks arrived, and I felt some relief as I had something on the table to distract me from William's conversation.

I began slicing into my perfectly cooked steak and slurping on my cold gin cocktail.

'So, do you go on many dates?' he asked.

'Hmm . . . not too many. I work a lot so I don't have much time. What about you?' I had learned from the months of dating that men seem to make unfair assumptions about women who serial date like myself; it seemed far easier to tell a little white lie in these situations.

'God, no. My wife and I split last year and this is the second time I've been out the house. I don't like rushing into anything, and I really feel like there has to be a spark there before any sort of physical intimacy takes place.'

I was nodding in agreement, still chewing my sirloin. *What a pussy! Still, at least there won't be an awkward convo at the end of the night full of rejection.*

'Yeah, absolutely. I'm the same, although I'm not sure what I'm looking for. My work life is so full on. I obviously have Dubai and things coming up now and who knows where that will lead?' I said, attempting to plant the seed of letting him down gently.

'Great. I'm glad we're on the same page. Another drink?' he asked.

I shrugged. 'Emm . . . OK, why not?'

The night was flying by. I wasn't sure if it was the alcohol content rising in my bloodstream or the fact that I knew William didn't like to have sex on the first date that relaxed my nerves a bit, but I started to enjoy his company. He was fairly funny, despite some cringeworthy jokes which at times I didn't know how to take. But still, I could tell he was a nice man. I didn't feel like we were flirtatious, just enjoying each other's banter, and when he offered to pay the bill, I was grateful for a good night.

'Right, after you, Zara.'

We were heading out of the restaurant and I couldn't help feeling relieved when he tossed his jacket on, concealing that horrendous waistcoat.

'Thanks for dinner, William. I had such a lovely time.'

As soon as I hit the cold, frosty air, my head began to get the gin spin and I clumsily bumped right into my date. My hands gripped both his arms as he broke my stumble.

'Oh sorry,' I giggled, feeling uncomfortably close to him.

We were facing one another head-on and all I could feel was warm breath hit my face. *Salmon breath*. I broke away from his lingering stare and began to stroll merrily towards the stone archway of Royal Exchange Square to head home.

'Zara, hold up. I'll walk you home,' he called out, following me.

'No, don't be silly. I'm only down the street. I'll text you,' I insisted.

He grabbed my arm. 'Zara, let me walk you. It wouldn't be good manners.'

'OK then, but watch that puddle, it's pure ice. I don't want you breaking a hip on me.'

We both laughed as William pretended to tickle my waist, avoiding the frozen puddles along the way.

'You're getting brave, Zara! You'll get yourself into trouble!'

I turned round to face William, who raised his snowflake brows at me suggestively. *Oh, hold the fuck up!* I thought. *Is he hitting on me?* I began questioning his good guy motives and suddenly, as he smiled at me under the dark starry sky, I was questioning my own. Was I beginning to find William more attractive? Or were my beer goggles well and truly on? I mean, he was very masculine, with cheeky patter and a great set of broad shoulders. Yes, ideally, I would like to place a bag over his face if it eventually came down to the deed. But it got me thinking – *how old was too old?*

My head was swirling into overdrive and I wasn't sure if I was imagining the sexual chemistry, but he seemed to get closer as we walked, telling the same shitty jokes then making excuses to touch me. All of a sudden, it dawned on me – *I think William wants to be fucked!*

We approached the entrance to my building and for the first time that night my date looked tense. His hands were back in his pockets and I could see his cold breath in the dark night.

'This is me then. Thanks again, William.'

I leaned over to kiss his cheek but at the last second, he turned his face, landing my kiss directly onto his peachy lips. We shared a peck, and I chuckled at his bravado, pulling away and smirking up at him. I didn't have much time to gather my thoughts before he was pressing me up against the door, kissing me hard and passionately. *Oh, hello, grampa!!! Where the fuck did this come from? Jesus!*

Without a second thought, his tongue was touching my tonsils and rummaging about my mouth. I was taken aback and trying to gather my thoughts. He had me pushed against the door, holding my wrist tightly above my head. I couldn't help but immediately feel my fanny tingle at the strong man caressing me so openly in the middle of the street. After a while, I could feel his hard dick push into me, pleading for my attention. One thing was for sure, this OAP certainly didn't need Viagra!

'Do you want to come upstairs then?' I managed to blurt out, still kissing him.

He bit my bottom lip and tugged it out, gently nodding his head. *Damn,* this old dog had the fucking moves. I could feel adrenaline pulsing through my body. I hadn't expected this to happen, not tonight and certainly not with him.

I opened my bag, retrieved the key and led William all the way up the stairs and straight to my bedroom.

Chapter Three

I opened my bedroom door with one hand while gripping William's tightly in the other. Nerves crammed my belly, but I was still lustful and intrigued by how this experienced man would perform.

Giggling, I walked over to my bed. The bedside light was still on from earlier, and I turned to see my date begin to take off his coat, staring at me with a seductive grin on his face. The crunch of misplaced Quavers I had dropped on the floor the previous night didn't seem to bother him as he crumbled them into my carpet and continued looking at me, almost as if he was in a trance.

'You sure about this, Zara? I know you don't normally do this.'

I nodded back, innocently agreeing with him but wondering if I had even changed the sheets since my last encounter only a few days prior.

'I'm sure. Come over here.' I patted the bed for him to join me.

He threw his coat to the ground dramatically and leapt towards the bed. We began kissing again, but this time it was more intense. He was a very passionate kisser, and I was impressed. My mouth was drenched from all of his spittle, but he was biting my lip and sucking my tongue and I couldn't help but enjoy the sheer graft he was putting into it. He continued teasing me with his tongue, and after ten minutes of kissing and dry humping I couldn't help but think I had made the right choice. He started grabbing my tits, rubbing them aggressively through my woollen dress. I was baking enough as it was and could feel myself getting blotchier as he continued. I stopped the kissing momentarily, stood up, kicked my boots to the side and yanked my dress and tights off.

Finally, relief! I could get a breath.

I turned to William, who looked like he'd enjoyed the spontaneous striptease as he ogled me intensely.

'Jesus, Zara! HIYA, baby!' he yelled and pulled me down on top of him.

We kissed more deeply now, his fingers squeezing my nipples and slowly making their way down towards my honey pot.

Bingo! He slowly began slipping his fingers in and out of me. My body squirmed as he teased my clit. He was rubbing it fast, then slow, then fast then slow.

I was on the brink of coming every time, and then he'd stop and whisper, 'Not yet.'

Jesus Christ, I hadn't been this horny for a long time. I wanted him, and I wanted him immediately! I began rubbing his hard bulge through his jeans and tried to pull them down.

'Take them off!' I moaned impatiently, and he grinned like the Cheshire Cat at my request.

William slid his worn jeans down his muscular legs, and next tackled the dreaded waistcoat. Each individual buckle seemed to be an effort. I wasn't sure if it was the actual fastenings or the fact this old bastard probably had arthritis beginning in his decrepit fingers, but just when I thought he was almost done, he turned to the loops at the back. *Oh, for fuck's sake!* A straitjacket would have been easier to escape from. I waited below him, watching him eagerly, my left foot tapping with impatience as my fanny dried up. *Finally*, his clothes were off, and my hot muscly mature man was on top of me with his impressively thick dick standing to attention. I couldn't believe how I'd underestimated this man. My heart was beating hard as he leaned over me, positioning his dick to its target with real precision, and with one slow hard push, he was inside of me. He paused for a second and stared directly into my eyes before bellowing loudly, 'Oh hiya!'

I smiled back and whispered, 'Hello.'

I was keen to get this rhythm started, but again he slid in and out, shouting 'Hiya!' directly into my face. I was so confused – surely all of these immediate pleasantries had happened at dinner – but he was looking at me like he wanted an answer, so again I replied, 'Hey.' He continued slipping his big dick in and out, getting more aroused each time as he began groaning, 'Mmmmm . . . hiyaaaaa.'

I felt unbelievably uncomfortable. I was spending more time thinking up replies that consisted of 'Hi there' or 'Howdy' than the fact I had a large knob inside me.

Each time I responded, I would see the fire blaze behind his eyes. He would pick up the pace then start all over again in a seductive tone of voice: 'Hiya.'

I had to take control. I pushed him over and climbed on top of him, then began bouncing hard up and down while he continued yelling.

'Aw HIYA! Yes, hello, baby!'

Shut the fuck up, I thought, but still, 'Hi, hi, hi, hi, hi,' with each thrust he would continue.

I was now trying to block out the noise as I rode him hard, shutting my eyes tightly and angling my head to the ceiling, desperately frustrated and wanting to orgasm.

'Look at me, baby, hmm . . . hello? Let me see your eyes,' he panted beneath me.

I pretended not to hear, but again he begged me to look at him. I shook my head, unable to talk from the exertion. My breathing was becoming shallow and my thighs were beginning to seize.

'Open your eyes!' he wailed.

'I can't! I'm too . . . er . . . tired!' I shouted back.

I continued bouncing, and still the hiyas came, keeping perfect time. Nevertheless, I persisted, trying my hardest to block him out and not allow him to distract me from finding my orgasm. But, no, unfortunately the old bastard beat me to it, and came with one last, loud, resounding, 'HELLO!'

I was utterly dumbfounded. Physically and mentally exhausted.

William lay on the bed like he was the one who'd

done the hard day's work, while I hobbled off his now deflating penis and made my way to the bathroom.

'Baby, where are you going?' He bolted upright on the bed and watched me waddle out of the room.

'I'll be back in a second. Just nipping to the loo.'

I entered the bathroom, confused and disappointed. I didn't know what just happened or if it was even a big deal. If anything, I felt more annoyed at myself for giving in and shagging again. I went out for a civilised meal in a fancy restaurant, but a few gins later and I'm riding a pensioner with a catchphrase. I wiped myself down and reluctantly returned to the bedroom.

William hadn't got dressed and was lying comfortably on top of my covers. Legs opened wide, still enjoying his session. *Well, he's certainly not shy. I'll give him that.* I couldn't help but notice how much smaller his dick looked, shrivelled up like a little raisin. I edged my way to the side of the bed, trying not to gawk too much.

'That was a lot of fun!' he said, turning his head to face me.

'Yes, it was!' I replied, feeling like a terrible liar.

'I hope you don't think I do that all the time, Zara. It's just . . . well, I think, in fact we both know there is a special connection here. I could feel it from the moment we met. You're a bloody keeper!'

My face fell as alarm bells rang in my ears just as the sound of his hiyas were fading.

'Can I grab some water? I am parched! Too much fish for one night, eh?' He began to chuckle as my face fell further. *What a cheeky bastard! He better have been*

35

referring to the salmon. But that comment alone made me shudder.

'Eh, yeah sure, ha! I'll get one for you.' I went to move off the bed when he rolled around suddenly.

'No, no, you stay where you are. I'll get it, baby.' He stood up and went to the door. I watched his peachy bum strut out the room before he paused and turned back around.

'Zara, I hope you don't have plans this week. I need to see you again!'

I looked at the overeager man staring at me, bollock naked. I couldn't help but admire his ripped body, especially for his age. My eyes dropped lower as I examined his dick again. Even if it did resemble a raisin when off duty, it was a good size when erect, with an excellent girth. Maybe I could see him, just have him as a fuck buddy option. Perhaps the hiyas were just first-time nerves.

Then, peeking out from behind the dick, I spotted something I hadn't noticed before.

A set of curly white balls. I had just shagged a guy with silver pubes. Why hadn't it dawned on me that his curtains would match his carpet? I smiled sympathetically at William, who was awaiting my reply.

'Oh, William, remember I'm going to Dubai to work . . . for a while. I should have spoken more about it, but it was only finalised today.' I blurted it out so naturally, as if I was genuinely upset.

'What? Oh my god! I didn't realise it was so soon. When are you going?' He looked frantic.

Shit, I felt under pressure all of a sudden.

'I'm going . . . in the morning actually.' I began stuttering, 'I, eh, I haven't even had a chance to pack or anything. It was all so last minute.'

William placed his bulky arms on top of his head, disappointedly.

'I knew this was too good to be true!'

He took a large sigh and walked back over to me as I tried my hardest to appear sombre.

'How long will you be away, Zara?' he asked.

The room fell unbelievably quiet as I thought up my next lie.

'I'm not sure. I wouldn't want or expect you to wait for me or anything silly like that. It could be months.'

He nodded.

'God, I can't believe it. Tomorrow though? Wow. You must be stressed out with all the organising. Do you need me to leave? Or I could help you? Packing or anything?'

'It's OK, but I better start soon, I suppose. I know I should have said before this happened. I just didn't expect it.'

'Listen, don't apologise. I'm fucking glad it happened. I'll go, eh? Let you get organised. Why don't you call me when you've packed, and we can have a good chinwag? And, Zara?'

I lifted my eyes from the floor and faced him.

'Never say never. In a few months' time you could be walking down Argyle Street and we could bump into one another. You'd get a big hug and a HIYA from me!'

I had heard enough fucking hiyas to last a lifetime and knew then he had to leave immediately. I politely hugged the naked man, avoiding direct contact with his ageing ball sack as it swung towards my thighs.

William began buckling up his chainmail and eventually made his way towards the front door. His eyes seemed sad, and I tried my hardest to look devastated myself. I waved him out, shut the door and felt an instant stab of anxiety. *Am I a horrible person? I've just had sex with that guy and told him a pack of lies to get him to leave my house.*

Fuck, this time last year I would have probably arranged a wedding with the sheer amount of interest he was feeding me, but now I felt nothing. Whatsoever.

I wrapped my dressing gown tightly around my shoulders and headed back to the bedroom to rejoin *The Vampire Diaries*.

Chapter Four

The following morning, I thundered through the clinic doors, running late, feeling hungover and exhausted from my night with William.

'Morning,' Ashley called out. 'God, you look rough.'

I shot her a death stare, not wanting to comment on my current situation, and headed straight to the staff room to crack open a cold can of Irn Bru to help relieve my hangover.

The clinic had its usual morning buzz and my clients helped take my mind off my worsening headache with their latest dramas at work or at home. Around twelve I made my way back through to reception, craving some calories. Ashley was swivelling idly on the reception chair, staring at the computer screen.

'Hey, have you got lunch in with you?' I asked.

'So, you want to talk now?' She stood up, deliberately flicking her hair out so that it brushed my face and I could smell her coconut shampoo glide past my nostrils.

'Oh, stop! OK, sorry. Don't make me feel worse than I do. I had far too many gins and a weird fucking night last night.'

'You need to stop drinking on a school night. Will we go to Greggs and you can tell me about it?' she asked.

'Yes!' I blurted, feeling surprised as Ashley had been calorie counting since Christmas.

We collected our jackets from the staff room and began walking through the busy square towards the bakery. The weather was miserable, but my body felt an immediate relief stepping into the cold, fresh air. The alcohol was finally departing my system. We carefully crossed the roads, linking arms while stepping over the deeper puddles left by last night's rain.

'So, how was your date?' Ashley asked, clutching my arm tight as we dodged the cars.

'Oh my god, Ash, his hair! It was completely silver – not at all like his pictures. He was really old.'

'Shut up!' Her face screwed up, unimpressed. 'What a catfish! And what a bloody cheek. I can't believe that – fucking creep, Zara! So, what time did you get home?'

'Like half ten. I think.' I shrugged my shoulders, still battling the wintery wind blowing directly into our faces.

'Well, that's not too late. I thought it would have been worse. You looked like shit this morning,' she added, giving me a sarcastic smile with her bright teeth.

'Well . . . I kind of brought him back to the flat though, didn't I?'

'No. You didn't. Did you pump him?' Ashley stopped, unlinking her arm, and held her hands to her mouth in shock. 'Zara, did you pump a pensioner?' Her voice seemed incredibly loud as she was ready to erupt into laughter.

I suddenly became paranoid about the stares of passers-by.

'Shhh! Seriously, shhh, come on.'

We walked into Greggs and stood in line to be served. Ashley was still in need of more information.

'Yes, I did,' I whispered. 'And I'm slightly traumatised. Not only did the rug match the curtains, but he had a fucking catchphrase.'

Ashley gasped in disgust.

'Oh no, it's something weird, isn't it?'

'Not weird in any other context. But he continuously shouted "Hiya" during sex!' I began to giggle as I heard how bizarre my night sounded out loud.

'*What*?' Ashley said.

'Like, constantly,' I said, keeping my voice low. 'I was answering him back too, like a right fanny. I had no idea what to do. But he was grunting, like, "Oh hiya . . . hiya . . . hi . . . hi . . . hi".' I looked around us and closed my eyes doing my best impression of William's voice.

We both cackled so loud that the other customers began to gawk and I stopped feeling embarrassed. As I approached the front of the queue, I lifted a tuna and sweetcorn baguette from the fridge along with some Lucozade for a much-needed sugar burst.

'Maybe he had Tourette's?' Ashley suggested, still trying wrap her head around the situation.

'I think I would have picked up on that at dinner, Ash?' I said.

'And he couldn't have looked that old, or surely you wouldn't have done it! You must be exaggerating.'

'Ash, I'm telling you. He could be a grandpa; I'm not even joking.'

'Next!' the cashier called out, sounding impatient as Ashley and I were too engrossed in conversation to notice it was our slot. Our chat halted as we approached the till and the cashier rang up our lunches and put them in a carrier bag.

'Any cakes or pastries?' she added in a monotone voice.

'Zara?' Ashley asked.

'I'm fine, thanks.'

'Are you sure? She's pretty fond of a snowball or two.'

That set us off laughing loudly in the shop again. We quickly paid for our lunches and headed back to the clinic.

We sat down in the staff room and began munching our lunch. Ashley had a salad and I devoured my large baguette.

'So, are you going to see him again?' she asked, unscrewing her water bottle.

'No way. Well, he wanted to, but I told him I was going to Dubai for work *and* made out it was long term.' My face scrunched up as I felt bad once more for my late-night lies.

'Aw, Zara! That's a fucking sin!'

'I know. Stop. I feel bad enough.'

Ping.

'Oh no! Is that him?' Ashley asked as my phone lit up the table.

I smiled when I saw Luke's name appear on the screen.

'Zara! Is he texting to say hiya?'

'It's Luke. The young guy. I swear I like this one, Ash, he's so sweet and clever. Look at this fucking body.'

I turned my phone round to show Ashley an eight pack of pure muscle he had just sent as this little delight had just finished his training session. My stomach had butterflies from watching the sweat drip from his forehead in the photograph.

'I mean, ooft. Mate, he is hot!' Ashley said.

I nodded in agreement as a large piece of baguette was preventing me from speaking.

'When are you seeing him?' she asked.

'Between my late nights now, and his shifts, I can't see him till next Thursday night.' I stuck out my bottom lip briefly before stuffing the last piece of baguette in my mouth.

'Eh, that's the night before Dubai! It can only be for a couple of hours and nothing else. You can't miss that flight, Zara, or bring him back for an overnight. Imagine Raj if you messed up.'

'For god's sake! Of course I won't. I'll get organised for Dubai this week, then I'll enjoy a nice, quiet date with Luke, nothing wild. I'll meet you guys first thing in the morning, and we can head to the airport together. It'll be fine,' I said reassuringly, taking a long gulp of my Lucozade to wash down the sandwich. I was starting to feel human again after last night, and now I felt buzzing for my date with Luke, immediately followed by the trip of a lifetime.

But Ashley stayed looking concerned. 'Please don't fuck it up, Zara,' she said.

Chapter Five

That week my days were filled with work, online shopping hauls and lots of sexting with my new love interest, Luke. He would send me innocent selfies from his lectures, wearing his fashionable glasses, looking overly intellectual, and then every bathroom break he would proceed to send a picture of his rock-hard dick. This boy was always solid, and I wondered if it was an age thing. I had high hopes for Luke in the bedroom department – for one so young, his chat was filthy. One evening we were sexting so intensely I even considered an underwear change because his words got me so damp. But with a folder already dedicated to his dick on my iPhone, I began to wonder if our whirlwind lustfulness had lost some of its excitement. I knew exactly what I was getting: five, maybe six inches with great potential. After our weeklong sexta-thon and seeing his dick from every conceivable angle and in every lighting condition, there wasn't much mystery left. But even so, I was intrigued. This lad had clearly bedded a few women in his short lifespan, and he promised to ride me like the Waltzers, so I wasn't going to pass on that one.

In between my suggestive messages, I was getting organised for Dubai, excited by the thought of being away from the cold, wet Glasgow weather. I had stocked up on Femfresh and plenty of factor fifty as my pale Scottish skin couldn't handle the heat on the east coast, never mind the fucking desert. By the next Thursday evening, my case was packed, passport and documents looked out the night before the flight, and all that was left to do was meet my toy boy for a few hours of innocent cocktails before heading home alone for some beauty sleep.

My hair was washed, body exfoliated, and pubes gone. My right nipple wire was plucked, holiday nails done, and I was all set to go. I was looking forward to meeting Luke, especially after my date with William the previous week. I had seen so many photographs I was confident he wasn't a catfish and I felt so excited for some light-hearted banter. I studied myself in the mirror, wearing ripped jeans, high top Converse and a tie-dyed T-shirt. I would never usually go on a date in such casual attire, but I felt an overwhelming urge to appear younger for anyone observing us. I ran my fingers through my hair, gathering my thoughts. My long dark locks flowed neatly down to my waist; it was the only thing I liked about my look, having only visited the salon a few weeks before. I studied my teenage-inspired outfit again. *Am I hitting a mid-life crisis? I look ridiculous. What's next, Zara? Fucking space buns?*

Ping.

My pitiful thoughts were interrupted as I glanced at my phone and saw Luke had messaged.

Outside your flat. I think lol xxxxx

Shit. I ran to the living-room window, which over-looked Royal Exchange Square, and saw him sitting on the benches awaiting my arrival. *No time for a change, Zara! You have to live with your ludicrous choice to dress like JoJo Siwa.* I took a deep breath, swung my short puffer jacket on and headed downstairs to finally meet my date. The air was crisp and the sky was becoming duller as it had just passed 8 p.m.

Luke stood up and approached me when he saw me walking out.

'Awrite, shorty, nice kicks.'

Jesus, I forgot to google the lingo.

'Hey, how are you? Thanks,' I replied, feeling nervous but surprisingly pleased at how handsome this young man was in the flesh. He had blond hair pushed back and styled well, sallow skin and was wearing an outfit almost identical to mine except with a lot more designer labels attached to it. He looked like Justin Bieber with more of a bristly growth around his jaw.

'So, where do you want to go?' I asked, walking to the main road.

'I was thinking of a pub closer to mine? I borrowed my dad's car. It's only twenty minutes away.'

I was surprised he hadn't suggested this before in the messages, but I was certainly up for a change of scenery from my usual haunts. I was desperate to accept immediately, but hesitated as I remembered my promise to Ashley: a sensible night. I looked at my watch and smiled; I suppose it was still early and I had at least a few more hours before I had to worry about time.

'OK, sure, let's go,' I shrugged, still not able to take the beam off my face.

Luke stopped walking and put his hands on top of his head.

'Right. I'll be honest with you, Za. It's not the best place in the world. I was pub-watched a few years back so I can't go into most bars or clubs in Glasgow or Lanarkshire. My uncle owns my local so we'll be cool in there.'

My eyes widened. Not only had he already given me a nickname, but I also realised my baby-faced date wasn't as innocent as he looked.

'So, you're effectively banned from pubs and clubs in this entire area?' I asked, my voice coming out more high-pitched and surprised than I'd intended.

'Aye.' He started to laugh. 'I know it's not a good start. But I want to be honest with you straight up. You can always turn back if you like, pretend this didn't happen?'

I looked up from the ground, considering my options. As much as I knew this should have set off alarm bells, I was enthralled by him. And, let's face it, I had always been a sucker for a rulebreaker.

'Bad boys are my downfall. Let's do it,' I said.

He began to nod, looking impressed.

'Come on. I'm parked over here.' He pressed the key fob and a large Audi estate car flashed from the double yellow line. Parking in a no-parking zone? I couldn't help but feel strangely aroused at his total lack of regard for other road users and pedestrians. He was getting naughtier by the second. *Rarrrrrr* . . .

'So, you have to explain. What the hell did you do to get this pub ban? I mean, it must be pretty bad,' I said, giggling as I opened the car door and sat down.

'Aww, Za, honestly, I'm just a bit of a hothead. But enough about that. Tell me about Dubai. You must be buzzing!'

We continued our chat on the short journey towards Paisley, where Luke parked in his driveway and we walked around the corner to his local pub. The place was empty and as soon as we entered, the smell of beer, stale cigarettes and poor hygiene filled the room.

'It's a bit of a shithole, eh? I should have warned you, but it's free drinks.' Luke seemed embarrassed by his past behaviours, and I couldn't help but feel sorry for him, even if my brand-new Converse were firmly stuck to the well-worn carpet already.

'No, not at all. I don't suppose they do cocktails though,' I said. He raised his brows. 'Or gin, even?'

Luke laughed and small dimples appeared on his cheeks. *Wow, he's so cute!* I thought.

'You can have beer, cider or vodka,' he said.

'I'll start with the vodka!'

The night continued and as the drinks flowed freely, I began to realise Luke and I had an undeniable chemistry. Occasionally he'd say a phrase I didn't comprehend or mention people I had no idea existed, which resulted in me frantically googling in the bathroom to try and keep up. But language aside, he was sweet, clever, well-mannered and extremely sexy. My initial plan to head home for an early morning flight was slipping out my mind as my body craved Luke more than ever. Yes, I knew what I was getting, I had seen his hard dick so many times, but with this unexpected connection which made my body quiver with pure desire, there was only one thing on my mind. Him. He'd wink at me while he sipped on his pint and I felt my fanny rattle my jeans like a Tasmanian devil, desperate to escape and devour his meat.

Five rounds of unmeasured drinks later, Luke turned to me and whispered, 'Zara, want to head back to mine? I know it's forward, but all your pics were with underwear on! I think it's time you showed me a wee bit more.' His eyes widened as I felt him daring me to break the rules, and I began to overheat with sheer lust.

'Ha, oh god, I'd love to, but I'm going on this work trip. My friends would kill me if I missed this. In fact, I'd lose my job,' I insisted frustratedly.

Luke leaned over to me and gently turned my face so he was speaking into my ear. 'Just come back to mine. I'll fuck you so good and you can leave for your flight a happy woman. Honestly, you have no idea how hard I want to be inside you, Za.'

My underwear instantly turned soggy and all good intentions had departed. The next thing I knew, I was waltzing down Paisley Main Street, hand in hand with a baby-faced bad boy and his rock-hard dick.

It had just passed midnight and I was walking back to Luke's home feeling frisky and foolish. The fresh air was sobering me up and at times I was questioning my decision.

'I really will have to go soon. I need to be at the airport in a few hours,' I said.

'Don't change your mind now. Come up. Don't be a spoilsport.' Luke placed his forehead against mine, and the touch of his breath against my cold skin began to make my heart race.

'Come on,' he enticed me.

'I want it too, but I know I should be sensible,' I moaned, still keeping my forehead against his.

'Well, you won't be wanting any of this then?' I felt Luke's warm hand gently taking mine to feel his bulging jeans.

With one feel of that throbbing cock, my brain went foggy and all I craved was him.

'Hmm, I suppose I could make an exception, but I really can't stay long.'

Luke grabbed my hand and we walked straight upstairs as we entered his home. It was a large, newly built house. As we entered, I could smell the remnants of homemade cooking, which made my stomach rumble from the three-day crash diet I had embarked on for Dubai. Everything looked immaculate. I was impressed. I studied the family pictures hanging on the wall above the staircase as Luke tugged me on.

'Aww, is that you there?' I pointed to a photograph, and he turned to me sharply, holding his finger to his mouth.

'Shhh, my dad's still up,' he said.

My heart began to beat fast.

He didn't tell me he lived with his family. What the fuck. My face fell as my instant horn turned to fear at the thought of having sex in my thirties with someone's parent in the next room. I shook my head aggressively.

'You never told me that!'

'You never asked,' he responded, shrugging his shoulders. 'It's not a big deal, Zara. Chill the fuck out.'

We were at the top landing now when we heard a voice call out from the living room downstairs.

'Luke, is that you?' His dad's deep voice echoed up the stairwell.

'Aye, I'm in. I'm with . . . ma mate, Dad. We're going to watch a film, right?' Luke turned round to me, raising his eyebrows suggestively.

I felt like I was back in high school. I stared back at him with my arms folded, feeling incredibly uncomfortable. Noticing my reaction, Luke pushed me against his room door and started to nibble my ear.

'Aye, that's fine, son,' his dad called back. 'Did you see the fitbaw highlights when you were out?'

I let out a large sigh of frustration. *I need to leave. This is a bad idea.* But Luke's eyes lit up with mischief as he placed one hand tightly over my mouth and began rubbing between my legs with the other.

Holy fuck. I wiggled slightly to break free, unsure of what to make of my unexpected submission. Luke shook his head with a sexy smirk on his face and I smiled back, enjoying his hand massaging my clit. This wee bastard seemed to have the moves; he was taking me pleasantly by surprise.

'No, what was the scores, Da?' he asked, giving me another wink as he started aggressively unbuttoning

51

my jeans and throwing them to the ground while my body was still pressed hard against the door, throbbing for him to touch me. His dad began recalling every score in the bastard premiership as Luke placed two fingers in his mouth then started ramming them deep inside me. My body squirmed, and I could hear my fanny squelch with excitement. *What the fuck were they teaching the kids at sex ed these days?*

Luke was visibly more aroused as his fingers went deeper and faster. I could feel myself building up for an orgasm as the sheer sense of exhilaration was all too much. He ignored the rest of the football highlights, opened his room door, pushed me on to his single bed and stripped off his jeans. I finally saw his dick in the flesh, and it was every bit as solid as it had been in all his messages. He bit his lip as he proudly pushed his foreskin back and forth, staring at my fanny lips hungrily.

'You want me to fuck you good, ya wee fucking cow?' he grunted, still pulling back his foreskin now more aggressively. I nodded back and then felt him pounce on top of me. With one slippery thrust, he was inside, drilling away like a jackhammer.

My jeans were falling from my ankles, and I felt alive as the idea of getting caught by his family was oddly thrilling. I was screeching, and the headboard was banging loudly off the wall as his pelvis was thrusting as vigorous as Tom Jones. My fanny felt throbbing from the ruthless beating and I felt myself cum all over him with one deafening orgasm.

'Shhh! Keep the fucking noise down, eh,' he hissed from above me.

I looked up at his cute little face, which was now red and sweaty with anger. He was no longer warm or attentive towards me, he was rough and furious, which was strangely arousing. I began to think that perhaps Luke's thuggish rule-breaking days weren't behind him after all.

Still, I couldn't help myself – the thought of shagging a felon was driving me crazy inside and once again my breathing was getting heavy as his dick thrashed in and out of me, and I could feel another orgasm on its way.

'Ahhh fucking hell!' I yelled. As soon as I let it out, I felt conscious I'd pissed off my little toy boy with my noise level, but he quickly joined me, releasing his own angry load, shouting and banging the side of his wall in enjoyment.

'Fuck. Yes. You wee fucking skank yeh.'

He eventually stopped moving. Looked down at me and began laughing.

'Well, well, did you enjoy tha—'

We were interrupted by a thunderous knock at the door, and I immediately hurdled out of bed in search of my jeans.

'Gonnae keep the noise down, son. That's not what I want to hear when I'm catching up with *The Chase*.'

I shut my eyes in utter humiliation, wishing the ground would swallow me as quickly as my vulva digested his son.

'Right, Da, sorry! Fuck's sake,' Luke tutted back, then began cackling.

'Oh my god! This is not funny,' I whispered. 'When will your dad go to bed?'

'Fuck knows. Chill out. We could watch *The Chase* up here. See if the Vixen's on?'

I shook my head in astonishment.

'Fucking chill I said. I'll roll us a joint?' Luke slid to the end of his bed and pulled out a small tray of marijuana from underneath. I took a minute to examine his bedroom and sat back down on the bed questioning my last-minute decision. His small bed was pressed against the wall and his TV stacked on top of his uni books. PlayStation games took up the majority of the space around us, and Luke seemed to have a thing for collecting McDonald's Happy Meal toys, which were piled up in an old washing basket in the corner of his bedroom. I was squashed to the edge of the bed, allowing Bob Marley extra elbow space to roll his doobie with a substantial amount of concentration. *No, no no. What the fuck am I doing here? I need to leave.*

'Luke, I'm sorry, I really need to go. I'm literally going on holiday in a few hours.' I glanced at my watch. Almost 2 a.m. *Shit.*

'But my da's downstairs,' he snapped back. My toy boy seemed pissed, but I wasn't prepared to hide like fucking Anne Frank all night at one stroppy teenager's request.

'I'll quickly run out when a taxi comes. He doesn't have to see me. I seriously need to get home.' I had the fear and a pounding vodka-induced headache on the way.

I lifted my phone from my jacket pocket.
Six missed calls from Ashley.

Fuck. My stomach ached with anxiety. I had to pick Ashley and Raj up for three-thirty to catch the flight and had at least a half-hour drive home. I discreetly swiped onto the Uber app and ordered a ride, not wanting to piss off my date further by phoning in and making extra noise. Thankfully Luke's joint seemed to be doing the trick as his eyes were gradually getting heavier and slowly closing over. After ten minutes of pacing the floor of his two-metre dungeon, I heard a car horn peep outside, and I gently shook his shoulders.

'I'm off, Luke. That's me. Can you walk me to the front door please?'

He began nodding his head, barely rousable, but with another lively shake he hesitantly stood up, pulling a pair of shorts on from a pile of laundry at the side of his bed. We quietly crept downstairs, reminding ourselves that his dad was in the living room.

'So, when will I see you again, Zara?' Luke whispered, tapping me on the shoulder from the step behind.

'Oh god, who knows? I mean I'd love to make arrangements, Luke, but I don't know when I'm going to be back from Dubai . . .'

The lies once again rolled off my tongue so effortlessly.

'What!' he roared. 'Are you having a fuckin' laugh? I didn't know it was fucking permanent, Zara! You didn't fucking tell me that!' His voice was getting deeper as I felt his eyes pierce me from behind. He stopped on the stair and began rubbing his forehead aggressively.

I watched on, confused and unsure if I should console him when he suddenly punched the wall angrily.

What the fuck!

I let out a squeal and soared in fear, running past the living room towards the front door. Luke dropped to the step, rocking himself back and forth.

The living-room door swung open, and instantly I felt relief as I saw a large male figure belt out, observing Luke perched on his naughty step.

'Is everything all right, son? What's going on?'

I stood still, watching the commotion unfold.

'Fuck. Aye. I'm sorry, Da. I just had a bit of bad news. Dad, this is Zara.' He pointed towards me still witnessing the drama.

His dad turned round to greet me. At first, I felt relieved that he was there to intervene in his son's tantrum.

'Oh, hiyaaa.'

My heart paused. *Wait.*

'Zara?' It was William, and he recognised me. 'What are you doing here?'

My whole body froze in disbelief as I watched the penny drop for him. His head twitched, then shook, glaring between me and his son as his face grew in horror.

'Wait,' he said. 'Oh no, tell me that wasn't you who was . . . Oh god, NO!' His face twisted in disgust as he continued to waggle his head aggressively.

From outside, the Uber driver beeped the horn again. *Saved by the fucking bell.*

'I'm sorry, guys, I need to go,' I said and turned to face the closed door.

'How do you two know each other?' Luke barked, confused at his dad's reaction.

'That was *my* date, son. Zara, the girl that told me she was moving to Dubai.' William was pointing his arthritic finger at me, looking irater than his son as the situation worsened.

'Wait. No. No fucking way. That's *my* Zara. She's just told me the same, Da, that she's moving to Dubai.'

Both of them scowled at me like I had just took a shite in their kettle.

All I could say was, 'I seriously am going to Dubai, like right now.' I looked at my watch; I didn't have time for this debate and I could feel the buzz of my phone ringing in my pocket.

'So, you're telling me I'm sitting up this late so I could text you a "good morning" message because of the time difference, and meanwhile you were up my fucking stairs?' William shouted. 'With my fucking boy!' he bellowed.

'Sorry. I need to go now.'

I turned around, trembling and striving to breathe, then opened the front door and immediately threw it shut behind me. I stood on the step for a second listening to their blaring voices shout from inside the house and caught my breath as my heart thumped. The Uber was thankfully still waiting outside, and my shaky legs just managed to make their way towards it, too terrified to turn back to the family I had just shafted.

'The Italian Centre, driver, and please be quick. I'm about to get fucking ragdolled.'

Chapter Six

A few hours of rushed taxi rides, security checks and duty-free later, our arses were finally sat on a luxury Emirates flight to Dubai. My two friends were looking forward to a well-deserved break from the gloomy Scottish weather, whereas I was just thankful for a faraway refuge from a possible lynch mob attack.

We were one of the first groups to be let on the plane, and I found myself wedged between my pals as Ashley demanded the window seat and Raj preferred the aisle to stretch his long legs. Ashley had strutted out of her flat that very early morning dressed in a loosely styled cream maxi dress and an oversized floppy sunhat, which she insisted on keeping on for the entire journey to Dubai, along with a huge pair of sunglasses, even although it was a pitch-black January in Glasgow. The flight was filling fast behind us, and we sat impatiently, observing the remaining groups of people boarding the plane.

'He's not bad, Zara, eh, eh.' Ashley nudged me and lowered her shades for a better view of the man walking up the aisle. I pushed my neck out carefully before seeing a wedding band.

'Married,' I shrugged.

'What about this one coming? Don't look just now. Don't look,' she whispered quickly, but it was too late. I was staring directly at the stranger pushing his case along to his seat.

'You made that too obvious!' she hissed.

'You were the one who told me to look in the first place,' I snapped back, feeling too hungover for her games.

'Will you two be quiet!' Raj muttered to both of us, interrupting our pastime. 'Ashley, you have a partner, and you're checking out every man on this flight, and by the looks of you, Zara, you've not long finished with one! Let's just relax, get our headsets on and stop gawking at strangers. I'm not listening to boy chat for the next four days. This is a very important work trip, girls.'

As Ashley and I fell silent from our telling off, I looked down self-consciously at the childish outfit I had just been judged on from the night before. I'd had no time for a change when I arrived back at my apartment and suddenly felt insecure. Raj rummaged through the pouch in front of him and popped his headphones into the TV frustratedly as the plane began heading to the runway. As soon as he had them on, Ashley nudged my arm.

'What's up with him? He'd better not be a miserable cunt all holiday!'

I giggled at her doing evil eyes at Raj's head, while he innocently concentrated on the safety video.

'He's just stressed because of the clinic; we're really struggling to keep afloat.'

Ashley rolled her eyes. 'So, how did last night go?' she asked.

'If I told you, I'm not even sure you'd believe me, Ash.' I shoved my head in my hands, still in total disbelief myself.

'Oh, come on. Try me.'

'Well, I went back to his—'

'OK, well, I can believe that so far,' she said sarcastically.

'We shagged, but his dad was awake, overheard us and started chapping his door.'

'OK, cringe. But so what? He's a grown man – *just*. Maybe his dad wanted in on the action,' she giggled.

Her choice of words made me die inside all over again. 'Wait – I'm not finished.'

'OK . . .' She lowered her sunglasses as her interest grew.

'I can't believe I'm saying this out loud, but his dad was William.' Ashley shrugged, looking puzzled. 'William! For fuck's sake, the old guy I pumped last week!'

Ashley let out a gasp of disbelief, followed by the loudest scream. It felt like the entire plane suddenly turned to us in panic as she eventually erupted into laughter. Raj shot us a stare, but we both continued laughing frantically while he put his hands over his headphones.

'No. No. No. Have you pumped the father *and* the son? Naw, STOP IT! I cannae cope,' Ashley shrieked, bursting into infectious laughter again.

'Shhhh. Keep it down, Ash. It honestly wasn't funny. They were fucking livid!'

She had tears of foundation streaming down her heavily painted face.

'I'm not surprised. I would be too if Dave shagged my maw! No! How could this happen?' she asked. 'Tell me the truth, though, who was better? Because let's face it, that's exactly what's going through their heads right now.'

I didn't even have to think about it.

'Luke,' I replied.

I could tell from the way she was looking at me she was trying to recall which one he was.

I huffed. 'The young one. It certainly wasn't his da.' I started giggling before doing my best seductive impression of William discreetly into Ashley's ear. 'Hiya, hiya, mmm . . . hiya, hiya.'

'Ahhhhh!' Ashley cringed away from me and pushed her body against the window as the plane paused on the runway.

'Seriously, that's so creepy, Zara,' she shivered.

Beneath us, the engine rattled powerfully as the plane suddenly began to pick up rapid speed and roared down the flight strip. I gripped the armrests tightly along with my two friends. Raj smiled briefly to me then shut his eyes, looking anxious, as the plane finally lifted off the tarmac and into the air, heading for Dubai.

We weren't long into the clouds before I became engrossed in the fragrance selection of the *Duty-Free*

Guide magazine. Ashley, however, was still wrapping her head around last night's family affair.

'So, have you heard from either of them since you left?' she asked.

'I blocked them in the taxi as soon as I left the house,' I admitted, still scanning the selection of perfumes on offer.

'Savage, Zara!'

'They would have pelted me with abuse, and I wasn't prepared to let them ruin my holiday buzz.'

'Maybe give them an explanation? Like, admit it was an honest mistake.' She was thinking about this too much while I was trying my best to forget it even happened.

I closed the magazine in frustration and turned to my best friend. 'Ashley, I have no explanation. Like seriously, what would you like me to say?'

'What about something like . . . "*Guys, I'm sorry, but as you've probably guessed I'm a massive slut atm! I've not stopped shagging ever since getting my heart broken last year! I now find it difficult, in fact, I find it impossible to commit, or have interest in anyone whatsoever now. So much so, my family background check didn't occur, and you guys paid the ultimate price. Take care, Zara.*" How's that?'

'Well, it's a little lengthy. I mean, a few words would be sufficient.'

She laughed and attempted to rest her head on my shoulder, but her colossal sunhat was still firmly fixed to her head, and it squashed into my face uncomfortably.

'Really though, I'm sorry. I didn't mean to make you feel bad.' She pushed out her large, freshly filled bottom lip.

'You can't make me feel worse than I already do, Ash.' I stared down at the floor, feeling ashamed as my hangover fear was kicking in.

'You don't look bad, Zara. Please forget I said anything. I'm such a Debbie Downer and if anything, you're in high demand! Maybe I'm just jealous you're getting all the attention. I swear Dave didn't even bat an eyelid when I said I was going to Dubai. He looked pleased with the bloody break.' Ashley shrugged her shoulders and turned her attention elsewhere, spotting people beginning to walk around the plane as the seat-belt sign turned off.

'Oh, sorry, let me past, Zara. I hate queues. C'mon move, I seriously need to pee.' She unbuckled her seat-belt and scurried past Raj and me towards the bathroom.

Raj shook his head in amusement as he watched Ashley frustratedly wait in line. He took down his headphones and smiled.

'She'll be lucky to get that hat in there.'

I began to grin, watching people having to edge away from Ashley and the sheer circumference of her accessory when they passed her still wearing her sunglasses.

'You OK, wee yin?' he asked.

'Yeah, I'm good. You?' I replied.

'I'm good. Looking forward to some hot weather!' Raj raised his eyebrows, making a fed-up face.

'Are you sure? You seemed a bit touchy earlier.'

'I'm honestly fine. I'm just stressed out we've closed, not unnecessarily, I hope.'

'I don't think it will be, Raj. Andrew's always been spot on with his advice so far.'

'Ooh, Andrew,' Raj teased as my cheeks blushed just from saying his name. Everybody seemed to know how much I crushed on him.

'I know, Zara, but we're struggling with the volume of new clinics opening offering cheaper, shitty products. I don't really need to be jetting off to Dubai when I should be working.'

'Raj, it's a free trip to Dubai! These clinics are dishing out humungous duck lips for practically nothing. We're the crème de la crème of aesthetics. Fucking hell, man, we're going to Dubai! Just relax. There's virtually nothing that could go wrong.'

'Thanks, Zara.' He smiled. 'If one more girl asks me for duck lips, I swear to God . . .' He paused for a second and faced me. 'I don't know why you're single, you know. You have so much to offer someone. I know it's cheesy but I wish you could realise that, you know?' He pressed the tip of my nose gently, then closed over his eyes while I felt my heart buzz with warmth, completely grateful to have such a great friend.

I rested my head on Raj's shoulder, thinking over the last few months. I really didn't want to be *that* girl, but the sheer thought of letting anyone else into my life to potentially hurt me the way Tom did was utterly terrifying. Surely this is a normal reaction following a break-up? I didn't intentionally try and hurt anyone after all. I needed to be alone, I needed to have fun and let my hair down. I needed this holiday.

As the plane soared through the sky, leaving Glasgow small and twinkling behind, I pushed back on my seat, pulled down my complimentary eye mask and eventually got some rest.

Chapter Seven

A few hours later, we arrived safely in Dubai. As the plane descended and I peeked out the window, my eyes widened with delight. I was instantly captivated by the ultra-modern city, crammed with skyscrapers, luxurious cars and scorching hot weather. It felt surreal that we'd left Narnia behind only a few hours earlier, and now we were transported to one of the most beautiful cities in the world. My stomach ached with excitement, and I couldn't wait to hop off the plane and start exploring.

When the plane doors opened and we were allowed to disembark, I immediately regretted my lazy decision of not changing out of last night's jeans and T-shirt combo. As I walked down the burning steps with the stifling sun beaming directly into my eyes, I felt the hot, humid air attack my foreign pasty body. After accomplishing the stairs with my hand luggage, I stopped on the tarmac, panting for water as an extreme BO and excess sweat spell occurred. I peeled my jacket off my damp skin and caught a glance of Ashley, who casually promenaded past me, looking as though she was just off a catwalk. *How can she still look so good after seven hours on a fucking plane?* I thought.

We eventually reached the terminal building to collect our luggage, and I was thrilled.

'Wow, fresh air!' I cried out, enjoying the air con. 'Thank fuck we're out of that heat!' I puffed, placing my hands on my knees for breath. Jesus Christ, that was terrible. Hopefully it's not as warm as this the rest of the trip.'

My friends looked at one another and began to laugh.

'You were outside less than three minutes, Zara,' Raj said.

'Eh, it was at least five. And I swear, I thought this terminal was a fucking mirage at one point. It seemed to get further and further away.' We all began giggling while I patted my sweaty forehead with my soggy sleeve.

'And this will be it cooling down too – it's 3 p.m. Good luck for tomorrow, kiddo,' Raj said.

'It'll be better when you get your pins out and a bikini on. Both of you are wearing jeans – honestly!' Ashley tutted as she tapped away on her phone, keen to join the local mobile network and *'check us in'*.

The thought of wearing a bikini next to Ashley made me shudder, and I felt my insecurities creep back in. Suddenly, standing in the airport, I became aware of every girl's perfect figure around me, their top-to-toe designer clothing and their handsome partners draped over them. I looked down at my own atrocious child-like outfit and general physical appearance and I felt my stomach sink. I hadn't even showered off my rendez-vous with Luke yet, and here I was, with frizzy hair, puffy ankles and my chronic singledom in the midst of the most glamorous city in the Northern Hemisphere.

Finally, the luggage belt began moving, and we collected our cases and headed for the exit. To our surprise, we were greeted by a driver holding up a card with 'Individualise' written across it, who then led us to a private Mercedes to escort us to the hotel.

During the half-hour drive from the airport to Palm Jumeirah, our eyes remained fixed on the sights passing by the tinted glass windows, awed by the state-of-the-art city jammed with palm trees, construction sites, high-rise towers and wide, dusty streets. We pulled up outside the hotel and looked up in wonder at the sheer size of the grandiose entrance.

'Guys, this is insane!' Ashley took out her phone and immediately began snapping.

'Andy's certainly pulled it out the bag!' Raj said, looking dumbstruck.

As soon as the car stopped, he jumped out to get a better look while I sat there in awe. I couldn't agree more – it was by far the most extravagant place I had ever seen. Eventually, I picked my jaw up and got out of the car, admiring the arched, glass-tunnelled entrance as an entourage of staff came out to greet us. We were escorted directly into the hotel, and our cases followed with the bellboy. The hotel lobby was glazed in marble and gold. Ashley entered with her phone stuck firmly in her hand, capturing every inch.

'Checking in?' a voice from the reception desk called out, and we headed over to a smiling gentleman behind the desk. Raj pulled out the documents and started to fill out the forms for our stay.

'Zara, this is the most incredible place ever. I can't believe this!' Ashley screeched excitedly.

'I know, I'm seriously speechless. Look over there! Oh, and there.' I began pointing out the features of the hotel I loved. Best of all was the huge pool area, which led out onto a sandy white beach. Beyond that, the sea glittered and stretched out to touch the sky.

'Girls, I need one of you over to sign the papers!' Raj interrupted our excitement. 'You need to sign here.'

'Yes, sorry, of course.' I retreated to the desk. The receptionist was staring at me.

'Where do I sign then?' I asked, trying to break up the awkwardness.

'Here.' He pointed to the page in the front. 'And, lady, please read this.' He turned to a laminated sign on the desk and began tapping it sassily with his ball-point pen.

'All guests should dress appropriately or will be asked to vacate the premises.'

'Ahh, okey dokey.' I scrunched up my eyes, reading his name tag. 'Adam. Well, I promise to keep them covered up!' I placed my hands over my chest, jiggling my breasts gently for a joke to break the tension, when Raj kicked my foot under the desk.

Adam's face fell with surprise. 'Please do.'

I was stunned. I had no idea why he would think I was planning to wear something disrespectful. I mean, my jeans and T-shirt were not my favourite combo but they were hardly offensive.

'Yes, she'll be mindful of it, Adam. Thank you.' Raj turned to me. 'Zara, just sign the thing and we can get to our room!'

I did what I was told and dropped Adam's pen back in his hand with a slight thud.

'Thank you, sir, madam. Your luggage will be delivered to your rooms shortly.'

We retrieved Ashley, who was in search of the best lighting for her selfies, and headed to the lift.

'I can't fucking believe the cheek of him!' I shouted as soon as the lift door was shut.

'What? What did I miss?' Ashley darted her head up from her phone.

'Adam basically warned me about the clothing policy! Why would he think I'm going to dress badly!' I spouted.

'He probably smells you from last night and was giving you a heads-up.' Ashley started to laugh hysterically with Raj while I stood, arms folded, allowing them to giggle at my expense.

'Aye, very funny. Haha.' I rolled my eyes at the pair of them.

'Seriously, though. Your jeans are looking a little crusty,' she continued, but fortunately I didn't have to answer as we had arrived at level five and the doors opened.

Ashley burst out the lift like a five-year-old, desperate to find our room. She skipped down the corridor, carefully examining each door's number.

'Zara, Zara! This is us!' she screamed, and I followed her excitedly up the hallway.

'And . . . this is me. Right across the hallway!' Raj rolled his eyes, mocking our excitement before popping his key card in. 'When are we meeting for dinner? About an hour? It's five o'clock Dubai time and I'm starving.'

Ashley and I began to giggle.

'Make it at least two hours – remember, Raj, you're on a girls' holiday now. See ya!'

She snapped the key card out of my hand and opened our room door to the most magnificent suite.

'WOW!' My jaw fell to the thick luxurious carpet.

The room opened directly into a lounge, which had a large double balcony overlooking the sea. There were doors at either end of this space, leading to mine and Ashley's separate rooms, each with our own en suite. This place was heaven! I lay my tired, achy, well-travelled body on top of my bed like a starfish, feeling incredibly grateful.

'Zara, I'm gutted we aren't sharing a room – I was looking forward to our drunken chats!'

I looked up at Ashley standing in my doorway.

'You know what this means though? If I pull, you don't have to put up with all my moaning and groaning sex noises!' I turned onto all fours and pulled my pillow between my legs, pretending to shag the stuffing out of it. 'Oh hiya, hiya, hiya, Adam, HIIIII!'

Ashley doubled over laughing as I smacked the pillow like a bucking bronco, making my kinkiest orgasm impression when we suddenly heard someone clearing their throat behind us. Ashley stopped, turned around slowly and squealed. My face immediately turned scarlet.

'Sorry, madam, your luggage. I didn't mean to scare you!' A young teenage worker was standing in the living area with our cases neatly stacked up beside him.

'Do you need anything else?' He was staring at the floor, probably too timid to look up.

'No, thank you,' I replied, attempting to demount Adam the pillow.

'Can you bring a few more towels, please? I only have two, and I need to wash my extensions for tonight,' Ashley asked.

'Certainly,' he said. After a brief bow, he walked backwards out of the room, shut the door, and we both started laughing.

'If he tells Adam, you're on your own. I'm not moving digs,' Ashley said.

I threw the pillow at her, and we both collected our cases and began getting ready.

Two hours later, I was sparkling clean, dressed and excited to spend my first night in Dubai. I walked out of my room to see a smartly dressed Raj watching TV in the lounge with his feet up.

'Finally! And weet wheel, Zara! You look incredible!' he said, admiring me while I turned slowly, showing off my black playsuit with backless lace detail, enjoying the compliment.

'Is Ash still not ready?' I called out above the sound of her music. Raj shook his head, returning his focus to the television.

I walked into her bedroom to find all her clothes scattered around. She was sitting in concentration with her dressing gown wrapped around her, searching through one of her cases. Her rollers were firmly in place and make-up looking flawless, with the sound of her Spotify playlist blaring through her phone.

'Ash!' I said, to which she screamed, having not noticed me walk in.

'Fucking hell.' She reached for her phone, pausing the music. 'You scared the fucking life out of me!'

I started to giggle back.

'No, seriously, remember I asked for towels? I came back to my room when you were in the shower, stripped down to FaceTime Dave trying to be all sexy, then the next thing, that wee pervert who keeps sneaking about with our cases walked straight in here to hand me the towels!'

I gasped then started laughing again.

'Well, you did ask him to bring them, Ash.'

'I know, but he should at least knock on the fucking door.' She looked harassed in her mounds of clothes.

'I'm thinking this little dress? Be honest. What do you think?' She held up a miniature, low-cut, silky dress which looked stunning. I'd be lucky to get it past my cankles from the flight.

'Perfect. I love it.'

'OK, I'll be fifteen. You look amazing by the way!' she called over to me, pulling her dress on above her tiny, tanned frame.

I smiled back and rejoined Raj on the sofa.

'So, how's your room?' I asked him.

'It's nice, really nice. It has a view of the skyline instead of the beach, which is awesome. It's only one room though. Mine doesn't have a living room or anything like that, just a bed,' he said.

'Ohh, sounds nice all the same! What's the dinner plans?'

'Has Miss Organised in there not WhatsApped you the itinerary for the weekend?' he asked, making me realise I hadn't looked at my phone for a few hours.

I walked through to my room and retrieved it from my hand luggage, still nervous in case I had any hate mail from the father–son duo I had fled from.

One new WhatsApp from Ashley and one new Instagram message from Andy.

I opened my Insta DMs and was surprised to read Andy's message. My heart began to beat quickly inside my chest, and I clicked on it straight away. I couldn't help but smile when I read it.

Hey, hope you lot have arrived safely! Any issues give me a bell! Andy x

I ran, grinning, out of the bedroom to see Ashley finally ready.

'Andy DM'd me, guys.'

'No way! What did he say? I bloody knew he liked you!' Ashley waved her hands excitedly, making her jewellery jingle.

I read the message aloud, and Raj started to chuckle. Ashley shot him a disparaging look.

'OK. Have you replied?' she asked.

'Not yet.' My fingers were twitching, desperate to start a conversation up.

'Don't. Well, not yet. We need to be careful about how we play this one. Is his Instagram private?' She was pacing the floor in deep thought.

'Yes . . .' I nodded slowly and took a deep breath to calm my nerves.

'Listen Cilla, enough matchmaking for the night,' Raj said. 'The guy sent us on a business trip and said any issues to let him know. He's hardly proposing. Can we eat now, please!'

'Oh, for fuck's sake. Maybe you should just like his message and keep him hanging – you're in Dubai, mate!' Ashley said. 'And Raj, *yes*. All you ever think about is your stomach. Right, everyone stand at the mirror with me before we go. We need a pic!'

I walked over and examined us all in the shot, still hot with excitement over Andy.

Ashley held her phone above her head and pouted into the mirror. Her legs looked even longer with her tiny dress on. Raj stood smartly with linen trousers and a shirt, and I felt plain. My playsuit felt even tighter than last week when it was delivered. *For fuck's sake Zara*. The Pringles from the plane were seriously taking their toll on me.

'OK, everyone, ready.'

We all held our poses, me sucking in every inch of my body hoping for a decent take. There was the sound of the camera snapping.

'Let's eat, then hit Barasti!' Ashley screamed.

Chapter Eight

We ate at the hotel and ordered a taxi to Barasti, a lively beach club crammed with loud music, hot men and fruity cocktails. We entered under an exotic archway of Hawaiian flowers and strolled down a decked area jam-packed with young couples, holidaymakers and businessmen, following the music off the deck and onto the beach. *Wow*. The sky was dark, but I watched my shoes sink into the sand in the light cast from the elevated DJ set at the other end of the beach. We were in the middle of a techno tropical paradise. It was beautiful and modern and by far the most incredible club I had ever been to. The beach was crammed with large crowds of people from diverse backgrounds, mixing and mingling, dancing around. There were large beach beds spread out with tables, loungers and shisha pipes all present. I had never been anywhere like this before in my life, yet I felt welcomed by smiling partygoers dancing casually around me. It was certainly nothing like my days at Colour Fest or the Arches, where smiling at a stranger meant accepting it could end up in a square go.

I turned to my friends, who looked equally mesmerised.

'Ash, this place is amazing!' I yelled over the trance music blaring around us.

She nodded enthusiastically as Raj beamed.

'I know, it's insane! Look at all the talent as well, Zara!' she winked.

'Yeah! Especially the girls! Look at the arse on that lassie! It's got to be fake.'

I couldn't help but notice the skimpy outfits the girls wore. I was shocked, having heard so many horror stories of people getting arrested for flashing the gash innocently in the Middle East.

'I didn't think you'd be able to wear half the clothes these girls are wearing. I honestly thought the way Adam was acting you could get arrested over here for having your shoulders out!' I admitted.

Ashley laughed and called back over the music. 'Zara, that's ancient history. Dubai is with the times now. As long as you respect their culture and don't do anything too wacky, then you're fine. A wee bit of cleavage is completely fine nowadays.' She sounded wise and sure of herself as she rolled her eyes at my naivety.

'Would you girls like a drink?' Raj asked, delving into his pockets for some dirhams.

'YES!' we yelled at the same time.

'Two cocktails?'

'Aye, each,' Ashley called back. 'It saves us going up to the bar all the time.' She smiled angelically at Raj, who shook his head before shuffling his feet through the sand, making his way to the bar.

'This is probably the coolest place I've ever been to, like look at it,' I yelled to Ashley, and we hugged tightly with excitement.

'Should we take that table? I think that group are leaving.' She pointed to a large circular bench situated at the centre of the action.

'Yes, let's go.'

We hovered around the table waiting for a few minutes, then finally sat down just as Raj joined us with a tray containing four strawberry daiquiris and a bottle of water for himself.

'Good spot, girls!'

I gave him a smile. 'Thanks for the drinks, boss.'

'Oh my god! Guys! Guys!' Ashley was screeching at the top of her voice. 'That's the entire Celtic football team behind us! Footballers literally surround us!'

I turned around to gaze at a group of young men enjoying themselves, jumping around the sand to the music.

'We have to get pictures with them!' Ashley said.

'Ashley, do you not support Rangers?' I recalled seeing photographs on her Instagram of her draped in a Rangers scarf at the last Old Firm, and in Glasgow, we take the rivalry of football incredibly seriously.

'Awk, I don't bother. Dave supports Rangers, but who gives a shit? It's good for the gram! Come on!' She stood up, pulling me out of my seat. I looked at Raj for help, but he was laughing.

'I'll watch the drinks. On you go!' He stuck his tongue out at me while Ashley kept on tugging on my arm.

'OK, OK!' I said.

We coolly walked over behind their table and stopped.

'Now what?' I asked.

'Just dance, look easy-going,' Ashley hissed under her breath, so I started moving, awkwardly sober, to 'Horny' by Mousse T.

I watched Ashley pout and pose seductively, trying to attract the footballers' attention. There was a definite buzz in the air as the chorus dropped, and the crowds of people on the shore began jumping together, moving like a current through the strobe lighting. We were completely caught up in the moment. The more we bounced around, the closer Ashley edged to the football squad, and I cringed as she 'accidentally' crashed into them then winked at me. I was looking pleadingly at Raj for back-up, who laughed hysterically in the distance.

'Ash, I'm going to get my drink,' I yelled out after the second verse, now developing a stitch.

'Zara, wait!' she said, but I was already making my way back to the table.

'She never fails to amuse me,' Raj snorted.

'I know. I've never felt so uncomfortable.' I was panting from the effort of dancing in the heat and took a huge, cooling gulp of my strawberry daiquiri. 'Oh, where's she got to now?' I searched through the busy crowd and spotted Ashley chatting away to one of the younger players.

'Ah, she'll be happy she's finally got someone's attention,' I said and went back to sipping my fruity daiquiri with pure delight. The frozen slush immediately cooled me down from the hot, humid air and I brought my phone out, eager to respond to Andy with some cocktail confidence behind me.

'Awww thanks Andy! We're loving it! Thanks again for this. X'

'Sheesha?' A voice interrupted my lust just as I hit send.

I turned around to the barman who was asking to light up our pipe and grinned at Raj.

'Shall we?' I asked. I had never done sheesha, but I was craving the complete Dubai experience.

'Yes, let's go for it,' he replied. Raj paid the gentleman, and our sheesha pipe began bubbling on the table between us. I lifted the hose and started to inhale the vapour furiously before erupting into a coughing fit. I hadn't smoked since high school when I would occasionally purchase a fifty-pence fag that would guarantee me a nicky buzz that lasted the whole of lunchtime.

'My turn?' Raj lifted the pipe as Ashley returned to the table, holding her phone out, ready to capture the sheesha's victory. He started puffing on it like Snoop Dogg, exhaling the steam from his nose.

Ashley and I gasped at his expertise.

'You girls underestimate me!' he exclaimed, before expertly puffing out a trail of smoke rings.

'Naw, no way! I really want a shot, but there's no way I'm putting my mouth around a communal pipe. That's fucking disgusting,' Ashley said as she sat down again.

'I'm sure you've had your mouth around worse,' I teased. Raj nodded in agreement.

'So, guys, that footballer has added me on Instagram!' Ashley said.

Raj waved his hands in the air and began cheering mockingly.

'Is that shit making him high or something?'

'No, it's just steam,' I replied, shrugging my shoulders.

'First time for everything, I suppose – Raj finally gets steaming!' Ashley blew him a sarcastic kiss across the table, and we carried on with our cocktails and sheesha.

The Barasti buzz continued, and a few hours later, we were stumbling to and from the bar, dancing on the loungers and hugging anyone who walked by our station. My cocktail intake was becoming uncountable, and despite regular checks to my Insta DMs and feeling slightly disheartened Andy hadn't replied, I was still having the time of my life.

'Zara, I think I'm going over to talk to that Celtic player. I really, really like him,' Ashley said as we stood in the queue for the bathroom. By this point in our alcohol fest we had well and truly broken the bladder seal.

'What? The one in the picture with you?' I felt confused by my friend, who had never before shown a hint of interest in any other man except Dave for the past five years.

'Yes. He's lovely, and I wasn't going to say anything, but he's been sending me mails since I added that picture.' She bit her lip suggestively as I gasped, having been completely unaware of what was transpiring.

'Noooooooo.' I held my floppy drunk hands to my face. Then I looked at her.

'What about Dave?' I asked.

'What about him? I'm in fucking Dubai, hen!' she screamed with drunken happiness.

'That bastard doesn't appreciate one thing about me, do you know that?' Ashley pointed in my face aggressively. 'I sent him about ten fucking pictures since I got here and not once has he said I looked nice!' She shook her head, now looking upset. 'So, I say fuck him!'

'But the Celtic guy is not hot, Ash. At least pick someone hot.' I thought back to the young player, who had thick bobbed hair and the biggest set of teeth, who looked more like a horse in a huff than a person.

'Hey, he is fucking hot! Plus, it's not all about looks, Zara. He likes me. And I like him!' She looked at me grudgingly.

'You've just fucking met him. Ash, honestly, you're pissed. Look, let's go back, have a drink of water and calm down a bit.' I was slurring my own words but trying my best to appear rational while my fuzzy head attempted to tackle this critical situation.

'I don't need to calm down, Zara! And I don't need to pee!' she yelled at me frustratedly and turned her back on me, stumbling her way back to our spot.

As much as I wanted to, I couldn't follow her; I was desperate for the toilet and instead had to squirm and jiggle about till it was eventually my turn. While pissing in the pan, I began wondering what the fuck Ashley was on about. *Maybe I should let her enjoy the holiday and let her hair down?* But I didn't want her to regret her decision. Ashley was such a loyal person, who seemed to have it all; I didn't want her fucking her entire life up because of a few daiquiris in Dubai. As I walked back to the table, I watched my best friend swaying in the moonlight, still wholly engrossed in her phone.

'Is she OK?' I asked Raj.

He shrugged, waving his hands in the air to the music.

'Ash, are you OK?' I called out.

She nodded, not breaking eye contact with her phone.

'Ash?' I probed her for a better response.

'Yeah, I'm sorry. I just felt sick. I've drunk way too much.' She eventually glanced up to me, smiling, looking a little teary.

'OK, good! Do you want to dance?' I held my hand out towards her.

'No, honestly, I'm OK. I feel really fucking sick. I think I'm going to walk down to the water and call Dave.' She stood up and kicked off her Louboutins.

'Wait, I'll come with you.'

'No, Zara. I need to have a chat with Dave in private.' She turned and began wandering down to the water.

'Watch my shoes. I'll be one minute,' she called back, bouncing down the beach.

'Wait. Please let me come,' I called out after her.

Already in the distance, she shook her head.

'What's up with her?' Raj asked.

'She was moaning about Dave and considered chatting up the Celtic player,' I said, holding up my hands, still in disbelief.

'Ouch. Which one?' Raj asked.

'The one in her selfie.' I raised my eyebrows at him.

He burst out laughing. 'The one with the teeth!'

I nodded back, laughing with my floppy palms hiding my face.

'She must be blotto! He could chew an apple through a letterbox with them wallies.'

Raj and I started to howl loudly.

'C'mon, another dance?' He held out his hand just as 'Insomnia' by Faithless struck and the lights began to flicker.

'Ahh, YES!' I screamed.

The flash of strobe lighting took over the beach as everyone began bounding around like they were listening to GBX on a Friday night.

We carried on partying for another few songs, laughing, dancing and screaming, before finally noticing Ashley hadn't returned.

'Raj, I think we'd better find Ash. She seemed unhappy.'

He glanced around the crowd and nodded back. 'Aye, c'mon then.'

I swiped ahold of Ashley's expensive shoes and held Raj's arm tightly, keeping my balance as we moved down the sandy beach together. The further we walked, the quieter it became, and I was starting to get worried.

'What if she goes back to the loungers and thinks we've left her?' Anxiety crept up in my chest as I realised I shouldn't have left my best friend alone.

'It's Ashley. We'd hear her before we see her. Try her phone.' I tried but there was no answer.

We continued walking until we reached the water then looked at one another nervously. *Where the fuck was she?* I called her phone again, and we both stood static, hoping to hear her voice. But nothing. Raj and I stared along the shore; it was still. No passers-by, no crowds of people. No one.

'What if she's been kidnapped?' I was panicking.

'She'll be fine, Zara.'

'Or sold into white slavery?' My mind was going mental with possible scenarios.

Raj smirked towards me.

'What? You read about these things happening all the time!' I spouted.

'But Ashley, a slave! She'd be the worst slave in history . . . Zara, sshh . . . I think I heard a faint buzz coming this way. Keep ringing that phone!' Raj picked up the pace and I walked quickly to keep up.

His face was serious with concentration as we walked along the water's edge, hoping to hear anything to lead us to our friend. Finally, a hazy noise buzzed in the distance, and we both began to walk quickly towards it. The beach was dark, and we hadn't passed anyone else for a while. I continued to let the phone ring out until I saw a shadow in the distance.

'There, Raj.' I pointed towards the figure. It was someone kneeling up in the sand. I adjusted my eyes and recognised the clothing. *It was Ashley!* My body exhaled the largest sigh of relief.

'It's definitely her, Raj. It's her dress. Fuck, she's bloody vomiting!'

I raced towards my friend, who I could hear retching in the sand, hoping to hold her hair or offer some assistance, but as I got closer the moonlight seemed clearer and I noticed that she wasn't alone. And she wasn't being sick. Ashley was, in fact, sucking dick.

I gasped when I recognised her star striker standing so proudly behind her with his hands rummaging through her weave.

'Ashley, ew, what the fuck!' I shrieked as Raj stopped a couple of steps behind me.

She turned around, looking dishevelled.

'What are *you* doing here?' she snapped, swaying from side to side, still on her knees.

'You've been away for ages! We thought you got *murdered*!' I looked up to the player who watched on, proudly holding his penis. 'Hi, I'm sorry, can we have a word with our friend, please?'

I snatched Ashley's arm and pulled her to her feet, marching her a few metres away.

'What the fuck are you doing? You said you wanted to call Dave!' I exclaimed.

'Listen, Zara.' She pointed in my face. 'I'm on holiday, and I can do who or what I like. He's fucking famous. He has a blue tick on Instagram.' She looked over seductively at Bugs Bunny like an infatuated teenager.

'I don't care if he has a blue dick, Ashley, he's fucking bogging.'

Raj stepped over, clearing his throat. 'I can assure you his dick is not blue. I have seen it, all of it.' In a more assertive voice, he said, 'Ashley, we need to get you home now. You've had far too much to drink.'

'No, I'm not going anywhere, Raj. I'm old enough to make my own decisions.'

'And you're old enough to remember you're here on a business trip, representing my brand. Tomorrow is a big day and your hangover isn't wasting it for the company. Get it together, Ash,' he snapped back.

Ashley grumbled and finally agreed, bowing her head. She signalled back to her athlete, who was frustratedly zipping up his trousers.

'I'll call you later. I better go back. I'm working tomorrow.'

She shoved her arms around both our necks to be steadied as she walked.

'I love you guys,' she said and kissed us both on the cheek.

I watched Raj squirm as he knew where her mouth had just been. It didn't bother me. I was just glad to have my best friend back safely in our arms. After all, what was one more dick between us?

Chapter Nine

I woke the following day to the racket of Ashley retching across the apartment. *Great.* Surprisingly, I didn't feel that hungover. Perhaps the shock of seeing my best friend on her knees gorging on some random guy's dick had sobered me up. I rolled over and checked my phone: 9.30 a.m. Following her wails of distress, I made my way into Ashley's room, unsure just how much of a mess I would find.

'Ash, are you OK?'

Instantly I was greeted by the smell of vomit. I peered into her en suite where she was lying with her legs dangling out the door, head still inside the toilet pan. When she lifted her head up to look at me, I saw that she was sporting two enormous bloodshot panda eyes.

'I think I have food poisoning – this isn't just a hangover.' She turned again and sobbed into the toilet bowl.

'I think it's just the fear, doll,' I said, struggling with the smells to get close enough to console her.

'Trust me, Zara, I've had hangovers before. It was that dinner. I must have eaten something dodgy; my stomach is on fire,' she moaned.

I knelt down on the carpet outside the bathroom. 'I wonder what you could possibly have eaten.'

She shot me a look.

'Tell me last night didn't happen?' She seemed exhausted, mentally and physically.

'I wish I could, trust me. But listen, we don't have to talk about it just now. Wait till you're feeling better.' I smiled over at her.

'Zara, I could have been arrested! And it would probably make the papers!' She was running her fingers through her long hair extensions nervously, thinking of all the possibilities.

I nodded back.

'Well, I would have been more embarrassed by your choice of player.' I raised my eyebrows disapprovingly.

'No. Stop. Was he that bad?' she whimpered.

'I mean, I'm not one to comment on looks, Ash, but that cunt would seriously get his money back on the ghost train. Dave is so . . .'

I watched her bottom lip tremble. 'I can't believe I've done this to Dave!' She looked defeated.

I stopped myself from saying another word. I just let her cry it out. I knew she was hurting, but just being there with her was all I could contribute. We sat in silence for over half an hour, with the odd sob and sniffle being the only noise echoing throughout the suite. Just after ten, the front door chapped, and a bright-eyed Raj marched in with his beach bag stuffed to the brim with essentials.

'Ah, good morning?' He stopped and took a big, exaggerated sniff of our apartment.

'Don't, Raj. It's too soon for a lecture,' I said, stopping him before he went into full dad mode.

He grinned widely. 'What? I never said a thing.'

I stood up from the floor and came over to him. 'You're up and ready very early. The job isn't until three,' I reminded him.

'Yes, but if you checked our itinerary for today, Zara, you would see we have loungers booked in at Zero Gravity.'

He paused for me to react.

'The most exclusive beach club in Dubai? No? OK, so, glass infinity pool, everyone stands at the edge and takes photos?'

'Eh, I know what it is!' I lied. I had never heard of it but didn't want to be completely out of the loop.

'It's the place to be, Zara. Very Instagrammable,' Ashley called out from the toilet pan.

'And it's only a few minutes away from the hotel we're working in this afternoon, so pack your things for the entire day.' Raj flapped his hands in front of my face, shooing me to get a move on, keen for us to leave.

'What about you, Ash?' I turned to my friend, who was still retching.

'I have a virus! You both go. Just take lots of stories for the Individualise Instagram, that's all I'd be doing anyway.' Ashley manoeuvred her leg and shut the bathroom door with a bang.

'Come on then, looks like it's just you and me, kiddo. Hurry and I'll wait here,' Raj said.

I hovered, unsure of what to do. I felt guilty leaving Ashley alone but I had to set up the injectables for the photoshoot anyway.

'Give me ten minutes and I'll get my shit together,' I said.

He nodded and then shook his head, rethinking his decision.

'I'll meet you in the lobby, Zara. This place fucking stinks!' Raj stepped out with a disgusted look on his face.

I chuckled then cracked open the balcony doors, keen to get rid of the uncleanness of the apartment too. However, as the doors widened, I was immediately engulfed by humid, fiercely hot air that would only encourage the stench. Just for a second, I missed the crisp freshness of the Scottish air, to be able to take a long deep breath in the morning and feel it coolly travel down your body. The only thing I was tasting right now was Ashley's vomit vapour.

Back in my room, I squeezed into my swimming costume and slid into a pair of Nike sliders, throwing on a black and neon green–striped Aztec dress. I didn't have time for a shower so ran the dry razor up my slightly stubbly legs, winching slightly. I grabbed the deodorant and applied an overgenerous amount to mask any sweaty scent, before breaking out into a coughing fit at the fumes. My hair felt dry and tuggy from the night before, and with a mound of extensive brushing, I managed to pull it back tightly into one neat French plait. *Nothing worse than dealing with stray hairs when you're trying to enjoy a swim*, I thought. Before I left, I had one last check on Ashley, who was lying asleep on the bathroom floor. She had pulled a pillow off the bed and looked peaceful. I gently shut the door, leaving the 'Do not disturb' sign swinging on the door handle.

Raj was waiting in the lobby, slumped back on one of the grand sofas, scrolling through his phone. I walked over to him and nudged his knee with my bag.

'You ready?' I asked.

'Yep, let's go.' He bounced up energetically. 'Have you got everything? Your bag's tiny!' He stared at my small wicker beach bag, which had my essentials packed inside.

'Yes. I don't need much. I'm sure the club will give us towels and things when we're there. What do you think? Have you got the products for the shoot?' I stopped briefly, rummaging through my bag of sun cream, AirPods and magazines, now feeling paranoid I had forgotten something.

'Yes, I have the work things. Zara, what's that?' Raj pointed towards my swimming goggles dangling from the edge of the bag.

'Goggles. For a swim,' I shrugged and pressed them firmly back into the bottom of the bag, then continued towards the taxi line.

Raj laughed loudly behind me. 'Oh, Zara, you never fail to make me laugh!'

The car drove the fifteen-minute journey towards Zero Gravity, and as we pulled up outside, I immediately understood Raj's hilarity. The loud techno music echoed from afar, and I glared at my colourful Aztec ensemble and sensible plait and immediately felt self-conscious.

'So when you said beach club, you meant . . . it's a club.'

'Yes,' he laughed. 'On a beach, of course.'

'Great.' I could feel my heart sink to the bottom of my masculine-looking shoes. 'I feel a mess, Raj. I look like an enormous fucking wasp.' I peered out of the taxi window, disheartened. 'Look at all the other girls strolling in here with their fucking high heels and metal G-strings. I can't go in like this.'

Raj let out an almighty frustrated sigh. 'Zara, we're in Dubai. You don't know anyone here except me. *Plus,* you look great. Trust me. You will regret ruining a full day out in a fancy beach club because of your low self-esteem.' I knew he was right and I didn't want to ruin his day either but the thought of stripping down beside these perfect model girls made me shudder. 'Besides, when that forty-degree heat hits at one o'clock, do you think the girls with the metal G-strings will be laughing then? I can foresee third-degree burns happening in places they should never be.' He smiled and gently squeezed my hand.

'You coming? Don't leave me doing the robot by myself in there.' He opened his door, and began getting out of the car.

'Yes, of course,' I simpered. I wiped my sweaty arse cheeks across the leather seat and followed a step behind my friend towards the Zero Gravity entrance.

I craved a relaxing day at the beach, I wanted to enjoy myself. I also knew I couldn't let Raj down, so instead of hiding in the taxi, I took a deep breath of bravery and attempted to make the most of my day in the sunshine.

Chapter Ten

Zero Gravity was surreal. The freshness of the architecture combined with the banging music gave me goosebumps walking in, it was such a voguish vibe. The bar-restaurant area was entirely white, overlooking the pristine beach and ocean. Behind it stood the city and its soaring skyscrapers.

We were seated in the first row of loungers bordering the sand with the glass infinity pool just behind us. I couldn't help but feel sad Ashley wasn't here to experience this. She would have soaked it in, enjoying every photo opportunity and relishing the atmosphere. Raj and I got comfortable. I flipped off my sliders and watched Raj pull his shirt off.

'Nice abs, boss,' I giggled. I had never seen Raj with his top off and I had completely underestimated his body. *Where has he been hiding that?* I thought.

Raj jokingly stroked his trim, toned torso and lay back on the lounger.

'Are you not taking that dress off? You must be boiling,' he said.

'No. I feel too heavy.'

Raj turned his head and pulled his shades down, shooting me a disappointed look, and then retired to his sunbathing.

I lay back in an attempt to get comfy but almost instantly could feel sweat stream down my face. My thighs were sticky too. I turned my head slightly and tried to take a discreet whiff of my oxters. *Am I beginning to smell already?* The temperature was unbearable, and it was only eleven in the morning.

'Can we put the umbrella up, Raj? I'm too warm.'

'Seriously? We've only just arrived. I've come to sunbathe, not sit in the shade.' He looked over to my melting corpse. 'Take that fucking dress off. You're on a beach, and it'll cool you down.'

I let out an angry grunt and attempted to open my *OK!* magazine. I was only a couple of lines into the first article when I saw my sweat drip down Molly-Mae's face as I was trying to uncover the secret to her life with Tommy. I couldn't bear it any longer. I stood up and tugged my dress off over my head, and sat back down.

'Better?' Raj asked.

'Hmm . . . The umbrella would be even better. I can feel my scalp burning already,' I tutted back.

'Well, go to the shop and get a hat because that brolly ain't going up, Zara.'

He sounded serious, and I began to count how many more hours I'd have to stay here. Three, maybe four. I would be a puddle of eyes and teeth by then. I stood up, unable to settle, and thrust my feet into my sliders frustratedly.

Raj sat up.

'Where are you going?' he demanded.

'The gift shop – I need a hat or a fan or something. Will you order me some water for when I get back?' I hadn't even moved yet and I was panting the words out.

'Sure,' he chuckled, reclining back on his chair.

I marched up the decking towards the shop, feeling my expanding thighs chafe painfully with every step until I reached the gift shop. They had a poor selection of hats on offer. Most of the skip hats were branded and worn by the lifeguards or bartenders on duty. *I can't look like I work here.* I rummaged about a bit and found an old-style gangster fedora. *Oh, nice,* I thought. I pulled it down and admired myself in the tiny circular mirror situated on top of the hat stand. It gave me a very nineties pop vibe, and it matched my black swimming costume perfectly.

'I'll take this, please.' I handed it to the cashier, paid and strutted back to the lounger with my new prop.

Raj was still lying down peacefully, enjoying the sun, now with two giant jugs of water on our table.

'Well, what do you think?' I pulled my hat on over my plait and smiled down at him.

'Wow, very . . . erm . . .' He sat up, considering his response.

'Alicia Keys?' I suggested.

'Hmm . . . I was going to say Danny DeVito, but I suppose Alicia would work too.' He burst out laughing as my face fell.

'Is it that bad?' I asked, feeling more self-conscious than ever.

'Zara, no. I'm only winding you up. Sit down.' He patted the lounger.

'OK.' I handed him my sun cream. 'Will you do my lotion? I can feel myself cooking.' I leaned forward, arching my back towards my friend.

'Sure thing.' Raj squeezed the lotion onto his hands.

'What fucking factor is this, Zara? It's like an emulsion,' he said as he stretched the cream over my back.

'Fifty – I have pale skin, Raj,' I replied defensively.

'You look painted,' he laughed, watching me cover my arms and face as well. 'Like a geisha or something.'

I started to giggle as well.

'We're not all blessed with your skin colour, you know.'

'Can you do mine now?' He handed me his bottle and turned his back to me.

I started to spray Raj's carrot oil on his broad brown shoulders, then worked it up his neck and down his back, feeling envious of his colouring.

'Done.'

I patted my greasy hands together, and we lay back once more, finally appreciating the beach club. The sun was intense, but I immediately felt relaxed, listening to the ocean hit off the sand.

'To think we would be working back home in the bitter cold, eh,' Raj said.

'I know. This is just amazing. Cheers, Andy, eh,' I giggled.

'Oh, Andy again,' he teased in a high-pitched tone as I grinned back. 'Did you message him back last night?'

'Yeah, I just said "Aww thanks," or something, but he didn't reply. He was probably just being nice sending the first message anyway.' I shrugged down the situation.

'Yeah, maybe. Plus, even if he had other intentions, would you really want to go there again with a co-worker?' Raj snickered, referring to my ex Tom.

I lowered my sunglasses and blasted him a stare.

'He's hardly a co-worker, is he?'

'Well, he is. Besides, the way the aesthetics business is going, we need all the inside help we can get, Zara!'

'Is it that bad, Raj? Like, surely there's enough business to go around the clinics?' I peeled my arse from the plastic lounger to turn around and face my friend, who was rubbing his forehead, looking concerned.

'It is bad. The younger clientele goes to the cheapest clinics that are offering deals or who are completely free to influencers, and they end up with shitty sub-standard results. People get what they pay for, and it's just fucking annoying because I know we're the best. I don't see why we should lower our prices or offer discounts. I've worked too hard to get the clinic where we are with a stellar reputation.'

I smiled back warmly, completely understanding his concern. 'Yeah, you're right. The good old duck look, which makes everyone look identical.' I paused for a second, recalling a shower thought I'd had recently. 'Maybe we should try a new treatment?' I waited and watched Raj, who seemed to be only taking in half of my words. 'I've seen this new thing American practitioners do on YouTube. It's called facial balancing. Rather than sticking a mil of filler in lips and two mils in cheeks just because *everyone* is doing it, we would provide a full consultation of each individual face. Like completely measure it, making it as symmetrical as possible. It's basically like a person-centred approach to aesthetics. That way, we could advise the best treatment uniquely based on a client's features. We could pitch how we could enhance their natural features and balance the profile. The clinic is called Individualise after all. Whether it's the jaw, the cheeks, the ey—'

'Zara,' he interrupted, 'I know what facial balancing is but no one in Glasgow would pay that amount of money each visit. It wouldn't work. The younger clientele doesn't care about balancing their original features. They want the opposite. They strive to look identical to influencers and girls off the television,' he said.

'I don't think so. I honestly don't think the millennials want to look the same. They're quirky and fun *and* individual. Honestly, maybe we could ask Andy to see what—'

'I'd rather we kept doing what we're doing already, to be honest,' he cut across me again. 'I'm just so stressed with work now. I hardly see my wife and son and it's impacting massively on my life now. I'm never home. I'm working in the hospital, at the clinic, meeting with banks and you guys. And here I am in Dubai when I haven't spent any time with my family for god knows how long. The last thing I want to do is retrain on something that's a big risk,' Raj huffed. 'We just have to advertise more. I'd rather spend money on an ad campaign than new treatment packages and expensive courses that just wouldn't pay off.'

I raised my eyebrows at him. 'OK, I was just trying to help,' I said, turning onto my back to face the sun.

'I know you were, Zara, and I appreciate it. It's all very stressful, that's all.' He sounded disheartened.

We lay in silence for a few minutes until Raj sat up.

'Zara, check out the pool. It is *very* photogenic, but you would definitely get caught having a piss in that, wouldn't you?' he giggled.

The pool was crammed with holidaymakers posing and relishing the photo opportunity.

'Oh my god.' I started laughing at the thought. 'How funny would that be? Thank fuck you said that. That's totally something I'd do.'

Raj twisted his face up in disgust.

'Ashley would have loved this place, you know,' he said, admiring the beautiful beach and luxurious surroundings.

I took a long sip from my cold glass of water. 'I know. We would all be ordered in the pool till we looked like prunes just to catch that perfect snap!'

'Go in, and I'll send her some pics to make her jealous,' he said, nudging my arm and standing up.

'No way. Look at the nick of me!' I folded my arms in protest.

'Oh, here we go! Stop it. Go!'

He started pushing me off the lounger, and I eventually got up to walk towards the pool. I'd only gone a few steps when my feet began to nip from the burning sand and I winced and hobbled the rest of the journey up the stairs until I reached the edge of the water. I turned to see Raj, who had followed me to the poolside glass, wearing his sandals smugly.

I dipped my toes in the water and felt instant relief. I could almost feel the steam sizzling through my pores as I lowered myself down the stairs and my body finally cooled down. Pure bliss! The water was up to my waist, and I gradually battled my way through the pack of posers to reach Raj, waiting at the poolside.

'Ahhhh . . . This water feels amazing, Raj. You need to get in.'

'No, I'm concentrating on my suntan today! Right, c'mon. Give me your hat and I'll take some snaps.' I passed it over the glass partition and began beaming my happiest, most contented pose while Raj clicked away on his phone.

'Don't make me look fat, Raj!' I warned. 'Fuck's sake, take it from a higher angle!' Rolling his eyes, he raised the phone higher into the air. 'Did you put a filter on it?' I called out. I could see the frustration build on his face until he eventually called an end to the shoot, and he headed back to the edge of the pool to show me the results.

'What do you think?' He was scrolling through the phone as my eyes scrunched up, struggling to see with the glare from the sun.

'Turn this way.' I grabbed his arm and turned so my pasty white back was to the sun.

'Wait, I'll adjust the brightness on the screen,' he huffed.

As Raj fiddled with his phone, I cast my gaze out and admired the beach once more. The sand was almost white, and the ocean washed up so rhythmically as the techno music played in the background. My eyes followed the horizon, admiring the relaxed vibe of the club, and I was quickly drawn to the most stunning-looking couple strolling along the beach, his large arm draped over her. She had sandy blonde hair and wore a tiny white bikini with an oversized white shirt covering her petite, muscular frame. The guy had dark hair, pushed back from his face with a fantastic set of fuck-me shoulders and a sculpted, hairy chest. His large Ray-Ban sunglasses were taking up the majority of his face but his glare was fixated on his partner. Both of them seemed fascinated entirely with one another, and completely oblivious to the magnetic sex appeal they were radiating.

'Jesus, check out Posh and Becks, Raj.' I nudged him. 'Look, three o'clock,' I whispered, continually tapping his shoulder.

He looked up. 'Wow, she's like a movie star.'

'I know, so perfect,' I muttered enviously as the entire beach was now staring at the handsome couple.

'Wait.' Raj stopped dead. He dropped his arms and edged away from the poolside. 'Is that . . . no . . . it can't be . . . ha, it bloody well is. Tom! TOM!' He started roaring. 'Tom, over here!'

My heart began to pound heavily. *It couldn't be*, I thought. My hot sweat suddenly turned cold as my head went dizzy. I felt clammy, sick. This must be a misunderstanding. But when I blinked and tried to refocus my eyes, it was, sure enough: Dr Tom Adams, Sugar Daddy, my bloody ex who had ripped my heart out, shat all over it and threw it back to me. And he was striding towards us.

Shit. Shit! I felt wheezy. He couldn't see me like this, not here, not overweight and half naked. Not when I was plastered head to toe with factor fifty, and had an alarming case of prickly heat spreading rapidly over my body. Not with absolutely no make-up or lashes on, and certainly NOT when his date looked as if she'd just strolled off a Victoria's Secret's runway. *Shiiiit.*

I started to panic and splashed around the pool in despair, moving backwards and forwards, flapping my arms, feeling entirely trapped by selfie-driven tourists. I had to disappear. In a blind panic, I inhaled an almighty deep breath and plunged under the water, pinching my nose. With my body fully submerged, I could hear my heartbeat pounding into my ears, along with the faint distant chatter from the busy pool. I started to wonder how long the average person could hold their breath underwater for, as right now it was the only escape strategy I could think of. I watched in horror through the blurry water as Raj shook Tom's hand and kissed his girlfriend on the cheek. Then he began pointing towards the pool, scanning the crowd, searching for me. *Why the fuck would you look for me, Raj?* I suddenly became aware that the three of them were tilting their heads towards me, Tom slightly crouched to my level before waving and Raj awkwardly rubbing his forehead. It was only then I remembered that I was in a glass fucking infinity pool, clearly visible to the entire beach. And here I was hiding like Shamu in a tiny glass tank. There was no avoiding him. I kicked off the bottom of the tiles and emerged from the water with my dripping wet hair now firmly glued to my face.

'Oh, Zara, would you look who it is? Can you believe it?' Raj spoke first, raising his eyebrows at me sympathetically.

I carefully picked the stray hairs from my mouth and pushed my hands back through my slippery locks. My eyes were nipping from the chlorine, and I could feel myself shaking with nerves.

'What? Oh wow, Tom?' I attempted a shocked laugh. 'What are the chances, eh?' I tried my best to sound convincing, avoiding any eye contact with the couple.

'Raj, could you pass me my hat, please.'

Raj bent down and handed it to me. *At least this will conceal my Amish hairstyle*, I thought.

'Zara, it's very nice to see you again.' His posh English accent immediately sent twinges to my fanny. I could smell his familiar scent, the masculine musky smell of him that I once lavished in, but now didn't belong to me. Tom approached the edge of the pool to embrace me. I hovered gawkily, unsure of how much physical contact we were about to have. His arm reached out and he was coming closer, and I embraced him quickly to relieve the tension. I was hugging him tightly at the waist before realising he was going in for a handshake. Shit.

'Jesus, you're soaking.' He vaulted back, wiping down his shirt. 'Erm, this is Claudia. Claudia, Zara.'

I smiled at the stunning woman standing beside him.

'So, why are you out here, Tom? You guys on holiday? Or work?' Raj caught up with his friend but I couldn't keep up. I was nodding at times, joining in with random giggles, but the entire time wished I had stayed back at the hotel with Ashley. I felt angry at Raj, who was acting as if the full clinic takeover hadn't happened. Not to mention the fact the cunt almost broke me, his so-called 'best friend'.

'If you're free tonight, we should all catch up over dinner,' Tom offered.

I almost gave myself whiplash with the stare I darted towards Raj but he was too pre-occupied with his old friend to notice.

'One hundred per cent. It would be great to catch up. We're actually here on work and setting up the products for an aesthetics photoshoot, but it shouldn't take too long. We could arrange for something after that?'

I gritted my teeth and attempted a grin as I watched Claudia rub her freshly polished fingers down Tom's sun-kissed arm.

'Ideal. I'll text you, mate. Well, I guess I'll see you all tonight then. Raj, Zara.'

Tom turned his back to walk off, only taking a few steps before he spun back around.

'And, Zara, nice hat.' He chuckled. 'Very . . . um . . .'

'Alicia Keys?' Raj interrupted kindly.

'Hmm . . . I was going for Indiana Jones, but hey.' He lifted his hand briefly in some half-arsed attempt to wave, then turned back, promenading through the sand with his perfect princess giggling like a hyena behind him.

I remained still. Unable to move.

Raj's face was wincing for me.

'I'm so sorry, Zara, if that made you uncomfortable,' he said.

'Uncomfortable? You have no idea how I feel right now.' I could feel my breathing get heavier and quicker as my heartbeat throbbed sickeningly.

'Why the fuck would you shout him over here? Why would you even break breath to him after what he did to you? Or me, for that matter,' I barked angrily at Raj.

'I've forgiven him, Zara.' Raj shrugged his shoulders. 'He's been my best friend since uni. He was the best man at my wedding, for god's sake.' Raj held his hands up in despair. 'Like I said, I'm sorry if it made you feel uneasy. I just couldn't let him walk by without saying hello. We're all in Dubai!'

'And what? I wouldn't give that cunt a nod if we were the last two people left in Dubai. And there's no fucking way I'm going to dinner with him and Twiggy to sit there and get laughed at all night,' I said, feeling anger rage through my body.

'No one would make jokes about you, Zara. Don't be so childish,' he spouted back.

'Indiana Jones?' I could hear my voice get louder. 'He slagged my fucking hat, and you said nothing.' I was pointing in Raj's face aggressively. 'Meanwhile, he's stoatin' about Dubai like the fucking big man with Skindiana Bones on his arm. Aye, well, I've had enough, and I'm not fucking going anywhere with him, OK!'

I began wading through the water, my feet occasionally slipping on the tiled floor as I tried to get out of the pool in a hurry.

Eventually I surfaced, soaking wet, and stormed to the loungers. I could feel my emotions surging, and I wrapped both my and Raj's towels around me. I was shocked, embarrassed, envious and sad. Out of all the people in all the places on the whole entire planet, I had to see him when I looked like this.

Raj returned to his lounger, but we sat in silence. I pretended to sleep, shutting my eyes tightly while my salty tears dribbled down my face. Suddenly I felt trapped in this beachy paradise and craved my home. I missed the cold, grey weather. I missed the layers of clothes I could wear to mask my unpleasant body shape from the outside world. Most of all, I missed the comfort of being able to hide away from every person when I felt like this. My friends surrounded me, but today, more than anything, I wanted to be alone.

Raj nudged me just after two o'clock.

'Time for us to go to work, kiddo,' he whispered.

Chapter Eleven

Just before three, Raj and I walked into the luxury Palm Hotel's grand suite to set up injectables for the influencers. The room felt chaotic and was alive with noise from an overwhelming number of camera operators and make-up artists. I tried my best to blend into the background and spotted a small space to wait in until required. I sat down on a small leather bucket chair, and Raj followed closely behind. We hadn't spoken about Tom, or our argument, solely about the necessary arrangements for work.

'Sorry, who are you?' A small English man approached us, looking overworked and stressed. He was wearing a cotton turtleneck with a suit jacket and matching handkerchief hanging from the pocket. I couldn't help but wonder why anyone would wear a turtleneck in the fucking desert.

'My name's Raj, and this is Zara. Andy sent us. We've got the filler for the aesthetics shoot?' Raj answered politely while I continued to scrutinise this man's choice of clothing.

I could see the stress drain from his face immediately as he puffed.

'Thank god,' he muttered under his breath. 'Everyone, hello. Everyone, they're here.'

The room suddenly swarmed around us, and I peered up at Raj, who looked as baffled as me.

'What's going on?' he asked, looking uncomfortable as the assemblage eyed us up and down.

'You're here for the shoot? Yes?' the photographer asked.

'Yes,' we both nodded.

'Well, you'd better get ready then. This is a major campaign. We don't have time for you two to sit around. A lot of money is behind this.'

'Get dressed?' I said. 'Sorry, there's been a misunderstanding. We're only here to set up the injectables; we're not actually in the photographs.' I began to chuckle loudly at the confusion, but no one joined in.

'Yes, you are. There's been a change of plan to the shoot. Get to make-up and hair straight away. Both of you!' he added, wiping away the smirk which had begun to form on Raj's lips.

I rose as one of the make-up girls hurried over and ushered me to the side. *What the fuck was happening?* I couldn't be part of a photoshoot. I looked a mess.

'Raj, what is happening?' I hissed to him under my breath as I was led in another direction.

'I have no idea,' he called back.

A tall girl stood at the make-up station with her entire collection laid out in front of us.

'Zara, right?' she said.

I nodded to her, still completely confused.

'I'm Stella. Just relax, I'm going to do your make-up,' she said with an American accent and patted the chair for me to sit on.

'Stella, I think there's been a mistake. I can't model.'

'Girl,' Stella popped one hand on her hip, 'once I'm finished with you, you're gonna feel like a model. Besides, have you seen any of them model gals without a filter or an airbrush?' She paused sassily. 'Trust me, you don't wanna. You're going to be fine, girl.'

Before I could say anything else, she started wiping my skin thoroughly with a cleansing wipe.

'What the hell kind of product you got going on your skin? Y'all like Casper right now.' She sneered at me.

'Factor fifty,' I replied.

'Good god, it's like toothpaste!' she winked at me jokingly and I immediately felt at ease. She was warm and laid-back, and right now I had to trust her. 'The other girls are ready, so I have a bit more time with you. They're popping champagne in the bedroom,' she giggled.

'I honestly don't think I can do this, Stella. I'm freaking out. I have no idea how to pose or look pretty,' I admitted. I could feel my breathing getting shallow as my mind raced, and I felt dizzy.

'Hey, hey. Stop it! You look pretty all on your own. You will be holding the product like you would every day. You're not there to look like a model, you're the practitioner, which you already are. Plus, the photographer is the one who tells you how to pose. That's his job description, girl. *Hey,* trust me, he'll be more worried about easing off that guy.' She pointed across the room to Raj, sitting on another chair, getting pampered, seeming restless and profoundly uncomfortable.

Stella continued to paint my face. Her laid-back manner helped me relax, and she convinced me this was a once in a lifetime opportunity. My face was bronzed, and she gave me smoky golden eyes with a clear glossy lip. I felt like a beautiful sculpture and somewhat unrecognisable from the beast who roamed the beach. Next, Franco, an Italian hairdresser, blow-dried my hair, leaving it bouncy and alive. I felt like a different person.

When their work was done, Stella escorted me through to the bedroom, where the influencers were relaxing, sipping on their drinks.

'Hey girls, this is Zara. She's the aesthetics nurse.'

I waved shyly to the three picture-perfect girls perched on the bed.

'Hi!'

'Hi, Zara.'

'Come and sit with us. Champagne?'

The girls were friendly, and I immediately liked their vibe.

'Erm . . . sure.' I shrugged and smiled at Stella as I joined the three blonde bombshells. My eyes skimmed around the surroundings but I couldn't see Raj. *Huh, probably away looking for someone's arsehole to kiss*, I thought.

'Wardrobe will be with you guys soon. Don't get too wasted,' Stella called out as she left.

The girls cheered and poured me a drink.

'Zara, I'm Indie. This is Laureen and Skylar.' All three girls smiled with their pristinely white veneers.

'It's so lovely to meet you all. God, I'm sorry.' My voice was shaking and I lifted my glass, downing the champagne. 'It's just that I'm so nervous. I've never done this before. I've had the worst day in history, and I had no idea I'd be part of this shoot, surrounded by you three absolute stunners.' I was babbling with nerves.

'Oh my god, you poor thing. Tell us what happened.'

Indie rubbed my shoulder and the other two listened in as I spilt my guts about Tom and how shocked I was to see him today. They sympathised and immediately took my side. Before I knew it, I was on my third glass of fizz, discussing and scrutinising Indie's manipulative relationship with her ex, Chris, because she made an OnlyFans account. The girls were so kind and fun that after a while, I completely forgot that I was working.

'Costumes!' the small man with the turtle neck bellowed as he came speeding into the room with a dress rail, looking even more harassed than he had earlier. The girls flew to the clothes with enthusiasm, while the overwhelming dread of fitting into anything filled me with complete terror.

'You.' The small man pointed to me, as I was building up the courage to walk over. 'Could you pick something, please? Come on.' He guided me up from my safe spot on the bed, and I cautiously approached the rail. Everything was red.

'Oh, Zara, this would look lush on you,' Indie said, holding up a stunning velvet skintight dress.

'I like this one for Zara,' Skylar said, throwing a one-shouldered jumpsuit over my shoulder.

'She's got to look the best ever, girls. Tom will see these pics!' Laureen reminded them. 'This is the one,' she announced. She held up a wet-look knee-length dress. It was incredibly eye-catching and very low cut.

'Wow. It is beautiful. I just don't think I could wear something so . . . out there. It's so . . . sexy and—'

'Hello! You're sexy! Get it on you!'

Laureen passed it to me, and I held the dress in my hands. The other girls stripped naked so confidently and pulled dresses on and off. There's no way I could do that. I slid into the bathroom to try mine.

My swimming costume was still on from the beach club, and I looked down at my lumpy figure. *Why am I even doing this?* I thought. But I had to do it for the clinic. I had to do it for Raj, even if he was in my Burn Book right now. I took a deep breath and pulled on the short, sexy dress. *Thank fuck,* it fit. Very snugly, but I was sure it was supposed feel snug. I tugged on the tight synthetic material to haul it down and gazed in the mirror. *Wow,* I actually looked decent. I felt voluptuous and sexy. I took my phone out and sent a quick selfie to Ashley. *Hope you're feeling better! Check me out a pure model! Please say we can go out tonight! I've had a shitty day* 😩 *xx.*

Send.

I opened the door of the bathroom to my three new friends, who were in the next room adjusting their outfits.

'Well . . .' I shrugged my shoulders, immediately feeling less confident when I saw them dressed up like supermodels.

The girls began jumping around screaming.

'Oh my god, I love it!!!!' Laureen screamed.

'Me too,' Skylar echoed.

I couldn't help but smile. Maybe it was their energy, perhaps it was the bubbles, but I felt like I was finally experiencing Dubai the way I had hoped.

'Zara, one thing. What the hell is going on with your granny pants?' Indie giggled, staring at my arse with confusion.

I laughed. 'I've still got my swimming costume on. From Zero Gravity, remember? I thought the elasticated material would act like Spanx, you know, suck me in a little,' I shrugged, pinching my stomach flab jokingly.

'Oh no, it's making lines, hun, take it off!' Skylar exclaimed.

'I don't have any underwear with me. I didn't have any idea about this.'

'So what? I'm commando too. Look.'

Indie lifted her mini skirt and casually flashed her flaps, *wow*. She had the most flawless vagina I had ever seen. My mouth gaped wide. I couldn't help but tilt my head to examine it from extra angles. The other girls watched on as if it was entirely rational to flash your gash on a Saturday afternoon to a complete stranger, but with a fanny so perfect, I was sure I'd flaunt mine too if I was her. I couldn't help imagining the looks on their faces if I had flashed my ingrown, fiery pube line, never mind my overhanging udder lips. These girls did have it all – from face to fanny.

'Zara?' Indie gazed at me while my eyes were still fixated on her groin.

'Yes. OK. Sorry.' I lifted my finger in the air. 'I'll try commando.'

I trudged back to the bathroom and ditched the swimwear. Pulling the dress up felt more uncomfortable this time around without the Spanx effect of the swimsuit to help glide it up, but eventually I got there. My phone screen lit up in my hand – it was Ashley.

Wowwwww you are stunning mate! Sorry Z I really can't come out, I'm vomiting non-stop. What's up? xx

I huffed sadly and slipped my phone back into my beach bag, ready to show off my smoother figure to the girls. Coming out, I noticed they were gone, and I could see flickering from the lounge. I took a deep breath. *This is it, Zara. Don't fuck it up!* I turned to my half-full champagne glass, took a large swig of confidence, and then marched into the lounge.

I stood for a few seconds watching from the corner while the crew set up, experimenting with the flash on a selection of cameras. The influencers were holding their phones up, taking selfies against the bright backdrops behind them. I felt someone tap my shoulder.

'Well, would you look at you?' I smelled Raj's sweet aftershave from behind and turned to face him. He was dressed in an all-red suit with a white bow tie.

I took a step back. 'Well, that's some get-up you have.' I could feel my mouth hanging open in shock.

'I have been assured it will work for the purposes of the promotion. Very eye-catching.'

'It isn't half,' I said.

'Maybe like a sexy devil,' he giggled.

'If the shoe fits,' I couldn't help but add.

He sighed back.

The photographer waved us over to the set, and as my chub rub chafed together, I started to feel a prickly pain. The material was sticking to my inner legs and arse. I wobbled as both legs felt wholly restricted, clumped together with some sort of sweaty bodily paste, and I struggled to move.

'OK, I want the three blondes in the middle. Laureen, you're the smallest, so you stand out front. Raj and Zara, I want both of you on the outside – you'll be holding up the needles.'

We all fell into position as I continued to adjust my dress. It was crawling into the crack of my arse, and I was desperate for relief.

'Zara, stop moving,' the photographer bellowed. 'OK, hand them the needles.'

The blazered man delivered both Raj and I the needles while the three models held the filler product.

With a few streaks of fluorescent flashlights, the photoshoot was off.

The other girls seemed to pose and pout so naturally, while my heart thrashed as I attempted to imitate their poses, still continually having to fidget with my dress.

Nothing was easing the pain and the more I stayed static, the nippier my skin became; I could feel a new burning sensation flare between my thighs.

'Zara, stop fucking moving,' the photographer called out once more.

Indie rubbed my arm sympathetically from behind. I angled my head, trying my hardest to concentrate. *OK, you can do this, just stay still and smile*, I thought. My eyes were blinking wildly from the flash, and my arsehole was throbbing. *What the fuck is going on down there?*

'STOP! STOP! This just isn't working. Raj, could you kneel on the floor and stare up at the girls. Zara, stay where you are! You three girls, you are all doing wonderfully.'

Following his directions, Raj proceeded to walk around the set. I was glad for a few seconds rest and seized the opportunity. I'd had enough of the discomfort. I forced my legs open, shoved my hand up my arse crack and freed the dress with a jerk, happy to relieve the wedgie that was eating me from the outside in. I was clawing at the material, making sure there was no chance of it returning and praying a little bit of fresh air would help extinguish the fire raging between my legs. As I rotated my hips around, finally free of my shunkie, I felt something dislodge, my body was instantly soothed, and I could feel my insides completely ease. *What the fuck was that?* My eyes darted to the floor as I witnessed a large pile of sand fall straight out my arsehole and pile up like a fucking pyramid directly between my legs.

No one was aware but me. I paused, hoping it would stay that way. *Shit, shit, shit. Maybe they won't realise,* I thought. *Maybe they'll assume it's blown in through the window, after all, we are in a desert.* But as I tried to kick the last few grains free from my leg, Stella waltzed by briskly, heading towards the door. I gasped in fear as the air whirled and my little sandcastle started to take flight. At the same moment, Raj kneeled to the ground, and I followed its journey as it flew directly into his face.

'AGGGHHHH . . . My eyes! My eyes!' he screamed.

I gasped a second behind everyone else, striving to look concerned.

'Water, I need some water. Someone fetch me some water.' Raj was moving his head wildly, unable to open his eyes.

'Someone get a medic. For fuck's sake! I need to get on with this shoot. And why the fuck is there sand on my set? Joseph, get a brush!' the photographer screamed.

A young boy ran over and immediately brushed up my sand baby as I continued to play the shocked role.

'Raj, are you OK?' I called out.

'Zara, is that you?' His eyes were shut tightly and he was now lying on his back rolling around the ground.

'Yep, it's me,' I answered, rubbing my forehead.

'It's my right eye; I need to irrigate,' he said, trying to whisk the remaining grains of sand from his face.

'They're getting someone to help. Don't worry. Come here.' I bent over and held his hand, helping him stand just as a first-aider entered.

'Finally! Let's do this, people,' the photographer shouted. 'Zara, now you're in the middle. You're teasing these blondes with your needles. I want them to be surrounding you. Do you think you can do that?' he smiled.

'Yes, I'm pretty sure I'm up for it,' I grinned back.

'Let's do it then!' he yelled.

I felt a rush of adrenaline as I started to enjoy the attention. I was changing faces, poses and my arsehole was finally able to relax. With only a few more snaps, he called a halt.

'I've got enough content. These are great, girls.' The photographer was flicking through his camera roll, beaming. 'Yep, that's a wrap, everyone!'

I grinned from ear to ear, and the girls squeezed me tightly.

'You did so well, Zara!' Laureen squealed.

I was blushing, shaking my head at the flattery.

Raj walked over to us, forcing a smile. He had a large white patch secured to his right eye, held up with a bundle of bandages tightly tidied across his forehead. The girls gasped in horror.

'What's with the breast pad, boss?' I chuckled.

'Very funny. Well, you made us all proud, Zara. The shots are fantastic, well, from what I can see of them.' He pointed to his wound and laughed.

'Oh, Raj, I can't believe that happened to you. Maybe we brought some sand in from the beach or something?' I kept my voice low, trying my best to conceal the evidence.

'We're in a desert, Zara. It's just one of those things. I'll keep this on for a day or two, and it should be fine.'

I nodded back, relieved that my friend hadn't been permanently blinded by my sphincter's Sphinx.

'You set to go?' he asked.

'Yeah, sure. What's on Ashley's itinerary tonight? I'm gutted she missed this, you know.'

'I don't know about the itinerary but we have kinda scheduled a dinner – with Tom?' Raj sounded serious all of a sudden.

'No, you scheduled it. I'm not going. I told you that. I'm not going anywhere near him or her. I thought you understood that.' I could feel the anger slowly vibrate through my body, completely ruining my buzz.

'Stop being so childish, Zara. Build a bridge. Come on.' He shoved both hands on his hips, looking frustrated.

'Childish? Says the man dressed like a fucking pirate with a *wee* bit of sand in his eye.'

'A wee bit? My eye is in torture here.' He paused and took a deep breath. 'Get your stuff, Zara. Everyone's packing up. Please.'

I turned my back to him as I felt myself bubble up. *Don't ruin your make-up, Zara, don't ruin your beautiful make-up*. As I walked into the bedroom, the girls were standing at the mirror fixing themselves.

'Zara, oh my god. Are you OK?' Laureen rushed over to me while I flapped my hands in front of my face, trying to conceal the tears.

'Yes. Raj is just so determined to go for dinner with Tom tonight, and I don't want to. Ashley is still refusing to leave the apartment, and I'm going to have to go.'

'No, you don't! Come out with us. We have VIP to the Base nightclub. You have to come, it's R&B night,' Laureen said.

The other two girls were insisting too.

'I don't have anything to wear. I literally came in my beach clothes,' I huffed sadly but thankful for the invite.

'Take the dress. You look amazing. Once you wear it for a shoot, it's practically yours anyway,' Skylar called out from the mirror.

I weighed up my choices, and it became a no-brainer. If Raj was a true friend, he would respect my decision and cancel the dinner. This holiday was supposed to be fun and it was slowly turning into a nightmare. I'd had enough of people-pleasing and putting myself last. I wanted to let my hair down and finally experience Dubai!

'OK. Yes, OK, girls, I'm totally up for this!' I yelled. 'How the hell am I going to tell Captain Birds Eye, though?' I wondered.

'We can all tell him.' Laureen flicked her hair boldly and grabbed my arm. I leaned over, seized my beach bag, and headed to the entrance of the suite with her.

Raj was waiting outside, leaning against the wall and fiddling with his phone.

'Raj, I'm going out with the girls tonight. I told you I didn't want to spend any time with Tom, and the girls have invited me out instead.'

'Seriously?' He looked at me and shook his head, clearly disappointed.

'Yeah, seriously,' Laureen fired back. 'Let's go, Zara.' She squeezed my hand tightly, and we headed out of the apartment together with the other girls just at our heels.

Outside, some of the workers were packing up the van, and when they saw us, they started to chuckle. The girls were sorting an Uber and planning our wild night ahead, while I was zoning out until I suddenly overheard one of the boys.

'I swear, dude, the sand fell straight out that model's pussy.'

My heart stopped. *Shit, shit.* I was busted.

The other erupted, almost choking in his cigarette smoke. 'Which one?'

'The one with the dark hair!' the first one whispered back.

I smirked as I looked down. I was admiring my reflection on the freshly polished, shiny marble floor. That man may have known my secret, but that man also thought I was a fucking model! I felt my confidence rise as I stood tall, pulled back my shoulders and waltzed into the taxi like Naomi fucking Campbell.

Chapter Twelve

Base nightclub was insane. We marched straight past the queue and arrived through the VIP entrance. I watched the girls stroll in casually like it wasn't a huge deal while I tried my best to remain calm. On the inside, my eyes were wide, my enthusiasm was high, and I couldn't believe how fortunate I was. The interior was mainly white with a circular bar in the centre of the dancefloor. We were shown to a luxury booth with table service on a raised level overlooking the packed club.

'Zara, what do you drink?' Indie called over the table.

'Anything!' I waved my hands in the air, eager to start the night off.

'Can we have the large bottle of Cîroc, please?' Indie asked the waiter. The other girls nodded back, agreeing with her choice of spirit.

'This place is incredible, girls!' I blurted. My head couldn't stay still following the crowd's dance below us while acrobats flew from the ceiling above – not to mention the unbelievable amount of talent swaggering by.

'Yeah, it's always a good night! Right, dolls, selfie!' Laureen squealed, and we bundled together to try and squeeze into the shot. I suddenly felt self-conscious wedged between the three attractive girls as my triple chin took up most of the photo.

'I'll take it. Give me your phone.' I rose and grabbed Indie's phone.

'No, you get in. Come on, Zara.' Laureen ushered me back.

I shook my head and began their photoshoot.

'OK, OK, go!' I began clicking the button, standing tall, then small, conducting my little shoot animatedly. The girls were laughing as I screamed, 'Oh yes, yes! Beautiful girls!' imitating the photographer from earlier.

I took a step back and felt a clatter from behind. A massive ray of light blinded my eyes, and my body swerved as I felt heat on my skin. The bottle of Cîroc came with a gigantic firework stuffed in the top, and I had almost knocked it out of the waiter's grasp. I stumbled back and fell into the next booth, landing with my hands flat on the table for support. I panted for breath and looked up, slowly cringing, as the four men at the booth grinned.

'Bonjour.'

I turned to my right where a handsome man with a cigarette hanging from his mouth was watching me.

'Bonjour. Eh, hello. I'm sorry, I'm so sorry about this.' I blushed as I wiped my hands down my dress, which were now damp from the table as I had sent their drinks rocking.

I could hear the girls screaming with laughter while the waiter holding the bottle of Cîroc looked as traumatised as me. I swivelled back to the table and my cackling group of friends, feeling mortified. As I sat down, I glanced back towards the group of men. The handsome Frenchman was looking over, still smirking.

'Right, let's get this party started!' Skylar screamed as we raised our glasses together with an almighty clash and began our night.

The drinks flowed freely as we partied to our favourite R&B old school classics. My jowls ached from smiling as we knocked back another round of Tequila Rose shots. The girls mingled with some of the regulars while I stayed put to rest my feet and watched over our drinks. I felt relaxed and happily drunk as I lip-sync'd to 'This Is How We Do It' by Montell Jordan when I was approached at the booth by a young man dressed in a tailored all-black suit.

'Miss, I am one of Mr Beaumont's security guards, and he was wondering if you would like to join him while your friends are away.'

I was confused. Perhaps the message was meant for one of the other girls, I thought.

'I'm sorry, I don't know anyone by that name. You must be mistaken.' I shrugged my shoulders. The man grinned and pointed over to the next table – the one I had dived into earlier that evening.

'Oh, right.' I bent my head, realising who Mr Beaumont must be.

'I'm fine sitting here just now, but tell him thanks,' and glanced over the booth towards the attractive stranger, watching keenly.

The security guard headed back to Mr Beaumont's table as I lifted my glass and sipped my drink, feeling flattered. *I'm here with my friends; I am trying not to have one-night stands,* I told myself. I resisted the urge not to stare over at the booth while Beaumont got his message, taking out my phone instead to fiddle with and check in with Ashley. I was having the most amazing time, meeting new people, hitting cool clubs but I wished more than anything my best friend was here to experience it all with me.

'Bonjour. Hello,' a deep voice called out from above.

A solid, masculine, musky smell enveloped me and I smiled as I saw the beautiful Frenchman I almost mounted earlier stand before me.

'Bonjour,' I giggled.

'May I join you?' he asked.

'Sure,' I replied, watching another three security guards accompany him to the table.

'Eh, what is your name?' He took out a cigarette and lit it up so coolly. I watched the smoke gather between our faces. There was something weirdly attractive about his filthy habit.

'Ah, hold on.' I pulled my shoulders back and cleared my throat cockily. 'Je m'appelle Zara.'

He clapped his hands. 'Bravo, Zara. Mon nom est Henri.'

'Nice to meet you, Henri. I'm afraid that's how far my French vocabulary goes,' I smiled.

'Ah,' he groaned and came closer, whispering in my ear, 'it is a good job I'm very good at English then,

Zara. Oui?' I wasn't sure if it was the combination of cigarette smoke and his smooth sexy accent, or the fact I was in this glamorous, otherworldly club, but I felt complete and utter desire staring into Henri's large brown eyes.

'Would you like a drink?' I turned my head to the large bottle of vodka sitting on the table.

'No, no, I'm drinking water tonight, but thank you,' he replied, rubbing his stomach.

'OK, more for me then,' I giggled.

'What brings you to Dubai, Zara? Business or pleasure?'

'Business, believe it or not. I work in an aesthetics company and we were doing a photoshoot out here today. I'm guessing you're here for pleasure, Henri?' I couldn't help but blush as the words left my mouth.

'No, me too. Business meetings. I am an actor and I have a film being released soon. A lot of the production money comes from Dubai,' he said.

'An actor? That must be a chat-up line, surely?' I blurted and Henri shrugged.

'Oui, acteur. No chat-up line, Miss Zara. But I am hoping it's working!' Henri smiled over to me, showing his sparkling teeth. He then dived into his pocket and showed me YouTube clips of him in his latest film. *Ooh la fucking la,* I thought. I couldn't believe it! Here I was getting chatted up by France's finest actor. Not that I understood his videos or could hear the majority of his words over the banging music playing behind us in the club. But he was a fucking actor with an entourage of staff at his beck and call. Henri and I spoke for over an hour; he was kind and seemed engrossed in my 'normal' life, asking questions and actually listening to what I had to say.

When the girls arrived back at the table, my heart sank a little as I felt insecure compared to them. I watched them innocently wrap around his shoulders, introducing themselves, but Henri's warm, seductive eyes remained fixed on me.

'You've been away for ages, girls!' I stated.

'We were right over there! We just wanted to make sure THIS happened!' Skylar pointed to both Henri and I, and I instantly blushed.

'Ah, they are wing women! I like them, Zara,' he smiled.

'Me too!' I watched as the three girls topped up the glasses and moved back to the other side of the room to give us space.

'You know, Zara, I think you are very sexy. Your eyes are like le chocolat,' he said. The way he spoke made the words vibrate off his tongue, and I couldn't help visualising how his tongue would feel purring on my clit strings. Despite my determination not to have any more one-night stands, I couldn't deny the incredible amount of sexual chemistry between us. And this wasn't any guy trying his luck on last orders in the Savoy or The Horseshoe. He was a practically a celebrity – the possibilities were endless.

Henri gently pushed the hair back from my face, then whispered in my ear, 'I would love to taste you, Zara,' while caressing my upper thigh. I spontaneously turned moist. I began to imagine walking down the red carpet with this handsome man at award ceremonies. I was completely down for spending my life in a beautiful chateau in Paris. *Could this be the man I've been waiting for?* I smiled as I imagined Tom's face if he saw me now, getting chatted up by a fucking movie star.

Henri looked at his watch and sighed. 'I don't want the night to end, baby!'

I nodded in complete agreement. I felt the same. Every part of me craved his French fancy, and I couldn't let him leave without me.

'You could always come back to my hotel? Just for a coffee or something,' I said, trying to sound casual.

He squeezed my leg tightly, seeming pleased with my request.

'Oui . . . or something? You could always come back to mine too,' he suggested.

'My best friend is staying in my suite, so maybe yours would be better?' I replied, and Henri lifted his eyebrows cheekily.

'She's in another room, Henri. Don't get too excited,' I snickered.

'I only have eyes for you, my Zara,' he grinned lustfully, moving his hand further up my leg, making me throb.

'So, your place or mine?' He held his hand out for me to take.

I thought briefly, not knowing if the suite had been Febreze'd since I was last there this morning. I severely doubted Ashley had been fit for a clean-up.

'Yours.' I reached over, placing my hand in his. 'Can we lose the men in black following you, though? I don't need an audience, Henri.'

'Ha, oui! That would be a genre of film I'm not too familiar with, Zara.' He laughed noisily, then motioned to one of his men. Henri spoke quickly in French as he gave the man orders. There was something so powerful yet gentle about him, and just seeing how he instructed his entourage made me more aroused by the second.

'I told them Zara would protect me now. Shall we?' He stood up, and I felt butterflies attack my stomach like a swarm of midges doon the Strathy on a hot summer's day. This was real. It was happening.

'Should you tell the girls we are leaving?' Henri asked, glancing around the club for my new friends.

'It's fine. I can always text them when I'm back safely,' I replied.

You've got this, Zara. But all of a sudden, I had a nervous belly. I didn't want to fuck this up – this could be it for me. I took a deep breath, led my Frenchman to the taxi, and stared into his seductive eyes all the way back to his glamorous apartment.

Chapter Thirteen

Henri strolled casually into his six-star hotel apartment. He spoke in Arabic to greet the workers as we entered and I felt unbelievably impressed by his multilingual tongue. I couldn't wait to see what other talents Henri was hiding. The hotel was remarkably quiet, but there was a definite feeling of anticipation between my date and me as we waited on the lift to the penthouse. Henri brushed my hair to the side and kissed my neck tenderly. I could feel goosebumps travel down my left side as my eyes trundled back with pleasure. We entered the lift like randy teenagers, and as soon as the doors shut, Henri ambushed me.

'Let me taste your lips, Zara.' He leaned in and kissed me slowly. His lips were soft and full. I could feel my heart race, enjoying every second but craving more. I leaned into him, and the kissing became more passionate, his tongue caressing mine while he had one hand on my arse and the other stroking my face.

All too soon, the lift halted and the doors opened. We both jumped with surprise.

'I hope this is somewhere a little more private?' I smiled.

'Oui.' He raised his eyebrows suggestively.

Henri grabbed my hand and we walked into an open space. The room was dark but as soon as it detected movement, golden shades of light warmed the apartment.

'Wow.' My eyes widened with the huge open-plan space and sea view. I quickly slipped off my high heels to avoid marking Henri's plush white floor tiles; he held my hand and supported me as I did. 'The view is phenomenal.' My hands were stuck to my face in shock.

'It certainly is, Zara.' Henri was looking at me with utter desire.

Usually, that patter would be enough cheese to turn me off, but hearing it in his sexy European accent made Henri even more irresistible.

Henri kissed my hand before leading me to his white leather sofa, where we began snogging once more. It didn't take long before his soft palms were skimming over my nipples. And I was looking into his warm eyes in complete awe.

'You are sexier than a chocolat-covered strawberry, baby,' he panted.

What a comparison, I thought. However, given the intense level of horniness and the obvious language barrier, I happily overlooked it. His hands continued moving down my dress, carefully unzipping it at the back. As he pushed it up from the bottom towards my waist, his eyes lit up.

'Ahh, commando. Scottish girls don't wear lingerie?' he asked.

I shook my head sexily, not wanting to admit my earlier sandcastle disaster.

Henri began rubbing my clit with a firm, confident touch, my body twitching as I watched this handsome man tease me. I was wincing and could feel his fingers become saturated the more he played with me.

'Voulez-vous coucher avec moi?' I muttered, feeling ready to hit Christina's legendary scream the more he continued.

'Oui, oui.'

He stood up, removing all his clothes. I watched on, not believing how blessed I was to have this stunning, naked, famous man in front of me. Henri boldly held his long thick dick in his hand.

'Do you want Henri's baguette, Zara?'

I smiled, feeling slightly awkward at his phrasing yet again, but there was no denying it – I wanted it. The entire footlong. I nodded.

Henri moved his naked body on top of me, gently kissing my lips. I could feel his dick swelling between my legs and was praying he'd put it inside me soon. I reached down and tried to position it into place.

'Henri's not finished with you, baby,' he groaned.

He was taking it slow, which made me crave him even more.

Henri moved lower and started to kiss my inner thighs. *Halle-fucking-lujah! He's a licker!* I thought as he ran his tongue seductively around the rim of my vagina. I glanced down at his dark eyes between my legs, and he grinned on all fours, with his tongue buried deep down inside me. He didn't seem to care about the obvious amount of stubble down there, if anything he was enjoying it.

'Your pussy tastes as sweet as honey,' he purred.

Fuck me, this guy is a serious foodie! I thought.

His tongue softly began going in and out of me, teasing my clit as it throbbed in his mouth. I could feel myself almost come from the torment alone when I heard a slight *ping* from the elevator and suddenly the doors burst open.

'Fils de pute!' A tall, blonde-headed woman was standing with a suitcase looking irate.

Henri jumped to his feet, immediately suppressing his semi.

My body felt rigid as I froze for a few seconds. The alcohol was making me react slower than usual as I wondered what the fuck was going on. I started to pull down my skin-tight dress, suddenly aware that my vagina was very much still a centrepiece of the apartment. I tried hard to comprehend the situation, desperately examining my Frenchman's face for reassurance. Instead, Henri ignored me and began to chase after the stunning woman while waving his hands in the air dramatically. They were speaking so quickly in French that I had no idea what was happening. However, it didn't take me long to put two and two together, and I quickly realised I wasn't the only girl Henri was dipping his meatloaf in. I stood up, trying hard to zip up my dress as quietly as possible without disturbing the domestic. I watched as Henri began weeping while kneeling for forgiveness in front of this furious woman who was now pointing towards me.

Shit, why did I cancel his security? I thought.

Suddenly, the woman came lunging towards me in some form of attack. I screamed, covering my face at the commotion, but Henri grabbed ahold of her mid-air as she fell to the ground in a dramatic puddle of snot and tears. She was hissing towards me, yelling in French with an almighty bright red burning face.

What the fuck?

'I'm leaving, I'm leaving, OK?' I screamed as my heart pounded through my chest.

'Oh, a fucking English girl, seriously! Another fucking English girl?' The woman turned to Henri, who was still trying to restrain her from hurting me and began slapping him ferociously.

'Oh no, I'm Scottish,' I mumbled, clearing my throat, and she flashed me a look of disgust for even articulating. 'Look, I have no idea what is going on here. I am going to go and leave you two alone. I'm sorry for whatever this is, you know.' I walked cautiously towards the door, sheepishly anticipating another attack at any given moment and slipped my feet back into my heels.

'What are you standing there for, Henri? You better pay the bitch! She will tell the papers.' The woman tutted while Henri hovered in the distance.

'No payment necessary.' I pressed the elevator button, frantically tapping my foot to flee the situation. *Hurry the fuck up. Hurry the fuck up. Please, God!* I thought, gradually observing the lift numbers stop at every floor bar the penthouse.

'Pay your mother-fucking prostitute, Henri!' she bellowed.

Prostitute? I gasped in shock. My eyes slowly scanned down my body at my low-cut skin-tight dress. Maybe French girls don't dress as risqué, I thought. I glimpsed back around to the woman shrieking and compared my outfit to her bright pink Versace power suit. I let out a slightly drunken shrug. Fair enough, I thought.

I heard Henri's feet storm towards me, patting off the cold tiles. He was ransacking through his jean pocket before bringing out his wallet. He seemed unbelievably enraged.

'Take your money and never come back here! You eh . . . fucking bitch.' Henri's eyes were no longer kind or lustful. Instead, he stared down at me as if this entire situation was my fault. I knew he was an actor, but I felt betrayed by his callous attitude. I couldn't reply. My mouth was as wide as the Clyde, and my vagina was still soggy from his tongue. *How could he become so heartless so quickly?* Henri suddenly threw a bundle of notes at me and prompted me to go. Before I knew it, I played along in his little game, picking the paper up from the ground, feeling half offended, half glad, of some form of compensation from my horrific ordeal. I couldn't work out the exact currency exchange rate, but I thought of mine: a lick-out and a hand full of dirham for some shitty insults that I couldn't even translate. I certainly wasn't passing that up.

The lift door opened, and I flew in, pressed for the ground floor and belted out of the hotel straight back to mine.

The taxi ride took less than ten minutes to get back to my hotel, and the driver was trying to chat along the way, but I couldn't engage in any form of conversation. Twice in the last week, I'd had to flee dangerous situations due to my ravenous bearded clam. I couldn't help but feel that the carefree fun I thought I was having had suddenly turned complicated and cold. As I walked through the foyer, I spotted Adam at the desk. His eyes lit up with disapproval at my latest wardrobe choice, but I had no fight left in me, so I waved, hoping for a free pass or some sort of truce. Instead, he nodded back and didn't say a word.

Ashley's sickly stench immediately greeted me as I entered the apartment. Great, I thought. I kicked my heels off at the door and let out an almighty sigh. As I did, tears started drowning my face. What was wrong with me? I couldn't stop. I held my hand over my mouth, not wanting to wake my friend, but a few minutes into my meltdown, I heard the screech of Ashley's door.

'Zara, you OK?' she whispered, sounding sleepy.

'I'm . . . so— sorry. Go back to sleep,' I sobbed.

Ashley staggered into the lounge area and sat on the tiled floor beside me.

'Obviously, I'm not leaving. What's up?' she asked.

Sat on the hard tiled floor, we blethered on, me telling her about my hellish day at the beach club with Tom, then about the photoshoot and the night at the club. I could see Ashley feel every bit of my drama and she looked gutted she had missed out. I explained about Henri and his crazy girlfriend attack and how I'd had to race out of that apartment with a wad full of cash.

'I can't believe I've missed this day, Zara. I should have been there.' Ashley had her arm round my back as I rested my head on her shoulder.

'But don't feel bad because Henri has a girlfriend. That's on him. You didn't know,' she continued.

'But how much did you get?' she giggled.

I smiled. 'Like three thousand dirhams – I gave the taxi guy a big tip!'

Ashley gasped. 'That's a lot! Look on the bright side – if you are a prostitute, you are a high-end one, babe.'

I sniffled back. 'Aw, thanks. But it's not that. It's just . . . When I left the club with him, I started to think I really like this guy. Maybe, like just maybe, this could be it. I felt excited to start something again, but here I am. Hurt again.'

'It's amazing you want to start something again, Zara. But not with Henri. He's not the one. Maybe seeing Tom with someone else has made you realise it's time to move on and find a nice decent guy?'

Time was getting on, and we both realised we couldn't linger in the suite any longer. The stench was beginning to permeate the whole place and we decided to tackle it in the morning. While Ashley waited patiently at the door, I headed back to my room and changed into a fresh pair of pyjamas, and with our tails firmly between our legs, we went out to the corridor and chapped on Raj's door. It was 4 a.m., and after a couple of minutes we eventually heard Raj stumble to the door.

'What's happened?' he asked, still wearing his eye patch and scanning all over the place.

'Can we sleep here tonight?' I asked, sticking out my bottom lip.

'Why? What's happened?' he said again, looking concerned.

Ashley nudged his arm from the door and marched into his room.

'Zara nearly got battered. That's what happened.'

'Wait, what? By whom?' he asked, allowing me in and shutting the door.

The three of us laid on Raj's bed and faced the ceiling while I filled him in on Henri and the crazy night I'd had. When I finished, we lay there together in a few moments of silence.

'Raj, I'm really sorry about today,' I admitted.

'No, I'm sorry. I would never have called Tom over if I'd known it would upset you, Zara. I just sort of blurted it out before realising what I was doing. It's been a while now – I had no idea.'

He held his hand out as a peace offering and squeezed mine tightly over a cosy Ashley, who was wedged between us.

'This is nice eh, everyone's kissed and made up,' Ashley murmured.

'So, Zara, are you going to tell him how he got that sand in his eye or am I?'

Chapter Fourteen

On Sunday morning the three of us woke to the hot sun beaming through the blinds. Raj tossed and turned, then eventually sat up, pulling his eye patch to one side.

'Morning,' he managed through a yawn.

'Morning,' I replied.

Ashley groaned and rolled onto her side.

'What's on the itinerary today?' I enquired cheerfully.

Raj sighed loudly. 'Yoga on the top floor of the Burj Khalifa followed by a day of sightseeing.'

'Yoga? Seriously!' I moaned.

'Yoga in the middle of the desert, and on the top floor of the tallest building in the world. Sounds perfect on paper, but really who can be fucking arsed?' he said.

Still curled up and trying to snatch a few more moments of sleep, Ashley giggled while I gasped at Raj's language. In all the years we'd been friends I could count on one hand the number of times he'd sworn.

'Raj!' I shouted.

'What? I say patch it. Let's all enjoy our last day chilling by the pool together, no drama,' he said.

'No drama? Ooft, I'm well up for that!' I leaned over to the bedside table and sipped on some tepid warm water, seriously craving my Irn Bru fix to take away my dehydration.

Ashley raised her hand in the air. 'I'm in! As long as we don't need to talk about Friday night ever again.'

Raj and I glanced at one another.

'Deal. Come on, ladies, let's get organised then.' He started clapping his hands, and I covered my tender ears quickly.

'Stop!' I moaned.

Ashley sat up, rubbing her eyes.

'Why are you always so awake!' she huffed. 'Fine, I'll go get ready!' Ashley threw back the duvet and made her way for the door, with me following a few steps behind.

We sank into sun loungers just before midday. Considering she'd spent most of the previous day spewing her guts up, Ashley looked glam with her cut-out swimsuit and gigantic shades on, wholly engrossed in the latest gossip magazine. Raj was successfully frying his skin, macerated in coconut oil, while I lay beneath the brolly scrolling through YouTube videos of my famous French 'almost-husband' from the previous night. I finally felt relaxed and at ease in Dubai. No glitz, glamour, fancy parties, and it was the happiest I'd been; lazing about with my best friends, chatting shit by the pool.

'Zara, have you checked out Botox Boxx's Instagram? Your client Peter is on their grid photos and had his lips filled! Badly, may I add.'

'Let me see!' I peeled my sticky arse off the sun lounger and grabbed Ashley's phone.

'Is it him?' Raj asked, tilting his sunglasses. I nodded, too shocked to speak.

'Sly bugger! Didn't think he had it in him! They must be poaching our clients,' Raj tutted, looking incredibly disappointed.

'They are probably adding them from our socials, sending our clients messages to go there. It's simple but genius, when you think of it. Like, they almost have ten thousand followers and they've been open a few weeks. That's insane!' Ashley sounded impressed.

'Well, you're the head of Individualise media and marketing – you should be putting in the same amount of effort,' Raj replied.

'Don't worry, I intend to, boss!' she sniggered.

'But play fair. I don't want our reputation getting tarnished because of dirty tactics.'

'Oh you're such a spoil sport!' she replied. 'You know I like to play dirty!' She winked over to me playfully, trying her best to make Raj feel uncomfortable.

'Aye, and look where it's got you, lady! Enough!' he joked back.

Ashley rolled her long black eyelashes at him sassily, choosing not to retaliate and ended the conversation.

'If it's worth mentioning, guys, after last night's fiasco, I'm completely over dating and in fact, I'm over men in general. I'm going to give it at least a good six months to a year before chatting to anyone else. My head is firmly stuck on saving the clinic!'

I turned to Raj and Ashley who remained silent and then burst out laughing.

'What? Stop it!'

'No, I love your dedication, Zara. I really do. *But,* I'll believe it when I see it,' Raj replied.

The entire day raced by, and we spent it laughing and revelling until the sun began to set. We returned to our rooms to get organised for home. Our suite had been deep cleaned, and as soon as we entered, Ashley and I inhaled the clean scent.

'Finally!' Ashley screamed. 'Fresh air and fresh bedding!'

'Yep, just in time for us leaving.'

Ashley slumped down on the sofa in the living area, dropping her beach bag to the side.

'Zara?' she mumbled.

'Yeah?'

'What am I going to tell Dave?' Her eyes seemed heavy. I sat alongside her and sighed.

'You know, you don't have to tell him anything. What happens in Dubai and all that . . .' I smiled, gently squeezing her thigh.

'I honestly don't know if I can face him knowing I did this. Thank fuck you guys found me or it could have been worse.' She ran her hands through her thick extensions, looking distressed.

'Technically, you just kissed,' I said. 'Dave doesn't need to know the location of your lips. If you need to tell him something, tell him that,' I shrugged, and she attempted a grin.

'And if you don't want to tell him anything, then don't. Raj and I can keep a secret. Don't make a crazy decision from a moment of madness. Sleep on it.'

Ashley rested her head on my shoulder.

'Zara, can we get room service for our last night?'

I nodded hungrily, having eyed up the chicken tikka on the menu since we arrived. Raj knocked on the door and was pleased with the change to our dining plan. He spent most of the night giving us life advice while Ashley mocked his wisdom every time he turned his back. Around ten, Ashley started to gather up her clothes to begin to pack, and Raj went back to his suite for an early night. I headed into my room feeling completely exhausted from a lazy day at the pool, and curled up into a ball, ignoring my empty suitcase on the tiled floor. I squeezed my phone out from the arse of my back pocket and sat up as soon as I noticed: *one new Instagram message from Andy.* When I saw his name, my sleepy head woke up in an instant, and I frantically clicked the message received an hour earlier.

Safe flight home tomorrow. Hope Dubai was fun 😄 *I got sent the proofs from the shoot and it looks amazing! Everyone at Juju loves the content. Nice one! A*

Again I wondered, was he being friendly, professional or flirty? I had no idea, but I knew I wanted to reply immediately.

Awww, you will need to send me the proofs! Was a shocker to be part of the shoot! Dubai is insane but weirdly missing Glasgow! See you when I'm back, and thanks again for this opportunity! x

My eyes remained fixed to my screen for the next few minutes, wishing for a reply. I could see Andy was active, and my heart sank, wondering if he was messaging someone else. *Finally*, seven long minutes later, he read the message. I waited for him to start typing but he simply liked it. No reply, no conversational starter. I flopped onto my back. Yep, it's professional.

I woke the next morning to my alarm ringing loudly from the pillow beside me. As I turned to switch it off, I immediately thought about Andy and leaped to check my messages. Nothing.

I went through to the lounge and found Ashley already dressed with her suitcase propped against the door.

'Morning,' she muttered as she tidied up the living area.

I yawned. 'God, you're organised.'

'I know, I couldn't sleep. I'm just excited about seeing Dave, I think.'

I smiled over to her, while she pretended everything was OK.

'Yeah, he'll be dying to see you too!' I responded.

'You better get organised, Zara. Raj is meeting us in the lobby in forty minutes. C'mon!' Ashley ordered, and I turned back, plodding through to my bedroom to get packed up.

I threw the combination of wet and dry clothes in the case, shoved a plait in my sticky pool hair, and forty minutes later, the three of us had checked out and were headed back to the airport.

★

I'd had such high hopes for a fun-packed holiday, but in the end the only part that went to plan was the job itself. From blow jobs on the beach, to unexpected collisions with an ex, fall-outs and fall-ins – Dubai really tested us all. As we boarded the flight, I couldn't help but feel awful for Ashley, who remained painfully silent, riddled with guilt as she trailed behind me, with Raj dragging her case. Raj seemed more at ease strolling in front; he knew the photoshoot had gone well, and he looked less tense on the journey home. Juju planned to release the images as part of their summer campaign, and as much as I couldn't wait to see me starring on a billboard, part of me feared Individualise wouldn't last till the summer. We couldn't afford to lose any more clients in the meantime, and heading back home, we all knew we had our work cut out to keep the company afloat till then.

Raj spotted our row, and we noticed a young woman was sitting in the third seat.

'Check your tickets! We must be split up,' Raj sighed.

Ashley's head darted up from the ground. '29D. What are you guys?' She was panicking.

I scanned over my ticket.

'29C,' I replied.

'29B for me, kid,' Raj said.

'Sorry, Ash, we're in this row.' I shrugged. 'But you're only across the aisle.'

Her eyes filled up with dread.

'What if it's the Celtic player?' she hissed.

'I'm sure he'll be flying first class! And, what if it's Tom?' I retaliated.

Ashley's voice got higher as she mocked me, 'I'm sure he'll be flying first class too!'

'He is, and he leaves tomorrow. It's a Tom-free zone!' Raj added.

'Zara, please, I don't want to sit by myself!' She huffed. 'Raj?'

'Don't look at me. I'm not a Nigel for no one,' he giggled and sat down firmly in his allocated seat.

'Zara?' she moaned. 'Go an' ask that girl to move then!'

'Ash, no way! She's probably paid extra for the window seat,' I whispered. 'You literally have an aisle separating us. Two foot of space. We're all practically next to one another.' I tried to sound positive while Ashley stared back frostily. A brief stand-off ensued as we each waited for the other to back down.

'OK, fucking fine! I'll swap!' I budged by her as a queue was forming from all the commotion. There was no way of winning the argument when Ashley was being so stubborn, but part of me didn't want her to be alone for the flight, overthinking and worrying about things with Dave.

'Yay!' She cheerfully nudged past Raj and grinned across the aisle at me.

Great, I thought, *I'll presumably be stuck next to the worst person on the entire flight, unable to move for the whole journey. Or even worse, a honeymoon couple.* I sat down and clipped myself in, preparing for the worst. *Oh shit no*, I thought as I observed two troublesome twins battle one another down the aisle towards me. *Please, God, not the twins,* I prayed.

'Excuse me,' a solid Highland accent came from behind me. I turned to see an exceptionally tall, bearded man standing shyly, looking down at me.

'I think you're stuck with me,' he said.

Oh, I fucking wish, I thought. My jaw was still gaping as I attempted to stand for the third time before realising, I was seat belted in.

'Shit, I'm sorry.' I finally managed to unhook myself and make room for the stranger. 'I'll let you in.'

I stepped out of the row while he placed his backpack in the overhead compartment. Across the aisle, Ashley was hanging over Raj for a better view while nodding her head frantically, watching the hunk slam shut the luggage door and take his seat.

Slipping back into my seat right beside him, I watched him expand his seatbelt to make more room for his muscular physique. His hands looked strong and sun-kissed.

Jesus Christ, this cunt was hot. He had dark brown hair, which was ever so slightly thinning at the front, a short, neat beard, and by the looks of his tight grey top, an incredibly athletic physique.

My eyes darted between his sizeable bulge and his empty ring finger, relieved only one was packing.

He spotted me staring and looked slightly flustered. 'Good holiday?' he asked while fishing his phone from his pocket.

'Yes. Well, no. It was work. What about you?' I responded, feeling my heart hammering harder in my chest.

'Aye, the same. Work.' He looked up and squinted at me. 'I think we've met, you know. Were you at Base nightclub the other night?'

I gasped and held my hands to my mouth.

'Oh my god, *yes*. Were you there too?' I hoped he hadn't seen me leave for some Eiffel Tower action.

'Yes. Well, I was working – I do private security.' He shrugged it off, but the thought of him being a bodyguard sent shockwaves to my fanny. 'I was working for a famous French actor. I'm pretty sure he liked you.' He snickered and gazed down at his phone.

'Oh.' I felt my face flush with warmth. 'Yes. God, that guy wouldn't give up. But I left early with my girlfriends,' I said, trying to sound convincing.

'I got off early too that night, actually,' he said.

Aye, thanks to me, pal. I thought.

'Suppose that's the perks. I can't complain about a job that lets me hit the best nightclubs and stare at pretty girls all night long, eh?' he laughed.

'I'm Cameron, by the way.' He was fidgeting with his jeans.

'Zara,' I replied. 'Nice to meet you, Cameron.'

'Nice to meet you *properly*, Zara,' he said, as I briefly gazed into his warm mysterious eyes.

Chapter Fifteen

Flying back to Glasgow beside the hunk from the Highlands was exhilarating. We giggled clumsily when our arms bumped against one another in the small confined space, and every time we made eye contact, I felt my vagina drizzle with desire. *God help the poor cunt sitting on this seat after me,* I thought. As we talked, I quickly forgot about my two friends across the aisle. Cameron was from Aviemore, which was way out of my usual Tinder boundary restriction, as it took far too long to travel to from Glasgow. In his early twenties, he had worked as a sniper in the army and retired to Dubai at thirty-two, where he now worked private security for affluent targets. As Cameron described his job in detail, my clit twinged and my imagination raced at the thought of sharing an armrest with my very own Kevin Costner. I couldn't help but feel safe and protected in his company. Cameron explained how this journey was in fact his connecting flight to Turkey where he was travelling for a holiday.

'So, do you travel a lot to Dubai then, Zara?' he asked, offering me one of his sour cream and onion Pringles.

'No, this was my first time. Eh, no thanks,' I refused the snack through good manners, although my stomach grumbled with hunger, knowing fine well I could demolish the tube in ten seconds if I had the chance.

'First time, eh. If we'd met earlier, I could have shown you all the best bits.' Cameron blushed, looking a little shy at his flirty remark.

'That would have been so much more fun,' I said, unable to stop myself from smiling.

We continued chatting for the first hour until a comfortable silence came over us and Cameron tilted his chair back and made himself more cosy.

'I'm going to try and catch a wee half hour. However, if the snack trolley appears then please waken me!' he joked, then dived into his tight jeans, popped his AirPods in, and closed his perfect eyes.

'Zara! Pssst, Zara!' Ashley hissed, leaning across the aisle. 'Oooft, fucking hell! What a babe!' She and Raj giggled.

I glanced discreetly at Cameron, making sure he was unaware of our gossiping, and turned back to my friends, rolling my eyes and sighing with satisfaction.

'He is so fucking hot!' Ashley continued. 'Like mile-high-club hot.'

Raj darted her a disgusted look while I burst out laughing.

'Sorry?' I heard the strong accent behind me, and my body went stiff with panic.

'Did you say something, sorry? I had my AirPods in,' Cameron said.

'No, no. Not to you, sorry. My friends are just across the way there.' I felt my palms sweat with nerves at the realisation he may have picked up on our conversation. Cameron grinned over at Ashley and Raj, who waved back enthusiastically.

'Would you like an ear?' He held one of his AirPods out.

I was caught by surprise. 'Erm, OK, sure! I hope you have some Beyoncé on that playlist, though,' I teased.

Cameron laughed. 'I not only have Beyoncé, I *also* have some original Destiny's Child on here, Zara.' He began flicking through his phone; I watched his fingers move quickly and I imagined how good they'd feel inside me. 'And here is some "Bootylicious", just for you!'

'Wow, I'm impressed.' I popped the AirPod into my ear and faced him, feeling intrigued.

He leaned over and whispered, 'Zara, can you handle this? Cammy, can you handle this? I don't think you can handle this,' while wiggling his shoulders with attitude.

I laughed out loud as I watched him. Cameron was adorable, and I felt utterly captivated by him.

Over the next couple of hours we listened our way through his assortment of tunes. I chuckled at some of his poor selections, but overall enjoyed being whimsical and flirty, and being complimented by an absolute ten. I positioned my back towards my friends, keen not to catch Ashley's eye or allow Cameron to see the immature, hilarious yet repulsive hand gestures she directed my way. I knew she was attempting to make me uncomfortable and I only dared to engage in conversation with my friends when Cameron nudged past me to go to the toilet.

Ashley seemed frantic, leaning over Raj.

'OH MY GOD! He's perfect!' she gushed.

'I fucking know,' I said, unable to take the grin off my face. 'Well, almost. He lives in Dubai!'

'He's just so manly, Zara.' Ashley was not listening to any of my cons.

'Like, I could imagine him up in the Highlands chopping wood or shearing fucking sheep or something.'

I knew exactly what she meant. Cameron was tall and robust, not in a working out kind of way but more genetically favoured. He wasn't a pretty boy, draped head to toe in designer labels, no Rolex watch or Gucci belt in sight, but he had an aura. He was a manly man who naturally oozed one hundred per cent raw sex appeal.

'Oh my god, he's legit the spitting image of the Scott's Porage Oats guy!' Ashley said, having an epiphany.

I snorted loudly, and observed a few sniggers from other passengers listening into our conversation.

'You're forgetting he stays in Dubai, Ash,' I reiterated, hoping she'd listen this time around.

'No one stays in Dubai for ever; it's a stepping stone. Ask how often he comes back to Glasgow. Go, shhh, here he comes.' Ashley rested back in her chair, smirking at Cameron as he returned to his seat.

'So, Cameron, do you spend much time in Glasgow?' I asked once he'd sat down.

'To be honest, on my holidays I like to travel. I have a few friends in Glasgow, so occasionally, I suppose.' He buckled up his seatbelt and faced me.

'I could be inclined to spend more time there if I had something to go back for though.'

'Or someone?' I murmured, feeling all the heat rush to my face.

'So, I know this is unusual, and I'm probably going to sound like a massive weirdo in a minute, but I'm getting this other flight in a few hours, so I won't even be able to leave the airport. But, when we land, I don't suppose you would like to grab a coffee with me? It would be an airport special, so nothing fancy, just to pass the time. I completely understand if you're too tired and have a million other things to do, but it's just a thought . . .'

'I'd love to,' I replied quickly, not needing a second to think about it.

'OK. Good. I'm looking forward to it already.' Cameron put his strong hand on top of mine and gently squeezed it. I turned to Ashley, who was still spectating. When she saw me, she started to thrust her hips excessively and mouthed over, 'Mile-high club!' I screwed my face up at her before popping one of Cameron's AirPods back in.

The flight eventually began its descent into Glasgow, and I had butterflies. I knew my journey with Cameron wasn't over, and I hadn't felt anything like this with anyone else for such a long time. Maybe it was my holiday buzz, or maybe it was the atypical place we'd met, but one thing was for sure, it felt right. I had always heard people say you meet the man of your dreams when you least expect to, and perhaps they're right. For the first time in my life, I was more concerned about the clinic, then this hot bastard catapulted straight towards me at thirty thousand feet. I tried not to get too carried away, but something felt real and pure. Maybe this was *my* time? Maybe, this was *my* movie.

It was approaching 5 p.m. when I shuffled down the small plane staircase with my friends and Cameron. Fuck, it felt good to inhale cool air once again. My body was entirely drained from the wild long weekend, but my head was glistening full of hopes and dreams with Cameron at the forefront. We walked through passport control, and the four of us stood together, awaiting our luggage.

'So, Cameron and I are going for a coffee. I'll grab a taxi home and catch you guys in the morning?' I tried my hardest not to smirk with delight as my friends looked thrilled for me.

'Sure. If Dave's finished work, he'll be collecting us anyway.' Ashley held up her phone for a better signal. 'Not that he's even texted to tell me. If not, we can grab a taxi together, eh, boss?' Ashley rested her head on Raj's shoulder, and he briefly patted her head.

'Will you be OK tonight, Ash?' I asked quietly, still unsure of what her plans were for her and Dave.

'Why wouldn't I be?' she replied, brushing me off.

A large beep echoed through the building as the baggage belt began churning, and the hall full of impatient, sun-stroked, hungover Glaswegians squeezed together, hoping to reclaim their belongings first. I peered through the cracks between people and pinched my way to the front when I spotted my large pink case. But as I went to lift it, I felt a tap from behind and looked up to see Cameron.

'Let me, Zara.' With one slight tug, he hauled my suitcase off and lifted his khaki green holdall too.

'Shall we head?' Cameron asked.

I looked up to the hot, strong, masculine man in front of me and nodded.

'Yes, sure! See you later then, guys.' I called over to my friends who were paying more attention to their phones than their luggage.

Ashley glanced up briefly and winked, and I pulled a face, feeling nervous.

Cameron held his hand out to grab mine. My heart thumped loudly as the blood flooded my entire body. I grasped his hand tightly and pushed my case with the other.

'So, do you make it a habit, chatting up girls on flights?' I asked as we walked towards the concourse.

'No, never,' he laughed. 'Well, when you consider I was married before, I suppose that means I would never have looked at another woman, never mind chat her up.'

My psychologically disturbed heart immediately sank at the thought of the man I had just met being married to someone else, and I felt nauseous.

'Oh, right, OK,' I replied, nodding, as we approached the coffee shop.

'So, are you separated?' I probed further, trying my hardest to sound laid-back when I knew this bitch was about to be severely stalked.

'Divorced, yes,' he said. 'I took some time out, travelled and enjoyed life, I suppose. Anyway, enough of that, eh.' We were approaching the empty coffee shop and we stopped at the entrance. 'What would you like to drink?' Cameron asked.

'Oh, can I have a hot chocolate, please?' I smiled at the handsome man who had let go of my hand in search of his wallet.

'Oh, great choice. Choose a seat, and I'll bring it over.'

He gestured towards the empty chairs, and I whizzed my case over to a small booth, waiting restlessly. I observed Cameron greet the barista with impeccable manners and some friendly chat. He ordered the same drink as me and topped them both off with cream and marshmallows.

'Here you go,' he announced as he brought the drinks over.

'Aw, thank you so much,' I replied, immediately stirring the cream, hoping to avoid it catching on my moustache.

'So, tell me about you, Zara. I want to know everything.' Cameron gazed at his watch. 'Well, maybe not everything. I have a flight to catch in just over an hour,' he giggled.

I began to tell him about the clinic, my nursing, my friends and our unexpected trip to Dubai. He was a great listener. Every so often, he drew his hands to the top of the table and squeezed mine. I asked him about himself and he revealed how he was married for three years to a girl he met at school. As he worked abroad, they grew separately as people and fell out of love. He had been single for almost two years now. His honesty about his situation and his warmth towards me felt real. There was no second-guessing his intentions, no girl code I had to follow, just meaningful chat. Maybe it was because he was so new to the dating scene, or perhaps it was because he was genuinely a nice guy, but I couldn't help feeling comfortable with him.

'So, tell me about dating? Have you had many since the split?' I slurped my drink, keeping eye contact with the attractive man.

'Well . . . hmm . . . I had Tinder, *briefly*. I had lunch with one girl in Dubai, but nothing *happened* happened.' He blushed as he opened up.

'So, nothing's happened *happened* since the split, Cameron?' I was intrigued, hoping we were using the same code for sex.

'Well . . . I was in Brazil, and I sort of dated a dancer for a couple of weeks. Something happened *happened* there, but not since then,' he chuckled.

'Wow,' I gasped. 'A Brazilian dancer! Congratulations!' I was fascinated yet utterly intimidated as I imagined a half-naked, six-packed belly dancer grinding her perfect puss all over my new man's beard.

Cameron shrugged, seeming a little flustered. 'I suppose I had to tick it off the bucket list.'

I joined in with his awkward laugh, and we drank some more of our hot chocolates.

'What about you? What's your story?' he asked.

'Well, I suppose I've been single for a while,' I said. I suddenly felt a stab of anxiety thinking about Tom. I tried to put him to the back of my mind but seeing him so recently made me feel sick. 'So, I dated a guy, fell in love, fell out of love and have been partial to a Tinder date or two recently!' I played down the fact that I was a serial shagger since we split, who'd *also* had her fair share of South Americans exploring her jungle.

'So, you could teach me a thing or two about dating?' he asked.

'I would love to.' We paused and stared into one another's eyes; I could feel my clit throb, desperate to get to know Cameron. 'If only you were staying a bit longer, eh.'

Cameron agreed and raised his eyebrows.

'God, it's so annoying, but I've had this trip booked for a while now. Depending on how it goes, I might be finished sooner. I mean, I could always try to fly by Glasgow on the way back to Dubai. Meet for another coffee?'

'Really? Wow, yes! I mean, of course, I'd really like that,' I gushed.

'You could take my number, and we could chat? Try cross paths?' He shrugged his shoulders, looking nervous.

'*Hey*, are you asking to be my new pen pal?' I joked, biting my lip at the hot sexy gentleman facing me.

He grinned and put his hands to his mouth jokingly.

'You know, I think I might be!'

We continued our chat effortlessly and exchanged numbers. The moments zoomed by so swiftly, and I dreaded each time Cameron glanced at his watch because I knew it was almost time for him to leave.

He stood up and groaned after what turned out to be almost an hour-long chat.

'I need to go. I don't want to, but I really need to go!'

'I know, *yes,* you do. I can't believe how random today has been.' I shook my head.

'Come here.' Cameron stepped towards my seat, and as I stood up, I gazed into his chocolate eyes. His flawless smile glistened through his dark brown beard, and he looked so sexy. Cameron pulled me in, and we hugged for a few seconds. I heard his heart pound heavily in his chest, and I felt the soft touch of his kiss against the top of my head. I grinned against his chest, feeling almost euphoric as he squeezed his body close to mine. He smelled of masculinity, and when I was wrapped in his arms, I didn't want him to let me go. I felt so comfortable with him, like I had always known him.

Cameron's head moved towards my ear, and he whispered, 'Maybe you could lay off the Tinder dates and let me work something out about coming back?'

I glanced up at him in total surprise.

'I'm sure I could do that,' I said, and we broke free from our hug.

He seemed pleased with my reply, as he couldn't take his eyes off me.

'Goodbye then, Zara. I'll text you.'

'OK, speak soon. Safe flight.' I shuffled backwards, not wanting to break eye contact with my latest crush until he entered the check-in terminal. I immediately felt pumped. *What a glorious day!*

I strolled towards the airport exit, my cheeks hurting with happiness, and took a long, deep breath of the cool, damp air. Fuck me, it felt good to be home!

Chapter Sixteen

Heading to work the following day in the cool, moist weather with a loaded WhatsApp chat stuffed with Cameron's sweet words and cute selfies felt invigorating. I hadn't heard from Ashley since leaving the airport, but I knew she'd been so desperate to see Dave and catch up with him that they probably ended up shagging the entire night. I couldn't wait to spill the juice on my airport date and night of non-stop messaging. I'd only had around two hours of sleep, but still, I managed to spring out of bed, keen to start up our conversation once again.

As I jogged across the busy road to the clinic, I saw Raj was opening up. His timekeeping was habitually as poor as mine, and I wondered where Ashley was.

'Hey, morning!' I buzzed as I bolted through the door behind him.

'Where's Ashley?' he replied, glancing at his watch.

'I haven't heard from her. I assumed she'd be erm . . . *busy* with Dave.'

'Hmm, weird, though. She's the only one among us with good timekeeping. Maybe she's slept in from jet lag. I feel totally done in too.' Raj stretched his arms in the air and let out an exaggerated yawn. I leapt up jokingly behind him and tickled his armpits. We both burst out laughing, crouching over one another, him slapping my arms as I continued to annoy him.

The front door swung open behind us, and in burst Ashley. Her face was scarlet as she sobbed, wearing a bright pink velour tracksuit with a leather jacket thrown on top and wheeling her Dubai suitcase after her.

'Ash, what's up? Are you OK?' I ran over to console her.

She was nodding her head, whimpering into my shoulder.

'Me and Dave are over. I told him about Dubai. Please can I stay with you, Zara?' she bubbled. 'Just for a wee while.'

'What? Of course, you can! Please don't cry, Ash. We will fix this!' My heart agonised for my best friend as I felt her pain. Raj stood with his hands on his hips, looking sympathetic.

'Take the day off and get some rest, Ashley,' he offered.

Ashley lifted her tearful face from my shoulder. 'What? Are you sure?'

'Of course!' Raj replied.

'Wouldn't you mind? I could go get some make-up on at Zara's, square myself up and come back in an hour or two?'

'No, I insist. Go to Zara's! I can drive you if you like.'

'I'll be fine walking. It's only round the corner. I'd better go before the clients come.' She sobbed again.

'I'll pop up at lunch if I can. Oh, here.' I delved my hand into my jeans pocket and handed Ashley my house keys.

'Thanks. I'm sorry, Raj.' She attempted a smile and left the clinic.

As the door shut, both Raj and I paused for a rare moment.

'God, I feel terrible for her.' I was in shock. I couldn't believe Ashley would own up to her escapades. Part of me felt proud of her, but part of me wondered why she'd be so fucking stupid. Her and Dave had been together for five years and I didn't think he'd break things off so abruptly.

'What did she expect to happen, Zara? She blew a guy off in the middle of the desert! She's not a wee lassie anymore.'

Raj was heading into a full-blown lecture, and I rolled my eyes.

'Yes, she made one mistake. But it doesn't make her a bad person. Besides, she didn't *have* to tell Dave,' I shrugged, trying my best to defend my friend.

'I know it doesn't make her a bad person; she's a great person. Fantastic, in fact. But her actions still have consequences. It's that simple.'

'Right, Da,' I snapped back, and he sneered.

'Come and get set up, Zara,' Raj said. 'We've got Ashley's job to do today now too.'

I went through to my clinic room, changed into my scrubs and got straight to work.

Between balancing my own duties and covering Ashley's, the morning passed quickly, and I was grateful not to have a fully booked schedule for the day. I helped with bookings, telephone enquiries, *and* still managed to message Cameron in between. Raj finished his last client of the morning and popped back onto the shop floor.

'How're tomorrow's appointments looking?' He looked concerned.

'Pretty blah, to be honest. Botox, Botox, lips, more Botox,' I replied, scrolling down the computer screen.

'And are we full?'

'Nope, not even half full. But hey, it is mid-week.'

'I bet them across the road is full.' He tilted his head towards Botox Boxx, sighed and walked back towards the staff room. 'Go for lunch, Zara. Take ten minutes extra if you're going home.'

'Awww, thanks, boss,' I yelled.

I grabbed my jacket from underneath the desk and made the short journey home. Heading up the stairwell, I started to feel apprehensive about what I was walking into. I had never seen Ashley like this before. She was always the strong friend who had her shit together. She was the one who picked me up from the gutter and I wasn't sure what I could do to make her feel better. I opened the door quietly and immediately spotted Ashley's feet sticking out the end of the sofa.

'Hey, babe, how are you feeling?' I said, trying my hardest to sound as compassionate as I could.

'Shite,' she answered sharply.

I went over to join her on the sofa. Her face was still red from tears and she looked miserable.

'Do you know he's not even texted me? He said this morning that I should come to stay here with you. Like, that's it done. His decision was so final.'

I squeezed my hips onto the couch and sat beside her, gazing into her distracted, troubled green eyes. 'You know you can stay here for however long you need too, right?'

Ashley nodded.

'He's blaming you, Zara.'

'WHAT!!!' I jumped up, feeling outraged.

'I know. Fucking bullshit,' Ashley said.

'Did you tell him I was the one who prised you off the cunt's dick?'

'No, I didn't. *Because* I only told him I kissed someone.' Ashley began sobbing again. 'I saw how he reacted with a kiss. A blow job admission was out of the question. What am I going to do?' She roared with tears, and my heart dropped for her. There was nothing I could do or say to fix this, so I just wrapped my arms around her and allowed her to sob into my shoulder.

'You know, we covered that in Dubai. It was a kiss of his dick – end of. All he needs to know.'

She started to giggle and broke free, shaking her head, sniffing the wandering snot back up her nose.

'Why the fuck does he think it's my fault, though, Ash?' I muttered.

'He said the way you've been acting recently, all the different men, it's putting ideas in my head.'

'I mean, wow.' I was speechless. I felt like I had been hit in the face with a judgemental frying pan. 'For fuck's sake. The grass isn't greener over this side of the dating game, Ash, and I'll tell anyone that.'

'I know. He just looked so angry. He was screaming that I'm a slut and a skank. I've honestly never seen him like that before.' She looked traumatised, reliving her worst nightmare.

'Then he simmered down for a bit, and I thought I was getting through to him. I swore it was just a kiss. He begged me to tell him who the guy was and when I said he played for Celtic, then honestly, holy fuck! I thought he was going to fucking chemically combust or something. That was all he had to hear. As soon as I dropped the green and white bomb, my bags were packed.'

I couldn't believe Ashley had gone through this while I was happily texting Cameron. I felt sick for her.

'You're braver than me. I can't believe you told him about the Celtic player. His pride must be dented.'

'Aye, with a sledgehammer.'

I thought hard. 'You know, I think I would have rather told him about the blow job than the Celtic thing, no joke!'

'Mate, I know that now. I just felt awful. I didn't want to lie to him.' She started to bubble again but took a long, deep breath, stopping herself from getting out of control.

'Will I ever feel normal again, Zara? I don't think I can be happy without him.' Her voice shook.

'Ash, you don't need a man to make you feel normal. Look at you.' I held my hands up in bewilderment.

'You're the fiercest person I know, literally. You're the sassiest bitch all on your own.' I squeezed her tightly.

'I know I am. But it's going to take me a while to remember how to be just me again. I live with him, eat, sleep and shag him. He's all I know. I hate just having me already.'

'And that's fine. We all lose ourselves from time to time. But you will never just have you as long as I'm here. Cheesy but true!' I leaned over and lightly kissed her forehead. 'Fuck, last year I couldn't wash or anything with everything that happened with Tom. Now look at me, young, free and happy!'

We were suddenly interrupted as my phone began to ring in my jacket pocket. I rolled my eyes, expecting an impatient Raj, but was pleasantly surprised to see Cameron's name appear. A smile radiated across my cheeks.

'Who is it?' Ashley questioned.

'Cameron!' I boasted.

'Eh, get it answered! Go! Go!' She wafted her hands up at me, and I answered the call, stepping through to my bedroom.

Cameron had just finished a stroll through the Turkish markets. He'd met up with one of his old workmates and they were planning a trip the following day to Istanbul to explore the capital and its culture. We chatted for around ten minutes before I reluctantly called an end to our chat, knowing I'd better check on Ashley. As I wandered back into the living room, I found her engrossed in *Keeping Up with the Kardashians*.

She sat up and looked at me. 'Well? What happened yesterday?'

'It was nice. We spoke for ages, laughed, drank hot chocolate and got on really well. He seems pretty amazing, to be honest.' I didn't want to praise my date too much when Ashley felt so low, but I couldn't help but break out in a huge grin, thinking of the stranger on the plane.

'The catch? There must be a catch?' she said, knowing my attention span for men rarely reached the forty-eight-hour mark.

'I suppose it's that he lives in Dubai . . .'

'So it's the "not being able to have him" element. There's always something with you, Zara,' she chuckled. 'Wait, where is he now, again?'

'Turkey – he's on leave from work and likes to travel. He's into sightseeing and exploring.'

Ashley cackled.

'To Turkey? Have you been to Turkey? Like, what's he exploring? The fake goods? Coz it's hardly the sightseeing holiday, is it?'

'He's not going to sit on a lounger in Marmaris, mate. He's travelling to Istanbul. The city is full of history.' I shot her a smug look, and she burst out laughing. 'What? Stop! What's so funny?'

'Istanbul? You know he'll be getting his gnashers done? No one has ever gone to Istanbul for a holiday, Zara, period. Like ever ever ever.'

'Well, Cameron is cultured and well-travelled with a respectable set of teeth already. Trust me, he's there for the city.'

'If you say so.' But Ashley laughed cynically, and I threw her a dirty look from across the room.

'Right, lunch, arsehole. What would you like?' I glanced down at my phone for the time. 'I have about twelve minutes before Raj has a flaky!'

I went into the kitchen and opened the fridge. *Shit.* Empty.

'I know what you're going to say. I've checked the cupboards already. It looks like it's a Monster Munch sandwich for us, eh?' Ashley said from the sofa.

My face twisted as I peeked inside the bread packaging, full of blue mould.

'Nope, you're wrong, babe. It looks like it's just a packet of Monster Munch – the bread's off.' I threw the crisp pack over to Ashley and headed for the door. 'See you tonight. I'll bring the shopping in!'

I rocketed back to the clinic, hoping to squeeze in a flirty text to Cameron, but found Raj swivelling restlessly on the stool behind the desk as I arrived.

'Hey, everything OK?' I asked.

'Hmm.' He was buried in thought.

'Raj?' I probed.

'Two cancellations this afternoon. I can't keep doing this, Zara. It's soul-destroying. You should just take the rest of the afternoon off. Be with Ashley or something.'

'What?' I was astounded. 'Have I done something wrong?'

Raj snapped out of his dwam and smiled.

'Of course not, but there's just no point in both of us being here. Spend the day with Ashley, get her back to her crazy self, and we can talk about social media strategy ideas next week. We're going to need something to turn this place around.' He looked dampened.

'You know, I could come in tomorrow and we could brainstorm together?' I offered.

Raj raised his eyebrows. 'I have a few scattered clients, don't be silly. Just enjoy your days off.'

'Or . . . I could do some research about the facial balancing idea I was—'

'Zara!' he snapped. 'Just take your days off. We'll talk about ideas next week with Andy and Ash. And I've already said before: facial balancing isn't suited to younger clients. Drop it.'

My face fell in disbelief. *Wow*. That was me told.

'Sure thing. See you Friday.' I turned around, opened the door and headed back out to the street.

What a dick! I thought, as I stormed across a bustling George Square. I mean, I knew things at work had quietened down since Botox Boxx had opened right across the street, but I never realised how stressed Raj was about it all. Then it occurred to me: maybe it was my fault? I stopped dead as I realised I was the most recent aesthetics practitioner hired. What if Raj was beginning to regret training me up altogether? There were never any issues booking enough clients when Tom worked with us. I found myself doubting my abilities more and more as my head scrambled, thinking up lips and cheeks that weren't up to scratch. What if Raj felt my work just wasn't as good as his, and that's why he told me to leave?

Before I knew it, my worried legs had cut off to the right of the square, and I was standing directly outside the window of Botox Boxx.

The clinic looked fresh, inviting and utterly packed full of younger clientele. A selfie station was set up in the corner, and customers were queued up to stand with the cardboard cut-out of Jackie Stallone holding the *'I'm with her'* props. My eyes squinted through the window, admiring the on-trend décor, from pink shaggy rugs to golden chandeliers to a spray-painted mural of Mona Lisa smoking a joint in the corner. Wow, I got it. I completely understood the buzz.

I moved closer, aching to examine their clinic rooms.

'Zara?' Andy had marched out of the clinic and collided straight into me.

'Andy, wow, hey,' I giggled clumsily.

'What are you doing here?' He began to laugh at how misplaced I looked.

I edged away from the window. 'Honestly?' I cringed. 'I was kind of spying.'

'On me?'

'Oh my god, no! No, not at all, sorry – on this clinic.' The words were pouring out of my mouth at a million miles per hour. 'This place is so cool and lively, and I suppose I wanted to know why!' I put my hands to my face, trying to conceal my rosy cheeks.

'Mon walk down here a wee bit before your cover gets blown, Bond,' Andy said, ushering me away from the window. 'What's going on?' he asked.

'Raj sent me home today; there's not enough work. And I thought I would have a look at the competition, you know. Suss them out.' I pretended to punch his arm jokingly, before realising how weird I must seem.

'You know,' Andy said, placing both hands on my shoulders, pulling me in and whispering in my ear, 'if you wanted to see inside it, you could have asked me to take photos. I could be your double agent!' He burst out laughing and started to walk again. I felt the hairs on the back of my neck stand up as the smell of his Creed Millésime lingered between us. 'I sell Juju products to them too, Zara,' he said.

'Would that be unethical?' I asked, walking alongside him. 'Besides, Raj said we'd all have a meeting about it next week.'

'No really. Fuck it, I won't tell if you don't. Do you know what it is – Raj's brand doesn't tailor to that age group. Maybe that's your problem. Botox Boxx is cool and hip; you guys are classy, high-end and—'

'Struggling, it seems!' I interrupted.

'I'll tell you what. I'll get my thinking cap on for you guys next week. The ad campaign shoot is out in a couple of months too and you're the fucking star! Honestly, your picture is *ooft!* They will be lining up at the door for you!' Andy stopped and leaned against his grey Mercedes casually; I couldn't help but admire the shape of his large muscular arms. 'So, hey, how was Dubai? I bet you're gutted to be back?'

I felt my face pulsate at Andy's compliment. 'Yeah, it was pretty amazing.' I smiled up towards his tall shadow.

'Any dramas or anything I need to know about?' he asked, raising his eyebrow suspiciously.

'Emmm . . .' I paused for a second. 'Nothing that comes to mind.'

He exploded into laughter. 'I don't believe that for a fucking minute!'

We continued to chat for a few more moments before he jumped into his car to head back to work. It felt so straightforward and effortless speaking to Andy. No airs or graces, no secret trips to the bathroom to google his vocabulary. Just basic Glaswegian patter, and I liked that.

After our goodbyes, I wandered round to Tesco, feeling much better about the clinic situation. I wondered if the problem was less to do with me, and more to do with our branding. Individualise seemed to cater more for the older age range of clients. Maybe the younger clientele wouldn't pay our prices? Or perhaps the luxury clinic vibe was less appealing to the younger market? I scooped a notepad and pack of scented gel pens from the shelf directly into my shopping basket. I was determined not to let Individualise go down without a fight.

Chapter Seventeen

After two days of stalking flourishing clinics on Insta, texting a potential boyfriend in Turkey, and emotionally consoling my best friend, I returned to the clinic bright-eyed and eager to get to work. I'd spent my days off YouTubing *'How to make a business stand out'* and had jotted down a few ideas about rebranding to attract a younger clientele. Raj had the weekend off, but I'd already briefed Ashley on the importance of an action-packed weekend with social media marketing and customer satisfaction being at the forefront.

Ashley had been relatively OK since splitting with Dave. She had her teary moments every so often where she would well up on the couch, but nothing compared to my pathetic, self-destructive experience last year. I was proud of how well she seemed to be coping. Although, every time her phone pinged, I could see her heart levitate out of her chest, then crash back down to the floor when she realised it wasn't Dave. She had sent him umpteen apology messages, voicemails and even an email just in case he blocked her number, but so far, she'd heard zilch back.

As we walked to work that Friday morning, I could see the weight of the world topple on my best friend's petite little shoulders.

'I'm so proud of how well you're coping, do you know that?' I studied Ashley's green eyes, which were watery and lifeless.

'I don't feel like I am coping, Zara. I feel terrible. I miss him so much, but what can I do?' she replied, shrugging her shoulders as we crossed over the street.

'Nothing. You'll hear from him when he's ready,' I said, trying to stay positive. 'You know, Emily's asking if she can pop by at lunchtime, hear the Dubai chat?'

I hadn't caught up with my sister since the holiday and had missed our weekly gossip brunch gathering.

'Yeah, cool. Just, please don't tell her about what happened, Zara – I don't want to talk about it anymore. OK?' Ashley said sternly.

'Yeah, of course. Sure!' I replied casually, trying to play down the event that had left her single and homeless.

In between my morning procedures, I began studying the Individualise client portfolios. I was on a mission to find out the average age of our customers and the treatments they preferred. I called a few of our regulars, finding out how they initially heard of Individualise and asked them for ideas on what they would recommend to improve our clinic. I was on a fucking roll. My hand was throbbing from writing and researching. I hadn't done any data analysing since leaving school, but I felt invigorated and determined to turn this place around. I couldn't wait to share my findings with Raj.

Emily popped in around half twelve, and I was pleased to see Ashley smile for the first time in days.

'Hey, guys,' Emily greeted us, radiating positive energy as she walked through the door laden with sandwiches and drinks.

'Ahhhh, I've missed you, Em.' I hugged my sister tightly, and Ashley followed a second behind.

'Where's your tan, Zara?' she giggled as the three of us headed into the staff room to start dishing out lunch.

I smirked at my sister, who always seemed to have the better skin tone. Not to mention the better hair, teeth, hygiene and brains overall, but I did take pride in inheriting the family's humour.

'God, I must have left it in Dubai, along with your present. Whoops!' I stuck my middle finger up at her before unscrewing the bottle of diet Irn Bru she'd delivered.

'That's cool. You can transfer me a fiver for your lunch then, eh,' she shot back as Ashley tittered.

'Stop! How're things with you, Em?' Ashley asked.

Emily huffed, unravelling a salad roll. 'Work, gym, kids. Basic! But I want to know all about Dubai! I haven't been since my honeymoon! Make me jealous!' she gushed.

'Well . . . erm . . .' Ashley and I stared at one another. I was scared to start spilling in case I dropped something she didn't want me too.

'Well . . . Zara met a guy!' she blurted.

'Shut up! A guy who you're still talking to?' Emily looked shocked, and I couldn't help but feel slightly offended.

'Erm, yes, who I'm still talking to!' I snapped back. 'His name is Cameron, and he's a fucking babe. Oh, and . . .' I pulled my shoulders back cockily. 'He's a bodyguard!'

'Noooo way!' Emily gasped and turned to Ashley, who was nodding her head in confirmation.

'To who? Like who does he guard?' she demanded.

'Well, different folk like . . . eh . . . diplomats and . . .' I tried to think back, wondering if Cameron and I had covered this chat on the flight or if I was too distracted by his protruding biceps and bulging crotch.

'No, to a French guy who almost pumped your sister!' Ashley burst out laughing, and I joined in briefly while Emily looked utterly confused.

'Stop!' I snorted, trying hard not to choke on my chicken tikka sandwich. 'He basically works for an agency and guards whoever needs protecting at the time. Hot though, eh?'

'But he stays in Dubai,' Ashley said, shattering my vision.

'*Yes*, but he is currently on holiday in Turkey. We're talking like twenty-four hours a day. He phoned me last night for like two hours.' I stuck out my bottom lip, feeling nostalgic for my late-night call with Cameron.

'So, like, have you done anything? Like anything physical?' Emily enquired.

'Eh, no. We met on the plane on the way home from holiday. We went for hot chocolate afterwards, and he asked me not to see anyone else until we work out what's going to happen with us.'

'Wow, Zara. I'm shocked. Like a good shocked, but still shocked.' We paused briefly, all munching on our food, then Emily continued, 'So you haven't even seen a picture of his dick or anything sexual?'

I giggled. 'Well . . .'

My friends joined in immediately.

'Last night, he said he was getting horny, right? I sent him the overedited unbuttoned booby pyjama picture, one of my favourites from the archives. The poor cunt had no idea – he thought it was just for him. Anyway, the conversation was growing heated, like . . . what he wanted to do to me and all this. I told him to send me a sexy picture of him, but he didn't want to. He doesn't take selfies or any of that shit, but I was saying it's not your face I want to see.' I rolled my eyes as my friends listened intently. 'So, he sent me a picture of like his rock-hard abs and his dick – sort of.'

The two of them gawked, waiting for further information.

'Well, he put an emoji over his penis, so I couldn't actually see it.' I held up my hands disappointedly.

'No!' Ashley gasped, looking slightly disgusted. 'That's weird, Zara. Do you not think, Emily?'

Emily swayed her head from side to side.

'I'm not sure. Maybe he's just shy?' She shrugged.

'Or, more likely, he has a tiny penis.' She held up her pinky finger, waggling it around. 'What emoji did he use?'

I grinned. 'The wee guy with the shades!' As soon as the words left my mouth, I shut my eyes, cringing for poor Cameron.

'Noooo. He thinks he's been cool. Ditch him, Zara. Creepy!' Ashley said.

'But I like him. He's sweet and kind and so fucking sexy. Plus, he said he's going to try and re-route his travel plans and visit me soon! Is that not the most fairy tale-like thing you've ever heard?' I tried my hardest to stick up for my latest flame.

'No, I think you're right, Zara. I say go for it! I've not seen you like this with anyone since Tom, and . . .'

Both Ashley and I erupted into hilarity, and I turned back to face my sister.

'About Tom . . . You'll never guess what happened!' I said.

We spent the remaining lunch break chatting about Tom and the photoshoot in Dubai. Emily was in her element, and it felt great to watch Ashley become animated as she shared the gossip with me, having a slight distraction from her heartache with Dave.

The rest of the afternoon was slow. Yet again, we had further cancellations. Ashley asked the clients to rebook but they all had similar excuses: they'd call back later, or they couldn't afford the treatments just now and so on. The social media drive Ashley had promised was lacking, but I didn't want to push her when she already felt so shitty. I spent a large part of the afternoon staring jealously through the damp square towards the high activity going on in Botox Boxx. I returned to my notepad, writing down ideas, competition plans, and statistics. I felt my optimism dwindle as the day progressed and began to feel more intimidated at the edgy new competition from across the road. Despite this, I had a plan and I couldn't wait to share it with Raj and hopefully get him on board.

Cameron's day seemed less gloomy than mine as he sent scenic photographs of Istanbul combined with cute messages about how pretty my WhatsApp profile picture looked. This pleased me, as I had changed it about twenty fucking times that day, all for his benefit.

Ping.

I was in the middle of a YouTube seach for '*How to turn your business around in 24 hrs*' when another WhatsApp from Cameron came through.

So, what if I told u I had booked a flight to Glasgow on Tuesday? Would that b crazy?? xx

My stomach flipped, and I screeched.

Ashley jolted upwards, looking concerned, but I couldn't engage with her. I was fixated on my screen. I typed quickly.

Please say you mean it!!! OMG, so crazy but so AMAZ-ING!! xx

I was practically panting with excitement, refreshing my phone screen every few seconds as I waited for his reply.

'Zara, for fuck's sake, what's up?' Ashley was stomping her feet like an impatient child in a bid to get noticed.

'Shhhh, Ash. I think Cameron's booked a flight for Glasgow!' I yelled. 'Oh my god, he's typing! Shhhh. He's typing!' I was out of my seat, jumping up and down.

'AHHHHHH! Shut the fuck up! For when? When?' She bounced up and down with me.

I mean it Zara! See you Tuesday bby! I don't have a date to restart work (as yet)so it looks like you'll have me for a few days at least xx

I started squealing as my eyes skimmed the message. 'He's staying for a few days! Mate!' I was thrusting the air jokingly.

'Oh my god! What the actual fuck! This is a big step, Zara. Are you sure about this?'

'Of course I'm bloody sure, Ash! Please get on board with this!'

I didn't have time for Ashley's concerns to dampen my mood. I got it, and I knew this wasn't the best timing for me to find someone given her circumstance with Dave, but I needed to take my chance. I felt unbelievably nervous and extremely apprehensive, yet happy and outrageously excited all swirled into one. *Someone* was flying halfway across the world just to see *me*.

Chapter Eighteen

Tuesday seemed to come around exceptionally quick. Ashley and I spent the weekend hauling bags of old bobbled clothes from my wardrobe to charity shops, striving to create space for her things. We double hung and squeezed as much clothing as we could back into my wardrobe and drawers. Then, together, we scrubbed the flat, took out the bins and even changed the old crumby bedcovers, all to make way for my special visitor, Cameron.

My stomach appeared slightly less flabby as I scrutinised it in the bedroom mirror that particular morning. I had, after all, participated in a dramatic four hundred calorie per day deficit. The idea of stripping down naked for my Mr Muscle was horrifying me, and I could feel my anxieties build. I had gotten used to stripping quickly with confidence, not giving one single fuck what my Tinder fuck boys were thinking. If they judged my body or not, I didn't care, the only thing I desired was a big old orgasm, and a commitment-free one-nighter. However, today was different, Cameron was different, and I wholly accepted the likelihood that when he saw my cellulite jiggle and my hairy big toe wiggle, he would be on the quickest flight back to the United Arab Emirates.

I was nauseous at the concept of seeing him again, but I couldn't help but feel swept away by such a bold move. I didn't want to get too excited, but no one had ever done something so romantic for me before. Fuck, I couldn't even get Tom to acknowledge me in the hospital canteen and this cunt was flying across an entire continent just to see me. I hadn't wanted to make anything work with anyone else until now. I felt goosebumps climb up my arm just thinking about his stunningly handsome face. He had the most muscular arms, perfect dimpled cheeks hidden behind the macho beard, and today I'd finally get to explore what was underneath that emoji, and I couldn't fucking wait. I pictured seeing him at the airport and leaping towards him like they do in the movies. He'd drop his luggage and spin me around. I imagined taking him back to my house and allowing him to undress me slowly, throwing me onto the bed then pleasuring me with his turbulent tongue. I had thought of it all. Every single part. Hours upon hours of phone calls finally came down to this day.

I woke early that morning, butterflies prancing around my belly. My fake bake had developed nicely, and within half an hour, I was freshly showered and smothered in Molton Brown moisturiser. I planned to collect Cameron from the airport at five, which meant I had to organise my work outfit around an appropriate number to pick him up in as well. Something sophisticated but sexy. After much deliberation over the weekend and a two-hour late-night catwalk show in my living room, Ashley and I decided on a black V-neck knee-length dress teamed up with a blazer. My rollers were in, and after I showered, I released them, revealing bouncy luscious locks. My pubes were eradicated, and a generous amount of Femfresh was slathered over my poontang, guaranteeing a healthy pH balance fit for an excellent late-night kebab munching.

I felt unusually organised for such sexual events. I hadn't had my usual quota of men since ditching Tinder, and I was looking forward to a meaningful shag. All that was left to do now was go to work and stay focused on saving Individualise. At ten to nine, Ashley and I hovered, having one last studious look at the flat. She had pyjamas and a change of work clothes stuffed in her favourite Chantelle case ready for an overnight at Emily's to give me and Cameron time alone.

'What do you think? Looks OK, doesn't it?'

She tilted her head. 'Yeah, not bad. One last Febreze before work?' she suggested.

'Go for it!'

Ashley dashed through the flat, clip-clopping in her heels as she over-spritzed the fabric refresher.

Coughing on the fumes, we left the fresh yet misty flat behind.

'How are you feeling, Zara?' Ashley asked as we left the close.

'I feel . . . worried. What if he doesn't like me? What if he doesn't fancy me? What if—'

Ashley let out an almighty groan. 'And what if he does? Don't ruin this moment because of your insecurities! Fucking own it, man.' She stopped in the street and turned to face me head-on. 'Maybe I've been distracted and a tiny smidge jealous of this relationship forming with everything that's going on with me, and I'm so sorry. But as your best friend, I understand you need regular pep talks and I've been off my game recently, so here it is, listen – OK? There is a man – a fucking hot, stunning man – who is leaving a warm country to spend a few days with you in this cold wet city! God, he only met you for a few hours, Zara, and he's already smitten. And to be honest, I don't blame him. You're fucking fabulous. Now, push back your shoulders and just *be* confident. I'm so sick of your negative body chat. It's exhausting. You attract what you feel, remember?'

I paused for a second, taking on board how inconsiderate I must have sounded since arriving home from Dubai, finding any excuse, twenty-four hours a day, just to mention Cameron's name when Ashley's been in torture.

'He sounds like a keeper. In fact, I know it! So, stop for one second, and believe that you deserve this shit. I don't want to hear one more negative thing leave your lips today, OK?' Ashley's warm, excitable grin was contagious, and I felt reassured after her lecture.

'OK, you're right!' I rested my head on her shoulder. 'Ashley, thank you and I'm sorry if I kept going on and on about him. I don't know what I'd do without you,' I said, and we walked arm in arm to the clinic.

Raj was sitting on the sofa, engrossed in his phone as we arrived.

'Morning. How's my girls?' Thank fuck he appeared to be in a better mood than the last time I'd seen him.

'Morning, boss! Good thanks,' I grinned.

Raj looked up from his screen. 'Holy shit, Zara, you look phenomenal! What's the occasion? Oh, wait.' He started to giggle.

'Why are you laughing?'

'It's because Andy's coming for the meeting, isn't it?' He shook his head, tittering to himself.

'Andy? Ha, *no, no, no*. This,' I pointed to my carefully selected outfit, 'is all for my handsome, stunning, ripped, bodyguard man, who is flying into Glasgow because he misses me so much. *Yes*, Raj. Cameron from the plane is coming to town! And we're almost an item,' I was boasting, slightly exaggerating my relationship with Cameron to wipe the smirk off Raj's face.

'No shit!' His face fell in disbelief. 'He's really coming back for you?'

Ashley tutted. 'And why wouldn't he? Fucking look at her, mate!'

I smiled gratefully at my friend and turned back to Raj. 'Yes, he is. Tonight at five, and he's staying for a few days!'

'God, your gaff is filling up fast with all these home-less folk.' Raj raised his eyebrows at Ashley, who darted an evil stare back.

'No, Ash is staying with Emily tonight, giving us some alone time,' I winked. 'And then she'll need to crash on my sofa until he heads back to Dubai.'

Raj looked stunned, like he had missed out on so much drama. He stood up and began pacing the clinic floor. 'So, long term, you think this is going to work?'

Ashley cleared her throat to grab my attention before I responded, and as I glanced over to her, she mouthed *POSITIVE*. I couldn't help but smile.

'Raj, I know this is going to work. We're perfect for one another, and Dubai is only a few hours away on a flight. It's no big deal!'

Right at that moment, the door swung open and Andy burst in.

'What's happnin', troops?' He was wearing the pale blue Ralph Lauren shirt I loved, as his tattooed sleeve would still be visible through the light-coloured material. I started to twiddle with my hair and pout seductively as much as I could.

'You OK, Zara?' he asked, walking by.

I looked curious. 'Yeah?'

'Aw, sound. I thought you were ready to sneeze. You bunged up?'

I watched him make his way towards the sofa.

'Yeah. Oh, oh, achoo.' I rolled my eyes at the sheer embarrassment of hitting a new low of faking a sneeze because I looked so much like a dick trying to pout.

'Wow, you bouncin' doon the dancing tonight, Zara?' Andy gave me and my overdressed appearance a suspicious look.

'She's not bouncing down the dancing, but she will be bouncing!' Ashley exclaimed, and Raj erupted into laughter.

'Guys!' I blushed.

'Sorry, Andy. Zara met a guy in Dubai, and he's coming back to Glasgow today to stay with her. Don't ask her questions. She's far too much in love at the moment to take straightforward criticism or accept any what ifs,' Raj said, pushing his hands through his hair and taking a seat again.

'For god's sake!' I could feel my cheeks growing hot as I watched Andy giggle with my friends. 'It's nothing serious! Stop it.'

'Nothing serious? She's literally just told me how perfect they are together.' Raj let out an almighty laugh. 'Ahhh, Zara, you crack me up. Come sit and let's get this started, eh.'

My hands shook with humiliation as I thumbed through my bag for my notepad, feeling embarrassed that Andy had just witnessed that conversation. I wanted him to take me seriously and understand how professional I've been, gathering my research for today. My phone pinged, and I slid my finger across the home screen.

One new message from Cameron.

Good morning baby. Can you talk? I have a confession about something. Ps can't wait to see you xx

I felt my face drop. I grabbed my phone and sat down on the sofa. Andy went through the sales figures for the month, and then the meeting began. I remained engrossed by my screen, rapidly typing. What the fuck did he have to confess?

Morning! Oh no, what's up? I can't talk but I can text! Can't wait to see you too xx

I rested my phone on my knee and attempted to concentrate on the analysis Andy had prepared for us all. I was nodding, agreeing with his advice but taking absolutely nothing in, too busy refreshing my screen every spare second that I could. The others cut me a few glances as I fidgeted. I was beginning to sweat. *What if he's still married? Or perhaps he's changed his mind about me?* My legs started bouncing around nervously. I couldn't stand the heat. I stood up and peeled my blazer off my perspiring pits.

Ping.

Fucking finally! All I could hope was that my fantasy hadn't fallen apart.

OK! Well, I didn't go to Turkey for a holiday – I had a small procedure! I might look a wee bit different for you 😣 *xx*

I let out an almighty sigh. The group turned to me, and I wafted myself with my notebook.

'Sorry, guys, I'm just warm,' I mumbled, feeling an overwhelming sense of relief. When their focus returned to Andy, I picked up my phone again.

I kind of thought you did! Well, Ashley did! Haha she said no one goes to Istanbul for anything else. You will look hot regardless, but I didn't think you needed them done! Just at a meeting, will call you afterwards xxx

I raised my head, finally able to concentrate and incorporate my figures, when Andy peered over.

'What do you think about that, Zara?'

Shit. I had no idea what I was supposed to be thinking about but noticed Ashley nodding eagerly behind him trying to give me a sign.

'I think, eh . . . I think it's a great idea!' I tried my hardest to sound convincing.

'Amazing! Just when you said your boyfriend lived out there, then I thought why not, eh? So it would be four weeks to begin with, great pay, stunnin' hotel, and you're only talking five- or six-hour workdays. Piece a' piss. Great coverage for your social media and things!' Andy looked excited.

'Wait. What? Sorry, I'm lost. You want us all to go back to Dubai? To work?'

'No, just you. For the four weeks initially, which will probably continue, as of next Friday.'

My heart hammered in my chest.

'Four weeks is an awfully long time. It's like—'

'It's like . . . an amazing opportunity, Zara,' Raj interrupted. 'You would represent us, the first recognised clinic to collaborate with Juju independently. They won't just be selling us product anymore, you'd be over there with Juju, working as their brand ambassador. Individualise will be part of huge marketing campaigns. Fuck, they make over ninety per cent of all filler worldwide. This is a really big deal. Andy's pulled it out of the bag for us.' He looked up at Andy gratefully, as if he had just handed him a golden fucking vagina.

How would I cope for so long away from everyone? Fuck, the heat over there did not agree with my peely wally skin tone. I felt like my friends had made this massive decision for me and hadn't given me a second to decide for myself.

'Zara, Juju have over two million followers, plus you have Cameron out there. You could make a real go of it,' Ashley said, but the whole moving away thing still had me taken aback.

'But what about all my clients here? You work in the hospital some days, Raj, and we can't cancel them. We don't want to lose real customers while gaining social media followers in Dubai.'

I could see the cogs turn in his head.

'You're right – absolutely. I'll just have to get a temp, someone who can fill in for a few weeks. It's too good an opportunity to miss.'

'You mean Tom, don't you? You'll ask Tom?' I replied.

Raj looked uneasy. 'Well, I'm not sure. Realistically it does make sense – he knows the clients, how we operate, and it would only be for four weeks, well initally. I'm sure he'd help us out, and it's not as if you'll have to see him.'

'Thank fuck for that,' I snapped back immaturely.

The room fell silent, and Andy cleared his throat.

'So, are you up for this, Zara?'

I laughed, uncertain of what I thought of it all. The fact Raj had picked Tom out as my replacement all in a matter of seconds hurt. Maybe he wanted me out, and this was an easy option. After all, the clinic was busier when Tom was here. The only plus side for me was Cameron, but I hadn't even consulted him about this life-changing decision. I glanced up and Raj was nodding his head eagerly. Then Ashley, who appeared captivated by their plan.

'Well, it looks like I'm going to Dubai! Woo!' I tried my hardest to sound pleased, raising my fist in the air, but my heart plummeted inside; maybe Cameron wouldn't want me there. It was a massive step, and he'd probably think I'm nuts following him to his country of residence like a love-struck immature teenager. I had a sudden flashback of starting my placement on Tom's ward last year, and how it ultimately ruined our relationship. Fuck, I didn't even know if I enjoyed Dubai. I struggled with the heat for a weekend over there, never mind four weeks. I looked at Raj, who was clapping his hands happily, as if a weight had been lifted from his shoulders.

'Does anyone have any other suggestions or plans they want to discuss?' He scanned the room. 'Zara, what were you working on?'

'Nope, I'm all good. It's honestly nothing,' I replied, keeping my notebook firmly shut over.

There was no way I could reveal my research now. What was the point? I'd be injecting famous influencers in Dubai while Raj and Tom profited from more clients back in Glasgow. My plan was much less extravagant than that.

The meeting carried on longer than planned as Andy explained the technical information on working with aesthetics in Dubai. He outlined a list of colleagues from Juju who would be supporting me throughout my visit and where I'd be living. When the meeting finally finished, my head was bursting and I felt defeated. Andy collected his folder, and we waved him out the door.

'I'm so excited for you, Zara!' Ashley whizzed over to me, wrapping her arms around me tightly.

I attempted to look happy and hugged her back.

'You're really helping us out, Zara. I'm so grateful. Do you know that?' Raj added.

My eyes filled up, and I took deep breaths, trying to conceal my emotions.

'Hey, what's up?' Ashley asked.

'What's up? Are you OK?' Raj marched over and kneeled to my level.

I was wiping away the stray tears carefully, not wanting to ruin my make-up but feeling embarrassed at my outburst.

'I'm OK. I do want to try things with Cameron, but I just feel a bit pushed out. I don't know what I'll do without you guys for god knows how long. And what if . . . well, what if you prefer Tom working here rather than me when I get back, and what if I lose my job?' I sobbed loudly, no longer able to hold back the tears.

Raj laughed and pulled me into his shoulder.

'Tom couldn't lace your boots, kid. You have nothing to be worried about. Listen, if you don't want to go, we'll think up another plan. I don't want you to be upset. We just thought with your almost-boyfriend being over there that it was a win-win situation.'

'You think it'll really help the clinic?' I bubbled.

Raj shut his eyes briefly and kissed the top of my head. 'I really do.'

I tried hard to grin. 'I'll do it. But I want daily FaceTime and constant reminders of how much you want me back.'

'Done.' Raj giggled and Ashley sniffled, struggling to hold back the tears.

'Don't you fucking start now!' he huffed.

The reality of leaving my friends, my home and my job to move halfway across the world was slowly sinking in. I didn't have a time frame on this new venture and part of me felt disappointed that I hadn't shared my pitching idea. Everyone seemed so pleased about Andy's elaborate plan. We sat there chatting about the endless possibilities that collaborating with Juju could mean for Individualise. When we had finished, I picked up my phone.

One new message from Cameron.

Getting on the plane. See you soon beautiful!!!!! xxx

My heart began fluttering once more. If Cameron could fly halfway across the world to see me, perhaps I should return the favour. I smiled as I allowed some of the positives to swell in my head. Maybe this was the universe's way of bringing me closer to him as well as helping the clinic at the same time. I was undeniably apprehensive but, for the moment, enthusiastic about what the future might hold. Maybe Ashley was right, and if Cameron was the one for me, living in the same city under the sun would be a pretty perfect way to begin our journey.

Chapter Nineteen

Before I knew it, it was 5 p.m. and I was pacing the arrivals hall of the packed Glasgow International Airport, scanning the screens as updates flashed up. Cameron's flight UAE113 had landed at 4.20 p.m. so he would be here any minute. My mouth felt dry, and my breathing was rapid. Why the fuck did I think this was a rational decision? Ashley was demanding updates, but I couldn't concentrate. I was beginning to forget what the hot cunt looked like, wondering how much more handsome he could possibly get with his new set of gnashers. Every person that strutted out of that arrivals hall made my stomach drop and arsehole twinge with nerves, and as soon as I realised it wasn't him, I'd let out an enormous sigh of relief. I wasn't ready for this. What would I say to him? The questions and self-doubt began to flood my mind.

Hey, Cameron, how are you? Nope too basic. *Hey, Cammy, how was the trip?* No, too casual. *Hey, sexy, I've missed you!* My ideas were getting worse the more I panicked, and I eventually reached for my phone, hoping for a last-minute pep talk from Ashley.

'Zara? How are you?'

I looked up to see a tall bald man standing in front of me. Everything about his face seemed swollen and completely distorted, and he had the most enormous head I had ever seen. His eyes were so puffy and bloodshot he looked like he'd gone ten rounds with Ricky Burns.

'Hi,' I replied politely, trying my best to recollect him in my fuzzy, distracted brain while watching over his shoulder, still keeping an eye out for Cameron.

He continued to grin down at me, and the expression seemed to cause him pain as his face grew tighter. I couldn't think of how I knew him at all. God, his face was humungous. I gasped as I wondered if the poor cunt was perhaps in full-blown anaphylaxis, and I was just standing there observing.

'You don't recognise me, do you?' He sighed disappointedly, and looked at the floor.

I also glanced down, trying my best to avoid staring any longer. Then I spotted his luggage – a khaki green holdall, the same as the one Cameron had on the flight back from Dubai. My head snapped up to examine the bald man before me, and as it all came together, I let out an almighty gasp.

'*Cameron*?' I held my hands up, wondering what had happened to my hot hunk from the Highlands.

'I know, I know. I'm pretty scary. I'm so swollen. I think the pressure from the plane's made it worse.'

I was frozen, completely fixated on his gigantic face and trying my hardest to see some resemblance of the handsome man I'd met.

'I'm sorry, I can't believe it, it's just . . . all of this is from veneers?' My voice was incredibly high-pitched as I was in complete shock. How did such a handsome man leave last week, and Quasimodo return?

Cameron attempted to laugh but his eyes closed over and wholly disappeared into his mangled mush.

'My teeth? What? No, Zara, I had a hair transplant. Why, do you think I have something wrong with my teeth?' He held his hand over his mouth insecurely.

I reached for his hand, wanting to comfort him about the miscommunication. 'No, not at all. And your hair was fine too. This is all just a shock for me. A bit of warning would have been better, maybe a FaceTime,' I giggled.

Cameron agreed and looked embarrassed. 'I'm so sorry. My head wasn't anywhere near as big as this when I left Turkey. I'm mortified you didn't recognise me, Zara.' He turned his head to the side but it looked just as big from every angle. 'I imagined you standing there with a little sign to pick me up and a friendly welcome. This was a bad idea. I'm so sorry.'

I looked at his Bo' Selecta face, all puffy and bald. Behind that inflammation was still the kind, warm guy I met on the plane, and I couldn't help but feel like I still wanted him to stay.

'I'm so glad you're here, Cameron. This is sweet and cute. It just took me by surprise. I love the fact you've flown across Europe with your head so raw, and wow, it must be absolutely throbbing, which kind of makes all of this even sweeter.' I paused and smirked. 'I'm still into this. That's what I'm trying to say.'

Cameron held out his hand for me to take and kissed mine gently.

'Really?'

I nodded. 'Of course, I've been counting down the days till I saw you again.'

'Me too, he said. 'Let me just turn this phone off and enjoy every minute with you,' he reached into his pocket, switched off his phone and smiled towards me.

We wandered through the airport to the taxi rank like Beauty and the Beast. I spotted holidaymakers gasping in horror as they spotted Cameron. He didn't seem to notice the stares or the kids wailing with terror; he was oblivious and laid-back. I was thrilled he was here, but part of me felt disheartened. I just wanted one aspect of my life to go smoothly, but the only thing that was smooth in this situation was Cameron's ever-expanding, red-raw, entirely hairless coupon.

We travelled home in the taxi and laughed about the misunderstanding. Then, as I led Cameron up the stairwell to my flat, he suddenly seemed nervous.

'Zara.' He cleared his throat. 'I've not stopped thinking about you since the moment I met you.' His strong Highland accent echoed up the close, and I immediately blushed and turned to face him.

'Awww. Me too.'

We stared at one another on the staircase, then he leaned towards me for a kiss. His lips were soft and tender. A rush of warmth and happiness subdued my body. Cameron lowered his holdall and ran his fingers through my hair. The moment felt perfect and natural, and although I didn't know Cameron very much at all, once again I felt that strange comfort with him.

The kissing came to a halt, and I giggled and nudged him into my immaculate home.

'This is it!' I declared, shrugging my shoulders, still feeling his touch linger on my lips.

'It's fantastic, right in the town centre too.' Cameron seemed impressed as he roamed the living area.

'So, Ashley will be back tomorrow night. She'll sleep on the couch, obviously,' I said.

Cameron smiled. 'Of course. She seems fun!'

I made my way over to the kitchen for a drink of water, feeling parched from all the kissing. 'Can I get you a drink?'

Cameron placed his bag down and walked towards me at the sink. I turned my body round to face him, and he bent down to hug me, then suddenly lifted me onto the worktop. His teeth glistened cheekily behind his swollen face.

'I have been on that plane for five hours, and all I've thought about is how blinking amazing it will be to strip you down. I want to make love to you, Zara, all day and all night.'

He was only a few inches off my face, and I felt his breath bounce off my skin as he spoke. I relished it. He wanted to *make love* to me! Was Cameron trying to tell me something? Normally this phrase would make me run for the Campsies but I thrived on it with him. I wrapped my arms tightly around his neck and started to kiss him more aggressively.

'Ohhh, gentle. Gentle with my head,' he whimpered.

Cameron's hands began to massage my thighs. My body squirmed as I felt him get closer to my voracious vagina.

'Am I going too fast?'

I shook my head, feeling like he'd almost hypnotised me. Then, I tugged my dress upward around my waist giving him more room to explore. He moved his hand closer to my vagina, and his thumb began rubbing through my underwear in circular motions. My breathing turned short and sharp.

'Do you want to go into the bedroom?' I asked, still squirming from all the kissing. Cameron didn't reply, but with a tug I was being lifted towards my boudoir.

He held me up, kissing passionately, then lowered me to the ground. I started to unzip my dress and dived under the covers, watching him strip down. His body was toned, and I could see a glimmer of abs as he lifted his top up over his torso. *Jesus,* he was fitter in person. My chest thumped as Cameron walked towards me with purpose burning in his eyes. His dick looked hard and ready for action under his crisp white boxers. He stood for a second, then pulled down his underwear as my eyes lit up. No micropenis! *Thank fuck.* I mean, it wasn't the largest dick in the world, small- to medium-sized with a smallish girth, more of a baby carrot than a micro dick. Cameron pulled back the covers. His expression was hard to gauge with the trauma, but I'm sure I recognised a grin as he then soared on top and, without a word uttered, began to thrust his dick inside of me. In and out he stirred, and I moaned each time.

'Mmmmm . . . Fuck me. Fuck me,' I murmured.

Cameron still hadn't said a word. He put the graft in but his eyes remained fixed on the headboard. Everything felt good but something about it was disconnected. Was he shy? Or perhaps in pain from his immense head wound? I hauled him closer, kissing him while he continued to thrust in and out of me.

'Oh sorry.' His dick fell out. I looked down, smiling and he fumbled a little, pushing to reposition it and eventually continued. Without warning, Cameron finished with a tiny whimper, pulled out his dick, and kissed my forehead.

'Wow!' he said.

I rolled over to kiss the sweaty man lying in my bed.

'You were amazing!' he said, kissing me back, then elevated his arm, gesturing for me to lie on him. *I mean thanks, but I didn't have to do much*, I thought. As I snuggled in, however, I felt peaceful and strangely relaxed. I couldn't believe how natural it felt lying in the arms of a man I had just met. Yes, the first-time sex was basic, but I supposed he was used to marital sex, and we presumably needed to find our groove a little more. I mean, it wasn't bad, but perhaps a little less exciting than the late-night fuckboy hook-ups I had been accustomed to. Maybe this was normal, and I was the overexperienced kinky one? I wasn't sure. But I knew I liked him, boringly quick sex regardless. I wanted this to work.

'Cameron?' I whispered, still slightly panting for breath as we both faced the ceiling.

'Zara?'

'So, today, I found out something in that meeting I was telling you about. I didn't have any idea about it before today so don't think I've been keeping it from you. But, as of next Friday, I'll be working in Dubai!' I could feel my eyes squint with dread, not knowing how Cameron would take the news. When I told the last man I was seeing I was coming to work beside him, he threw a wobbler, and I uncovered his secret love affair.

Cameron sat up, plopping my head flat on the mattress, and looked into my eyes.

'You're joking!'

I shook my head, still finding it difficult to make sense of his wonky expressions.

'Zara, that's bloody amazing!' His smile lit up the room, and he seemed thrilled. I felt a surge of relief.

'I wasn't sure how you would take it. And it's not like you're obliged to see me every day or at all, even. It's a work thing. I don't want you to think that I'm following you or stalking you. But, oh god, I'm so glad you're happy! Phew!'

Cameron started to laugh, leaning down on me. I could feel his hot sexy body sticking to mine.

'I have just flown hundreds of miles to see you. If anyone is a stalker, it's me. This is great news.' He kissed my forehead and snuggled into me.

That night we ordered a Chinese takeaway, watched *The Wolf of Wall Street* and made love twice more. I shut my eyes at midnight, and for the first time in months,

I felt content. Somehow, Cameron seemed different from the previous men I had dated. He seemed interested in me as a person, not only in what was between my legs, and I was finally willing to let someone in. If mediocre sex was a price I had to pay for having a thoughtful, loving, kind man then I'd happily take it. My head whirled around with hopes and dreams of how we were about to spend the next month together in Dubai, and all of a sudden, my anxieties of leaving were gone and I couldn't fucking wait!

Chapter Twenty

The following morning Cameron and I lay around the flat, spending my time off tangled in one another's arms. We watched the series *Shooter* on Netflix, which I recommended because of his sniper days in the army, but secretly was just craving a Ryan Phillippe fix. We ordered pancakes from Just Eat and got to know each other better. Cameron described his plans to settle down and have kids soon, and I felt utterly swept away by everything he said. More than ever, I wanted his visions to include me, as I daydreamed on the sofa beside him, hoping our kids had his colouring with my strong hair line. In the afternoon, he put on a YouTube documentary about Dubai, educating me on the most wondrous experiences I would be undertaking with him in the next few weeks. He promised to arrange skydiving, desert safaris, and even hiring a yacht for the day. I suddenly felt ridiculous that the weekend I had just spent in Dubai with my friends consisted of far too much alcohol, prising my best friend's jaw from a footballer's penis and getting thrown out of a penthouse when all of this was on offer. I wasn't an adrenaline junkie by any means, but the way Cameron spoke with passion about experiencing new things and pushing personal boundaries made me want to try anything with him.

His swelling seemed to be going down a little, and I reminded him to take regular anti-inflammatories and pain meds. He frequently had to layer up a concoction of creams and apply it to his head. I found myself watching him throughout the day, wholly engrossed in the television even with his painful face, and couldn't help but relish how adorable and innocent he looked. I admired his confidence above all. God, if I was due an eyebrow wax or a root touch-up, I could never go on a date, never mind rocking up with an overgrown tatty growing out my head. I found it admirable, and I felt utterly smitten regardless of his look. Everything seemed to be going to plan. It was easy, uncomplicated and peaceful.

The front door buzzer rang around 7 p.m. We were slumped into the sofa with Doritos and dip, and I immediately remembered about Ashley. I hadn't checked my phone since picking Cameron up from the airport, feeling slightly guilty because he had switched his off to enjoy our time together, but with the loud buzz I was shot back to reality.

'Oh, shit. That'll be Ashley!' I announced, throwing my legs off Cameron and standing up.

He smiled and stood behind me, getting prepared.

I hurried over to the buzzer.

'Hey, come on up, Ash. Door's open!' I said in my friendliest voice. Usually, we would greet each other with grunts or funny insults, but I wanted to be on my best behaviour in front of my new bae.

I quickly felt apprehensive. This was a big moment, my best friend meeting my kind-of-boyfriend properly. I heard her footsteps echo up the close, and opened the door to her cheesiest grin.

'Hiiiiiii, I have tried calling you a million times! I know, I know, you would have been busy, but . . .' She hugged me carelessly, then pushed by to get to Cameron. 'AAAARHHHGHH!!! Jesus! WHAT THE FUCK has happened to you?' Ashley screamed.

Shit, shit, I hadn't told her about the hair transplant.

I tried to make a face to Ashley but she was too busy staring in amusement.

'Hi, everyone.' I felt a tap on the shoulder, and was surprised to see my sister holding Ashley's case. Ashley's mouth was still wide, gawking at Cameron, who looked completely flustered.

'Emily, this is Cameron. Cameron, this is my sister,' I smiled.

Emily went over and shook his hand. 'Oh, ouch. Sorry, it's so lovely to meet you. I've heard so much about you.'

Cameron laughed. 'Aye, you too. Lovely to meet you, and you again, Ashley. Hey, listen, why don't I go out and get some fresh air, let you girls catch up. I haven't looked at my phone all day, and no doubt my boss will be wondering why I haven't checked in.' His voice was genuine, and he kissed my forehead and grabbed his zipper from the bedroom.

'See you soon,' I said, my eyes trailing after him as he winked and left the flat.

As soon as the door shut, Ashley opened her mouth again.

'Right, what the fuck happened to him? Did he get a beating? A Glasgow kiss?' She looked traumatised, holding her hand to her chest dramatically.

I shook my head and sat down.

'Remember we thought he was away getting his teeth done?'

Ashley laughed sarcastically. 'No, no, *I* called that one, Zara. You thought,' she cleared her throat and put on a snooty voice, 'he was cultured.'

Emily rolled her eyes at us both and joined me on the sofa.

'Well, it turns out he got a hair transplant. It was so bad, guys. I didn't even recognise him when he came up to me at the airport! God, Ash, I can't believe you shouted that when you walked in.' I burst into guilty laughter.

Emily covered her face. 'Ashley, you're terrible and Zara, ouch! That's such a shame! Did he need one?'

I tried my hardest to think back to the handsome man from the plane and shook my head. 'I don't think so. Maybe he was thinning a little, but honestly not bad.'

Ashley burst out laughing. 'Thinning? A little? His hairline was back further than Christmas. How did you not notice that? I don't think it's a bad thing; I respect that. I mean, yes, bad timing for you, clearly. But this time next month, that cunt will be cutting about with more hair than Jesus.'

Emily and I buckled with laughter.

'So, what have you been doing? Have you pumped him?' Ashley seemed to be doing overtime with interrogations.

'Yes, we have. Practically straight away!' I answered proudly.

Emily's face twinged, not wanting to hear about her baby sister's bedroom antics, but I continued anyway.

'It was nice.'

Emily and Ashley exchanged a glance. 'Nice?' they said together.

I huffed a little and nodded.

Ashley rubbed my shoulders. 'Tell us. Why wasn't it amazing? Do you not like him as much now he's actually here? Do you wish he had a bit of that swelling downstairs? Is that it?' She chuckled, and I slapped her arm.

'No, he's completely perfect. Honestly, so sweet, caring and kind, and I think he likes me too. But he's really shy during sex, like, he doesn't even look at me, and totally silent. Not a word is spoken. It feels a bit awkward. But maybe I'm overthinking it all.'

Emily made a face to Ashley, which I caught.

'What?!' I yelled.

Emily tittered. 'That would make me feel weird as well, but you have literally just met him. If it's going well in every other department, then stick this one out. You haven't liked anyone since Tom. I'm proud you've made this commitment, Zara.'

'No, of course, like it doesn't put me off him. It just makes me wonder if he fancies me or something because he doesn't engage with me. Like, no filth, no moans or anything.' I blushed, realising how uncomfortable my sister looked.

'Right, this morning he was really going for it on top and honestly, if I didn't have my eyes open, I wouldn't know I was getting shagged. I hardly felt anything, physically, and certainly didn't hear anything. Does that ever happen to you guys?'

Emily giggled. 'Yes, that's happened to me! If I get too excited, you can't feel the dick at all.'

Ashley threw her arms in the air. 'Of course it's happened to Emily, she's had two kids! She'll be like a sausage getting threw up a close! You should still feel his dick, Zara!' she exclaimed.

Emily snorted. 'I beg your pardon. My pelvic floor is tighter now than ever!'

'Maybe I was just too wet!' I replied.

'I'm surprised you could get wet with that big fucking face on top of you!' Ashley erupted.

I gasped and launched a Dorito in her direction.

'Stop it! That's a sin! He is honestly such a nice person.' I was beginning to wish I hadn't confided in them at all.

Ashley squeezed onto the sofa and wrapped her arm around me.

'You know I'm only joking. Why don't you instigate it? He's maybe thinking the same, and he doesn't want to push you if he's a gentleman. Slip in some role play or dirty chat. Ask what turns him on. You'll never know until you ask him, Zara!'

She was right, and I was grateful to have some advice at last.

'Right, well. I'll have a few drinks with him on Saturday night and see what happens then. I'll need some gin confidence if I'm going all sexy!'

'Exactly!' Emily said, getting to her feet. 'OK, I need to go home – you're both giving me a headache! Zara, can we organise a leaving drink next Thursday for you both, maybe in the Corinthian?'

I clasped my hands excitedly. 'Eh, yes! Of course. That would be awesome!'

Emily leaned over to pat my head and then left towards the door.

'No doubt I'll see you before, but good luck getting your freak on!' she called out as the door shut behind her.

Ashley looked around the living room.

'You don't think Cameron will seriously make me sleep on the sofa, do you?' She turned her nose up in disgust.

'I do. And trust me, after hours of sex, you don't want to sleep in that bed anyway!' I declared, standing up and lifting dirty dishes over to the kitchen.

Ashley followed. 'I'd take your jizzy bed over a couchful of mushed-in cheesy crisps any day! Zara, please!' she moaned.

I grinned back.

'Not a fucking chance!'

Chapter Twenty-One

After a few more magical days of endless hugs, late-night winching and romantic walks doon the Barras, I was utterly convinced Cameron was the perfect man. We had sex a few times each day, but as much as I became accustomed to his rhythm and pounding technique, the caveman passion was still seriously lacking when we got our freak on. I found myself moaning his name loudly, trying hard to awaken the macho beast trapped somewhere deep inside him. However, my minimalistic tactics were failing, and I was getting nowhere. Cameron remained tortuously quiet as he shagged away in his own little fantasy, staring high up towards the sky with no eye contact whatsoever. I wondered if he was embarrassed because one time his eyelids almost shut over during sex because he was so swollen. Was it just a preventative measure to save his eyesight for the rest of the day? Or maybe this was just how he had sex? I wanted to feel that heart-throbbing, close connection that we enjoyed in every other aspect of our relationship. Like the way we finished one another's sentences, or how he turned his phone off when I finished work to ensure I had his undivided attention. How he put brown sauce lovehearts on my morning roll and would run me a bath for finishing work, just in case I was tired. He was perfect, but part of me craved an intense, leg-tingling, filthy orgasm with him staring deep into my eyes, but as soon as we got past foreplay, all I was guaranteed was a few pumps and a squirt.

Cameron's facial swelling was still slowly improving each day, which I was incredibly grateful for as our leaving dinner was less than a week away and I was desperate to show him off to all my friends and family. As Cameron's warped features slowly diminished, I began to see glimmers of the handsome man I'd first met on the aeroplane.

Emily had booked one of the private rooms in the swanky Corinthian Club, just a stone's throw from my flat in the heart of the city. Its modern, grandiose décor and delicious cocktails made it one of the most elegant venues in Glasgow. My family, friends and some VIP clients had all been invited for a special Individualise evening, and I couldn't fucking wait. Only Emily and Ashley had met Cameron properly, and I was excited about parading the sexy bastard around to everyone else like a scud book in the jail. He seemed eager too, constantly asking who would be there and how he couldn't wait to celebrate the start of our lives together in Dubai.

That Saturday afternoon, following another quiet morning at the clinic, Cameron and I walked hand in hand down Argyle Street. He was on the hunt for a fancy new suit, eager to match my navy tailored dress

I'd bought especially for our leaving do. While Cameron shopped, I was desperate to find sexy underwear to poke at his dragon. We decided to split up, Cameron going to scour the men's department in House of Fraser and me running across the road to Ann Summers.

I was in my element searching through racks and racks of voluminous bras, crotchless undies and devilish lingerie sets, wondering what kind of look would get Cameron going. So far, he hadn't taken much interest in my underwear but I knew it was probably because he was desperate to get past the clothes and hit the jackpot. Was he a lacy or a leather type of guy? Maybe he enjoyed a bit of role play – a sexy secretary or a naughty nurse. I was more than prepared to play a stereotype if that was what it took, but I wasn't convinced he'd even like that. I stumbled through to the over-18 section, hoping to find something truly irresistible, and giggled at the huge cocks sticking out from every angle. But beyond those, nothing in particular caught my attention. Eventually, I selected a black thronged bodysuit that zipped up from the crotch. It was guaranteed to conceal my muffin top, lift my saggy tits and flaunt my ever-growing arse all at the same time – it had to be a winner. My body squirmed, knowing I'd have to be extra vigilant and tuck my flaps in just in case we had a *There's Something About Mary* incident with the zipper. Still, this ensemble was bound to turn him on, right? God, I felt horny just looking at it.

Happy with my selection, I took it to the cashier and smiled.

'Would you like a bag?' she asked.

'Yes, please.'

'Can I interest you in any bullets, condoms, anal beads? They're all reduced.'

I smirked and blushed at the word 'anal' being spoken so openly in public. 'Oh, no, thank you. This is fine.'

She rang up the bodysuit, waited for me to pay, and then slipped it into a bag. 'OK, have a nice night.'

'I intend to! Thanks.'

She handed me the bag and I rushed across the road to meet back up with Cameron. He was standing at the cashier himself, paying for an elegant suit.

'Hey, beautiful. Did you get anything nice?' he asked, leaning over and kissing my cheek.

I smiled mischievously and raised my Ann Summers bag in the air.

'Maybe,' I whispered.

'What have you got there now?' he asked as the cashier handed him his shopping bag. He looked pleased and curious as we stepped away from the counter and headed towards the exit.

'You're going to have to wait and find out, aren't you!' I said, discreetly brushing my hand past his penis.

Cameron let out an almighty laugh and held me close, looking both thrilled and mortified. 'You are terrible, Zara Smith. But that's what I love about you!'

I felt my heart stand still. *Did he just say . . .?* Suddenly time was passing in slow motion as we continued along the street and my mind floated up out of my body, flying way up in the sky with the gods.

Cameron loves me!

My entire body felt electric and alive, and an obscenely large grin expanded over my face as I walked alongside Cameron. Should I tell him I loved him back? I was almost certain I did. I mean, the man was perfection. But by the time I thought of this, the moment was gone. It had been so unexpected, but so wonderful.

I walked back up the hilly city centre towards my flat, with a handsome, beautiful man and a declaration of love weighing happily on my shoulders.

That night we tackled the last few episodes of *The Originals* boxset with Ashley and a bowlful of Sensations. I hadn't confided in Ashley regarding Cameron's declaration of love for me as she seemed so down about Dave. I didn't want to boast about my fantastic relationship when hers was in tatters and decided to play it down. She was aware of the sexy night of passion I had preplanned for my man and knew to have her headphones at the ready. Cameron and I sat cuddled up on the couch, while Ashley stared at her phone most of the night. As soon as the credits rolled on the last episode, I shot to the bathroom, keen to get my freak on.

I retrieved the sexy bodysuit from under a pile of folded towels, having carefully hidden it there earlier. Through the door, I could hear Ashley debate the best vampire series with Cameron while I squeezed out a pee, drenched the edge of a towel in warm soapy water and started scrubbing my fanny, arse and armpits. Next, I yanked the bodysuit on, loosened my ponytail and gazed at myself in the small circular shaving mirror

Cameron had brought with him. *Ahhh too close.* I gasped as I was magnified one hundred times and all I could see was my hairy nostrils and abundance of blackheads. I swivelled the mirror and looked at myself again from a little further away. I felt sexy but self-conscious. What if Cameron didn't like it? What if he wondered why I was going to such measures? I ran my sweaty hands over the black shiny plastic material. *You can do this, Zara!*

I slipped out of the bathroom and headed for my bedroom, calling on Cameron, who was still passionately arguing the merits of *The Walking Dead* with Ashley. As he lifted his head from the couch, I watched him immediately stand to attention.

'We're er . . . going to bed, Ashley. Night.' His strong highland voice sounded surprised, and he practically leapt over the sofa.

Ashley giggled, remembering my plan, and called out, 'Keep it down, shaggers!'

Cameron marched in the door behind me and grabbed hold of my waist from the back. He pulled me against his chest and kissed my neck.

'Zara, what are you trying to do to me?' he panted.

I turned around and faced him. 'Do you want to fuck me, baby?' I said as seductively as I could.

His eyes widened at my profanity. 'Erm, yes. Of course. I would very much like that indeed!'

I dropped my hand down to his tartan pyjama bottoms and stroked his hard dick. 'Mmm . . . I can tell you want to,' I whispered over his lips, teasing him as he followed my every word.

Cameron propelled his legs out of his pyjamas, then grabbed the zip of my bodysuit and lowered it down, gently exposing me.

'You are so beautiful, baby,' he said and smiled down at me.

I felt warm with desire inside. 'So are you!' I gushed, lifting his T-shirt over his head.

I stepped back a few steps and lay down on the bed.

Cameron looked unbelievably handsome, his warm, bright eyes gazing down at me. No swelling, no redness. I just had to look at him to get turned on, and tonight I was determined to have some dirty, fun sex – *finally*.

He lay down on top of me and we began kissing. His touches felt loving, and as his tongue met mine, I wrapped my legs tight around his waist, wanting more. 'Fuck me!' I demanded.

He looked shocked but pushed his erect penis straight inside me. No foreplay, no airs and graces, I wanted one hundred per cent raw shagging.

'Ahhhh.' I moaned extra loud as I felt him, and glanced up to see his reaction.

But he was assuming his usual position, eyes upward, unconnected.

For fuck's sake, here we go again!

'Mmmm, is that good, baby?' I asked as he thrusted in and out.

Cameron glanced down, an expression on his face like I was distracting him, and nodded ever so slightly.

'Ohhh, keep fucking me like this, YES!' I screamed exaggeratedly, hoping for a response.

But Cameron remained quiet as he continued.

'Oh, Cammy, am I your dirty little slut? Eh? Do you like FUCKING me like your filthy little whore?' I bellowed at the top of my lungs. At this point, I wanted his dick to be ready to explode with desire.

Instead, the thrusts abruptly halted and Cameron leapt off me.

Then he lay on his side towards me, and held my face, looking concerned. 'Zara, you know I would never think you're a dirty slut or anything of the sort! Oh my god, come here.' He held me tightly, and I felt shamed.

I could feel my head stick to his naked body and sat up, needing to get a breath of distance for a minute.

'No, no, I know you don't – it was just sex chat,' I explained.

Cameron held me tighter, lavishing me with empathy and I couldn't take it anymore.

'Cameron, hear me out. I know you don't think I'm a slut, and you're so so respectful, and I love that. But on the odd occasion, I like some dirty talk during sex. It turns me on. In fact any chat, actually. But you don't make a sound. Like at all. You don't even look at me.'

Cameron sat up now too, unable to make eye contact, yet again.

'Oh, all right. I'll be honest with you, Zara, I've never understood it. I'd just hate you to think I was disrespecting you. Not when I like you so much.' He sounded sweet and sincere, and suddenly I felt like a sex-mad fucking pervert.

I groaned.

'God, I'm so sorry. I sound like an absolute rocket.' I held both hands up to my face with embarrassment.

Cameron kissed my hands, trying to squeeze his head into my face to make me feel better. 'You do not, miss. We all have little things we like that are a little weird. I don't mind trying it for you, Zara. OK?' His voice was soft and understanding.

Why was I such a fucking deviant!

'Well, the moment's kind of gone now, eh?' I giggled. 'But I'm now more intrigued to find out your little kink then.'

Cameron waggled his head and flopped back down on the bed. 'Nope!'

'Oh, come on! I've just told you mine! How do you know I won't like it too?' I pleaded, gently shaking his broad shoulders till he laughed.

Even in the darkness, I could see he was considering his next words carefully. 'Right, well . . .' he began, 'there is one thing that I like to do.'

I nodded, anticipating the hot night of passion I was about to be subjected to. Was he a sixty-niner type of guy? Or maybe he liked to watch porn together? Shit, maybe he wants a threesome! I was starting to feel nervous at his answer.

I let out a huge sigh. 'Just tell me!'

Cameron leaned over and tapped my arse. 'That!' he whispered.

I grinned, bopping up and down like an excitable puppy. 'Oh, I'm partial to a little spanking too!'

He shook his head and grinned. 'I don't want to spank your ass, Zara. I want to . . . you know . . . have sex with it.'

My face fell in shock as the PG-perfect prince unveiled his fantasy, and I hadn't foreseen it at all.

'Ohh. OK,' I laughed, feeling nervous at the thought of my haemorrhoids bursting all over him, but slightly relieved he didn't disclose a darker secret. I suppose most men seem to enjoy anal but it was something I'd never tried. I heard so many horror stories in the hospital with patients becoming incontinent and all of a sudden, I had another fear. *Would Cameron still love me if I wore a pad.* I knew I was being dramatic; one time surely wouldn't cause permanent damage, would it? I always thought it would be something I would only consider in a serious relationship. But this is as serious as I'd ever gotten, maybe this is the time, I thought. But fuck, I didn't fancy getting ghosted after leaving a skiddy on a penis after all. I really didn't know what to do.

I sat quietly for a few more seconds, keeping Cameron fully in suspense and eventually shrugged.

'I mean, I've never done it, but I'll try anything once, I suppose!' I wanted to sound upbeat, but a sudden nervous belly overcame me.

Cameron's grin took over the room, and the cunt looked like I'd just handed him a night with Beyoncé. 'Are you sure? Tonight?' he said.

'Erm . . . yeah. To be honest, I'm worried about the pain,' I admitted.

He nodded. 'If it's too sore, I'll stop. I'll be gentle, baby.'

I looked at the man I wanted desperately to keep and make happy, and thought, *What's an arsehole between two lovers, really?*

'Fine, I'm just going to nip to the loo first. I suddenly feel worried!' I laughed, swinging my legs out of the bed and tossing my dressing gown around my shoulders.

As I entered the living room, I saw Ashley still engrossed in the TV.

'Pssst, Ash!' I whispered.

She perched up and turned around, looking sluggish. 'What? I'm trying to sleep, Zara!'

'Come here!' I went to the bathroom, holding the door open for her to join me.

She eventually stumbled in, and I shut the door behind us.

'What's up?'

'I tried the dirty chat with Cameron, tried to get him to loosen up a bit, then basically begged him to tell me his secret fantasy, and now he wants to shag my arse!' I exclaimed all in one breath.

Ashley shrugged. 'You did poke the bear, Zara.'

'Well, I don't want the bear poking my bowel, and I've agreed to it! What will I do?'

Ashley was laughing, and I stuck my hand over her mouth, not wanting Cameron to know how childish I was being.

'Shh! Stop, he'll hear you!'

Ashley grunted, then took a deep breath. 'If you don't want to, don't do it. No big deal. But honestly, it's quite good when you get into it. I think you'd enjoy it!'

I rolled my eyes. 'I have the worst piles in the world. I could haemorrhage! My friend who works in A&E said one night a couple came in stuck together. Imagine if we got stuck, I'd know half the doctors in the waiting room,' I cried.

She began giggling. 'Stop being so dramatic. It's no big deal. He's the nicest guy in the world. He'll understand if you shit out of it.'

'Aw, great choice of words, Ash,' I said sarcastically, flapping my hands in panic.

Was this what I needed to do to break the connection issue? Maybe Cameron would see how hard I was willing to go for him. If he saw me trying something new for him, hopefully he'd try with the dirty chat too. This could be a win–win for us.

'OK, I will try but will you check my arse? Please, Ash. Make sure I have no piles?'

She screwed her face up in disgust. 'Fuck right off, Zara. No chance!'

I threw my hands down in a strop. 'C'mon. Please! I can't go in risking a growth hanging out my bumhole!'

Ashley put her hands on her face and huffed. 'Fine. A two-second check. Go!'

I turned around, lifting my dressing gown to my waist, and exposed my arsehole. She bent down, attempting to get a more favourable angle.

'I can't see properly! Hold on . . .' She delved into her pocket to click on the torch on her phone.

'OK, wait!!' I lifted one leg on top of the bath panel, spreading my cheeks wider in her face.

As she bent to look again, she paused and said, 'I swear if you fart, I will never break breath to you ever again.'

'Ash, come on! What do you see!'

'OK, OK!' she said.

For a few seconds, there was silence.

I curved my neck right under my legs and observed a horrified look on her face.

'What's up with the face?' I lowered my leg to the floor and turned to face her.

'There's a growth, all right.' She looked traumatised.

'Is it hanging outside my butthole? Like a wee bit? Maybe I could just push it back in?'

'Mate, the only hole that thing resembles is Brian May's fucking plughole – it's the hairiest thing I've ever seen. The cunt would need a sat nav to find your arsehole, Zara! I cannae see a pile, but sort out the fucking jungle, man!'

I carefully ran my fingertips up my bum crack and felt the dry, wiry pubes scrape against my fingers. *Oh, shit!* She was right. My arse felt like Hagrid's beard. Hastily, I grabbed hold of the nearest razor, parted my cheeks and ran it along my arse crack. *That's better.*

Ashley was leaning against the door, shaking her head at the commotion.

'OK, so you think I should go for it?' I replied.

She shrugged. 'If you like. It can be quite fun. Just don't shit on his dick.'

I shot her an evil eye, and she roared.

'I'm going to try to squeeze one out before I go in. I can't risk a brown boaby.' I lifted the toilet seat up and sat down with a bang and started squeezing.

'I'm outta here!'

'Ssssh, keep it down! Don't leave, Ash, he'll hear the door bang!'

'Zara, I'm not waiting till you stink out the bathroom. Go for it. Or don't. It's entirely up to you!'

She opened the bathroom door, and closed it behind her with a thud. Great, now he's going to expect me sooner. I tried my hardest to keep pushing but only managed to pass a little Malteser. I vigorously scrubbed my arsehole and finally felt ready. I took a deep pongy breath. *I can do this. I can do this. If Cameron wants bum sex, I'm going to give it to him!*

I marched back into the bedroom to find Cameron slowly pulling back his foreskin, keeping his dick hard and ready for action.

'Are you sure you want to do this, Za?' he asked as I crawled into bed with my back to him, assuming the position.

I nodded nervously. 'I'm ready! But . . . go slow, please!'

Cameron kissed my shoulders, and I jumped, not anticipating his touch.

'OK, bend slightly for me and stick out your ass.' He kissed my neck and then drew back, whispering, 'Just relax, baby.'

I took a deep breath to steady my nerves. His hands stroked my hips and then began to spread my cheeks.

A second later, I felt an uncomfortable tightness dig in from behind. *Ouch!*

Cameron cried out, sounding almost euphoric.

'Is that it in?' I asked, feeling an immediate gush of ring sting.

He breathed out sensuously. 'The tip isn't quite in yet, you're doing well, Zara.'

The tip? The fucking tip! *What the fuck!* I mean, he didn't have the biggest dick in the world, and I was struggling already!

Cameron moved his hands, gently raising one arse cheek and leaned further into me.

'Ohhh, fuck!' I winced. 'Oh, oh, can we have a wee break?' I said, feeling irritable and unsexy.

He kissed my shoulder. 'Of course. Thank you for trying this with me.'

I felt him pull out. Phew! What a relief!

'Did you get a lot of it in?' I asked.

Cameron giggled. 'I got like this much in.' He pointed to an inch off the tip of his penis and lay back down.

But my eyes were stuck to where he'd indicated. There was something on his dick.

Oh no! Oh no! What the fuck is that? Please, don't let me have shat on him!

I had no idea what the thing was, but it was a small circular-shaped lump hanging freely at the tip of his penis. Luckily, he hadn't seemed to notice yet. I had to get it.

'Mmm . . . your body is so sexy, Cameron, do you know that?' I leaned into him, trying to block his view of the foreign object stuck to his cock. 'I could kiss every last inch of you.' I smiled up at him and caressed his abs, slowly bringing my head down to his groin to examine the unusual item. *What the fuck is it?* It sat right at the edge, was lightly coloured and a peculiar shape. I grabbed the end of his dick tightly, capturing it in my hands.

'Ouch, Zara! What the hell!' Cameron grumbled, sitting up.

'Oh, sorry, babe. I thought you would like that. A wee bit rough,' I shrugged.

'Ouch, no, that was sore, babe!'

I giggled clumsily as I made my way back up the bed and lay back beside him, grasping my hand closed, unsure of what I was holding.

We lay for a few more minutes while my hand stayed securely shut over and sweaty.

'Do you want a can of juice or a drink of water? I'm boiling!' Cameron whispered.

'Mmm, that would be good, thanks.'

He kissed my forehead and wandered through to the kitchen, oblivious to it all. When the coast was clear, I released my hand. *Ew, Jesus Christ!* I sniffed it, knowing full well it wouldn't be pleasant. Luckily, or not, depending on how you saw it, it was most definitely not one hundred per cent shite.

I stared at it, and it was an inch from my face before I realised my arse had in fact gifted Cameron a large piece of sweetcorn. What the fuck?

Then I remembered: I'd had a chicken and sweetcorn baguette from Greggs the other day. I shivered at the thought, retching as I examined the leftover with utter disgust.

Fucking hell! I leapt off the bed, flicked the corn out the window and pored a generous amount of Micellar water over my hands. That was far too close a shave for me, I *never* wanted to try anal again. It had almost put me off Greggs for life.

Chapter Twenty-Two

On Monday morning, Ashley dragged us away from a home-cooked breakfast made by my sexy man to make the usual ten-minute journey to work. As we walked along the street, I tried to envision what my morning rush in the desert would look like and how my new life was only days away. Cameron was so optimistic and enthusiastic about it all, and I couldn't help but feel completely wrapped up in our little sandstorm. He was so eager to introduce me to his friends and I finally felt safe in my relationship, having never had that type of security before. Every night he'd divulge excursion plans, from travelling to Abu Dhabi to exploring the less occupied, cultural markets together hand in hand. At times I almost forgot I'd be working, but as I promoted the clinic from the land of luxury, I'd also be living like a princess with my love while Raj reaped the benefits back home.

I walked alongside the old sandstone buildings, running my fingertips over the rough edges and thinking of how perfectly things were working out. Ashley toddled along at my side, more engrossed in her phone.

'You know Dave's got social media?' she announced. 'He's never had social media. So why does he suddenly have it?'

'Oh really? Maybe he's trying to check up on you, or—'

'Or maybe he's putting the feelers out to get a new wifey. So that's what it'll be. What a fucking dick!'

I nodded awkwardly, trying to understand her over-reaction. 'Well, you don't know that for sure . . .'

'Oh, I fucking know, Zara. Has he added me? Naw! Has he added every other skanky lassie he can find – aye! Well, two can play that game!'

Right then, rain began to fall and splutter off the pavement, turning them shiny. I set a brisk pace towards the clinic, trying to avoid getting soaked.

'Oh shit, no! Ash!' I called out.

'What?' she answered, still staring at her phone screen, fingers rapidly swiping.

I nudged my head towards the Mercedes sitting outside the clinic with Tom's private registration plate: TA 1.

'What the hell is he doing here?' I asked, cold dread shifting through me.

'What? It's Tom,' she shrugged. 'People make mistakes, Zara! You can't hold a grudge for ever, you know!'

I was stung. Considering everything she knew I'd been through with Tom, this wasn't the supportive or sympathetic response I was after. I wondered if she was thinking of her situation with Dave, and decided there was no point in trying to argue with her.

I opened the clinic door and immediately spotted Tom's tall frame, standing with his back to me. The crisp white shirt, the posh English accent, his brown hair pushed back so effortlessly. And then he turned.

'Ah, morning, ladies.'

I smiled politely, keeping my eyes on Raj, who seemed uncomfortable at us all being under the same roof.

'Tom's just signing some paperwork for the payroll and things. We won't be too long,' Raj said, seeming flustered as his fingers dove through a pile of documents.

I cleared my throat as the room fell silent.

'Cool. I have a nine o'clock anyway – I need to set up. Ash, will you give me a shout when she arrives?'

Ashley nodded, still flicking through her phone.

I walked into my clinic room and closed the door. Then I pressed my back against it and felt my composed body crumble. When would it ever feel normal seeing that man? His aftershave filled the building, and even when I closed my eyes, he was there. Thank fuck for Dubai. I couldn't cope if he was back on Raj's friend list. Every time I saw him was a reminder of the old me, or the pathetic person he turned me into. A naive, heartbroken, needy woman, and I didn't want to acknowledge her.

My door chapped, and Ashley's voice echoed through. 'Laura's here!'

I jumped up. 'Yip, two minutes, just need to get changed!' I called back.

Take a deep breath, Zara! I thought. *Get it together.*

I changed into my scrubs and after a few deep breaths called for Laura, one of my regular clients. She was a stunning, twenty-five-year-old marketing executive, and owner of Gem Gyms in Scotland. She lived in Edinburgh but travelled through to get her treatments.

'Aw, Zara, you have no idea how happy I am to be here! My lips are completely deflated!' she said as she entered the room. Instantly the space turned fruity as her perfume swept in with her. She looked so glamorous with her bouncy blow-dry sitting perfectly with her tiny gym shorts. *How did anyone look so good after a workout?* I thought, reminding myself how I almost passed out at my last attempt to exercise, when even my Apple watch screamed 'warning of cardiac arrest'.

I giggled at Laura's exaggeration of her lips, feeling envious of her beautiful face.

'Is it just lips for today?' I asked as she sat down on the bed.

'Yes, please. I'll maybe get cheeks done next time.'

'Well,' I said, carefully wiping her make-up off, 'as of Thursday, I'll be working in Dubai! I will be back, but I'm not entirely sure when. Raj is amazing though; he'll take great care of you.'

Laura's face lit up. 'No way! That's fantastic, Zara! I love Dubai! Where are you staying and have you been before? Sorry, I'm just so jealous! It's my favourite place ever.'

Her enthusiasm and relaxed vibe made me almost forget about Tom outside. I applied her numbing cream and pulled my stool to the edge of the bed to have a chat while it developed.

'So, it's a bit of a crazy story,' I boasted. 'Basically, I was out there a few weeks ago for work, then I met an amazing guy on the plane who stays in Dubai but he's from Scotland, so we planned to chat and meet up when we could. But then the opportunity came up to live out there for a bit to promote the clinic.'

Laura's eyes were filling up with awe. 'OK, so this is like a bloody fairy tale! You're joking, right? It's totally meant to be!'

I shook my head, unable to stop grinning.

'I'm so happy for you,' she gushed. 'So, if I need an appointment, I need to get my ass to Dubai, that's what you're telling me!'

I laughed, gently clearing the cream off her numb lips. 'That's right!'

I took the small syringe and gently got to work on her top lip, injecting slowly in and out while we continued to chat.

'What about your love life, actually? The last time I saw you, I think you were dating the guy from the army?'

Laura eyes became heavy, and I gave her a break to chat.

'Yes, I still am! He's the sweetest, most amazing man in the universe! But he's in Baghdad at the minute. Ah, so annoying. He's due back home to the Highlands in four weeks, three days and about two hours . . . Not that I'm counting!'

I couldn't help but feel our soppy, romantic energy bounce around the room.

'That's so weird. My man is originally from the north too. I keep joking to Ashley it must be where all the good ones are hiding!'

Laura's bright green eyes were agreeing with every statement I said. 'Yes, yes, yes! I mean, Cameron is unlike any man I've ever met. He's funny, sexy, caring and honestly so masculine. He's just unlike any other man,' she said.

My mind froze at the coincidence.

'Yes, mine is too!' I said, dispelling the weird feeling. 'I've never met anyone so thoughtful. So, do you get a chance to phone him and stuff if he's in Baghdad? How does that work?'

Laura let out a slight puff. 'We can only text just now. He's been on an assignment for two weeks so I've not been able to FaceTime him, but we WhatsApp during the day and things.'

My heart beat stronger in my chest.

'Have you got a picture? I need a swatch, Laura!'

'Of course. He's my screensaver! I know, I'm such a saddo!' she said, radiating pure joy. She turned her phone screen around, and everything froze.

I stared, hoping the image would change. *How can this be?*

It was *my* Cameron.

My boyfriend.

My love.

But there he was lying in bed with this stunning woman, staring into her eyes with pure lust. He didn't look at me this way. This is what I've craved. From the second I met him. But he was doing it with her.

Still, I couldn't comprehend it.

Why did she have his photo stored on her phone?

I stood entirely still, feeling my eyes begin to water.

'He's hot, right? Superhot!' She beamed.

I opened my mouth, but nothing came out. Then I cleared my throat and said, 'Wow, *yes*! Super-duper hot!'

I couldn't tell her. I couldn't ask questions. I was in shock. I didn't want this to be the truth.

'OK, let's get crackin' with this bottom lip, eh,' I said, not knowing how to act or what to do.

I turned my back to Laura and faced the silver sterile trolley. I had to take a moment to compose myself. *You can do this.* I lifted the pre-filled syringe and watched my hand tremble, then immediately sat it back down. Quietly, I inhaled a large, deep breath, squeezing both hands into tight fists, and then slowly releasing them, watching my tremor disappear. I turned back to Laura and smiled.

'OK, you ready?'

I finished off the last few injections, making sure her lips were perfect. Laura continued to chatter while I nodded, taking nothing in. I couldn't think of anything; my mind had turned dark and hazy. Maybe the next person to touch these lips would be Cameron. How could he do this to me? How could I go away with him now? I wanted to bombard Laura with a million questions, but I couldn't risk losing any more clients for Raj. Not now. And to be honest, I was too embarrassed to confront her. She was stunning, far more attractive than me, and her energy was so uplifting, it was impossible not to connect with her. If it came down to it, I knew who Cameron would choose. How could I be so blindsided again?

Laura stood up from the bed, pouting and examining her face in the handheld mirror.

'Ohhh, thank you so, so much, Zara!' God, she was so lovely and bubbly. I attempted a smile back. 'And gosh, good luck in Dubai! I can't wait to stalk your Instagram and feel completely jealous!' she added, gathering her things.

'Yes, thanks for coming. Ashley will square you up and any issues, just give us a call.'

I felt Laura's arms wrap around my neck, completely unaware of the grenade she had thrown into my life. I gave her a light hug back.

When she was gone, I shut my clinic room door and lowered myself onto the ground. What the fuck just happened? My heart was pounding. I felt sick and dizzy.

'Zara! Zara! Your nine thirty's running late, can you still take her?' Ashley called out from the hallway.

'Erm . . . yes. Erm . . . no, actually. Tell her to reschedule. I need a minute.'

My body was stiff, and the room was spinning. I couldn't go out and face everyone. Not when Tom was there, not when I'd been boasting about my perfect life. Every single thing was just a lie.

The door bounced open, and Raj burst in. 'I'm sure you could still fit the client in . . .' He trailed off when he saw me sitting on the floor. His eyes darted around the room. 'Zara, are you OK?' He squatted down on the floor next to me.

'I'm fine. I just don't feel well. I don't think . . .'

Ashley walked in and gasped. 'What's happened? Are you OK?'

Tom's voice was close behind Ashley's. 'Is everything OK in here?'

I shut my eyes. 'For fuck's sake, Raj, get them to leave,' I whispered.

'She's fine. Tom, I'll pop round to yours later with the final paperwork, and Ashley, can you man the desk? I'll sort Zara! She's just feeling sick.'

'Yes, see you later then. Hopefully it doesn't have feet, Zara!' Tom added, and I heard him and Ashley giggle together, their voices growing fainter in the distance as they walked off.

Raj sat beside me and grabbed hold of my hand.

'Is this because Tom was here?'

I shook my head, feeling my face turn damp with tears. 'Of course not.'

'What's up then?'

I sighed, feeling humiliated that I'd allowed myself to be in this situation once more. 'My client, Laura. The one who travels from Edinburgh. She's been loved up with a guy from the army for a while now, and I was telling her all about moving to Dubai, meeting Cameron and all that. Anyway, she was telling me how her boyfriend is back home next month, and that his name's also Cameron.'

Raj's head swayed to the side.

'I asked to see a picture and . . .'

I watched Raj's eyes pop from his head as he realised what I was about to say. 'Fuck.'

'It's him. He's been lying to me. Mr Fucking Perfect is a liar and a cheat, and I'm the fucking fud that fell for it all.'

Raj wrapped his arms around me tightly. 'We all fell for it, Zara, not just you,' he said gently.

'I don't think I can go to Dubai. Not like this. I'm so, so sorry.' My body was beginning to panic, and I felt myself start to hyperventilate.

'Hey, hey, calm down. I don't expect you to go! But I want to kill him, Zara, seriously!'

I chuckled a little, feeling sniffly. 'He was a sniper. I'd put money on him, but I appreciate it.'

Raj huffed. 'Was he though? Who knows what he is? Or who he is!'

My mind boggled as I suddenly realised I had no idea who I'd been sharing a bed with for over a week. Who'd been living in my flat. Who'd told me he loved me.

'We should phone Andy, tell him as soon as. So they can replace me,' I said.

Raj laughed. 'Oh, I'll phone him and tell him there's been a change of name on the documents.'

I wriggled out of his arms and faced him. 'What do you mean?'

'I'll do it! God, I loved Dubai. I would need you to manage the clinic and try to keep us afloat. You'd need to be on top of things back here, but I trust you.'

'So, you'll go out there, and I'll manage the clinic!' I reiterated the plan, feeling my friend had just passed me a get-out-of-jail-free card.

'Yeah, I mean, as long as you can work alongside Tom.'

'I'd work alongside Harold Shipman if it meant I didn't have to go.'

Raj raised his brows at me and smirked.

'If it helps the clinic, I'd do anything, to be honest,' I continued.

'And you're one hundred and fifty per cent sure you're not going?' Raj checked, rising to his feet and helping me up behind him.

'I'm two hundred and fifty per cent sure!'

Raj nodded, already holding his phone to his ear. He kissed my forehead lightly and walked out the room. I heard him chatting with Andy, sorting everything out, while I caught my breath.

Raj offered to cover my clients that day to allow me time to sort things at home, but I declined. I wasn't prepared to fall apart over a man again. Besides, I was still struggling to comprehend what Cameron had done. Instead, I kept conversation to a minimum that day, pretending to my remaining clients that I had terrible cramps, while in reality my head did overtime working out ideas for how to confront Cameron.

Maybe I could cut up all his clothes and rip up his passport. That would snooker the cunt for going back to work for a while. Or perhaps I should let him explain himself. Maybe he had a doppelganger I didn't know about. I questioned if the photo was definitely him, but I knew deep down that it was. Maybe I could steal his phone and scroll through all his dirty little secrets.

There was bound to be more than Laura. Or I could smash it up, really piss him off.

I worked on autopilot all day, thinking up absurd ways of dealing with the burden back home, but knowing no matter how much of a retaliation I participated in, the damage was done.

It was after four when I finished with my last client. I changed back into my jeans and T-shirt, gathered my things and went out onto the shop floor. I appreciated Raj filling Ashley in, and found her waiting eagerly for her cue to erupt.

'Ash, I can tell you know!' I announced, staring at her tense face.

She threw her hands in the air. 'How can you act so calm? I'm ready to kick his fucking cunt in!'

'I honestly don't feel anything right now. I'm just so gutted.'

'But what did Laura say? And what did—'

'Can we please chat about it later? I just need to go home, take some paracetamol, and have it out with him.'

Ashley agreed, standing with her hands on her hips. 'If you're sure. I'll hang out with Raj tonight. He has some things to sort out. Text me when you need me.'

'We're here if you need us. Good luck, Zara,' Raj added.

I smiled back at the pair of them, swung my jacket around my shoulders and slowly walked home, feeling much less optimistic than I had at the beginning of the day.

Chapter Twenty-Three

I opened the front door to the warm smell of lasagne cooking in the oven. In the kitchen, Cameron was chopping a cucumber in between sips of red wine.

'Hello, gorgeous! How was your day?' he greeted me from across the room, and I couldn't help but sigh.

'Not great,' I replied, slipping off my shoes at the doorway.

Cameron stuck out his bottom lip sympathetically. 'Well, dinner will be ready in twenty. No Ash?' he asked, looking relieved.

I shook my head, coming into the kitchen.

'How do you know Laura Rinaldi?'

Just like that, I blurted it out.

Cameron was mid-sip of his Merlot and choked slightly at the question. He attempted to compose himself, but it was too late – his face had already turned white.

'Who?' he replied.

'Don't "Who?" me – I know everything. Laura is one of my regular clients and you could imagine my surprise today when she started showing me pictures of her amazing boyfriend, and saying how loved up you all are. I just don't understand why, or what the hell this big nice guy act is to you?'

Cameron's head bowed for a few silent seconds and then he came towards me.

'I'm sorry. I'm so bloody sorry. Yes, I've seen Laura since my marriage ended but not since me and you got together. I wouldn't do that to you, Zara. Please, please, believe me.'

I shook my head. 'You've been messaging her when I've been going to work? Yeah?'

He froze, not knowing how to respond.

'She thinks you're in Baghdad, and you're swarming aboot Braehead!'

He sighed.

'Don't just sigh, Cameron, fucking speak up! Why does she think you're in Baghdad? And why can't she speak to you?'

He shrugged his shoulders. 'I didn't want her FaceTiming me when I just had my hair done.'

I exploded into laughter. 'You didn't want *her* to see you like that? Yet you flew across Europe thinking aw, Zara will put up with the face? *Why?* Because I'm a downgrade. *Is that why?*' Blood rushed to my face as my anger grew.

'That's not it, at all. On that plane, we instantly connected. I wanted to see you,' he said.

'But you weren't honest. You continued messaging Laura every fucking day!'

Cameron agreed, acknowledging his blunder. 'But I didn't see her.'

'Aye, because you were too embarrassed about the size of your fucking face! I had to put up with the Elephant Man while she gets the hot hero apparently fighting for his country! I've had enough of men fucking lying to me. Pack your shit and go!'

But Cameron made no move to leave.

'I know I shouldn't have messaged her, but I didn't see or touch any women when I was with you, Zara.' As he spoke, his eyes filled with tears.

'But you kept your options open, and I don't deserve that. So, Cameron, I need you to leave now, please.'

'Is that what you want? To throw this away?' he whispered.

I sneered at him.

'*You* have done that, not me. Just leave before Ashley gets back. I'm over this conversation.' I turned my back and began shouting once more as the questions flooded my brain, 'So, what was your plan? Lead both of us on until what?'

'We were going to Dubai together. *You* are my plan, Zara!'

I started chuckling. 'So, you and Laura are over? Because she certainly didn't give me that impression today!'

'I promise.' He begged.

'Well, call her right now then. Tell her.'

He stood still, hesitating before me.

'No? Don't fucking bother, honestly. It's done! It's just creeping me out that the man I let share a bed with me, live fucking rent-free in my home is a liar and a cheat. The worst thing about it all is how much you pride yourself in being a nice guy. The thing is, I knew deep down my ex was trouble; I knew what he was from the moment I met him, but Jesus Christ, you deserve a fucking Oscar. Mr fuckin' nice guy, my arse! Now get to fuck, seriously.'

After a long, tense moment, Cameron finally seemed to realise I meant what I'd said. I spent the next ten minutes watching the man of my dreams gather his stuff and pack it all away in his holdall. Through it all, I remained composed. Eventually he walked out the apartment without saying another word.

I sat down on the sofa and my eyes began to trickle. It hadn't felt good to be so angry at someone I'd cared about, someone who'd told me he loved me not two days ago. For a brief moment, I questioned whether I'd been too harsh. Maybe there was some misunderstanding, maybe it wasn't as bad as I thought. Half of me wanted to chase after him and beg him to come back, but the better half knew it had to end. It had taken me a long time to rebuild myself after the break-up with Tom, and I wasn't prepared to lose myself again. So, instead, I gazed into space, wondering where he might go – wondering if he'd run to Laura's, fill her head with some heroic bullshit story about Baghdad. Or perhaps he'd head to the airport, meet another unsuspecting woman on the flight and fuck up her life as well.

I wept into the couch cushions until I smelt an unpleasant smell, then bolted to the oven as I realised the lasagne was burning. I was halfway unloading it when I heard the key turn in the lock, and Ashley popped her head round the front door.

'I'm sorry,' she said, catching sight of my tear-streaked face. 'I'll go if you want, but I needed to check you were OK.'

In spite of myself, I felt a smile pull across my face at her presence.

'It's fine. He's gone. You hungry?' I laughed at the crispy dish as she made her way to the kitchen.

'Gone? Just like that?'

'Flew into my life and kicked out, just as quick,' I shrugged.

Ashley walked over and gently rubbed my arm. 'Are you OK?'

'I think so.' I paused. 'I called him the Elephant Man, Ash,' I admitted guiltily, recalling my moment of pettiness.

'I hope you called him a shite ride, too! He deserves it all, babe. Who the fuck does he think he is?' She paused and looked into my face. 'You seem too well, it's unnerving. Cooking and shit. You know I can handle breakdown, Zara.'

'I just feel disappointed, like I'm empty. Every man that walks out that door takes a little piece of me with them and maybe now I'm sort of incomplete. I don't know.'

'You don't need a man to complete you, Zara. You've had rotten luck, but it'll pass. Besides, we have each other. I don't have Dave, which kills me every second of the day, but I still know I'm fabulous. You have me, and I'm not going anywhere.'

I attempted a smile. She was right, but I couldn't feel it yet. 'Did Raj manage to change the names and things over for Dubai?' I asked, wanting to change the subject slightly.

'Yes, he's all set. But I was going to keep the reservation for the Corinthian open if it's all right with you. Have a leaving thing for Raj instead? It'll be perfect for social media, but if you think it's insensitive, then I'll cancel. Raj isn't arsed anyway . . .' She rolled her eyes.

I shook my head. 'No. He deserves a leaving night. God!' My stomach filled with dread, wondering what I would tell the clients. All of them expected me to be leaving and now Raj was going instead. I had been boasting about my love life and suddenly it had crumbled.

I felt overcome with emotion. I was losing Raj to Dubai too.

'Fancy a bottle of wine tonight? I need to drink and drink till I feel more normal again!'

Ashley looked cautious, but then said, 'I'm game! But no late-night texting Cameron the Cunt!'

I laughed. 'Don't worry about that, hen!' I assured her.

'Right, well, pass me a glass already!' she replied.

In the days that followed, I continued to live off cheap wine and leftover lasagne. Work at the clinic continued as Raj prepared for the big move. I painted a brave face for my friends, but I felt more alone than ever, particularly at night. Even when Ashley ditched the couch and returned to my room, I insisted on using

Cameron's pillow and sleeping on his side of the bed. I felt Ashley's new hatred for Cameron and my situation seemed to lift her out of her depression with Dave as she comforted me and constantly checked in. Each night, I closed my eyes and thought only of him. His strong scent filled my lungs. I kept regular tabs on Laura's Instagram and composed several potential messages to out Cameron's lies. I even thought about an anonymous DM, but swiftly deleted it each time. I wanted to hurt him like he had hurt me or even warn Laura about him, but I couldn't risk any dramas for Raj, and I was worried her popularity might cause a negative reflection on the clinic. She was exceptionally well known in Scotland, with a great social media following, and business connections, so I remained painstakingly quiet, all the while stalking her perfect life from behind my screen.

Chapter Twenty-Four

Thursday night's leaving party came around fast, and the thought of awkward scenarios and answering questions from clients about the Dubai swap filled me with utter dread. I paced the floor of my flat in an old bobbly dressing gown, hoping Ashley would take pity and say I didn't have to go.

'I feel sick about going, you know.'

Ashley was straightening her hair, not paying any attention to what I was saying.

'Ash?' I moaned, needy for support.

'What? It's Raj. You have to come. Have a glass of wine and settle, petal.' She rolled her eyes in the mirror, and I trudged through to the kitchen. Ashley hadn't been out since splitting from Dave and it was the first time I'd seen her excited about anything since then.

But I knew she was right – I couldn't let Raj down. I opened the fridge to retrieve a chilled bottle of Prosecco a client had gifted me for the move, tore the packaging around the cork, and poured it into a mug sitting on the worktop. *Mmmm, that's better.* Next, I commenced my make-up and fake eyelash rigmarole, while having an occasional sip of the bubbles and playing through through possible scenarios in my mind.

'So, Zara, why did you change your mind about the job?'

'Well, I just love Glasgow that much, and the idea of working in that heat put me off!'

No, too apparent that's a lie, I thought. I tried again:

'Awk, I just thought I'd miss my friends too much!'

I chuckled out loud at that one. Everyone knew I only had one friend.

'Well, because my boyfriend was a liar and a cheat, and after I found out he was secretly living a double life, I didn't fancy being in the same country as the cunt.'

I took another long swig of Prosecco, considering that last one. Accurate but perhaps an overshare? I thought.

'Are you almost ready?' Ashley yelled out to me still standing in the kitchen.

I quickly let down my topknot of straggly hair and ran my fingers through to loosen it up.

'Just need an outfit – hair and make-up done!' I said as I went into the bedroom.

Ashley's skin was like porcelain with the layers of product she carefully applied, while I could still see a few of my chickenpox scars breaking through the cheap Rimmel foundation I used.

'Did you brush your hair?' she asked, giving me a look. Her own poker-straight blonde extensions rested like silk down her shoulders.

I grinned. 'I'm going for the cool, indie, "I woke up like this" vibe!'

Ashley burst out laughing. 'You're pulling it off, babe. You literally look like you just woke up!'

I glanced towards the classy tailored midi dress that hung so neatly in my wardrobe. I had it to match Cameron's suit perfectly for a *his* and *hers* inspired outfit. Now, I couldn't bear to look at it without my stomach feeling it was about to fall out my arsehole, so instead I began frantically rummaging through my wardrobe for another option, finally lifting out a mini boobtube dress.

'What do you think?' I asked.

'Ay, caramba! Very short! But fuck it! Wow!'

I stepped into it, tugging it past my hips and pushing it up past my boobs.

'Well . . .?' I smiled.

'Sexy. Really, *really* hot. I can almost see last night's kebab, but hey!'

I laughed and opened my thighs wide. 'Last night's kebab is probably my flaps wafting out my knickers. I'm not even lying! They seem to be getting bigger as I'm getting older, man!' I pretended to bend over tucking them in.

We were in hysterics in my room, and for a minute it felt like the last few weeks hadn't happened and it was just me and my best friend, happy and laughing.

Suddenly there was a knock at the door. Both Ashley and I looked at one another. I wondered why the intercom hadn't gone off.

'I'll get it.' I stumbled out of my bedroom across the living area and opened the door to a pale-faced Cameron.

'What are you doing here?' I gasped, feeling immediately queasy from seeing him.

'Thought I'd return these.' He held up the keys to my apartment and shrugged his shoulders.

'You look nice.' His voice sounded quieter than normal but I could hear his distinct northern accent echo up the stairwell. My heart immediately felt achy seeing him again.

'Thanks for returning them.' I sort of laughed, feeling uneasy at the tension.

'Can I explain? I know this is your big leaving party but I'll be a couple of minutes max.'

I shook my head, 'I'm not going anywhere now. I'm staying here – Raj is taking my spot in Dubai.'

Cameron let out a puff of disappointment. 'Shit. Well, I'm sorry for everything. I didn't intend to hurt you or Laura. We've had a relationship for a while now but it's long distance and I never intended to hurt you both.'

I stared through him. The last person I wanted to hear him speak about right now was Laura.

'I seriously blame myself – I should have known. You were too nice, Cameron. Good guys don't exist for girls like me. There was always something I couldn't put my finger on with you. I should have trusted my gut.' I could feel my eyes tear up so I blinked, determined to hide how much he had hurt me.

'Please don't say that, Zara. I didn't feel like I held back.' He reached forward to hold my hand but I stepped back.

'You switched your phone off, pretending to be in the zone but it was just in case Laura called. You weren't

251

honest the entire time. Fuck, you couldn't even make eye contact with me when we had sex, Cameron. Why was that? Were you picturing Laura?' My voice was getting louder and I was determined not to fall for any more of his bullshit lies.

'What? I don't know. Maybe. I don't know. Maybe I felt a tad guilty. But I didn't want to hurt you,' he pleaded.

'Are you still speaking to Laura? Have you told her all about this?' I asked.

Cameron remained quiet, not answering my question.

'If you didn't want to hurt me, you would have been honest with her. With me. You were keeping your options open, Cameron. And to be honest, I'm done with this conversation. You are a liar, a cheat and a fuckboy trying hard to disguise himself as a good guy. See you, Cameron,' I shrugged. 'Or, probably not, eh.'

With that line I shut the door and slumped to the ground.

'Zara?' he mumbled from outside but I didn't answer. Eventually I could hear his footsteps get fainter in the distance as I listened to him walk out of my life for good.

'Babe, fancy a quick glass of Prosecco before we leave?' Ashley called out from the bedroom, unaware of my unexpected visitor.

'Good idea!'

With a deep breath I stood up, walked through to the kitchen, grabbed another mug from the dish rack and lifted the half bottle from the counter. I started to glug the contents into the mug.

'Fuck's sake, go easy, Zara!' Ashley said.

'I need it tonight! Come on, let's go get this over with!'

'Who was at the door?' she asked.

'Long story. I'll tell you later. C'mon, let's go!'

In the hallway, Ashley grabbed my wrist for balance as we both slipped into our high heels. Then we did a last-minute check in the mirror, got our bags and made the five-minute journey to The Corinthian Club.

The Corinthian stood alone on Ingram Street, a grand sandstone building with an archway of flowers tastefully decorating the doorway. We walked up the marble stairs into the vast bar area and spotted Emily and Raj chatting to some clients. When Emily spotted us, she waved us over enthusiastically.

'We have the room next door booked out for us. Do you want to go in right now?' Ashley asked.

'Sure!' From across the room, I communicated to Emily that we were going into the function suite.

'This is better!' I puffed as we entered the less crowded room. 'I felt claustrophobic out there, I don't know why.'

The function suite was small, and clients were dotted around the tables, chatting and enjoying glasses of Prosecco. I smiled and waved as I wandered past a few familiar faces. Raj was wearing a black and gold embroidered suit. I walked up from behind him and gave him a little fright by suddenly slapping my hands on his shoulders.

'My two favourite girls have finally made an appearance!' He gushed as he turned around.

'Better late than never?' I held my hands up, trying to excuse myself.

'And you're half cut already!' He rolled his eyes.

'We were drowning our sorrows that our rock is leaving us!' Ashley leaned over and hugged Raj tightly.

'You'll have Zara! She has it all in order, don't you, kiddo?' Raj winked over and I grinned warmly to my friend.

I nodded back. 'I have my full "To do" list written down in my book. Don't worry about it! Plus, you're only a phone call away!' I tried to sound upbeat but my heart ached at the thought of Raj leaving.

'Exactly!' he laughed.

'C'mon, we'll get a drink!' Ashley was tugging my arm towards the bar.

'You two enjoy. I'm going to mingle,' Raj replied, heading towards his guests.

'Zara!' I turned around, surprised to see Sarah, my hairdresser and regular client.

'Hey! You look amazing!' I replied, admiring her golden floor-length dress.

'You two do as well! But what the hell, I thought you were going to Dubai? Now it's Raj? What happened there?' Sarah asked and I felt myself freeze on the spot with embarrassment.

'Erm, she changed her mind, Sarah! Nothing major happened! Oh, Zara, we'd better move — the queue is getting bigger! We'll catch up soon.' Ashley hauled me away and I felt my anxiety rip through the roof.

'Thanks,' I whispered, feeling my hands shake with nerves. 'I'll get these! What do you want?' I asked her, diving for my purse in my bag, feeling my chest pulsate.

'A large white wine! What do you fancy?'

I was still rummaging through my bag, stumbling to the side.

'*Shit*, I've brought my fucking work bag!' I hissed.

'Aw, fuck's sake, Zara.'

'Allow me, ladies.'

Immediately, goosebumps travelled up my arm as I heard Tom's deep voice from behind us.

I turned around, feeling flustered as he stood there calmly in a full tuxedo.

'What would you like, Zara? Ashley?'

My eyes continued to stare through him.

'Em, nothing. We're good. Ash, I'll walk home and grab my other bag.'

Tom huffed. 'Don't be ridiculous. I can pay for your drinks, Zara.'

I raised my eyebrows at Ashley, who looked uncomfortable.

'Don't call me ridiculous, Tom. I can pay my way. I've just lifted the wrong bag, OK?' I spouted back.

Tom shook his head. 'Whatever you say.'

I turned back to face him. 'Why are you even here? Everywhere I go now, you're there! Work, drinks, fucking Dubai!' I could hear myself getting louder. 'I'm sick of seeing you.'

Ashley cleared her throat and muttered, 'Zara, stop! People are watching.'

But I couldn't, I was on a roll. 'Nah, seriously, Ash, is it just me or is he everywhere? I swear there must be five of the cunt! Everywhere I fucking go!'

Tom leaned forward and smirked, keeping his voice low. 'You know we're going to be working closely, Zara. You're going to have to be civil at some point.'

'Is everything OK, troops?' Andy walked up to the bar and waited for a response.

I felt my Prosecco confidence backing me up once more and opted to ignore Andy altogether. 'No, you're going to be working for *me*, Tom. I'll stay civil during work hours, but I don't need you to buy my drinks *and* socialise with me as if we're pals. Comprendo? Yes, everything is fine now, Andy, thanks.' I lifted my hands in the air and turned to Ashley for some reassurance. She was facing the other way, smiling at clients who were watching the commotion.

'Well,' Tom cleared his throat and adjusted his jacket smoothly, 'you clearly do need me to buy them because you haven't brought your purse, have you?' he sniggered.

'Aw, fuck off! Ashley, Andy, I'm away. I've had a shit week and don't need this poor patter. See you at work, Thomas.'

'Can't wait!' he sneered sarcastically.

I gave him one last withering look and marched out of the room. My knees felt shaky as I continued back down the marble stairs, out into the cool night, feeling suddenly overcome with emotion. I hadn't even said goodbye to Raj. I paused briefly but knew I couldn't go back now. So, I stood until the traffic cleared and ran across the pitch-black road. The wind was strong and bitter; I could feel my body quiver with coldness.

'Haw, Zara! Is that you?' a voice called out.

I looked up to see Luke, my recent toy boy, swaying on the pavement. My face fell. I hadn't seen him since I legged it for Dubai. *Shit.*

'Hi Luke.' I attempted a polite acknowledgement and marched past him.

I felt a solid grasp on my arm. 'Hi Luke? Don't walk away. You never called me back! What was that all about? Eh?' He came closer, and I could smell lager and weed on his breath. The pavement was empty, and I started to feel nervous.

'I know, I'm sorry. But listen, I've had a bad week. I need to go. See you later.' I pulled my arm to head off, but Luke followed behind me.

'You can't be heading home alone dressed like that, Zara. You're forgetting I know you; I know what you like, darlin'. Mon, I'll come up to yours and make your week a bit better. What do you say?'

I continued to walk quicker, ignoring him, but my heart raced as I heard his swift behind me.

'What's the matter? Did you prefer shagging my da? Is that it?' He sounded irate, and I suddenly recalled all of his red flags – pub-watched, short-tempered, punching walls.

257

'Luke, please stop. I honestly just want to go home. Leave me alone!' I turned around and started power-walking.

My heart was hammering in my ears, my breath felt light, and I didn't know what was going to happen. My hand was diving into my bag, hoping to find my phone or my keys but the bag was full and I couldn't find either of them.

Suddenly, Luke grabbed me by the shoulders and pushed me against the shutters of a shop. The loud slam of my body hitting the metal echoed in the street. Luke pushed his face close to mine.

'Listen to me when I'm fucking talking, Zara!' He was speaking behind gritted teeth, and I closed my eyes tightly.

Please help me. Please help me. Please, God, someone help me.

'Why would you wear that dress and expect to go home alone, eh? I think we both know you're a wee slag, eh,' he smirked.

I shrugged my shoulders, pulling my face as far away from him as I could.

'Can you mind how much I made you cum? Eh, remember?'

I nodded, hoping if I played along, he'd maybe leave me be.

'Will I show you again? I know you were gaggin' for it the last time, weren't yeh?' Luke's eyes opened wide, almost manic.

I could feel my own eyes stream with terror. 'Please don't do this, Luke. Please! Please!' I cried.

I felt his hand move down roughly, grabbing hold of my thigh. My body squirmed as I anticipated the worst. I feared for my dignity, for my body and for my life. His weight was against me. I couldn't move. I closed my eyes, powerless to fight back.

'What the fuck are you doing?'

A voice from behind disturbed Luke, and I saw a shadow come closer.

'Mind your own business, pal!' Luke called back angrily.

Crack.

Suddenly, he was down. As the tension fled my body, I saw Tom standing there. He'd punched Luke to the ground and was standing with his hand out to take mine. I plunged towards him, my bag scattering its contents on the pavement.

'She'll be calling the police. You're a fucking scumbag,' Tom roared at Luke, who was rolling around in pain on the ground.

I couldn't speak. I was too terrified and overwhelmed at the same time. Tom's strong arms gripped me tightly as my legs gave way.

'Thank you, thank you, thank you,' was all I could whisper over and over and over again.

'Zara, is everything OK?' I turned around to see Andy standing a few feet away.

'I wanted to make sure you got home.' He looked confused, glancing at the commotion around us.

'She's fine now, thanks, mate,' Tom replied for me. I nodded back, too traumatised to speak.

'Wait – my keys, my bag . . . My bag fell. Everything's fallen out.' My voice was shaking, my legs trembling.

'Here.' Tom stretched down to grab hold of my keys and began tossing the rest of my belongings back into my bag. 'I've got it, don't worry. I'll take it from here, Andy.'

With his arm around my shoulder, finally I felt safe, and managed to walk despite my legs feeling like jelly.

When we approached my building, I pushed open the tenement door.

'Can I come in, just to make sure you're OK?' Tom asked.

'It's OK. I'll be OK, honestly, Tom. I'm so sorry about everything. I don't know what's up with me just now.' I was trying to hold my emotions in, but my voice crumbled and my bottom lip started to tremble.

'No, no. Zara, I'm sorry. I was coming to explain. I've had enough of this animosity. I want the clinic to work, and we once worked well together.'

I nodded, but I couldn't comprehend work just now. My entire body was shaking.

He must have noticed because he said, 'Listen, please, let me sit with you for a minute. Just until you calm down a bit.'

I smiled gratefully at Tom and began climbing the stairs to my flat, with him close behind. Truthfully, I didn't want to be alone, not now. My head was pounding, still trying to make sense of what had just happened. What *could* have happened. I was panicking in case Luke came back. Or what if he attacked the clinic or turned up here? He could follow me home one night after work. He seemed so angry, and Tom had probably added to his rage.

By the time we got to my flat, my mind was clouded by anxiety.

'I think you should call the police, Zara,' Tom suggested as I opened the door.

I nodded. 'Maybe.'

How could I? I thought. How could I explain what happened? If I tried to explain how I knew Luke, or his dad, I'd be laughed out the courtroom. I'd be judged in an instant, the way I was judging myself, and I felt like I deserved it.

'I'll sleep on it. Is your hand OK?' I asked, changing the subject.

Tom rubbed his knuckles. 'I'd love to act macho and say it's fine, but, my god, it's fucking agony! Any peas?' he laughed.

I smiled, thankful he'd made a joke, and went to the freezer. Inside was a pack of mixed vegetables that had been in there since I took the flat over from my mother.

'Did you know that scumbag?' Tom asked as I handed him the frozen bag.

I nodded sheepishly. 'I did. And what I did to him makes me think I kind of deserved that tonight.' I felt so ashamed, so dirty, so embarrassed. I could taste the salt from my wandering tears flow into my mouth again.

'Zara,' Tom said, 'no woman deserves that. I don't care what you did to that boy; you didn't deserve that happening to you tonight. Do you hear me? Fuck, I'm just glad I got there in time.'

I started to bubble. 'Me too.'

Balancing the bag of veggies on his sore hand, Tom placed his other arm around me. 'I'll call Ashley, ask her to take over here, eh?'

I nodded. 'Yes, please.'

Tom made the call while I got changed into pyjamas, awaiting her return. I sat on the edge of my bed feeling bewildered. I wanted to close my eyes and for all of this to be over, but it wouldn't go away. I relived every second the entire night.

Chapter Twenty-Five

The following day, I woke to a smiley Ashley holding a mug of tea at my bedside. Tom had left at just past eleven, and I went to bed immediately after. He helped to explain everything to Ashley about what had happened. I felt sick, at myself and the situation. I dreaded what could have occurred if Tom hadn't come along when he did.

'Morning! How are you feeling?' Ashley asked.

'Ermm . . . morning. OK, I think,' I yawned back at her.

'Why don't you take a duvet day?' she suggested, looking down at me kindly.

I stretched out and checked the time: 8 a.m.

'It's my first day running the clinic,' I replied, still adjusting to the light.

'I know, but I think after what happened, you should take a day off to recuperate! Or chill, or something. Get your head straight and come into the clinic ready to take it on.'

I shook my head, seizing the tea from her after sitting up a little. 'No way. I need to go in. I'll be fine. Besides, I kind of don't want to stay here by myself.'

Ashley sat down on the edge of the bed, seeming concerned.

'Are you sure you're OK? Just, with Cameron and now Luke. Everything's gone a bit tits up. I need to know if you're really all right.'

I puffed out a large gust of air, briefly letting myself feel the stress of the last few days.

'Yeah, I'm honestly feeling a bit shitty, but I know I'll be back to normal soon. And anyway, Dave has Instagram! That's the real fucking crisis here!' I didn't have the energy to think about the night before. I was too ripe right now.

Ashley shrieked and lunged for her phone, forgetting she hadn't checked his followers since boiling the kettle.

'Well, come on then, boss lady. Get ready!' she said, dragging my covers down the foot of the bed before leaving me to it.

My tired eyes stared across the room at nothing. I was zoning out, pondering about what Ashley had said. *Boss lady.* Shit, I was going to be in charge for the next few weeks, and suddenly I felt a surge of pressure. What if I made a blunder with the orders? Or if all Raj's clients went elsewhere? Shit. This was going to be challenging.

Luckily, I hadn't scheduled any clients today for myself, and only a couple were booked into the morning slots with Tom. My plan was to get familiarised with the paperwork and stick thoroughly to Raj's instructions. I lifted my work bag and rummaged around it to glance over my notes. *Shit!* My notebook was missing. My hands were hitting the sides of the bag as I desperately rummaged through it. Then I remembered – it must have fallen out last night in all of the commotion. I suddenly felt sick. I'm going to let everyone down. I began sobbing frustratedly.

'What's up?' Ashley ran towards me and put her arm around me.

'I've lost my holy grail of how to run a clinic! I've fucked up already!'

'Calm the fuck down. You know how to do this, Zara. Raj is a phone call away. You've got this!'

I gulped down the remaining tea Ashley had made me, got ready and then the two of us walked across the square, heading for the clinic. Inside the shop, the lights were already on and Tom's car was parked out front. I felt as if I had been hit by a bus. Tired, sad, violated.

'He's no shy, is he? Opening up on his first day and everything! Watch your job, hen,' Ashley said, giggling.

'It's not as if it's his first day, though. He's probably just keen to get started,' I said.

'Aw fuck, you're sticking up for him already! Round two, ding ding!' Ashley nudged my shoulder jokingly as we walked through the door.

My eyes popped out my head, hoping Tom hadn't heard. Fortunately, Tom seemed entirely preoccupied, standing with his shirt sleeves rolled up, chatting away to Andy.

Ashley flashed him a smile. 'Morning! Well, well, well, this is a nice surprise.'

I looked at both of them cautiously. What the hell

was going on? Shit, please don't delve into a safety intervention about my horrible experience last night.

'Morning. How's your hand, Tom?' I asked, taking a seat, noticing him rubbing his knuckles.

'Eh? Oh, it's fine, a little bruised but it's fine. Gives me more character, I think.'

Andy's usually calm, laid-back manner had disappeared, and he seemed strangely excited.

Exchanging puzzled looks with Ashley, we all sat down.

'When I left you and Tom last night, after you know, I was heading back to the Corinthian and found this lying on the street, so I grabbed it, and, I'm sorry, I don't want you to think for one second I was being nosey, but I had to make sure it belonged to you. Zara, you are brilliant. Your plans are fucking spot on!' He was gushing, holding my notepad in his hands.

I looked at Ashley, confused and speechless.

'What do you mean? My plans?' I laughed.

'Your plans to turn this place around. The facial balancing technique, the media strategy, everything you have written here, it's amazing. It's honestly beyond anything I would have even thought of. I started reading it and couldn't put it down.'

I blushed, realising he'd gone through my scribbles.

'I wrote that a while back, but then you suggested Dubai, so I left it.' I glanced at the notebook now sitting on the table and cringed at the thought of Andy reading my strawberry-scented gel pen notes. *Shit,* I hoped he hadn't seen the entire page dedicated to

'Zara loves Cameron' menchies. Or the three-page spread trialling Cameron's surname, just in case we tied the knot.

'We need this, Zara! Yes, it's a big fucking gamble, but it will work. It's distinctive, not all the pompous bullshit vibes this place has or the hippy shit across the street. It's individualised, person-centred treatments and that's what this place should be.'

I smiled at how animated he was about my ideas. 'Thanks. I mean, I'm flattered, but I mentioned it before to Raj, and he didn't like the concept at all.'

Tom stood up, looking shocked. 'This sounds astonishing, Zara! All of it, it really does. But if I may suggest one little thing?' He paced the floor for a few moments, then turned around.

'You're in charge when Raj is in Dubai and he doesn't do social media, right? He'll never know anything. We could have a trial transformation in the time he's away, Zara.' Tom smiled to Andy and they both seemed unbelievably keen, while I was still in shock to find out they'd enjoyed my ideas.

Tom moved closer then crouched down beside me. His hair, usually neat and pushed back, flopped to the side.

'I've actually attended a facial balancing course before for my plastic's clinical module. I know the principles inside out. I could teach you the techniques. It's not difficult; you'd be using less product than you do now. It's all about perfecting the angles and edges of the face. What do you think?'

I sat there glued to my seat, flabbergasted and speechless.

Ashley looked excited, not comprehending the conversation completely but infected by his upbeat energy. 'Zara, this sounds amazing!'

I wished I could share in her excitement, but somehow I couldn't help question Tom's motives. Did he really believe in my ideas that much? Or was he trying to get me fired so he could have his old job back? I rubbed my temples, trying hard to think, then turned to Andy.

'So, you think this could work? You believe in it one hundred per cent?'

Andy's smile shone towards me. 'I believe in you one hundred per cent, darlin', so aye, it's gon' to work.'

I blushed, still unable to break eye contact with the hot man across the room.

Tom let out a loud, echoing clap. 'I agree! Let's do this, Zara!' Tom's eyes were bright and alive with passion. I had never seen him so uncomposed before. He walked up to Andy and they started chatting and brainstorming ideas together like two kids in the playground. I watched their arms move around animatedly as they fed off one another's ideas. The room was filled with laughter and excitement.

Ashley turned to me, twirling her hair in confusion. 'Well, what was that all about?'

'Nothing that big, honestly. More about social media approaches and a focus on clients rather than trends.'

Ashley tutted. 'Jesus Christ, it was like you'd written the sequel to Harry Potter or something. That cunt had a semi with whatever was in that notebook, Zara! Nae joke!'

'Shhh . . .' I laughed as Andy's eye caught mine again briefly.

He cleared his throat and turned back around to us all, 'So, we all good here? I need to rush to work but I wanted to see you first.'

'Yeah, I'm good, and so grateful you like my ideas, Andy. But at the same time, I'm like, where do I start? Like, if we were to trial this?' I was still feeling overwhelmed by it all.

'You've done the hard part, wee yin. Everything is in there . . .' He walked by and tapped my head jokingly. 'You guys should have a team meeting, do the training, arrange the décor, the social media approach and I'll promote it on Juju's platforms. You've got this.'

I suddenly felt motivated and out of my slump from all this encouragement.

'I'd better get set up. My client will be here any second,' Tom said, walking away while Ashley walked towards her desk to prepare for the day.

Andy took a small sigh as we both began to talk at the same time. We laughed and I nodded for him to speak first. 'Sorry for bombarding you this morning. I hope I've not, like, overstepped the mark or whatever.'

'No, no. I'm so glad you did. That's the first time I think anyone has taken any of my ideas seriously. I am a bit speechless, to be honest.' I looked down to the floor.

'Why? They are amazing. Honestly, you could be stealing my job next!' He lifted my chin from the ground and smiled. 'Listen, I don't know what happened last night. It's none of my business. But one thing I have learned is everyone needs to work as a team in a small business like this. Especially with so much riding on a whole new concept. So, I'm hoping any beef with Tom is done and I hope that wee prick he punched for you is the only baggage you have. You'll need one hundred per cent focus if you want this to work, and then you'll have this in the bag.'

I agreed with his advice, feeling slightly vulnerable reminiscing about last night.

'I got this. No skeletons in my closet! Tom and I are honestly good now,' I grinned, trying to stay upbeat.

'Ha, I'm glad! Wish I could say the same. My ex-wife is enough skeletons for both of us, man. Right, I'll be in touch then. Good luck!' Andy winked and turned his back, leaving the clinic and waving to Ashley.

Tom returned from switching into his scrubs.

'Weet wheel!' Ashley called out.

Tom raised an eyebrow and sniggered at her.

'It's like I was never gone, eh, girls! Dream team's back.' His white teeth shone towards us.

I rolled my eyes jokingly.

'And we all know what happened then.'

Tom grinned. 'Yes, we do, Zara!'

At that point, the door opened and Tom's first client walked through.

'Ah, morning! You must be Sylvia! I'll take you through to the treatment room for your consultation,' Tom greeted his client effortlessly.

I smiled at Ashley at his charm and we both laughed loudly as they left the shop floor.

'So, I feel like I'm totally out of the loop. What the fuck are the new plans? Explain it all to me, Zara. And not in medical lingo.' She batted her false eyelashes.

'OK, so I was looking at our sales figures recently, since Botox Boxx opened, and that is unquestionably the more appealing salon. Their social media is insane. They have influencers on their client list, and cool, trendy, Instagrammable décor. Yes?'

She hastily nodded.

'But we are better at aesthetics; there's no doubt when you see the results. I was looking at their treatment menu, and they actually have social media influencing packages, so you pay to look like your favourite influencer. That's insane on so many levels! Why do they all want to look the same? It's a terrible message for young women – and men. So, anyway, I've been researching facial balancing for a while now, and I think we should promote it, like big style. Go back to measurements. Use small, subtle injections to slightly adjust the client's face but keep them individualised. Each client doesn't walk in like they do just now, and say I want one mil of filler. Instead, we measure their lips, measure the nose to the chin and advise an area that would help enhance their own facial structure, rather than them getting their lips done because everyone on

Instagram has their lips done. We could redecorate with positive body images all over the walls, stretch marks, real client portraits. Make *everyone* feel beautiful. Make everyone look like the best versions of *themselves*. You could head the campaign, of course!'

Ashley's eyes were glistening while listening intently.

'OK, so you're Individualising Individualise. But can we afford it? The way Raj was talking, this place sounded heavy skint,' Ashley replied.

I sighed. 'Well, if Tom has already trained in facial balancing, like he's said, then he could teach me, and in fact, we'd be using less product than usual. I can use my savings for the makeover. It might be a stupid idea, but if Andy liked it and—'

'Zara,' Ashley interrupted, 'I think it's fuckin' brilliant. Honestly.'

I gasped, clutching my hands excitedly. 'Shut up!' I screamed.

'I think it's clever, it's current and, let's face it, it's promoting better body positivity for younger clients. It's a win-win.'

My body bounced about the floor, feeling triumphant.

'But initially I'd keep it a secret from Raj,' I continued.

Ashley attempted an eyebrow raise. 'Surely he needs to know?'

'Well, yeah, less secret, more . . . surprise. Honestly, he'd do my head in, constant updates. He left me in charge,' I shrugged.

'If you think that's for the best.'

That night we ordered Chinese and squatted down on the clinic floor to plan. Tom set up his laptop and demonstrated the fundamentals of facial balancing, the techniques, the symmetry, the measurements. I took notes and began studying and understanding the method. Ashley flicked through her phone, searching décor ideas, selfie walls and inspiring artwork we could use to transform the bare clinic walls. It was the first excitement I'd seen in her eyes since her break-up. Tom seemed captivated by this project too, and his cool persona had lifted entirely. It felt refreshing to see his teaching side shine as he explained procedures in detail and patiently answered my questions. He was a terrific listener and put my mind at ease. I had built him up as the bad guy for so long, I had forgotten about this side of him entirely.

'Have you done rhinoplasties before?' Tom asked.

I sighed, kneeling up and, shifting my position while sipping on my Diet Coke. 'I've done the basic one, like across the bridge of the nose, but I've never lifted the tip yet.'

Tom shuffled towards me, placing his talented hands on my face. 'There is a significant artery that comes off here.' He used my face as a map and demonstrated areas to avoid by slowly running his fingers across my nose. 'Therefore, you have to be very careful injecting here and here impartially.'

I was holding my breath in case the smell of my curried noodles knocked him out. But inside, my

273

stomach churned. I'd forgotten how gentle his touch could feel. His hands were strong but soft. I'd painted him like the worst person imaginable, but maybe he was just a guy who'd made a bad mistake.

The hairs on the back of my neck stood up on end as he took his hands off me and continued the lesson. *Jesus*, why did I have a vague twinge from my vagina? *What was happening?* I hadn't thought about Tom like this for a while and had completely dismissed any feelings for him. Obviously my vagina hadn't got the memo as she drizzled like a custard doughnut, soaking my inner thighs throughout the session. I glanced at Ashley, who was smirking at her phone, clearly having seen the whole thing.

'I think another day of this and we'll be good to start practising on the public! What do you think, Zara?' Tom asked, diving back into his chow mein.

'Yeah, I mean, the principle of injecting is still the same, just the approach is a bit different. Not like, "A mil in the lips", "Right, three hundred quid, hen". More, "You have great lips, but perhaps we should pull your chin out slightly, giving you a more sculpted look".'

'One hundred per cent. It's more about taking our time and evaluating each person.'

'Yes, assessing is key. I also think it's really important to complement other features that the client has. Make it a positive experience to encourage their confidence.'

Tom smirked. 'And what if there's nothing to complement? I mean, occasionally we do get a couple of absolute munters!'

I rolled my eyes. 'Well, to complement their eye colour or shoes or something. Fuck's sake, Tom!' I tittered, trying to stay professional.

'Aye, and I bet you'd still stick it on them, Thomas!' Ashley cried out.

We laughed together, and for a second, it felt like the old times, like everything that had happened between us hadn't happened yet, and he'd never left at all. His fun, cheeky energy was welcomed back to the clinic, even though the dynamics had shifted.

That night Tom offered to drop Ashley and me off, and for once, I accepted. The hectic day had distracted me from the encounter last night with Luke, but I didn't feel brave enough to risk the walk yet. So, instead, I jumped out of Tom's car and skipped up the stairwell with Ashley hot at my heels, feeling fatigued but motivated and for the first time in my life, full of inspiration.

Chapter Twenty-Six

The next day, Ashley and I landed at the clinic earlier than usual. We set up the projector, which was hidden in one of the staff-room cupboards from earlier training days, and I connected my laptop, anticipating Tom's arrival. I had prepared a slideshow highlighting the key changes we were about to initiate at Individualise. Tom burst through the door ten minutes early, holding coffees for us all, wearing a crisp white T-shirt and jeans.

'Morning, ladies. Sleep well? Here you are,' he said, delivering the drinks.

'Aww, thanks, Tom,' Ashley said. 'Oh aye, I had a great sleep, thanks. Zara's an outstanding wee spoon!'

'She is that,' he said.

My heart quickened at the sudden flashbacks of steamy nights being spooned by him and his devil dick. *Jesus, stay focused, Zara. Be professional.*

'Tom, I've prepared a quick PowerPoint recap of the main points from yesterday. Just to make sure we're all on the same page,' I said.

Tom looked impressed. 'Absolutely! Nice work.'

I wandered over to the laptop and pressed the button to play the slideshow. *Shit.* Nothing happened.

I hit the button a little harder, hoping for a better response.

'Everything OK?'

'Yip! I think I just need to connect to the clinic's Wi-Fi. Maybe because I was using mine, it's all out of sync.' I was opening and closing the settings menu when Tom marched over.

'Allow me.' He leaned across me, and the sharp, sexy smell of him ignited an impromptu thought.

'Eh, no, it's fine. I'll sort it,' I said, quickly taking back control of the laptop.

Tom chuckled. 'Oh, is someone hiding some X-rated content on there? Someone hasn't deleted their search history, eh?' he grinned, playfully stretching back around me for the device.

I laughed nervously, trying to shut the laptop and hoping my late-night searching of *'Why do men always cheat on me?'* and *'What is the normal size of labia?'* did not appear on the screen. But by now Tom was clutching my waist, and I was laughing for real.

Eventually, Ashley called a halt. Tom relented, sitting back on the sofa, and I sheepishly took the floor.

'OK, obviously it isn't loading, so I just want to reiterate the crucial points during the consultation process from yesterday. Step one: find out what the patient does and doesn't like about their look. Step two: compliment them, make them feel good about themselves, comment on their most attractive feature. Step three: based on symmetry and measurements, suggest adjustments that can define their features. Yes?'

Tom was signalling his agreement. 'I've organised a couple of girls today to practise on, if that's OK with you?'

Ashley beamed, but I felt my eyes widen in surprise.

'Erm, sure, OK,' I said. I felt slightly awkward that he hadn't run this past me until now. I turned to Ashley. 'How are you getting on with the décor changes?'

She smiled. 'OK, so, the selfie wall we chatted about is going to be made up of real-life selfies! Like, get this, we'll have a Polaroid camera and let our clients take a selfie and add it to the wall. *Genius?* I know.' She flicked her long hair back sassily. 'And I have four stunning, beautiful and diverse clients who would LOVE to take part in a photoshoot for our pictures on the walls. I'm thinking we should basically print their images full-sized along the main wall, but I can't find a photographer who could have the prints available in the next week. Everyone I've spoken to sends them away, and it can take up to six weeks to get the prints back.'

I nodded. 'OK, I get that. Keep trying, though. And what about a painter?'

Ashley grinned, looking chuffed with herself. 'They can start tonight, and work through the night. No more white walls!'

I clapped my hands eagerly. 'Fab! What time did you book the girls for today, Tom?'

Tom glanced at his watch. 'I told them to keep a free schedule, so anytime you're ready for them, boss.'

'Well, ask them to come just now. That gives us time to work on our usual clients this afternoon. Then, from tomorrow, we'll slowly introduce the concept. Everyone happy?' I asked, looking between the two of them.

Tom and Ashley looked pumped and stood up eagerly.

'Let's do this!' I said, before strolling into my treatment room to get changed into my scrubs for a busy day ahead.

An hour later, Tom and I had constructed a mini-treatment room on the shop floor, complete with our sterile trays and equipment. Three tall, stunningly beautiful women sat patiently on the sofa, awaiting our instructions.

'OK, Zara. Do you want to take one girl each and do the last together? Or how do you want to work it?' Tom asked, pointing out the odd number of models.

'Eh, how about we both consult the three girls and let the models decide who does their treatments, based on our recommendations?'

Tom's eyes burned bright at the thought of some friendly competition.

'Bring it on!' he said, sauntering over to greet the girls. I followed a second behind, rhyming off the three-step plan in my head, over and over.

'Zara, this is Rheanne, Lisa and Ebony.'

Ebony was nibbling the arm of her glasses seductively, trying to keep eye contact with him. No wonder Tom looked so flustered. Fucking hell, I fancied all of these girls! Where the hell had he found them? Girls of this calibre didn't just stoat about Sauchiehall Street, that was for sure. I couldn't help wondering which of the girls had already been punctured by Tom's prick in one way or another.

'OK, ladies, my name is Zara, and I'm currently managing this beautiful clinic. Thank you all for coming at such short notice. I'm going to get straight to it because we have a busy afternoon. The plan for today is both Dr Adams and I will provide you with an individual consultation. During this time, we will each suggest treatments that we think would benefit your already sensational features. Then, when you've had both our recommendations, we'll ask who you would like to perform these procedures on you, and finally, you will get your treatments.'

The girls smiled brightly, and Tom seemed up for the challenge.

'OK, who's first then?' Tom asked, and Ebony rocketed out of the chair towards him. She was wearing a small red crop top and tight jeans. Her waist was as tiny as my wrist, and she finished her look with gold-plated earrings with an almighty letter E dangling off the centre.

'I think you should examine me, Thomas,' she said, her voice smooth and tempting, with a Spanish twang. I wanted to interrupt and make sure she was aware her face was getting examined and not her cervix, but Tom looked as if he'd just cum in his fucking Calvins.

I let out a small cough, breaking their lingering eye contact.

'OK, Ebony is with Dr Adams. Rheanne, shall I take you first?'

I brought Rheanne to my station and began to set up, aspiring to focus, but I couldn't help being diverted by the fireworks occurring at Tom's station. *What a prick!* I thought. *He's going to win this because he has a fucking penis!* Rheanne was sitting on the chair, patiently waiting for my attention to return to her. She was the smallest of the girls but still stood around five foot ten. She had a warm shade of vanilla-blonde hair and suited the natural look; no make-up or humungous lashes, plain but very distinct. It was hard to imagine what she could possibly want to improve about the face she'd already been blessed with.

'So, Rheanne, let's start with explaining to me what your favourite feature is? Or what you would like to change about your look?' I asked, sitting down on the stool beside her.

'Erm, well, truthfully, all the girls at shoots have really high brows, and mine are fine, but I'd like them higher. The problem is I do commercials, so I need my face to move. I know Botox totally freezes everything, though, so I couldn't get that. And also, I hate my nose. It's huge.' She covered it with her hand and blushed. 'But I know that's like a hammer-and-chisel job, not a quick one for you guys.'

'Aw, don't be silly. Let's have a look then,' I said.

Rheanne lowered her hand, and I examined her face, gently pressing my palms against her skin and slowly working out angles.

'OK, so firstly, your nose is the perfect size for your face. It isn't out of proportion at all. I think you have the most stunning cheekbones and structure to your face already.'

Rheanne nodded gratefully.

'But I do think defining your jaw a little would complement your appearance. Your face essentially gets smaller in the bottom half, which makes you think you have a big nose, but you honestly don't. You just have a smaller jaw. I could insert a small cannula and define the lower half of your face. It's all very non-invasive compared to a rhinoplasty! I also think raising your eyebrows slightly would give you the look you desire. I will use Botox, but without completely freezing your forehead, making sure you still retain movement at the sides.'

Rheanne sat back and smiled. 'Wow. Really? OK. Thanks, Zara! I never thought about the jaw thing before. Thank you!'

'Sure. Now you can swap with Ebony, if you like. Tom is fantastic too. Listen to his recommendation and make your decision at the end.'

Rheanne moved to Tom's bay, briefly chatting to him and Ebony. I felt elevated after only one consultation. This way of aesthetics didn't feel like the typical conveyor belt of patients telling me what they thought they wanted, like the bog-standard celeb face. Instead, I was listening and advising, using my own expertise, evaluating what would work for each individual face. My brain wasn't running on autopilot anymore, and it felt more rewarding.

Ebony strutted over towards me and sat on the chair.

'Hey,' she said, her gaze still sliding over towards Tom.

'It's lovely to meet you properly, Ebony. OK, you probably had this with Tom so I'll jump straight in. I'd love to know what your favourite feature is. And what would you most like to change about your facial appearance today?'

She sighed and ran her tiny Niknak'd fingers through her luscious brown locks. 'I like my face. I like the shape and structure. But I feel I look so tired all the time. I haven't had my lips done for maybe a year, so maybe my lips and like a facial or something.'

I couldn't help but grin towards her, 'OK, well, firstly, you are stunning. Like, I could probably cut my finger on that jawline. It's insane.'

Ebony's face hadn't changed at all. She was clearly familiar with compliments.

'I think Botox would be the only treatment I advise today. Your lips don't need to be treated. They're large and full with a striking Cupid's bow. You do, however, have small lines on either side of your forehead that I could even out and lift, and this would reduce the tired look. But honestly, you are stunning the way you are.'

Ebony twiddled her huge initialled earrings around and grinned. 'Is that me then?' she asked.

'Yes!' I replied, and called Lisa over to my station.

Lisa was the oldest-looking of the girls. I could tell she'd had work done in the past, but she was every bit as attractive, and her personality shone brilliantly as soon as she relaxed.

'Hi, Lisa, I'm Zara. Again, thanks for coming in today at such short notice.'

Lisa beamed. 'No, honestly, thanks for asking me! I love a wee freebie!'

I giggled, instantly clicking with her bubbly energy.

'OK, so what do you love about your face, and is there anything you really would like to change?'

Lisa burst out laughing. 'Eh . . . OK, I love feck all. Sorry!' she laughed. 'Just peel it off and make me look like one of them two, eh!' She giggled. 'No, eh. I suppose my face is feeling tired. I have a wee girl, and no matter how much Botox I get, I still feel like my face looks blah. Maybe I'm at that age, though, eh?' She rolled her eyes jokingly.

'Right, firstly, you are every bit as stunning as they two girls! Secondly, your features are incredible – the bright blue eyes, your complexion, just remarkable. What I think you might like is some cheek filler. That will return some shape and youthful plumpness to your face. Filler also massively decreases the wee signs of ageing. When we get older, we naturally lose shape here and here.' I ran my fingers down her cheeks. 'You don't need much, but a little bit of filler at either side, and you'll look twenty-one again!'

Lisa looked hopeful. 'You know, I've never considered cheeks before!'

'Honestly, two mils of Juju product will make a huge difference. I'll let you get your consultation from Tom now, if you like.'

She stood up. 'Thanks, babe,' she said and headed over to his section where the other two girls were standing.

I approached the desk and stood with Ashley. We watched Tom turn his charm on, completely dying to win the competition.

'What you thinking?' Ashley asked.

I shrugged. 'I was honest. I suggested completely different treatments than what they came in expecting. Maybe it will work.' But suddenly I was feeling less optimistic.

When his consultation with Lisa was over, Tom led the three girls back to the waiting area. They sat on the couch, and I joined Tom, standing in front of them. 'OK, ladies, who would you like for your treatment today?' he asked. He stood tall, confident as ever, crossing his arms and looking arrogant with his efforts.

Lisa smiled. 'Zara for me please. Sorry, Tom!'

Rheanne hid her face sheepishly. 'Zara for me too!'

My heart burst open with pride as I faced Ebony, hoping for a full house.

'Oh, Tommy, Thomas, of course, I would pick you. Always.' Ebony's eyes were mentally undressing him, and I felt incredibly uncomfortable being part of their moment.

'Thanks, girls, all of you. Now we'll get you through for your treatments.'

I walked proudly with my majority win trailing close behind, but I couldn't help observing Tom flirting ferociously across the room. Every now and then, he'd catch me staring, and his body stiffened, but as soon as I turned my back, he was all over Ebony again. The cunt hadn't changed one bit! He was entirely incapable of being professional.

The girls seemed satisfied with our new consultation twist, and delighted with the results of their treatments. Before they left, Ashley also unboxed the Polaroid camera, and the girls gave us great contributions to add to the selfie wall.

Later on that night, Ashley and I were rearranging the furniture in anticipation of the painters coming. Tom came bursting out of his treatment room, staring at his phone, looking rushed.

'Lift home?' he asked.

I shook my head. 'No thanks.'

Ashley looked confused, knowing how anxious I'd been walking anywhere in the dark.

'You sure? I don't want you girls walking alone,' he said.

'I need to wait on the painters. We're big enough and certainly ugly enough to walk home. Just . . . go enjoy your plans or whatever,' I shrugged.

Tom laughed loudly. 'Enjoy my plans? Why do I get the impression I've done something wicked, Zara?' He glanced at his watch, then slipped his phone into his jeans pocket and approached the pile of furniture we had accumulated in the centre of the room.

'No reason,' I shrugged but continued to avoid eye contact.

'We did great work today. I think we should be proud of it. Tomorrow will be an exciting day, too.' Tom reached for my chin, making it impossible not to look right at him.

I felt my body stiffen, trying to cut the moment short.

'Sure will. I'll see you tomorrow.'

He hesitated at the front door for a second, and then left. As soon as he was gone, Ashley leapt over towards me.

'What was the tension all about there?' she asked.

'Him, he's so sleazy, fucking hands all over the clients, flirting – it's inappropriate,' I huffed.

'Is that all? God, Zara, that's what he does. It's what he always does.'

'Well, maybe I don't like it when I'm in charge.'

'You sound jealous, babe! I mean, I get it. You guys have history, and a stunning woman is putting it on him. Of course you'll be ragin'.'

'She wasn't all that stunning, Ash.' It was all I could reply.

We looked at each other and burst into laughter.

'Oh, God, why am I jealous? I don't even want to be with him. Half the time, I want to punch his cheesy big face off, but I just don't want to see him flaunting his sex life in the middle of the workplace.'

Ashley laughed at my petty excuse. 'Aye, well, think how I felt with you two!'

There was a knock at the door.

'Oh, the painters! *Yes!* I'll get my coat!'

Ashley ran towards the staff room to get organised for home while I let the painters in and instructed them on what to do.

'Just post the key through the letterbox when you're done, guys. Thank you!' I called out, exiting the clinic with Ashley linking my arm.

It was after nine and Glasgow seemed dark and quiet. I tried to move, but my body seized immediately, thinking about Luke.

'Can we call a taxi, Ash?' I asked.

She smiled down at me. 'Course, my feet are throbbing anyway.'

The taxi took us safely home, and Ashley held my hand as we made our way up the stairs to get settled.

Ping.

Andy: *How did it go with the models?*

I instantly smiled in response to receiving his text.

Hey! Yeah great! They all seemed to love it. We have the painters in just now too. It's all coming together! Eek x

Ping.

Andy: *It's all down to you darlin. Can't wait to see the décor x*

Ashley and I FaceTimed Raj to check in and make sure he was surviving without us. He seemed to be less stressed and absolutely loving Dubai, but just chatting with him made me wish he was home and part of the buzz. It felt almost impossible not to be sharing our crazy few days at the clinic with our best friend but, ultimately, I just hoped the secrecy would pay off. We ended the call and headed to bed, discussing future plans for Individualise, how we could push the clinic to its full potential, delivering diverse treatments, using our expertise and promoting positive body campaigns all of the while. My mind was racing with optimism and opportunity. It felt wonderful not having a man being my last thought before bed, and there was a tiny spark twinkling in my gut, telling me that something much more exciting was just around the corner for us.

Chapter Twenty-Seven

The following morning as we walked through the clinic door, the potent smell of fresh paint caught the back of our throats. I turned the alarm off while Ashley ran for the light switches, keen to admire the new look.

'Wow, I love it!' she called out.

I turned to admire it all. The plain white walls had been transformed to an ivory cream colour. It was a small change, but the clinic seemed so much more homely and inviting already.

'I love it too! What about cushions or a throw or something?'

Ashley let out a wicked laugh. 'The accessories should arrive tonight or tomorrow.'

Tom burst through the door behind us and beamed. 'Well, ladies, I think I've solved our problem. Last night, I sped out of here to meet a particularly well-known Spanish photographer named Alfredo. He's visiting his sister in Glasgow this week, and he has use of a printing studio while he's here. I needed to check over his work before I got too excited, but he is phenomenal. He can photograph this evening and have prints available in a day or so.'

'Wow, Tom, that's amazing! Can you organise the clients to model for then, Ash?' I asked.

'I don't see why not! I have back-ups if I can't.'

'Thanks, Tom,' I said, feeling a tad guilty about my standoffish behaviour the previous night.

'I'm glad to help. One of the models from yesterday actually mentioned him to me and passed on his details. It was too good an opportunity to miss.'

I agreed and smiled back through gritted teeth.

So, Ebony must be the photographer's sister. A convenient connection indeed. When had she had the great idea about her brother? Was it over dinner, or after sex? My psychotic mind began overthinking, despite this connection working in our favour, whatever it was.

'Right, guys, we have ten minutes to push this furniture back before the clients come in!' Ashley interrupted us, and we all set to work, carefully coordinating the clutter back into order.

That day, Tom and I performed our innovative facial balancing technique on all the clients who booked in. We listened, complimented and suggested new ways of enhancing their appearances. The day sped by. I felt a buzz returning that I hadn't felt in a while as I added tiny, precise injections and witnessed the difference we were making. I felt as if I was empowering the women who came in, encouraging them to lean into their own uniqueness rather than encouraging them to look like someone else. I believed in the Individualise concept one hundred per cent.

Just after four, we'd seen our last clients for the day, and came out onto the shop floor to find an overeager Ashley encircled by boxes.

'What's all this?' Tom opened a box and began to lift out silhouette vases shaped like women's bodies. He was examining them carefully, both the curvy ones and the skinny ones.

'Watch you don't get a hard-on holding them, Thomas,' Ashley teased.

Tom laughed and then winked at me. My cheeks grew hot.

'Right, did you call the customers and ask them to model?' I asked Ashley.

'I sure did! They're meeting Alfredo at his studio in an hour!'

'What? Where's that? We better hurry!' I exclaimed.

Ashley turned to me. 'No way, I bags'd it! I'm an expert at that kind of stuff. I need you to wait here on deliveries. There are so many things getting delivered today. Oh, and the selfie wall needs to be put up.'

I huffed. 'What if they're shite? I need the pictures to be flawless, Ash.'

'Do you think I'd let them be shite? Calm it, Janet, and unbox.'

Tom crouched down beside me. 'I can help too. I don't have any plans tonight.'

Aye, probably because you emptied your balls last night, son, I thought.

'Aw, that's great, Tom. She'll probably need a hand,' Ashley said.

Fantastic, I thought, rolling my eyes at her.

Ashley left the clinic half an hour later, and Tom and I were left sitting on the sofa unboxing more deliveries. I had unravelled a magazine rack and Tom was opening *Women Don't Owe You Pretty* and *How to Embrace the Female Body* books.

'Are you hungry? I'm famished. Shall we call for some food while we're working?' he suggested.

'Sure. What you thinking?'

'That new noodle place is just around the corner. It's meant to be delicious. I could walk round and grab us something?'

'Yeah, that sounds good.'

He lifted his suit jacket and headed towards the door. Suddenly I felt a rush of anxiety at being left alone.

Get a grip, Zara, I told myself. Still, as soon as Tom had left, I galloped to the door and locked it, ensuring the place was secure.

I took a deep breath and returned to unpacking Ashley's spree of accessories. I loved the attention to detail she'd shown in her choices, from body-positive coasters to golden, fuzzy pampas grass in ceramic vases. She'd picked cream cushions with 'Individualise Me' printed in bold gold lettering. I adored it all. She totally got the concept and, if anything, added to it.

I glanced around the room at the chaos and couldn't help but smile. My vision was coming to life and I had a burst of proudness.

There was a loud knock at the door, and my heart plummeted. Through the glass, I could see Andy standing with his hand up for me to let him in. Relief washed through me. I unlocked the door and walked back to the desk.

'Hey! How are you?' I beamed.

'Aye, I'm good. I saw the lights on and thought I'd stop in. This looks great, bit cluttered but great.' He stepped over the boxes and admired the clinic.

'Thank you! I honestly love it. Can you believe how quickly this place is changing?'

'Aye. It just shows you what can happen when you have your head screwed on. You just staying back here by yourself?' Andy asked casually.

'Yes. Well, no. Tom went to grab some food. He's just unpacking boxes with me. Like, just unpacking and putting some frames up.' I felt my cheeks turn red as I couldn't stop talking.

'Well, you two sound like you have it covered then. But anytime you need a hand in here, I'm about and I'm pretty decent with a hammer.' Andy rubbed his hand over his bristly head, looking shy, and I instantly smiled at his offer.

'I bet you're a lot better with a hammer than Tom! I don't think they had tech at an international private school!' I laughed.

Andy giggled. 'Who's saying I learned my moves at tech! I'm from Castlemilk originally, hen. A hammer was part of your school uniform there.'

We both laughed loudly and Andy sighed.

'Well, the offer always stands. I mean it, anytime. I better boost. Got a busy day.' Andy winked and turned to leave the clinic.

'Are you just going home now by yourself?' I blurted out before he left.

Andy turned, looking confused at my random choice of words.

'I don't even know what I meant to say there.' I cleared my throat. 'Are you heading home then, I meant.' I could feel my face twist with embarrassment.

'Yeah, I'm heading home now,' he chuckled. 'And, I live alone. Well, sort of. It's complicated. See you darlin'.' With that, Andy about-turned and left the clinic.

'Look! Look!' Tom raced through the door, brushing past Andy, holding a paper under his arm. He sat the two boxes of noodles on the desk and opened it up. 'He's gone. Luke's gone.' He looked at me sympathetically as he handed the paper over.

'What? What do you mean?' I asked, feeling sick at the sound of his name.

'It was sitting in the window of the newsagents, and I grabbed it when I saw the photo. I recognised the bastard immediately. Read the article,' he urged, pointing the paper in my face.

My eyes skimmed the front page of *The Daily Record*: YOUNG THUG JAILED FOR KNIFE ATTACK.

'He's pled guilty. He's in prison, Zara,' Tom continued, and I could feel my body drain with relief.

'Oh my god, thank god. I mean, I hope the other guy is OK, but he's gone. He's actually gone.'

Tom nodded. 'He won't be bothering you anytime soon. An argument with a neighbour apparently.'

Without thinking, I bound my arms around him and squeezed tightly. I felt my heart warm, and I became conscious of how good he smelled. I opened my eyes and caught a glimpse of Andy observing our embrace as he entered his car. He smiled over when he saw me, then drove off. Our hug broke, but our eye contact remained. I was beaming at him as if he was my very own Dog the Bounty Hunter.

'Come on, let's eat.' Tom edged my tub of curried noodles towards me while smiling at how well he knew my order. He indulged in a more adventurous dish filled with shrimp and chillies.

While we ate, we talked about launching the social media idea behind us, and I felt as if the weight of the world had been lifted from my shoulders with Luke gone. Finally, a few more parcels arrived, and among them was the large black square for the selfie station. We laughed together as Tom rolled his sleeves up to tackle hanging the frame. I couldn't help but think of Andy while watching Tom's attempt to get his hands dirty.

'I thought she was using bloody Polaroids,' he said, holding the frame steady against the wall while I used the screwdriver.

I chuckled. 'Yes, but we need to attach the photos to a background,' I explained.

Tom nodded, looking flustered at a bit of DIY, and we eventually managed to screw the fixture to the wall.

'You know, I think we should take a selfie and hang it here,' Tom pointed to the centre of the wall, 'so that Ashley appreciates the struggle that took.'

'Excellent idea. I'll grab the camera!' I giggled as I stumbled across to the desk and popped the film in.

'OK, let's do it!'

We stood against the black backdrop, and I held the camera outward.

'Smile!' I shouted, a second before I felt Tom's lips squeeze into my cheek.

Click.

His lips were still there, and I gradually turned my face, peering straight into his eyes. In my hand, the camera was doing its job; in the silence, I heard the small square picture fall to the ground. Tom's face was just a breath from mine. Neither of us moved.

'We can't,' I whispered.

'I know.'

I puffed my cheeks out in frustration, still only a few inches from his face.

'But can we let this moment last a little longer, Zara?'

I shut my eyes, trying to avoid reacting to the mound of cream being released between my thighs, while feeling my heart twang. *Why does my vagina not understand girl code?* I knew he was bad news, and I wouldn't be duped by this man all over again.

He must have sensed my hesitance because I felt his soft lips kiss my forehead and then he pulled away.

He bent down, lifting the photo from the ground and smiled.

'Let's get this packed up, eh?' he said. 'It's been a busy day!'

Gently, he pushed my shoulder, and I giggled back. We lifted the boxes out the back and placed the goodies around the clinic.

After Tom dropped me back home, I showered and looked over invoices from the past few days. Ashley had headed to Emily's for dinner after the shoot, and was taking her time to return. As much as I enjoyed the peace, everything felt incredibly quiet without her. I continued to examine the figures, trying hard to concentrate before the Ashley madness returned. But no matter how much I tried not to, my mind swayed. I couldn't help replaying that moment between Tom and I. That enticing moment. My head was full of what ifs. *What if I had just kissed him?* Tom was undoubtedly wrong for me, I didn't want a relationship with him at all, but the connection I felt when I was with him was electrifying. *Why do I feel like this after everything he did to me?* After the months of cursing him and wishing I had never even met him, of building myself back up again. What did I actually want? Closure? An opportunity to fuck him over? Decent sex? I honestly didn't know.

I lay in bed tossing and turning, hoping for a moment when my mind would switch off Tom Adams and get back to business, but it never came.

Chapter Twenty-Eight

Over the next few days, my mind remained obsessed with my close encounter with Tom. I played it down, convincing myself it was nothing, but still found myself pining over his WhatsApp picture, carefully calculating when he went online and wondering who he was actually speaking to. More than once, I had to have a severe chat with myself, which left me feeling entirely in control of the situation. But the moment I saw him, I found myself laughing harder at his piss poor jokes than I ever had before. Maybe I was just enjoying the attention . . . I hadn't had any decent action in a while now.

I didn't reveal to Ashley how I felt because I found it difficult to comprehend it myself. After all, I wasn't entirely sure what I was feeling. Maybe I was just really horny and needed a good shag. After all, Cameron hadn't been up to much. Was I just craving a rebound?

But at the back of my mind, I was afraid it was more than that. Why was I rediscovering this unhealthy obsession with him? The cunt who almost cost me my career, diminished my self-love and provoked me into forgetting about personal hygiene entirely. Surely not?

I had to stay strong. The clinic was getting more productive by the day. We hadn't even revealed the new concept on our social media platforms, but Ashley had shared tasteful 'coming soon' videos, providing flashes of the newly refurbed clinic. Clients who were previously booked in got the complete facial balancing package and recommended it to their friends, causing waves.

Raj seemed none the wiser when he FaceTimed most nights. I was riddled with guilt as I kept the refurb of his business completely under wraps. My plan was to show him the figures first and hopefully he would understand the concept later. Raj luckily didn't ask many questions about the clinic and was more boastful about his current digs in Dubai. He worked only a few hours a day and said he spent more time socialising with Juju reps. He was devouring Dubai and seemed thankful for the change of prospect.

It had been almost a fortnight since Raj had left, and I'd worked every day since. Tom and Ashley insisted I took the morning off, and given the fragile state of my mental health, working every second with my sexy hunk of an ex, I decided some time away from the situation would be good. I found myself wandering to Coia's for brunch with Emily, keen to catch up.

'Hi, Zara,' she smiled as she greeted me in her tiny white tennis skirt and crop top.

'Hey, Em,' I replied, mimicking her high-pitched tone of voice. 'You look insane. Like tiny and straight off a Robinsons advert or something, but insane.'

She laughed. 'Thanks. I had a match at the gym this morning.'

I immediately felt put to shame. I'd been in such a hurry that morning I hadn't even managed to brush my teeth.

'So, how are you?' She looked concerned, given the last time she saw me I was trading insults with Tom and legging it out of the Corinthian.

'I'm good. Honestly, I'm kind of great just now. I've got some things going on with the clinic. We've completely refurbished it and we're rebranding it while Raj is away.'

Emily looked surprised and begged me to continue.

'What can I get you, ladies?' Marco, our usual waiter, asked.

'Full fry-up for me and a can of Irn Bru, please,' I said and patted my stomach hungrily.

Marco gave me an impressed thumbs-up then turned to Emily.

'Just toast, please, and a decaf coffee,' she smiled.

'Wait, I'd better make that a Diet Bru, Marco. Need to be good!' I said.

Marco bowed and walked back to the kitchen.

'So basically, I have so many ideas with the clinic, and everyone loves them!' I continued.

'That's amazing!' Emily seemed thrilled. 'How're things with Tom there?'

I had a sudden flashback to our lingering moment the other night.

'We're getting on great!' I exclaimed, completely compensating for how much I was struggling with understanding my feelings for him.

'And you are OK with him now? You don't feel weird or sad or . . .?'

My fanny once again contracted as I thought of his smug face.

'No, no,' I lied, shaking my head almost to the point of whiplash, wishing I could kid myself too. I needed to change the subject. 'Tell me about you and the kids?'

'They're good, they've started the David Lloyd kids' club and tennis lessons too. Honestly, the difference in one-to-one teaching is insane!'

Marco set down our drinks.

'I take them to court on a Thursday night, and you should see their swing. Why don't you come along one—'

I burst out laughing before she could finish.

'What?'

'Just this conversation, aye nae bother, Judy, fuck's sake!'

Emily and I burst into hysterics. We tucked into our breakfast when it finally arrived and spent the rest of the morning chatting about our lives. I loved catching up with her. Our days were entirely different, but she cared for me and was with me through it all.

Emily was interested to see the clinic, and after breakfast, she drove us back through the city so she could have a look.

As her car parked up, Ashley and Tom belted out of the clinic door to greet us.

'What's happened?' I sprang from the car seat, fore-seeing a catastrophe.

'Nothing,' Ashley said, but she was being cagey.

'We have a surprise for you inside,' Tom said.

I turned to my sister, who laughed as if she was thoroughly aware of what was going on, and followed my friends inside. The clinic was gleaming. The vases, the candles, the accessories were all arranged perfectly. I turned to the main wall and gasped – the prints of our clients had arrived.

There were four vast pictures of unique, wonderful women. Each woman wore only their underwear, leaving visible their scars, pimples, cellulite and stretch marks. The first photo was of my client Michelle, who had been coming to me for Botox for a few years. Michelle was born with a large, rosy birthmark on her face, yet she was confident and content in her own skin. Her bright green eyes and striking features made her one of the most beautiful and captivating women I knew. The second photograph that hung was of Ikra. Raj had helped fill in large areas of her skin after severe acne scarring, and she stood proudly in the photo, make-up-free and glowing. Joan was the third model. She was one of our older clients, around sixty. She stood in a white bra, pushing her breasts together and laughing, totally carefree. Her body looked insane. And lastly, Kerry-Anne was there, one of my first-ever clients, a schoolteacher. She came for regular anti-wrinkle injections. She had her glasses on and beamed a bright smile coyly towards the camera.

I felt my eyes tear up.

Turning to the others, I said, 'I love it! This is honestly phenomenal!' I was bouncing with happiness. I couldn't believe how proud I felt of my brave clients. How my vision looked so inspiring and unique. Normalising imperfections made me view my body entirely differently too. I suddenly realised that my arse crack may at times resemble Hagrid's beard, and my tits may sit like a spaniel's lugs without a bra, but that's perfectly OK, and normal. My friends had taken a massive gamble taking the clinic in this direction with me and it felt so wonderful to witness the results.

Ashley snickered. 'That's not all.'

She grabbed hold of me and hauled me towards the desk. Tom placed a hand on my shoulder, giving it a gentle squeeze.

'Look at this!' Ashley removed the dust sheet that had been protecting the desk from the decorating. It took me a second to realise that she was unveiling my photoshoot from Dubai. I stood in the centre with Indie, Laureen and Skylar, and beneath us was the Individualise logo.

'No way!' I screamed. 'I'm on the desk!'

'No, you literally are the desk!' Tom laughed, he ran around the desk excitedly and started typing into the computer.

'How the hell did you get that? The pictures aren't supposed to be out till spring!' I was in shock.

Ashley nodded. 'It was Andy's idea. He was rooting for you on that bloody desk! And, he's organised one last surprise!'

I glanced around the room curiously.

Tom smirked. 'Look at the screen.'

I hurried around to the iMac, and a Zoom call was in progress. It was my three friends from Dubai, and I exploded with happiness.

'Oh my god, girls, hi!' I screamed. I almost covered my ears with the volume of excitement I received back. 'How the hell?' I yelled.

'So, Andy from Juju DM'd us last night. He told us about how much of an awesome businesswoman you are. He sent us the pictures, but we had to see your reaction. Your clinic is fucking beaut, babe,' Laureen said.

'Oh my god, so beaut!' Skylar added.

'He told us all about your ideas, and we love it, Zara. We all love it.' The three girls were nodding, and I suddenly missed their wild energy.

'By the way, is that the same Tom you were talking about from Dubai, though?' Indie interrupted, looking confused.

I made a face for her to be quiet and quickly said, 'Thank you all so much. Please, please come and visit us when you're home.'

'We promise! Don't we, girls?' The three of them nodded simultaneously.

'Tell us when we can share this clinic on our socials, Zara. We want to spread the female empowerment message!' Indie said, and my stomach flipped. Each of these models had over one million followers. With this sort of promotion, the opportunities and coverage were endless for the clinic.

I burst out laughing as my jaw dropped. 'What, for real?'

'YES!' they screamed.

'What you guys are doing is amazing!' Indie said.

'Plus, our faces look so hot on your fucking desk!' Skylar added.

'Eh . . . well, I'll do the post today and tag you girls. I don't even know what to say. Thank you so much. This call has made my day, no, my week, honestly!' I gushed.

'We love you, Zara!' The girls blew kisses goodbye, and I clicked out of the call.

'They're going to share the clinic!'

Ashley and Emily squealed and wrapped their arms around me.

When the buzz simmered down, Ashley showed me more things she had added to the clinic. The treatment menu had grown, describing the new technique we were practising. The coffee mugs were all distinct shapes of women, and the selfie wall was hung with the image of Tom kissing my cheek in the centre, where he had suggested.

My friends had utterly outdone themselves.

We sat for a minute on the sofa and caught our breath.

'Do you ever get the feeling something big is about to happen?' Ashley asked.

'Yes!' I admitted, feeling a burst of butterflies.

Ashley's face lit up. 'I'm totally getting that feeling right now. Like, the way this place looks is insane.'

'Completely down to you girls,' Tom said.

'And you too, Tom,' I said. 'And Andy. He started this whole thing. It would never have happened without him finding my notebook!'

Tom squeezed my hand gratefully. Then he jumped to his feet. 'Let's stop this soppy shit and get some work done, huh, ladies?'

Ashley finished up taking photos of the clinic's new interior and finally prepared her launch post of our unique concept of aesthetics and treatments to the Individualise Facebook, Instagram and Twitter feeds. We huddled together and watched her large acrylic nails as they hit 'post'. I felt sick with nerves in case anyone disliked the idea. It was a risk, completely ditching our high-end reputation for a fresh take on the beauty world. Tom and I had back-to-back clients booked in for the rest of the afternoon. We didn't have time to check up on our phones or chat to Ashley about what was happening on our socials; instead, we kept our head down and stuck to our new three-step process.

The positive energy remained the entire day, and I felt butterflies swarm my stomach each time I heard the phone ring, wondering what was happening outside of my treatment room.

We finished with our clients at around five and came out to an unusually dishevelled-looking Ashley.

'Indie, Skylar and Laureen have shared our post and tagged us in their stories!' she began. 'They are amazing! All about the importance of self-identity and positive body image. Guys, we've gained four thousand followers in two hours, and we are fully booked for the next three weeks. I have four hundred DMs to respond to. What the actual fuck is going on?'

Once again, my jaw hit the floor.

'Something big, Ash, that's for sure!' Tom said.

Chapter Twenty-Nine

Individualise was thriving. Two weeks had passed since launching my new concept, and our schedules were full. Tom and I worked tirelessly on the injectables while Ashley was fully committed to promoting and cataloguing our days. We stayed open till late at night and cut down our breaks to fit in as many clients as possible, somehow managing to keep it all together, feeding off the thrill and buzz of it all.

Customers were turning up in person to make appointments because the phone line was constantly busy. People were only too happy to be featured on our selfie wall and were tagging the clinic in gushing, excited posts following their treatments. Bloggers and local magazines published our story and Laura Maginess from the Glasglow Girls Club even popped round to interview us for her channel. It felt like a dream, except it was entirely beyond my own mind's magnitude. Ashley seemed to flourish in the chaos and I could see how much it had taken her mind off Dave. Occasionally I'd hear her sniffle and tear up at night, but it was becoming less and less as she had a bigger purpose at work. I never imagined how many people would support our new branding, but as the piles of cash flew through the door, a sun-kissed Raj lay blissfully unaware of his clinic's success across the ocean in Dubai.

That Tuesday morning, the team gathered round the sofa with Andy for the customary sales meeting. He was dressed in a tight crisp white shirt with jeans and a statement Hermes belt. His warm smile shone when he began the session as we waited eagerly on the figures.

Finally, he glanced at his laptop and shrugged. 'I don't know why we're having this meeting, to be honest. You guys are killing it.'

I glanced at Ashley and Tom, who were beaming.

'How much have we taken in?' I asked

Andy scrolled through his MacBook. 'You've brought in more this month than you have the past three months combined.' He swung his head in disbelief.

'Long may it continue,' I replied nervously, hoping the novelty of it all wouldn't wear off.

'Have you guys got many appointments booked in advance?' Andy asked.

Ashley squeaked. 'Aye, full for the next three months. After that, there's a waiting list, plus a million DMs I've to sort through.'

'I don't think you'll need to worry anytime soon then, Zara!' Andy responded, winking in my direction.

I felt my shoulders being rubbed from behind as Tom moved closer to reassure me. My body stiffened, slightly uncomfortable as Andy glimpsed at the public display of affection. After a few silent, awkward seconds, I wriggled out of Tom's hold.

'So, Raj must've been buzzing when you told him, eh?' Andy asked.

Ashley giggled loudly. 'You would think, eh.'

Andy raised his eyebrow at me.

'I've kind of not told him yet.' I sighed and covered my face. 'Yep, basically, he has no idea.'

'What?' Andy's voice was high-pitched with shock. 'Why would you still not tell him? It's all good news!'

I agreed, feeling nervous at even the thought of coming clean. I had been so bold about my way of managing his shop. I thought about how mad Raj was when Tom betrayed him with the clinic before, and deep down, I wondered if I was just as bad. I knew I had to tell him but I was putting it off each day, trying to justify my rationale in my head.

'He didn't like the facial mapping idea. I pitched it to him while we were in Dubai, and he *really* didn't like it. Then he's away for a few weeks and here's me changing his entire clinic around the idea.'

'Aye, and it's paid off big time!'

'I know, but—'

'Listen, Raj is a businessman. He'll be over the moon about what you've done here. I know I am, and let's face it, he might want to come back from Dubai early because of it. Besides, you two are mates. Is it not a bit snide keeping it from him? What's the point in him being away? This place is top-notch and soaring. Raj is away from his family and business unnecessarily really. He doesn't need the extra promotion in Dubai when this place is doing so well, does he?'

I nodded guiltily.

'Why don't we FaceTime him just now? Together?' Andy suggested.

'Or I could call him with you, Zara. We can always play it down, make a few jokes and tell him how brilliantly you've done,' Tom suggested.

I agreed with both of them. Raj did need to know and I appreciated Tom's offer, but I didn't want Raj to think badly of the decision. Maybe if Tom was involved, he'd think there was something shady going on.

'Tom, I'd rather do it just now while Andy's here. Make it more professional rather than winding him up on the phone, if that's OK?'

'Yes, of course. Certainly. Excellent idea,' Tom smiled.

'Come on then. We could nip into my clinic room?' I took a nervous breath, and Andy stood up and followed behind me.

As I closed the door and thought about what I had to do next, I felt my mouth turn dry.

Andy saw the look on my face. 'Zara, you're telling him good news, hen,' he said sympathetically. 'Don't look as if you've just burnt the place to the ground. Let me do the talking if you want?'

'OK, thanks.' I started up the computer and aimed the screen round as I sat on a small swivel stool beside Andy. My chest ached with anxiety as I saw the call connecting.

Suddenly, a sun-glowing Raj appeared onscreen wearing Ray-Bans.

'All right, my man, how's it going?' Andy began.

Raj's smile faltered a little, curious as to why he was calling. 'Good, good. Everything OK?' Raj sat down, holding his phone.

I smiled in the background, waiting for my cue to speak.

Andy grinned. 'Everything's better than OK to be honest, mate. We have an update. While you've been away, Zara has gone and transformed the clinic. Messed around with the treatment menu, done a refurb of the shop floor, and you guys are currently my busiest clinic in the town.' Andy turned to me, and I felt my eyes fill with tears of anxiety, awaiting Raj's reaction.

On the screen, I watched Raj lower his sunglasses. 'You're joking, right?' He sounded shocked.

I shook my head, scrunching up my face.

'Zara Smith, you are fucking amazing! Ha, what the hell did you do?'

For the next twenty minutes, I took Raj through each step of the clinic's transformation. I explained the aim of each change and told him how it was all reflected in booked-up appointment slots and overwhelming client satisfaction. I wondered why I hadn't told Raj sooner. He's a great friend, after all. He was ecstatic and relieved, and for the first time in months, he looked worry-free. When we ended the call, I felt not only massively relieved, but also like my belief in the new approach had doubled.

Andy turned to me, grinning. 'I told you he'd be buzzing!'

'You did. Thank you so much for that. And for the push to do it. Honestly, you've been so great with us.'

'That's my job, darlin'.'

'It's all falling into place. I can't believe it.'

'Aye! You didny think you'd say that last month when you were spying through windows across the street, did you?'

I laughed loudly as we walked back out to the shop floor, suddenly remembering about Botox Boxx. For months I'd stared enviously through the glass, counting their customers in and out, but I couldn't remember the last time I did it. I had been so busy focusing solely on Individualise that I no longer compared it to the clinic across the square.

'How did it go?' Ashley yelled from the desk.

'Good, great. He's delighted.'

Andy gathered his things, and I walked him to the door.

'Keep going with this, Zara. You've got a great thing going,' he said.

I smiled. 'Thanks, Andy. Oh, and thanks for the Juju image for the desk.'

'Aye, no bother. It was my favourite picture of the shoot. You look great, pal.' I watched him blush at his flattery.

'Amazing what airbrushing can do, eh!'

'Nah, I see you a lot, man. You always look good.' He giggled nervously. 'Catch you later, Zara.'

I grinned towards Andy, then waved him off and re-entered the clinic.

'Aaaaahhhhh! We did it!' Ashley ran over and hugged me tightly as Tom rustled his hand playfully through my hair. 'What did Raj say then?' Ashley asked.

My phone pinged in my back pocket. It was a message from Raj, with a screenshot of flight details attached.

See you all Saturday! Tell Tom to clear out my clinic room. I'm coming home!!!

I read the message aloud, excited at the thought of seeing Raj again, but my enthusiasm plummeted a second later. Tom would be leaving.

I glanced at him. He looked completely calm.

'Saturday it is! It'll be good to see Raj again,' he said.

'Yes, totally. I'll genuinely be sorry to see you go though. Jesus, I never thought I'd say that again!' I chuckled and came closer to Tom, not knowing how to embrace him.

'It was great fun, Zara. Hey, we should celebrate! Friday night?'

'YES!' Ashley yelled. 'One hundred per cent in!'

'I'll take us all for dinner,' Tom said.

'No, no! No way!' I interrupted. 'I'm the boss at the moment, which means I have the business card! I'll be taking you guys out, to thank you both. I should invite Andy too.'

Tom smirked and gave me a salute. 'Absolutely!'

'I'm well up for this! Where are we thinking?' Ashley asked.

'I'll book somewhere nice. Don't worry, Ash,' I giggled.

We stood huddled together, happy but dampened, knowing that the dynamics would change suddenly at the end of the week. I grabbed my phone out of my back pocket and messaged Andy.

Hey! I'm taking Ashley and Tom out for dinner on Friday night just to say thanks for everything before Raj gets back. We would all love if you could make it too! X

Read.

My phone began ringing instantly from Andy and my stomach flipped with nerves. I stepped a few steps away from Tom and Ashley.

'Zara, I just got your message but Friday is a bad night for me.'

I felt my heart sink, not really understanding why.

'No, listen that's totally fine. It's short notice anyway,' I replied, trying to disguise my disappointment.

'I know, I'll deffo come to the next one. I've just got commitments every Friday night with Jennifer and Ty. I can't get out of them, you know.'

OK, wow. I was not expecting that. What commitments? Who the fuck were Jennifer and Ty? Did he have kids I didn't know about? Or was Jen his girlfriend? My head was racing with questions.

'No, of course. Listen, if your schedule changes, I can always add you on!' I replied calmy, despite my mental thoughts.

'I appreciate it, hen! Take care!'

I turned back around to Tom and Ashley who were chatting away casually.

'OK, Andy can't make dinner for Friday so it'll be a table for three! Let's get this show on the road. We have a busy afternoon ahead!' I clapped my hands, breaking the silence, and we got back to work.

For the rest of the day, the atmosphere was sombre, but none of us acknowledged it. We'd always known Tom's presence here was temporary, but in the few weeks we'd all worked so well together. We couldn't have changed Individualise around without him, and as much as I pretended to be OK, I knew then, deep down, I didn't want to lose him again.

Chapter Thirty

Friday sped around far too quickly, and each time I thought about Tom leaving, I felt my stomach churn. I composed a mental list of reasons to keep him on, which I would present to Raj, but realistically I knew there was no room for a third practitioner. At the same time, my head often wandered off about Andy. *What was his situation?* And had I imagined a flirtation brewing between us all along? I suppose he was the first man to ever see beyond my looks. He encouraged my ideas, my business skills and supported me. Perhaps his genuine personality and good guy attributes, combined with muscly pecs and a decent-sized bulge, made him intriguing for me.

That evening, after the last client had left, I swept and mopped the clinic, anticipating Raj's arrival the following day, hoping he'd give the new look his seal of approval. When the place was thoroughly Hinch'd, we closed the shutters, poured three glasses of champagne and scattered into the clinic rooms to get ready.

Ashley followed me into mine and we chatted about the day's clients while I compressed myself into two pairs of Spanx, ready to slip on my new House of CB black bodycon dress. Although I could hardly breathe, there wasn't a lump or bump in sight. I left my hair down with a slight wave, applied some more make-up to my face, slipped my painted toes into a pair of Valentino's, and threw a black blazer jacket around my shoulders. Ashley had changed into a pink shorts and jacket combo with lipstick to match. Her icy blonde hair was poker-straight, and her make-up was full. She looked incredible. As we put the finishing touches to our looks, her mouth was going like the clappers, but I was finding it hard to listen, preoccupied by the knowledge that it was Tom's last night.

'OK, you ready?' she asked, finally turning in my direction.

I nodded.

'Oh my god, you look amazing, Zara, so hour-glassy.'

'It's these, not me.' I lifted my dress, exposing the tight wetsuit I was contained by.

Ashley put her hand over her mouth, stifling a laugh. 'That's going to be a fucker to piss in.'

'Aw shit, I didn't think of that.'

'Come on,' she giggled, opening the door and walking out to the clinic floor.

Tom was already standing by the desk, pouring his second glass of champagne. He looked up at us and smiled.

'Ooh la la, ladies. You both look wonderful!'

I felt myself blush. The effort I'd made was obvious.

'Aye, you're a lucky man tonight, Thomas!' Ashley said as she sat down to adjust the band on her fluffy pink stiletto.

There was a sudden loud bang at the door, and we all jumped.

'Did you book a taxi, Zara?' Ashley questioned.

'No.'

Tom set his glass down and marched up to the door. I could see him simper as he turned the key, greeting the visitor.

'Dave, hello, come in.'

Dave?! I looked on in confusion as he wandered into the clinic, holding a bouquet of pink roses. Ashley's mouth fell open.

'Hey,' he said.

'Hey,' she responded. Her bottom lip began to tremble.

'Are you going somewhere?' he asked. He didn't approach her quite yet, and they stood staring at each other across the room.

'Yeah, well, kind of.' Ashley glanced at me while I watched on eagerly, almost wishing for some popcorn. He kept his eyes glued to her; he looked smitten.

'Zara,' Tom said, 'why don't we head out just now, and Ashley can catch up? If she likes. Give these two some privacy?'

I gave Ashley a look, checking whether she was OK being left alone with Dave, or if she needed some moral support. She nodded at us to go.

'OK, if you're sure. See you later, Ash.' I grabbed my bag and walked towards the door where Tom was waiting. 'Good to see you, Dave!' I added, touching his shoulder as I passed by.

He smiled briefly, still admiring Ashley from a distance. 'You too, Zara.'

I left the clinic with Tom a second behind me.

'I've got a feeling it's going to be a date for two tonight,' Tom murmured into my ear.

I raised an eyebrow. 'It's not a date. It's a business dinner.'

'I meant for Ashley! But if that's what you're planning. What a filthy mind, Miss Smith.'

My stomach twisted from cringing. 'I'm not planning anything!'

'Let's flag down a taxi,' I said. 'We can't walk to where we're going.'

I watched him lift an elegant arm into the air and effortlessly hail a taxi. As it pulled into the side of the road, he went to the door and held it open for me.

'Thank you,' I said, climbing in.

He got in behind me, and we settled together on the seat.

'Cut restaurant in Bothwell, please, driver,' I said, and just like that, we were on our way out of the city centre.

Cut was a delicious steakhouse situated in an affluent town just outside the city. We arrived just before our eight o'clock reservation and stood in the queue to be seated.

'Good choice, boss,' Tom said. 'Very swanky.'

I was glad he approved and smiled back. The restaurant was on Bothwell's main street, in an enormous sandstone building. The décor was dark and stylish with modern marble tables set against the classic period designs of the old-fashioned building.

'What would you like to drink tonight? Champagne?' Tom suggested.

'Why not!' I raised the credit card in the air mischievously. 'I'm buying, remember.'

Tom leaned in towards me, and I felt his warm body press against mine. 'I like this bossy side to you, Zara. Rarrrrrr.' He growled into my ear.

Immediately, goosebumps travelled up my arm and I felt my nipples turn hard. I shook them off.

We moved up the line to where the friendly hostess stood, holding menus and a clipboard.

'Hi, guys, do you have a reservation?'

'Yes, we—' Tom began, but I shot him a stare, determined not to allow him to take over.

'Yes, we do. Table booked for Smith at eight, please.'

'OK, perfect. Does any of your party have any allergies?'

'No, we don't,' Tom couldn't help but chip in once more.

I peered up at him again. 'Actually, I do.' I cleared my throat and turned back to the hostess. 'Penicillin.'

She seemed puzzled. 'Any food allergies, miss?'

I heard Tom choke on a laugh beside me.

'Well . . . eh . . . no, just penicillin, thanks.'

As Tom continued to laugh, my face turned scarlet. 'Follow me, please,' the hostess said.

We entered the restaurant and were seated at a small booth near the back.

'Can I get you guys any drinks?'

Tom held his hand up, gesturing for me to speak.

'A bottle of your best champagne, please.'

'Absolutely.' She handed us the menus and left the table.

As soon as she was gone, Tom burst into laughter. 'Penicillin! That was brilliant, Zara. Out of all the—'

Ping.

I seized my phone from my bag, glad of the distraction. It was Ashley.

Don't wait on me. I'm going to Dave's! WTF!!! xxxxxxx

I sighed. 'Ashley's not coming.'

'Hmm, I don't blame her. Hopefully those two can sort it out.'

I agreed quickly, texting her back with lots of sexy GIFs. 'So, what do you fancy?' I asked, picking up the menu, keen to keep the chat strictly platonic and distract me from gazing towards the handsome surgeon. Now I'd lost my chaperone, the pressure of snowballing back into a love bubble with the wrong man was weighing heavily on my shoulders. I had to stay strong.

'I'll, of course, have a fillet. What about you?'

I looked up from the menu and felt Tom's devilish eyes on me. 'Same,' I grinned.

'Let me guess. Well done?'

I nodded. 'What about you?'

'You know I like it raw, Zara!' he smirked, and I felt a sudden surge of warmth from my overly crushed clit.

'Too far, Tom. As always!' I tried to laugh it off, feeling flustered.

The drinks arrived, and we ordered our meal. The night was going well, and I was reminded again how much we enjoyed one another's company. Sex aside, we got on astonishingly well.

Tom glanced at his watch for the second time and I laughed.

'Do you need to be somewhere?' I asked, raising my brows.

'Not at all. I've just realised the battery is dead on my watch. Look.' He turned his wrist round to me, showing off his fancy Tag.

I suddenly cringed at my accusation.

'And let's face it, the only place I go these days is to work. You and Ashley are the only bloody women I see!' he laughed.

'No, erm, oh what was her name again – Claudia?' I murmured, pretending I had forgotten about the Arabian goddess he was with in Dubai.

'*Who?*' he sniggered smugly. 'No, she was a holiday romance. If you could even call it that. So, what's happening on the man front with Zara?' he asked.

I felt a little taken aback. 'We don't have conversations like this, Thomas.'

'Oh, come on. We're friends now. Friends chat to other friends about their dating lives, don't they? So, the Dubai guy? Spill.' Tom sipped his champagne.

I felt a sudden dunt of humiliation thinking about Cameron. I hadn't heard a single word from him since he'd left. 'Not much. He was a dick. I honestly think I'm not a relationship type of girl, destined to be single for the rest of my life. I suppose it would be a far less complicated life, eh.' I tried to make a joke of it.

'Me, yes, absolutely. You, no! That would be a waste!' Tom snapped back.

'Why is that then?' I asked.

Tom shrugged and sat back in his chair, looking serious all of a sudden. 'You're a great girl, Zara. Fantastic, clever, sexy, silly . . . it would be a real shame for you not to meet someone who appreciated that.'

I paused, waiting for a sarcastic comment to follow up his array of compliments.

When none came, I said, 'Thank you. But honestly, I think in this day and age, it's almost impossible to meet someone. No one is trustworthy. Even the nice guys end up being dickheads!' I added, still trying to giggle and lift the gravity of the conversation.

There was a moment of silence, and then Tom said, 'I'm sorry if I'm the one who has ruined your ability to trust, Zara.'

My head glanced down at the table, not wanting to remind myself of how much he had hurt me.

'It wasn't just you. But I appreciate that,' I replied, completely taken aback by his honesty.

'But there are trustworthy people out there, I promise,' he said.

I laughed at the thought. 'But decent-looking ones, I mean. Not complete munters who are just reeeeeally nice.'

Tom chuckled. 'You couldn't cope with a *reeeeeally* nice guy. Perhaps you're looking in the wrong places, Zara. They would bore you. You need someone cheeky, a little rough around the edges. You,' he pointed in my face as the lightbulb clicked in his head, 'you need a geezer!'

'A geezer?'

'No, no, you need a *good* geezer.'

'A good geezer?' I laughed out loud.

'That's precisely what you need.'

'Right, Cilla, I'll tell you what, as soon as you see a good geezer in this city, you let me know.'

Tom raised his glass in the air. 'OK, that's a promise. When I find one, I'll send him on to you.'

I hit my glass off his in a toast.

'But in the meantime . . .' He raised his brows, then sniggered before taking a swig of his drink.

My heart raced. He was speaking so openly about love, even acknowledging how he'd treated me in the past. *So why was he still so closed off to relationships?*

I drank my champagne as Tom leaned across the table towards me.

'Eyelash,' he whispered. I closed my eyes and felt his fingers softly whisk down my face.

When I opened my eyes again, he was still gazing, and I laughed, feeling nervous at his touch.

'You're mapping my face, aren't you? You're working out what I need done!'

'Shit! You know my work face!' he teased, breaking the tension.

'Do it – analyse me, Mr Adams. What do I need done?' I asked.

Tom looked at me warily. 'Ohh, I don't think so!'

'Come on. It's an order. I'm your boss until midnight, Thomas. I'll do yours, and you can do mine: a full consultation.'

Tom hesitated and then grinned. 'Pass me a piece of paper then, boss!'

I delved into my bag and handed him a small notepad and pen. He began writing immediately while staring at my face. I giggled nervously, doing the same with him. We fell silent for a couple of minutes until we both put down our pens.

'Ladies first,' he said.

I cleared my throat and put on my posh clinic voice. 'OK, Thomas, firstly, what do you like and dislike about your features?'

Tom rolled his eyes at our scripted routine. 'Absolutely nothing. It's bloody perfect. I'm more intrigued about what you think needs fixing, Miss Smith!'

'Well, firstly, you have the most inviting eyes and masculine jawline. You've been blessed with strong facial structure.'

Tom smirked and agreed modestly.

'However, you do have a small bump in your nose. It's ever so slightly out of alignment, and I could fix it.'

'A sporting injury at school,' Tom replied. 'Got hit in the face during a friendly polo match.'

I grunted. 'Polo?'

'You don't get polo at schools up here?'

I laughed. 'Naw, we don't. We get rounders, if we're lucky.'

Tom rolled his eyes. 'Continue.'

'And you have small frown lines when you laugh, just a subtle sign of ageing. I could straighten them out with a few injections, darling.'

'Quite finished?'

'Yes!' I laughed wickedly.

'OK, Miss Smith, what do you like? And what would you like me to change about your face?' he asked, looking right at me.

I thought about the question and suddenly felt insecure at what he might say. My head was messed up enough; my ex listing my physical imperfections could be enough to send me to Turkey or the fucking Priory.

'Ahh, stop! I don't want to do mine!' I blurted. 'Sorry!'

Tom gasped, holding his paper.

'I know, I've just slagged you for five minutes solid, and now I don't want to do me!' I admitted, covering my face. 'It'll make me even more self-conscious. I know it will, and I'm holding off from Botox for another couple of years at least.'

Tom huffed, seeming deflated he didn't get to share his consultation. He folded the paper up into a tidy little square, leaned over and inserted it into my blazer pocket.

'That consultation would cost you one hundred pounds, Zara. When you're ready, it's there!'

Just then, a waiter arrived with our food. He set the plates in front of us and told us to enjoy our meal. 'This looks amazing!' I gushed.

'It does! Cheers, Zara.' Tom held his glass up, and

I joined him in a toast. 'To Individualise!'

'YES! And to you believing in me. I couldn't have done it without you,' I said, smiling at him.

We took a swig each and tucked into our meal. The food was delicious, as was the champagne, and the conversation continued to flow into the night. As the restaurant began to empty around us, we decided it was finally time to go. The last night with Tom was over.

As promised, I paid for the meal, and the waitress called us a taxi. Outside, cold rain was bouncing hard down on the road, and the sky was dark and gloomy. We stood huddled under an arch at the entrance to the restaurant, glad of some shelter.

'That was a real treat, Zara. Thank you,' Tom said, his voice low and husky.

I became suddenly aware of how alone we were.

'You're welcome, Thomas,' I whispered back.

The atmosphere was quiet, and I rubbed my arms up and down my blazer as the wind blew towards us.

'Oh, you're cold! Come here.' Tom wriggled out of his jacket and draped it over my shoulders, gazing into my eyes. 'You OK?' he whispered. He was incredibly close.

'Yes,' I smiled back.

He didn't move away. We kept looking at one another.

'I think you're beautiful, Zara. In every way. Inside and out,' he said.

I laughed at his cheesy comment even as I blushed,

savouring it. 'You know you're handsome too, Tom. There's no point in me telling you that.'

'I know,' he smirked. 'If you weren't my boss and it wasn't deemed entirely inappropriate, I'd probably kiss you right now.'

Goosebumps sprinkled up my neck. It felt like the right thing to do in that moment. My eyes lingered on his as my thighs turned moist at the undeniable chemistry sparking between us. *What will I do?*

He seemed to want permission.

'Tom, I—'

Suddenly, we were blinded by headlights as our taxi pulled up.

'Well, it looks like you've been saved by the bell, Zara.' Tom leaned forward, kissed my forehead and jogged through the rain towards the taxi, once more holding the door open for me to get in first.

I jumped in quickly and sat down.

'The Italian Centre please, driver, then head to the West End.' Tom gave the instructions and I smiled towards him. He was pushing his damp hair back from his face, and gave the driver directions so quickly, without hesitation, there was no second-guessing where he was going. He wanted to go home.

'So, what do you think Raj will think tomorrow?' I asked.

'I think he will bloody love the clinic, and more importantly, love the books!' Tom leaned over and squeezed my hand reassuringly.

As the taxi ride continued, we chatted casually, not

acknowledging the tension growing between us. But inside I was racked with anxiety. *What if this was the last time I saw him?* Tomorrow Raj would be back, and we wouldn't need Tom at the clinic anymore. I wanted Raj home, but it was clear that I didn't want to lose Tom. I felt desperate, out of control and torn, but remained quiet, too afraid to say anything that would stir up my hurt from the past.

All too quickly, the taxi pulled up outside my flat, and I reached for my purse. Tom placed his hand on top of mine and shook his head.

'This is on me. You wined and dined me, lady.'

'It's the least I could do. Honestly, I can't thank you enough for the past few weeks.' I looked at him, at his perfect face, trying to take in the moment. 'Goodnight, Tom.'

He winked. 'Night, boss.'

I got out of the taxi, gave a small wave and watched Tom drive out of my life once again.

Chapter Thirty-One

I marched into my flat shouting loudly for Ashley, but heard nothing back. I needed to speak to her about my night with Tom. *Had I done the right thing?* I rummaged around my bag for my phone. No missed calls or texts from Ashley. She must still be with Dave. Agitatedly my fingers twitched, aching to phone her for advice. I needed reassurance I was doing the right thing. Surely kissing Tom would have been a bad idea? But, my god, he was the best shag ever. I mean compared to basic Cameron, I was in need of a decent dick. *Maybe I could have meaningless sex with him, like one last pump to get it entirely out of my system?*

I slumped onto the sofa.

Or would that bring back crazy, self-loathing feelings I've been trying to heal since the last time he fucked me over?

I immediately stood back up, pacing the floor. My gut told me I'd done the right thing, but my ravenous vagina was yodelling Tom's name from the inside. I couldn't think and felt dizzy with decisions. I had a choice to make, so I yanked my Spanx down, desperate for air, and felt my muffin top finally relax. Just like that, with a sudden sense of relief, I knew precisely what to do.

I hobbled out of my Spanx, tugging them past my shoes, then sprinted out of my apartment and hurried down the rainy streets of Glasgow, attempting to flag down a taxi. The icy rain was bouncing up my legs, and I could feel my dripping hair become flat against my face. Ubers were passing by, but no one was stopping. I continued walking up towards the city with my arm stuck out, and finally, a car pulled over.

'Head towards Kelvingrove please, driver.'

I had to tell Tom how I felt. I wanted to let him know that I felt something too, but was terrified. That no matter what had happened in the past, I wanted him in my life as a friend rather than not at all. Something at the bottom of my mind was telling me not to go, but my pounding heart was screaming with adrenaline, hoping for a happily ever after.

I stepped out of the taxi, facing the entrance to Tom's home. It looked smaller than I remembered, but just as grand. I took a step and felt a puddle soak the back of my calf. I was shaking, from the weather and nerves. What if he rejects me? I knew he enjoyed the chase, and I had been in torture from the 'almost' kissing moments, but he always seemed so cool. Perhaps it's all a game to him.

I walked to the buzzer, but noticed the door was slightly ajar. I pushed it open and approached the staircase. The plush carpeted staircase. As I held the railing, I had a flashback of me fleeing down the steps, dressed in candy underwear, and my mouth felt dry. *What if he's with someone else tonight? Maybe he hasn't changed.*

I've seen a different side to him this time around, a supportive side, championing my ideas and pushing me to deliver. When I was with him, fuck, I was lucky for the cunt to give me a nod in the corridor. *Had he changed?* I wondered. Or maybe I had. I could hear music playing as I continued to climb the steps. What would I say? I wasn't even sure what I wanted. To be friends, to be lovers, to fight or to argue. I had no idea, I just needed to tell him I felt it too.

I stood facing the door, took a deep breath and knocked on it. From inside, I heard footsteps on the hardwood flooring, and then Tom was standing there. His shirt had been undone a couple more buttons and he looked relaxed, clutching a glass of wine.

'Zara? Are you OK? You're drenched!' He came towards me and held my soggy shoulders, looking concerned.

'I'm fine, honestly.' I took a deep breath and laughed. 'I don't know why I'm here, actually. This is embarrassing.'

Tom laughed, looking confused.

'Oh, do you have company?' I whispered, suddenly fearful I had interrupted something for him.

'I only left you twenty minutes ago. Even I can't act that fast. Would you like to come in?'

I was hovering, not knowing what to do.

'Come on! What's up?' He pushed me playfully into his hallway, easing the atmosphere. I walked in and smelt the familiar fresh scent.

'I'm sorry I'm here. I just felt like I left you hanging before, and I didn't get to say to you what I wanted to.'

Tom studied the floor. 'What did you want to say?'

'I wanted to say that as much as I really want to kiss you too, I'm scared that I'll end up getting hurt again. Plus, I'm in a really good place with the clinic now, and you complicate things for me.'

Tom moved closer. 'And what do you want to say now?'

'I want to say . . .' I glanced at my watch, then smiled. 'It's twelve-oh-five. I suppose I'm technically not your boss anymore.'

Tom's face came even closer. I felt his breath hit off mine. My heart bounced in my chest as my clit winced with desire.

'Does that mean it's my turn to be in charge for a while?' he asked.

My eyes lit up, craving him more than I ever had before.

'Yes, boss,' I replied.

He turned to the side and placed his wine glass on the table, then faced me and smirked. He moved his arms behind my back, and in one large scoop, I was lifted from the ground. I wrapped my legs around his waist as he carried me to his bedroom. The room was dark, with only the streetlights peering in from the window providing any light. He lowered me to my feet and gently pulled at my coat; it fell to the floor. His strong hands ran through my wet hair. I could feel the raindrops still running down my body.

'I've wanted this for so long, Zara,' he whispered. Then he leaned in and kissed me.

His lips were soft, and his tongue felt passionate and sensual. I'd missed him.

His hands rubbed my shoulders and then lightly tickled down to my tits. My eyes were closed tightly, relishing this fantasy. I had forgotten how good it felt to be touched by him. He was taking his time with me, taking in every part of me. I leaned into him, requiring more kissing, and as he obliged, he guided me over to the bed. He turned me over, and I felt a shiver from behind as he unzipped my dress. I peered back at him. His eyes seemed darker.

'Are you sure?' he asked, unbuttoning his shirt.

I'd never felt more sure of anything in my life. I wriggled out of my dress, having unclipped my bra and was utterly commando. Normally I'd never have the confidence to stand there and be observed by a man, but I felt utterly amazing, exhilarated and beautiful. Maybe it was because of the body positivity campaign that I was promoting, or maybe it was just how Tom made me feel. Completely desired.

'I'm sure.'

With that, he sprang towards me, pushing me on top of the bed. He was licking down my front, sucking and biting my nipples. I could feel my toes curl with pleasure. As his hands wandered lower, my mind went numb with adrenaline. He caressed his way down between my legs, slow and teasing. In the low light, his toned body looked flawless. I felt like I was in a dream. I began to quiver with anticipation as Tom wrapped his strong arms tightly around my thighs. He held my gaze for a long moment, and then he spat directly onto my clit. I panted in shock. He slipped his fingers inside me, pushing in and out and tonguing my clit as pleasure hit in waves, overwhelming me. My back arched and my entire body contracted as I came, but his fingers remained firmly inside me, accelerating the pace until I came again and then again. I was in a euphoric cloud. He was reading my mind. I'd never felt this connected to him or to anyone.

By the end of the third orgasm, I was dizzy and completely breathless. I couldn't form a single thought except how amazing it felt to be with him. Suddenly I felt an almighty push as he thrust his cock inside me. *Wow.* He leaned over me, slapping in and out and shoving the fingers he'd just taken from inside me into my mouth. It felt filthy and insane.

'Turn over,' he commanded, and as I got on all fours, he ran his tongue right up my arse crack. 'I want every part of you.'

'Yes!' I panted back.

We had sex for hours. It was like we couldn't get enough of each other. I didn't know whether we were making up for all the time we'd spent apart, or if it was because we knew, deep down, this would never work. But I had never felt so desired, so sexy and so passionate. Finally, the barriers that I was struggling to hold with Tom were down. As we lay in bed after-wards, Tom kissed my forehead.

'You have no idea how fucking amazing that was for me,' he murmured.

I giggled, pulling the covers up. 'No, I do. I don't think I'll be able to walk for a week.'

'Don't walk then. Stay here in our little sex dungeon.' He smirked and ran his knuckle around the edge of my face.

'If only,' I whispered. 'I suppose I should really get going. I have work in the morning, and Raj is back.'

Tom sat up and glanced at his bedside clock.

'Zara, it's 3 a.m. You're not going anywhere. Stay, get showered in the morning and then head to work.'

I wanted to stay but didn't want to overstay. I wasn't sure what this meant for us.

'All right, but I do need to sleep, OK?' I warned, jokingly pressing his nose.

'Agreed. Now roll over and let me spoon you.'

My face was burning from smiling as I did as he told me. I could feel him pull me in tightly, smelling my hair. It felt so amazing to be entangled in his arms again.

I shut my eyes, hoping that tomorrow would take for ever to come around.

Chapter Thirty-Two

The following morning, Tom's alarm buzzed from the side of his bed. He groaned beside me, and I continued to keep my eyes shut tightly over. *Why the fuck am I still here?* I had morning breath, a champagne headache, and my wet hair had expanded into an afro overnight.

Tom gave me a gentle shake as he yawned. 'Morning!'

I smiled, sitting up. 'Morning.'

'Would you like some breakfast?'

I shook my head, declining his offer, feeling more uncomfortable than I had last night. 'I'd love a shower before work, though,' I replied, remembering his luxurious rainfall shower.

I watched his perky arse confidently strut over to the cupboard. He took out a fluffy towel and threw it over. 'I'll make us some coffee. You know where everything is.' He leaned over, kissed my forehead, rustled my hair, and strolled out of the room.

Wrapping the towel around me, I tottered off his high bed and entered the ensuite.

What the fuck did I do? Why didn't we have a conversation about *us* before the jumping straight on his dick stage? My head was pickled. I stood under the shower, lathering up his Molton Brown shower gels onto my tender vagina, disputing every decision I'd made last night. But then I'd suddenly have a flashback to how wonderfully filthy it was and I'd melt all over again. *Maybe we should have a conversation? Perhaps we could date initially. Take things slower this time around. I mean, if a life of sex like this was on offer, I'd be crazy not to consider it.* I switched off the shower, feeling a bit more optimistic than before and headed to the sink.

My mouth smelled like penis and pubes, so I went on the hunt for Tom's toothbrush. As I opened the bathroom cabinet and started rummaging around, any hope I had that things would work out slowly began to evaporate along with the steam. Behind the toothpaste was an oversized hoop earring. I held it in my hand to examine, tracing the initial E in the centre with my finger. Then I realised. It was Ebony's. She'd had it on on the day of the consultations. I fucking knew something was going on with them. Just like I knew the day I found Harriette's earrings in the same fucking place.

For some reason, I laughed. What the fuck was this cupboard? His little trophy room? I immediately felt like I had been punched in the gut. I couldn't even be angry at Tom, but felt disappointed with myself. Here I was back in the same place I had been over a year ago. This time fully aware of who and what Tom was. I felt numb, incredibly numb and sad at my over-imaginative desire to be loved by this man once more. He was Sugar Daddy, the Royal Gigolo, and I had to remember that, no matter how difficult it was for me to walk away from the connection.

I put the earring back, brushed my teeth and re-entered the bedroom to get dressed. My outfit still felt a little damp from the night before as I zipped it up at the back and headed towards the kitchen.

When I entered, I felt my eyes squint with the light shining in from the bright windows. Tom was sipping on a coffee at the breakfast bar with his dressing gown tied tightly around his waist. I couldn't help but cringe at the Hugh Hefner vibes he was emitting.

'I'd better go, Tom. I'm sorry about last night, just turning up like that.'

'Don't go yet. I'll drop you off. Raj has just messaged and asked me to come to the clinic too.' He turned his phone screen to face me. 'He says about ten? Presumably he wants to give me a gift for all my hard work.'

Fucking perfect, I thought.

'No, honestly. I'd rather not make this a big deal. We don't have to do any formalities. We both know what this was, so let's leave it at that, eh?'

Tom looked startled.

'OK, so no formalities. See you at ten, and call your own fucking cab then!' he laughed.

I smirked back. 'See you.'

As I walked down the stairs, I found it hard to keep it all together.

I knew deep down this couldn't be fixed. Tom was unavailable and would be for the rest of his life. As much as last night had been amazing, I knew it couldn't happen with feelings. I thought I could handle it, but the chemistry was too strong. I knew I deserved more than a hot-man head-fuck, and I knew this was going to be a nightmare to get over.

I headed to my flat and got dressed for work before walking round to the clinic. Despite how the morning had started, I was ecstatic to see Raj and hear all about Ashley's night with Dave. I was first to arrive, just after nine. I pulled the shutters up and deactivated the alarm. I wanted it all to be perfect for Raj to come at ten.

Ashley burst through the door around half nine, looking immaculate and bright.

'Well . . .?' I asked cautiously, never quite knowing what she was going to say.

She paused, bit her lip and screamed, 'We're back together!'

I rushed towards her and squeezed her tightly. 'I am so pleased for you! Oh, Ash!'

Ashley's eyes filled with emotion. 'Don't!! You'll set me off. I had the best night ever!'

'Go on . . .'

I pulled her over to the sofa where she divulged the entire night from start to finish. She explained how Dave acknowledged that he took her for granted, how she was so sorry for the incident and that they never wanted to be apart again. He promised to trade FIFA for fud and give her everything she desired. I felt a warm buzz for my friend. I hadn't seen her look this content for a long time, and it was infectious.

She had just started to rave about the insane sex she'd been having all night when the door opened. Tom was standing there with a white polo shirt and jeans on.

'Morning!' Ashley bellowed.

'God, you look radiant!' Tom replied, heading over to the sofas to join us.

'So bloody happy! You'll be gutted you've just missed me telling Zara all about the wild sex I had last night.'

Tom cleared his throat and raised an eyebrow at me. I immediately felt my face reddening.

'Lucky you!' Tom said.

'And how was your night, guys? Did you have fun?' Ashley asked.

We both nodded our heads awkwardly.

'I hope she gave you the send-off you deserved, Thomas!'

Tom chuckled. 'She certainly did, Ash. She certainly did . . .'

My phone began ringing loudly from the table, and I was thankful for the distraction. It was Raj FaceTiming.

'Hey, where are you? We're all here!' I gushed.

Raj's face was sun-kissed, and I could see tiny freckles had gathered sweetly around his nose.

'Are you all there? Tom too?' Raj replied.

I leaned my phone on the vase in the centre of the table, and the three of us gathered together.

'We're here!' Ashley shouted impatiently. 'Where are you?'

Raj flipped his camera around to a bright blue sky and a piping hot ray of sunshine.

'I'm still here. I couldn't do it,' he laughed, but his eyes were glazed with tears.

We looked at one another, confused.

'Still in Dubai?' I asked.

'Since you told me about the clinic, I've thought about nothing else. You transformed the place in a matter of weeks and I am so pleased, but part of me felt sad, like I didn't want to leave Dubai. The sun, sea, the laid-back lifestyle. But then it hit me: you lot don't actually need me at all. You guys have done it all on your own.'

'What? But I do need you, Raj, I honestly do,' I replied quickly.

The line fell silent for a second as we all took in the blow.

'Are you bammin' us up? For how long?' Ashley asked. 'Like, are we getting a holiday out of this?'

'Indefinitely,' he said. 'You know I've been so miserable and stressed lately, with you lot and with my family too, and they don't deserve it. I spoke to my wife last night and they are moving out this week. It's a done deal, and of course you lot are welcome to visit anytime. Just, erm, no footballers this time, Ash,' he giggled.

Suddenly my breathing ceased. This couldn't be happening. He was my rock, my mentor, my friend.

'And you're certain about it, Raj?' Tom spoke up, taking over for me.

Raj laughed. 'I've never been more certain of anything, mate.'

Ashley was furiously batting her long false lashes, not wanting them to get wet with tears.

'But what about this place? We've just got it off the ground. I want you to see it all,' I whimpered.

'No, *you* got it off the ground, Zara. If you'd listened to me, we'd never have made that move.'

I shook my head in disbelief. I couldn't imagine doing this without Raj.

'I want you to run it. Look what you've done already. I can fund all of your crazy expansion ideas but as far as I'm concerned, you've earned the clinic. I'm tied into a contract with Juju for the products, but I've asked them to change all the managerial paperwork to your name. They're dealing with the admin just now, and they've offered me a permanent position over here.'

I was speechless. My eyes were leaping out of my head, and I could feel Tom's and Ashley's arms clinging onto me.

'Zara?' Raj said after a few moments when I hadn't said anything.

'What? What are you talking about? I don't know what to say,' I answered.

'Say yes!'

'Of course, yes. But I want you to be here. I don't want you to leave me. I need you here!'

Raj looked on sympathetically. 'I'm only a phone call away, or a flight! But you have Tom, and you seem to be a great team. He'll be a fab right-hand man, Zara.'

'Of course he will,' I said, bowing my head to the floor. 'That's not the point though.'

'I'd love to stay!' Tom cut in. He looked ecstatic at the opportunity Raj was giving him. 'I could cut to some locum work in the hospital and spend most of my time here. Jesus, though, Raj, are you sure? It's a massive move.'

'I'll miss you all, but I'm sure.' Raj wiped away his tears while I watched on with a heavy heart.

'When you're settled, send us dates when we can all visit,' I mumbled, my voice still shaky.

'Absolutely!' he replied with the most glistening smile. 'I can't wait to read all about your new clinic, Zara. I believed in you the moment I met you.'

I nodded back humbly. 'I know you did, boss.'

The call lasted a bit longer, with us talking excitedly about the next steps for the clinic and how life would be for Raj out in Dubai, but I couldn't take anything in. Individualise was going to be run by *me*. I would be the boss of the most current aesthetics clinic in Glasgow. My body quivered from the rush of it all.

When we hung up the call with Raj, Tom and I sat in stunned silence, while Ashley couldn't stop babbling.

'This is like the best day ever! I'm back with Dave. Zara's got a business! Tom, it's your turn next!'

'I had everything I wanted when I opened my eyes, Ash. I'm a very fortunate man,' he said.

I glanced towards him, feeling slightly uncomfortable, having still not confessed to Ashley about the previous night.

★

344

The celebrating was short-lived as clients arrived, and in between appointments I was swamped with phone calls from Juju, finalising authorising signatures on the account.

That evening Ashley headed out on another date with Dave, and I waited on Tom finishing off his last client before locking up.

I observed him lead her to the front door, complimenting her every which way. *What does that man have over us women?* I wondered.

'Well . . . how does it feel?' he asked once it was just the two of us.

'Weird!' I giggled.

'Good weird?'

'Great weird!' I replied. 'Tom, about last night—'

He held his hands up, wanting me to stop. 'I know. It can't happen again. You'll be my boss, etc. etc. etc.' He rolled his eyes.

'Exactly. Plus, it's more than that,' I sighed, not knowing how to explain without sounding like a grade A psychopath. 'When we broke up, I was really messed up. I felt nothing with any guy for such a long time. It's taken me this long to *want* to feel something again, and I can't risk going back to where I was before.'

He pressed his thumb against his mouth, listening intently. 'I get it. And again, I'm sorry. For absolutely everything.'

I agreed. 'I don't need you to say sorry again. I forgive you. And besides, I was the one who turned up at your door last night. I mean, I wish there was no such thing as no-strings-attached sex with you.'

'I wish that too, Zara. Although, the way you sassily marched out of my apartment this morning made me think you were over this.'

The room fell silent as finding Ebony's earring was replaying in the back of my mind.

'Maybe I am. Like, over that part of us. I knew what last night was. I suppose that's what I mean.'

Tom's arms rested on his hips as he looked stuck in thought.

'Relationships in the workplace don't work for us, and right now *my* business is more important.'

We both stood silently.

'Well, touché!' he smirked. 'Come here, Zara,' he said eventually and pulled me to him. I rested my head against his warm chest and closed my eyes. I felt his finger under my chin as he turned my head to face his. We looked at one another, then kissed gently, softly, lovingly.

I forced myself to pull away from him after a few seconds, feeling my heart quicken in my chest.

He let out an exaggerated puff and said, 'Zara, Zara, Zara.'

I nodded, acknowledging the frustration.

'Technically you're not my boss till when?'

'You'll have to sign your full-time contract by Wednesday night.'

He smirked. 'I'll see you Wednesday night then? We could have a glass of champers, celebrate one last time, and *then* sign the contract?'

My heart ricocheted. Was he suggesting one last goodbye shag?

346

'Tom, stop!' I laughed at him chancing his luck.

'Oh, c'mon. Don't pretend last night wasn't fun. One last time before I can sue you for sexual harassment?'

Before I could think it through, I heard myself saying, 'I'll keep my diary free.'

Tom squeezed my hand tightly and stepped back. 'Keep the entire night free. There will be *a lot* of celebrating! Let's go out with a bang, eh!' He winked and headed back to his room.

Chapter Thirty-Three

Wednesday came around in the blink of an eye. The clinic was shut the entire day as I had meetings scheduled with Juju, the bank, my accountant and lawyers. Everything had fallen into place, and Raj kept his word as the paperwork arrived, officially handing me over the reins to Individualise. The clinic would still be owned by Raj, but I had full control over the work, the staff and any new concepts I wanted to explore, plus I had an exceptionally large pay rise to look forward to. I also had to keep up with paying the bills, liaising with payroll and honouring the commitment to Juju to keep utilising their brand. It all felt exhilarating, but at times I still struggled to wrap my head around it. *Why did he pick me?* I wondered. I loved Raj for this opportunity, but I knew how difficult it would be without him.

I hadn't heard from Tom for a few days, and as much as the proposition of one last night together was enticing, I wasn't sure if he'd changed his mind or if it was even what he'd meant at all. But I had taken no chances. My vagina to arsehole was shaved to the core, and underneath my floaty day dress I was wearing the sexy Ann Summers ensemble I'd originally bought for

Cameron. I was hoping it would be better appreciated by a throbbing Thomas, than it had been by my hiccup from the Highlands.

It was approaching five, and the shutters were down in the clinic. I was perched on the sofa, rummaging through tax returns when Tom strolled through the door.

'Thomas, you're early.'

'We have a countdown to adhere to.' He opened his jacket smoothly, presenting a bottle of expensive champagne. 'Tell me there are glasses in here. We need a night to remember!'

Instantly I felt relieved; clearly he was still up for our shag fest.

'They're in the staff room, the second cupboard from the right. Your contract's on the table too, if you want to sign!'

Tom growled. 'I love it when you speak so authoritatively. You're turning me on already, Zara Smith!' he called out, shoving the staff-room door open as I laughed at his mischievous energy.

I was gathering the paperwork when the front door opened again and a handsome-looking Andy entered.

'Hey!' I felt my stomach twist.

He was dressed casually in a plain white T-shirt and jeans. His Mowry tattoos were fully on show and no longer peeking through his work clothes.

He looked nervous. 'I'm glad you're still here, Zara. I saw the shutters were down.'

'Is everything OK?' I asked, feeling anxious at him unexpectedly dropping by.

He nodded.

'Is everything OK with the contract?' I panicked.

He sighed a little, edging a smile. 'No, no, that's a done deal. Don't worry about that . . . Fuck!'

I looked on curiously, waiting to hear what had brought him to the clinic. I'd never seen Andy look worried before. He was always so laid-back and chilled.

'I just wanted to say something to you,' he said. He sat down on the edge of the sofa, clasping his hands together.

'Go on . . .'

His warm eyes looked up and engaged with mine briefly, and I suddenly felt more unnerved.

'I just wanted to say that I'm glad you weren't the one who went to Dubai.'

'Aww, I am too—'

'Please, let me finish. I'm glad because I like you.' He looked right at me. 'The way you've handled the turnaround is so inspiring. You were determined to transform this place, and you did.'

'Aww, thanks, Andy. But I had all of you guys to assist me and, for what it's worth, I like you too.'

He swayed his head. 'Naw, I like you, *like you*! Look. It's everything about you, Zara. The way you laugh at the things that aren't even funny or find it impossible to eat something without wearing it for the day. You're so creative and so fucking smart. Everything about you makes me want you.'

I felt my mouth gape open.

'And I've never told a lassie how I feel before, so don't think I'm a pure bell end, but I had to tell you.'

The room was silent for a few seconds. Andy looked tense, waiting on my reaction. 'I . . . eh . . . I don't know what to say!' I said. 'I'm flattered, and of course, the attraction is one hundred per cent mutual. I'm just not sure I'm the type of girl guys want to have a serious relationship with though.'

When I said it, my belly dropped, realising how sad it sounded. But deep down, that's what I honestly believed.

'What? Of course, you are, Zara!' he said, shaking his head in disbelief.

'And what about Jennifer and Ty?' I added.

Andy looked confused, letting out a small giggle, 'What about them? Me and Jen are over. I only see her when she drops off Tyson. We share custody of the dog since the split, and I have him at weekends.'

Abruptly Tom broke out from the staff room, and both Andy and I jumped back.

'Oh, apologies, I'm interrupting,' he said, noticing the intense atmosphere.

I stood up. 'Not at all.' I looked awkwardly between Tom and Andy, wondering how much of the conversation Tom had overheard.

'We were . . . er . . . just chatting. You sorted?' I asked.

'Yes, absolutely, all done I think.' Tom glanced to Andy. 'I was signing the contract – I officially start tomorrow.'

I hesitated, not knowing what to do. 'I'll have to look over that briefly – excuse me one second, guys.'

'Right now?' Tom asked.

'I just need one minute.' I stood up and marched through to the staff room, and shut the door behind the two men. I could feel myself trying hard not to hyperventilate. My hands were sweating but cold as I heard the faint chatter of my two men behind me. What the fuck was going on? I felt my chest pounding every step of the way.

OK, get it together, Zara.

I plopped my two hands on the table in a bid to calm my breathing down and then noticed the contract sitting there, signed. Beside it were two glasses of champagne and a candy string bikini with a note.

'It's challenging to find anything as sweet as you – but I'm willing to try! T'

What the fuck did that mean? Try what? I wondered. Try the sweets? Try a relationship? I thought back to the last time I wore candy underwear for Tom, and I wasn't sure if he was trying to give me PTSD, a yeast infection or if this was a last-gasp attempt to redeem himself.

There was no getting away from any of this. Or from either of them.

I had a decision to make, and I was conscious of my time to make it.

I knew I had to do something.

I heard the sound of my nervous toes tap off the tiled floor.

'Tom,' I called out, covering my face, still swaying on what to do.

Tom opened the door and raised his shoulders. He seemed unusually unnerved. He waited till the door completely closed before speaking.

'What are you thinking?' His voice was soft and uneasy.

I shut my eyes briefly and whispered, 'I'm thinking this, like us, was never going to work from the get-go. Too much has happened. And honestly, I don't want to risk you not being part of my life anymore. I need you here, for my business and for me.' I could feel my eyes fill, hoping he understood.

'And Andy?' he replied.

I shrugged, waited a few seconds and said, 'What if he's my good geezer, Tom?'

He slowly walked towards me, kissed my head and let out a small defeated puff.

'Yes, he could very well be, Zara. I suppose you will never know until you try.'

We paused in one another's arms briefly. I could hear his heart beat against his warm chest. My face settled into his body, and there was part of me wanting to hold on to this moment for as long as I could. My eyes were shut tightly, realising everything was about to change.

'Well, I suppose I'd better go. Let you two enjoy the champagne. But if you don't mind, I'll take the undies.' He leaned forward, grabbed the candy and put them into his pocket.

'Really? Midnight snack?' I giggled, wiping away some wandering tears.

'I hope so!' His cheeky smile lit up the room. 'C'mon, you ready to go back out there? After that speech, the poor cunt will be shitting himself!' Tom joked.

I bowed my head, feeling awkward that he must have overheard all of Andy's declaration. Tom held the door open and ushered me out like a gentleman.

'Everything in order?' Andy asked, fidgeting with his phone case from the sofa.

I smiled back gratefully. 'Yip, everything is perfect.'

Tom winked to me encouragingly. 'Yes, well, I'll go home for an early night, and I'll see you tomorrow then, boss.'

He walked towards the clinic door, clutched hold of the door handle and turned back around to face Andy.

'Take care of her, Andy.' Tom gave one last smirk and left the clinic.

The smile radiated across my face as I looked at Andy, excited and nervous.

'So . . .' He stood up and took a step towards me.

'So . . .' I repeated.

He laughed and walked up to me, reaching for my hands.

'You up for giving this a shot, Zara?'

I faced the floor nervously, but nodded as I breathed a sigh of relief. 'Actually, I think I am.'

Andy's fingers raised my chin towards his face and he kissed me, lightly, sweetly, perfectly, once.

I couldn't keep the satisfied grin off my face as I stared at the man I had crushed on for months. I could feel an innocence radiate off us, apprehensive but eager to start a new chapter of our lives together. He held me closely in his arms, and finally I felt wanted.

'You know, I was starting to think good geezers didn't exist,' I whispered, looking up at him.

Andy smiled. 'I was here all along, darlin'.'

Acknowledgements

I want to start by thanking my mum and dad. For your continuous support, love and guidance. When I have been stressed, you have listened and talked it through. When I have been ecstatic, you are the first people to know. I appreciate all of your help, and I hope one day I write a book that will be clean enough for you both to read!

To Andy, Arlene, Joyce and Les for always being on hand when I need anything. You guys have helped tremendously when I'm writing and throughout my life. Thanks, Andy, for any legalities and brainy things I need to know. You genuinely are an encyclopedia of knowledge. To Arlene for being the best dog Meemaw to Wrinkles! And for being so creative with book promos and spreading the word. To Joyce and Les for watching the girls no matter what. Thank you for being on hand 24/7. For being proud of me and telling all the bingo gals about my books *(even if it puts them into an early grave)!* I appreciate you all so much.

To Rosie McCafferty for being my go-to wing-woman yet again! For proofreading my work and filling me with confidence throughout the process. You are an incredible writer, and I get so excited to see your comments throughout the process. My stories wouldn't have been the same without your input, and I appreciate all of your help throughout the last few years.

I'm also grateful to Orion Publishing, notably my exceptional editor Rhea Kurien. I couldn't have made this book without you. Thank you for having the patience to deal with my one million literacy queries! You have filled me with hope, passion and complete excitement about writing. I love how invested you are in my work, and for that, I am eternally grateful.

To Heather Suttie and the members of the Bookface 2020 group. I have met so many incredible, supportive, unique people there, and I'm eternally grateful for the opportunity to share positive book recommendations and conversations. To the Glasglow Girls Club for picking me up as an unidentified blogger and sharing my stories! You have the best feministic club, and I am so grateful to Laura for showing me endless support over the past few years. To the fantastic Waterstones staff in Glasgow for promoting the hell out of my book. In particular, to Erika and Clara, you have made all of us incredibly welcome in-store every time we visit and I appreciate everything you are doing for Scottish literature.

To my amazing friends and fantastic colleagues in ward one. The endless support and encouragement you have given to me to persevere and finish this novel is something I will never forget. When I'm having a shitty day, you guys always make it brighter. You never fail to ask about the book's progress or congratulate me despite the chaotic time we've had recently. I am grateful to all of you, from porters and domestics to doctors and nurses and the rest of the team. There are far too many staff members to name individually, but please know I appreciate all the daily comments of motivation, reassurance and dark twisty nurse humour *(which will occasionally make an appearance in my books)*.

To my besties, Lisa S, Sasa, Emma and Lisa M.

To Lisa Scott, for hearing me out and talking through my ideas. You always have a solution, and I can count on you for anything. You're definitely the most reliable out of the others and for that I thank you for keeping me sane when writing this. To my Sasa, my soul-sister. You make me laugh endlessly and there isn't a story you don't know. You are the kindest and most loyal person I know.

To my sister, Emma, thank you for your babysitting when I need it most! When I require some tough love, I come to you. Thanks for crying during book signings even when it's incredibly awkward. I love your lack of filter, and it's just what I need . . . most of the time! To Lisa Massey, my oldest school friend who has journeyed through every part of my life with me. Thank you for accompanying me to all my book events and giving me the best brows a gal could ask for.

To Aidan, Gabriella and Lucas for being a beautiful bundle of happiness in my life.

And to my beautiful girls, who this entire journey is for. Thank you for being so patient when I had to lock myself away to write this. For tolerating me working twelve-hour days in the hospital then coming home to write, and not even moaning about it! Thank you for making me laugh, putting up with my grumpiness and helping me in every aspect of my life *(except for the dog poo duties – that seems to be left for me!)* Thank you for waking up with a smile and telling me how much I'm loved every single day. I am so proud of the beautiful, kind, funny, smart little girls you are becoming, and all of this hard work has been for you! You are my true soul mates and I love you to infinity and beyond.

Love and eternal gratitude,
Sophie x

Credits

Sophie Gravia and Orion Fiction would like to thank everyone at Orion who worked on the publication of *What Happens in Dubai* in the UK.

Editorial
Rhea Kurien
Sanah Ahmed

Copyeditor
Clare Wallis

Proofreader
Kay Coleman

Audio
Paul Stark
Jake Alderson

Contracts
Anne Goddard
Humayra Ahmed
Ellie Bowker

Design
Rachael Lancaster
Joanna Ridley
Nick May

Editorial Management
Charlie Panayiotou
Jane Hughes
Bartley Shaw
Tamara Morriss

Finance
Jasdip Nandra
Afeera Ahmed
Elizabeth Beaumont
Sue Baker

Production
Ruth Sharvell

Sales
Jen Wilson
Esther Waters
Victoria Laws
Rachael Hum
Anna Egelstaff
Frances Doyle
Georgina Cutler

Operations
Jo Jacobs
Sharon Willis

Don't miss Sophie Gravia's filthy, hilarious and painfully relatable debut, *A Glasgow Kiss* . . .

A Glasgow Kiss [n.]
*A headbutt or a strike with the head
to someone's sensitive area*

Meet Zara Smith: 29, single and muddling her way through life as a trainee nurse in Glasgow. With 30 fast approaching, she's determined to do whatever it takes to find love – or at least someone to sext! Cheered on by best friends Ashley and Raj, Zara embarks on a string of dating escapades that are as hilarious as they are disastrous. From online dating to blind dates, hometown hook-ups to flirty bartenders, nothing is off limits.

But when Dr Tom Adams, aka Sugar Daddy, shows interest, it's a game-changing moment. Zara has had a crush on Tom since her very first day at the aesthetics clinic she works at part-time. As things heat up between them, Zara can't help but wonder: is this it? Or is it another disaster waiting to happen?